The monsters he faces are nothing compared to the monster within him.

Vell focused on one detail amid the confusion—a single blue eye staring out from an arrow slit in the fortress. He concentrated and threw his spear at it, but it missed, striking just to the left of its mark and bouncing off the wall. Below the eye, he saw thin lips twist into a smile, and an arrow flew from the window directly at Vell. He didn't have time to blink before it struck him between the eyes.

But Vell barely felt it. The arrow bounced off his skin as if it had struck iron. Vell gulped in confusion and whirled to face Keirkrad. The shaman's skin was covered with brownish, gnarly scales, for he had invoked a power the Thunderbeast bestowed on its priests. Keirkrad gasped and mouthed Vell's name through the noise. When Vell looked down at his hands, he realized that they too were covered with brown scales. His heart jumped at the shock, but he felt something else flowing from his core, overwhelming his fear. His senses began to cloud, and the confusion of war faded, replaced by the perfect clarity of rage.

Murray J.D. Leeder tells a fast-paced adventure of honor, will, and bravery, all centering on a man whose fierce heroism marks him as one of

THE FIGHTERS

FORGOTTEN REALMS®

THE FIGHTERS

Master of Chains
Jess Lebow

Ghostwalker
Erik Scott de Bie

Son of Thunder
Murray J. D. Leeder

Bladesinger
Keith Francis Strohm

Also by Murray J.D. Leeder
(as T.H. Lain)
Dungeons & Dragons®
Plague of Ice

FORGOTTEN REALMS

THE FIGHTERS

SON OF THUNDER

MURRAY J.D. LEEDER

Wizards of the Coast

The Fighters
Son of Thunder

©2006 Wizards of the Coast, Inc.

Cover art by Raymond Swanland
Map by Rob Lazzaretti
First Printing: January 2006
Library of Congress Catalog Card Number: 2005928108

9 8 7 6 5 4 3 2 1

ISBN-10: 0-7869-3960-5
ISBN-13: 978-0-7869-3960-2
620-95441740-001-EN

U.S., CANADA,
ASIA, PACIFIC, & LATIN AMERICA
Wizards of the Coast, Inc.
P.O. Box 707
Renton, WA 98057-0707
+1-800-324-6496

EUROPEAN HEADQUARTERS
Hasbro UK Ltd
Caswell Way
Newport, Gwent NP9 0YH
GREAT BRITAIN
Save this address for your records.

Visit our web site at www.wizards.com

Dedication

To Campbell, Roy, and my sister what's her name (and Alastair too!), for putting me up and putting up with me in Bournemouth for a large portion of the time during which this book was written.

Acknowledgements

Thanks must go to my editors, Phil Athans and Susan Morris. Also to Steven Schend, Eric L. Boyd, and Ed Greenwood for their enthusiastic furnishing of Realmslore—published and otherwise—when I asked for it; to Jesse Decker for the loan of Rask Urgek (a definite case of borrowing the car and failing to bring it back in one piece); and also to Elaine Cunningham for all her help and advice. And finally, thanks to Paul Jaquays, the creator of the Uthgardt, and all the other game designers who have detailed them over the years, without whom I'd have had nothing to play with.

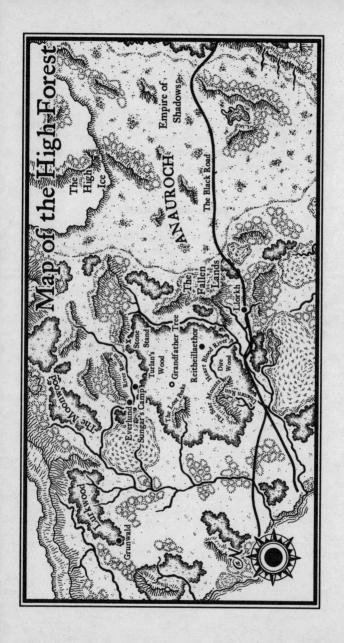

Map of the High Forest

Another bone cracked beneath Gan's foot.

"Ours wasn't the first army massacred in this place," the big hobgoblin growled at Thagalan Dray, one of the few humans sent on the most recent, ill-conceived expedition. Wearing a purple cloak over his scale mail, Dray was one of the Lord's Men of Llorkh, Zhentilar in all but name. So far as they knew, the two of them were the only survivors.

Dray ignored Gan and bent over to pick up one of the bones.

"Orc," he said, inspecting a thigh bone. He tossed the bone away and it clattered as it struck another one, half buried in the dirt. "This answers much."

"What do you mean?" Gan rumbled.

"This place used to crawl with orcs. Sometimes they'd come down and harass our caravans near

Parnast. But in recent years the activity has ceased. I think we've found the reason." The whole plain around them was covered with similar bones and rusted scraps of armor and weapons. A massacre had occurred here.

"The shades?" asked Gan.

"As likely a candidate as any," Dray said grimly. "But there are more than enough threats in this awful place."

The shades were the reason that Dray and Gan walked the battlefield on the western rim of Anauroch. Lord Geildarr had sent a force of Zhentilar troops into this gods-forsaken strip of moor—a place called the Fallen Lands. Their orders were to locate a Netherese ruin where the Empire of Shadow was encamped, and to excavate the site to discover ancient artifacts.

But Geildarr refused to commit his own men, beyond a few out-of-favor Lord's Men to serve as consultants. Instead he recruited humanoids—a local hobgoblin tribe that laired along the Dawn Pass, and some gnolls from the South-wood. This patchwork army never reached the ruin. The Shadovar forces attacked at night when they had all the advantages, and their smoky magic overwhelmed Llorkh's troops in no time.

So Dray and Gan found themselves trotting through endless dead fields of the Fallen Lands, facing an uncertain future back in Llorkh.

"What will Geildarr do when we return?" asked Gan.

Dray chuckled. "Return? We'd be mad to go back like this. He'll want explanations, and he'll want examples. We'll be hanging from a noose in front of the Lord's Keep the moment we set foot back in Llorkh."

"I could return to my tribe," said Gan, more orc bones cracking beneath his feet.

"And are tribal hobgoblins more tolerant of failure than Zhentarim?" asked Dray. "Perhaps this place is the answer," he said, looking over the dead plains. "Everyone knows that the Fallen Lands are full of lost magic. If we could stay alive long enough to find some of it, that is. But if we could provide Geildarr with something new, he might forgive us."

"You say 'we,' human," the hobgoblin said. "If you find

magic of such power, why not wield it yourself?"

"The truly useful magic can be unlocked only by mages like Geildarr. Such power would be lost on us. This battle didn't happen so long ago. Perhaps there's something here worth salvaging. Geildarr sponsors groups of adventurers to search lost ruins and dungeons for old magic—jobs that he doesn't trust to Lord's Men like us."

Gan snorted. "With good reason."

Dray ignored him. "There's a group of adventurers Geildarr's nicknamed the Antiquarians—he often hires them to search ruins and the like. I think they're somewhere down on the High Moor now. Geildarr's mad about ancient artifacts, especially things Netherese. Apparently the Fallen Lands were once a Netherese survivor state called Hlondath." He frowned. "I guess our whole army died to satisfy his hobby."

They spent a long time searching the battlefield. Orc skeletons by the hundreds covered the barren ground. Near the center of the field they found a small ancient ruin, little more than a few broken and fallen walls concealing nothing of value. Curiously, amid the nearby dead lay the cracked exoskeletons of two umber hulks, and what they guessed were the bones of a giant snake. But any weapons of interest were broken or rusted. Dispirited, Gan and Dray limped home.

Soon after, Gan noticed something glinting in the distance and pointed it out to Dray. "A trick of the light," Dray said, but as he studied the flash, he judged that it was the distinctive shine of metal. He and the hobgoblin raced toward it to find a most curious discovery.

"Tymora smiles today!" cried Dray. A collection of weapons and armor lay strewn across the dirt or half buried. All counted, at least twenty items awaited discovery.

"Nobody lost these weapons," Gan said, looking down warily upon their find. "They were thrown away. Probably for good reason. They're cursed, maybe."

Dray picked up a small silver helmet with an unfamiliar emblem on the side, then he dropped it into the dirt. "No, not cursed," he said.

"Perhaps they were so damaged that someone wanted to get rid of them," the hobgoblin offered. But the equipment, though covered by layers of grime, looked to be in fine condition.

"Or perhaps Cyric or some other power placed them here for us to find." Dray attacked the pile, throwing aside shields and hammers. At the bottom, buried in dirt, he uncovered a battle-axe, heavy and with a huge head of glimmering steel.

It was a weapon to inspire confidence and intimidate enemies—a leader's weapon. How many foes must have fallen to its thick blade? What battles had it seen? Gan could sense its age and its value, and he wondered what great heroes must have clutched it. Though the hobgoblin had only the faintest conception of such things, he wondered what dim forgotten age must have spawned it.

Dray anxiously rubbed off the dirt and then smiled up at the hobgoblin. "Does this look like a weapon someone would just throw away?" he asked. But as the Lord's Man went to lift it, he found the axe was beyond his strength, and he dropped it with a thud onto the ground.

Gan cast Dray a glare as he mishandled the weapon, then reached down and scooped it up himself, comfortable with its weight. A stiffness filled the hobgoblin's muscles as he held it, and a smile crossed his ugly face.

Dray inspected it closely as Gan held it up.

"Dwarven manufacture, I think. And look, it's probably been here for years, and there's no damage to the blade. I bet there's some dweomer on this."

"You think Geildarr will like it?" asked Gan.

"Well, magic weapons aren't really his favorites," Dray said, "but considering that if we stay here too long we'll probably be eaten by leucrotta or slaughtered by shades, I think this may be just the thing to save our skins."

"What kind of leader is Geildarr?" asked Gan.

"What do you mean?" asked Dray.

"Is he a strong ruler, worthy of service?"

"I suppose so," Dray said.

Gan looked at him more closely. "You say that if we give

this axe to Geildarr, he will let us live? Grant me a place in his service?"

"What did I just say?"

"I just wanted to be sure," said Gan. Before Dray could react, Gan brought the axe down in the middle of Dray's head. The axe smashed his skull and cleaved deep into the soldier's chest. The purple cloak around Dray's armor snapped free from his shoulders and fluttered to the ground.

The hobgoblin dislodged the bloody axe from Dray's body and examined it. He snatched up Dray's cloak and used it to wipe the blade clean.

"A fine weapon, indeed," he said, tossing the gory rag aside. But something felt wrong. He felt unworthy of wielding the axe. It was for a hero of the epic sagas, not for him. Steel such as this could lead armies.

It must be taken to one sufficiently worthy.

Till I find him, Gan promised himself, *I wield it on his behalf.*

With the axe clutched tightly in both hands, he set off for Llorkh.

CHAPTER 1

Vell the Brown tried to recall the last time he was at Morgur's Mound. He had been so very young back then. On this visit, he was met by distant feelings and scraps of memory. He recalled the roar that arose from the tribe as King Gundar stood before the altar, raising the great ceremonial axe above his head. In his mind, Vell saw his parents standing straight and attentive, gazing up at the cairn nestled amid the Crags. Because of all the stories his parents had told him, and all he had heard in the songs of the Thunderbeast skalds, he knew the cairn was the tribe's ancestor mound. Morgur's Mound was the most important place to any Thunderbeast, even one who had never seen it.

Surmounted by menhirs and within the rings of the outer mounds, lay the altar mound. It was here, said the skalds, that Uthgar died fighting

Gurt, king of the frost giants. Other tribes claimed that this cairn held Uthgar's mortal remains, but Thunderbeast legend held that no body was left behind when Tempus elevated Uthgar to godhood.

A ring of bones at the edge of the mounds, great thick bones—incomprehensibly large and set rigidly in the ground—were the bones of the Thunderbeast itself: a great behemoth lizard of legend and the totem spirit of the tribe. Some of the bones had been damaged or removed over the decades by vandals or enemies of the Uthgardt, but few dared disturb so sacred a site, protected as it was by magic and curses of old.

Atop a pike in front of the altar mound stood the skull of the Thunderbeast. Its empty eye sockets gazed out at visitors as a solemn reminder that although the place was held in reverence by all Uthgardt, the Thunderbeasts were closest to it. In turn, said the Thunderbeasts, they had the closest relationship to Uthgar, and he to them. As if in proof, the altar mound itself was shaped in the form of a great behemoth.

As a child told of these things by his parents, Vell had felt a swell of pride that had never been equaled. He loved his tribe and felt a deep connection to its history. While in his youth, his young heart had felt as if it might explode with the feeling.

Vell tried to dredge up those memories in the hope of finding the same feeling now. He reached into the past to try to silence his fears of the present, and he wondered how many others of his tribe were doing the same.

For most people of Faerûn, this day was celebrated as the feast day of Highharvestide, but to the Uthgardt, the day had a different name and significance. This was Runemeet, the holiest day of the year, most often celebrated with a Runehunt: a campaign against a ritual enemy. But this year, chieftain Sungar Wolfkiller had declared that the entire tribe should travel to Morgur's Mound for a rare ritual.

Word had gone out to all outlying clusters of the tribe, and now all were assembled at Morgur's Mound. Even the druid Thanar, green-robed and thick-bearded, had reappeared. Nobody knew how many years had passed since he had left the tribe to patrol the wilds, and no one had made contact with him since. In all, some six or seven hundred warriors, and just as many women and children, crowded the foot of Morgur's Mound. Their tribal relation was evident in the black hair and blue eyes of most all who were assembled.

Not even King Gundar, during his auspicious rule, had dared send out such a decree. But then, he had never needed to.

The gathering was joyous, but all present knew a strong tribe would have no need for such a ritual. The Thunderbeasts also knew they were not a strong tribe. As soon as they had arrived, they had met with the Sky Pony tribe—more frequent visitors to Morgur's Mound than the Thunderbeasts. The Ponies had been cordial and friendly, agreeing to Sungar's request that they stay away from the mound while the Thunderbeasts were assembled. King Gundar would have never needed to voice this concern. The Sky Ponies were almost as in awe of Gundar as his own tribe.

As the last light faded on Runemeet, the tribe stood within the bone boundary at the foot of Morgur's Mound. Atop the altar mound stood Sungar, just as Gundar had in Vell's memory, but without the traditional axe. Alongside him stood the ancient, thin-skinned Keirkrad Seventoes, the white-haired shaman of the tribe, and the Thunderbeasts' other priests and druids. Only with all of their combined might could they accomplish this ritual.

"Thunderbeasts!" shouted Sungar. "The beast is our guide, our light. It is our route to Uthgar, and it is our route to ourselves. It represents all that we are, and what we should be. King Gundar is with the Thunderbeast now, and I know that he will help us find the answer we seek."

A cheer went up from the assembled tribe at the very mention of Gundar. For many Thunderbeasts, Gundar and Uthgar were held in nearly the same regard. Whatever kind of leader Gundar's successor Sungar would prove to be, he would never escape Gundar's shadow.

As black clouds swirled overhead, and the residual light was finally extinguished, Sungar marched down the mound and stood with his warriors, signifying that he was one of them—a message he always tried to project. Keirkrad, dressed in ceremonial white rothéhide, turned to face the assembled tribe. He was so old that he could not summon his voice beyond a weak rasp. Only those standing closest heard him call upon the tribe members to focus their attention on the mound and lend something of their own souls to the ritual of communing.

"The Thunderbeast lives in all of your hearts. Now, you must let it free," he concluded solemnly.

With that, Keirkrad turned toward the altar stone, his head bowed and his arms extended. Specks of light coursed between his outstretched fingers and those of the other priests. A greenish ring of magic flowed between them, pulsing and glowing, lighting up the night with divine energy. The assembled Uthgardt stood straight and tall as the area filled with the crackle of magic, raising the hairs on their necks and arms, and releasing strange vibrations beneath their feet. The magic drifted to the bones at the mound's edge and set them trembling, the crackling rising until its crescendo crashed like thunder off the neighboring crags. Vell clenched his palms tightly and felt them fill with sweat.

The tribal assembly murmured with wonder. A tingling anticipation electrified the crowd. They awaited an explanation of why their number declined; they waited for their path to be shown to them.

But no response came. The racket dwindled to nothing, the skies parted above, and the ring of magic binding the spellcasters together winked out. A murmur of confusion wormed through the barbarians, and Sungar's face became a mask of shame. Vell's heart leaped in his chest. The worst suspicions whispered among the Thunderbeast tribe were true. They had lost their totem's favor. Uthgar had forsaken them.

Without warning, the bones came to life. They rose

from their places ringing Morgur's Mound and lifted high above the assembly, swirling in the air together, frantically trying to find the shape they had held in life. They eventually came together in the familiar form of a wingless dragon, a great bulky shape with a long serpentine neck. A collective gasp spilled from the tribe. Most had never seen the Thunderbeast before, but knew its shape well from the images that many of them tattooed on their bodies.

Vell's mouth opened wide. The Uthgardt were not trained to bow and cower in the face of their god, but to stand tall and stare in reverence. Vell felt his knees weaken and tremble at the spectacle of the totem come to life.

The skull was last to rise from its pike and find its place. Two brown lights flared into life within the vacant eye sockets, and they scanned the assembly, shining their radiance in the darkness. Swooping uneasily, the Thunderbeast encircled Morgur's Mound, casting its eyes over the throng. It turned to the altar stone and looked intently at Keirkrad. The shaman stood, his arms outstretched, his eyes closed in rapture, waiting to commune with his totem.

But the link never came. The Thunderbeast pulled away from Keirkrad and the altar mound, turning instead to the throng at the mound's foot. Its flaring eyes scanned the tribe, examining Sungar and many others as it slowly gazed upon the assembly. At last the creature came to rest in midair, its eyes trained directly on Vell.

Though his limbs trembled, Vell did not look away. The sounds of the world around him—the gasps of the warriors standing alongside him, the gentle wind blowing overhead—vanished. The unblinking gaze pulled Vell in. Something inhuman awakened in him, and he began to scream as he felt his own identity milked away. But his scream was cut short, and he stood rigid as a post: his face blank and his eyes empty.

Above, the bones of the Thunderbeast hovered but did not move, and the brown light vanished in its eyes. Most of the Uthgardt could not see Vell or the beast. A wave of confusion spread through them. Sungar pushed his way through the gawking Uthgardt to reach Vell.

"Can you hear me?" the chieftain cried, grasping Vell's face.

Keirkrad rushed down the altar mound to join them, his old bones carrying him through the throng with surprising speed. The shaman looked carefully into Vell's brown eyes.

"The beast has chosen a receptacle," he declared to the assembly. "This warrior—one of you—has received the beast's blessing. Let Uthgar be praised." His voice was tinged with astonishment and disappointment.

Sungar looked to Keirkrad for confirmation. "Speak to him," the shaman said. "Speak to him. He is the voice of the Thunderbeast."

Sungar looked Vell straight in the eye. "We beseech you. Our tribe needs guidance. We must know your will."

Vell's features remained impassive, and he showed no sign of comprehending or caring.

"What should we do to please you?" Sungar pleaded.

Vell's lips opened slowly. Sungar leaned closer.

"Find the living," Vell said. The voice was his, but the words were not.

"Find the living?" repeated Sungar. But no explanation came, nor any further words from Vell's mouth. His eyes closed, and he fell backward into the arms of some of his fellow warriors. Keirkrad leaned forward to tend to him. Above, the hovering construct tore apart in a whirlwind of bone, the skull taking its place on the pike once again, and all the other massive bones resuming their original places around Morgur's Mound, set and immovable in the earth once again.

"Is he safe?" Sungar whispered to Keirkrad. Keirkrad nodded. Sungar climbed the altar mound and looked out over the massive assembly of his tribe, all waiting for his words.

"The spirit has spoken!" he shouted. "It has told us to find the living."

A murmur of confusion spread through the throng.

Sungar yelled, "And find them we shall!"

A cheer went up, rolling off the distant crags and echoing into the night. The orders of the Thunderbeast were rarely forthcoming. Even words as cryptic as these were cause for much celebration.

A strange rattle sounded—faint at first, but growing louder as it echoed off the stone walls. It disturbed Kellin Lyme, asleep at her desk before a stack of books, her candle burned down to a stump. Since early morning she had been studying the account of Yehia of Shoon and his interactions with the Uthgardt during their early history, attempting to assess its historical veracity. Now, out of her window, she could see that the Way of the Lion was dark. But large portions of it would soon be awake if that rattling kept up.

Shaking the fog from her mind, Kellin paced the library—her father's own writings plus his collection, mixed with an increasing number of her own additions—looking for the source of the sound. She traipsed down the stairs into the archives, where she searched through the multitude of boxes collected by her father decades earlier. She was forced to open each crate carefully, to protect the priceless relics within. The noisy culprit was hidden at the bottom of a large stack. By the time she found it, she scolded the crate, telling it that every monk and scholar in the whole of Candlekeep was probably awake.

Kellin tore open the crate and found a heavy petrified bone rattling against the hardwood sides. It had already smashed and destroyed whatever other artifacts were stored with it, and when the lid came off, the bone jumped into midair. Almost automatically, Kellin reached out and grasped it, and when she did, the object's mysterious animation subsided.

Find the living. The words flashed through her mind as she clutched the bone. Something else came with it: an impression of terrible need and danger that washed over her and set her trembling. It would be a long time before she would feel right again.

Kellin held the bone up to her face and muttered, "Thunderbeast."

CHAPTER 2

Geildarr Ithym, Mayor of Llorkh, made his way
back from the Ten Bells tavern flanked by a few
of the Lord's Men. He cursed that even his own
drunken stumble home had to be moderated by
troops, but security was always of the essence.
No sooner had Hellgate Keep fallen, eliminating
one threat, than another—Shade—had appeared
in the desert in the form of a floating city. And
Shade was hardly the only threat Llorkh faced.
Agents from the Silver Marches, Harpers and
Moonstars, rival wizards from the Brotherhood of
the Arcane in Luskan, and rebellious townsfolk
who remembered a time before Llorkh was under
Zhentarim rule—all these threatened. Plus there
was the present danger of insane dragons sweeping out of the Graypeaks or the High Forest. It
wasn't so long ago that the phaerimm sent a force
of bugbears against the city, and not long after

that a rabble of dwarves thought to retake their old mines and stronghold—though their conspiracy was put down before any damage was done, it served as a grim reminder of how fragile Geildarr's rule really was.

Geildarr took his leave of the guards at the gateway to the towering Lord's Keep: his residence as Mayor of Llorkh, and the city's seat of power. The windowless Lord's Keep was the tallest building in Llorkh, and perhaps the dullest in a town filled with plain, utilitarian structures of stone. Beneath it was an extensive complex of tunnels and dungeons, the residence of many of Llorkh's enemies over the years. He could hear a few muffled screams from the torture chambers even now. Just before the gates, Geildarr lingered a moment at the spot where the previous lord, Phintarn Redblade, was found dead all those years before.

Lord's Men opened the iron doors. In the front foyer, a large painting of Geildarr hung on the wall, depicting him standing before the Lord's Keep and smiling as the happy people of Llorkh crowded around him. Geildarr climbed the staircase several floors to his private residence. He passed his custom-made golem in the anteroom and opened the sturdy iron door into a long hallway dotted with wall hangings and pedestals. Each bore an assortment of arcane and mundane relics, most recovered from the nearby ruins. Geildarr had personally studied each of them, learned something of their history and power, and applied many of their principles in the new magical items and weapons he designed. He relished being wrapped in antiquity. The items here hailed from dwarf kingdoms, elf kingdoms, and human kingdoms—all of them fallen and gone, remembered only by historians.

Lately, Geildarr had been wondering when he'd fall along with them.

A chill draft from his balcony greeted him when he reached the door to his wood-paneled study at the end of the hall. He found a missive waiting for him, likely arrived on the latest caravan from Zhentil Keep. It was marked with the new symbol of the Zhentarim—Fzoul Chembryl's symbol, Geildarr laughed bitterly—featuring Fzoul's own Scepter of the Tyrant's Eye.

This was the greatest threat to Geildarr's leadership in Llorkh: not the shades or any other external force, but his own superiors across Anauroch. He snatched up the letter and broke the seal.

"I can tell you what it says," came a voice from behind him. Geildarr spun to face the corner of the room and a tall man standing there in long, blue and purple robes, clutching a staff with a bat at its top. The wizard wore a smirk that showed just how pleased he was to have caught Geildarr by surprise. But Geildarr held his reaction in check and sized up the intruder with an aloof eye instead.

"I wonder," Geildarr mused, his voice slightly slurred from his earlier drinking, "am I drunker than I think, or is this Sememmon I'm seeing?"

"Is that all you have to say?" the raven-haired wizard asked. "There was a time when you would fall on your knees at my very presence."

"But I am not addressing Sememmon," answered Geildarr, "am I?" He began to gesture a spell of dispel, but Sememmon extended his hand.

"No need," he said. "Let's drop the masks." The form of the imperious wizard melted all around him, leaving a body half its height. A red tricorn hat topped a plump-cheeked gnome face. The figure wore robes of rich crimson—a small parody of nobility. The gnome clutched a thin blackwood cane at his side, and a mad, merry nature twinkled in his green eyes.

"What brings you here, Moritz the Mole? Do you need somewhere to sleep or something?" This wasn't the first time this peculiar emissary of the wizard Sememmon had dropped in on Geildarr unannounced since Sememmon had fled from the Zhentarim's prime western stronghold of Darkhold.

In the intervening years, Sememmon and his elf lady-love Ashemmi had scarcely been seen by anyone. Last he heard they were living in seclusion and traveling Faerûn, collecting magic and cementing allies for some endeavor as yet unrevealed.

Geildarr knew them both well from his own trips to Darkhold over the years, but never really came to understand them. Ashemmi was a heart-stopping beauty with flaxen hair and almond-shaped eyes. How had an elf woman ended up in the Zhentarim? He had heard she had been corrupted to evil by magical means. Geildarr couldn't even guess at the truth of this. What was clear to him, though, was that Sememmon and Ashemmi were utterly devoted to each other. Even such dark-hearted creatures as this pair were bound together by love. Geildarr yearned to trust another so completely.

Moritz laughed heartily in typically gnomish fashion. "I always enjoy visiting you because of that tongue of yours. You really ought to welcome my presence, for I come with a warning. Fzoul blames you for your failed incursion into the Fallen Lands."

"*My* failed incursion," Geildarr snorted. The plan had been Fzoul's order. "Doomed to failure. I minimized the damage. And now he thinks to make me his sacrificial animal."

"Fzoul courts dangerous enemies," Moritz said. "The might of Shade has Elminster shaking in his tower. But then again, you've served Fzoul well. Under your mayoralty, Llorkh has been one of the most trouble-free places under Zhentarim control. Most likely he'll keep you around a bit longer." Moritz took a step closer to Geildarr. "But let me ask. Have you ever considered working for another power?"

"Does Sememmon's customary offer follow? Am I to cast my lot against Fzoul? Hide in the dark like Sememmon?"

"I suspect it's this town you love, Geildarr," said Moritz. "You love being mayor, having that control. Llorkh is an inglorious post, but you love it all the same. I can respect that. You don't care too much for the Zhentarim any longer. That's why you refuse to sponsor that little girl Ardeth for membership. Or do you have other reasons for keeping her close to you?"

Geildarr's head swirled from the drink, and he was tired of playing games.

"Why have you come here, Moritz?" he asked testily.

"I may just be the truest friend you have, Geildarr. I've come here to tell you something. Fzoul wants a few changes in Llorkh. You can work with them, or end up like your predecessor Redblade." He extended his blackwood cane and used it to poke Geildarr in his pendulous belly.

"What kind of changes?" Geildarr asked, taking a step back.

"The same changes that are sweeping the Zhentarim. Bane is back. Would you like to see the Dark Sun replaced by the Black Hand?"

Geildarr shook his head grimly; he understood exactly what Moritz meant. The Dark Sun was both a title for Cyric, and the name of the god's temple in Llorkh. But Cyricists like Geildarr were growing unpopular within the Zhentarim as Fzoul—Bane's Chosen, and his mightiest priest—solidified power. This was a factor in Sememmon's flight from Darkhold.

"All this you know," Moritz went on, "but what you may not know is this: rumor has it that Mythkar Leng has already cut a secret deal with Fzoul to take your place as mayor of Llorkh."

"Leng!" protested Geildarr. The high priest of the Dark Sun had long been Geildarr's conduit to the Zhentarim leadership, charged with keeping him informed of directives from Zhentil Keep. Though Geildarr was officially a member of the Zhentarim, he was largely content to function as mayor of Llorkh, letting Leng handle the Network's day-to-day operations in the region. Leng would keep him advised on the Zhentarim's ever-shifting agenda, and Geildarr would try to react accordingly. "Why would they let Leng be mayor?" Geildarr demanded. "He's a Cyricist too!"

"Is he?" asked Moritz. "Cyric is Lord of Illusion—who would know better than I?—and Prince of Lies as well. Perhaps Leng learned the art of deception so well that he can fool his own god. It has been done before, after all. Leng was a priest of Bane before the Godswar, as you'll remember, and old habits tend to stick. But as I said, I know this only as a rumor. Something for you to investigate. If you wish to keep your job, I suggest taking it up with Leng.

"On the other hand," Moritz chuckled, "if you wish to keep your life, Sememmon offers his protection. Either way, he extends a message to you. I believe it was, 'Try to keep this town of mine in one piece.'"

"Llorkh?" asked Geildarr. "Sememmon's?"

"As much as it is yours, truly," Moritz said. "I'd wager you harbor fantasies of Llorkh passing from the Zhentarim as your private fiefdom. It's good to have dreams. The difference between you and Sememmon is his dreams have a chance of coming true."

"If you believe Sememmon has a prayer of wresting anything from Fzoul and his pet clone," Geildarr said, "then it's clear that all this toying with illusion has finally estranged you from reality. Bound to happen, really."

The gnome frowned. "You have no idea what kind of power Sememmon hoards. But know this—" Moritz aimed his cane upward at Geildarr's face "—Sememmon's patience is finite. His offer will be made only so many times, and you may find his friendship withdrawn just when you need it most."

"Then let your master show up here in person for once," Geildarr said. "Maybe I'll catch him in a bottle and hand him over to Fzoul as a present. I wager that would help preserve my rule in Llorkh."

Moritz cackled, bending over with laughter at this thought.

"And I'm the delusional one? Hear it and know it true, Geildarr—you may have some fun toying around with magical objects, but you are not the wizard Sememmon is."

And at that, he vanished from the spot, leaving Geildarr to his spinning head.

Thluna found Sungar just where he expected—standing on the outer ring of Morgur's Mound at the freshest cairn. The rest of the tribe was encamped just outside the Crags; it was forbidden among the Uthgardt to make camp at any ancestor mound, though the decadent Black Lion tribe had violated that rule by settling near Beorunna's Well. Thluna slowly stepped up to his chief and joined him in reverence of the dead.

In the last two years, young Thluna, son of Hagraavan, had become closer to Sungar than any other Uthgardt. Thluna had wed Sungar's daughter Alaa, and now stood to succeed him as chieftain, though such lines of succession were not always clearly drawn. Sungar and Thluna were among the few who had survived the shame and devastation brought down upon their tribe in the Fallen Lands. But more importantly, Thluna, though little more than a boy, was the sole member of his tribe who always told Sungar the truth.

"Has King Gundar any answers for you today?" asked Thluna.

"Silence only. I asked him how he became so loved by his people," Sungar told him. "Even those who disagreed with him. The songs don't tell that. Hazred and the other skalds tell of how he so impressed the Red Tiger tribe by slaughtering a leucrotta, armed only with one of their ritual claws. And of the time he and his warriors lay siege to the Black Raven aerie near Raven Rock, and smashed fifty raven eggs."

"Weren't you with him that day?" asked Thluna. "Was it truly fifty eggs?"

Sungar smiled. "That legend is for Gundar, not me."

"You must forge your own legends," said Thluna. "The Thunderbeast has told us how."

"No easy directive," Sungar said. "The shamans tell us that the behemoths still live in the depths of the High Forest, but they also say nobody has seen them since before the time of Uthgar."

"A great adventure in the making," Thluna said. "A chance to undo what has been."

"We did nothing wrong!" Sungar's voice echoed across the Crags.

"They don't see it that way," Thluna informed him, pointing toward the camp in the distance.

"They weren't there."

"No," Thluna said, "but they've heard the story. No songs will be sung of it, but the whispers will linger for a long time."

"Then we must find something for them to sing," Sungar declared, "and sing proudly. When we return to Rauvin Vale, I will pick a party and lead it into the High Forest. The Thunderbeast would not assign an impossible task. Now, how fares the chosen vessel?"

"Vell? He has not yet roused, but Keirkrad believes he is himself again."

"Odd that the beast should choose him. What do they say about Vell the Brown?"

"Apart from the color of his eyes, there's little exceptional about him. He is one of the warriors who generally stays behind to guard the camp during expeditions."

"By his own choice?" asked Sungar.

"I don't know," Thluna admitted. "He has few close friends. Though he has already reached the age to claim a mate, he has not. He defers to the warriors with more glory to their names."

"He may find himself with more friends after this, and women besides," Sungar said. "The beast chose him, and when we go into the High Forest, Vell will be with us."

Thluna nodded. "I will let him know when he wakes. For the moment, I have a recommendation." He looked down at the grave of King Gundar. "We are but a day's ride from Grunwald. Some of the men plan to visit it. Most of them were born there."

Grunwald was the abandoned dwarf hold on the edge of the Lurkwood, discovered and settled by the Thunderbeasts. For a few generations they forsook their nomadic ways and thrived at tree felling and lumber cutting. But when Gundar died, the first act of his successor Sungar was to withdraw from Grunwald.

"If orcs have settled in Grunwald," said Thluna, "then the men wish to clear them out."

Sungar stroked his beard. "They may go, if they wish. I will not prevent them."

"You should go, too," advised Thluna. "The men were denied a Runehunt, so let them have this instead."

Sungar cocked his head. "Is a chief to obey his warriors, or the other way around?" he asked, a trace of annoyance in his voice.

"Both, when the cause is right," said Thluna. "But a chief should not put his own considerations above those of his tribe."

"Is that what you think I'm doing?" snarled Sungar.

"No," Thluna said firmly. "But there are those who might."

Sungar paced. He saw the wisdom of Thluna's words.

"Why should I go to Grunwald?" asked Sungar. "To invite more comparisons between me and Gundar; or to let them all plead to move the tribe back there?"

"Neither. Show them you're above those concerns," Thluna said. He paused a moment, gauging Sungar's reaction. "You cannot make them forget Grunwald. Many of our people never had the opportunity to properly leave it behind. You need to give them that now. It is like a fallen comrade. Only when he is buried and grieved for, can we move on."

For a long time Sungar and Thluna stared silently at King Gundar's cairn. Though neither of them spoke, both thought of their dead fellows, buried so far away in the dismal earth of the Fallen Lands. They, too, could never be mourned properly.

"This whole trip is about embracing our history," Sungar said. "Consulting our ancestors to find our present path. Grunwald is part of that history."

"So we're going to Grunwald?" Thluna said. He erupted in a wide smile that betrayed his youth.

"You forget," said Sungar. "I was born there, too."

Images and thoughts swirled through Vell's mind as he floated in heavy unconsciousness. Something was lost when he awoke. When the darkness parted, Vell sensed places, faces, and ideas that he could not quite seize, though they would haunt the edges of his mind in ways he could never speak of with a fellow Uthgardt. He seemed to recall dreams of escape—of widening his horizons beyond his tribe and its way of life. These were not new dreams, but traces of something that was always there, now bursting into light.

When he awoke, he pushed those feelings deep inside himself. The sensation scared him. Something had changed in him—but what?

Vell found himself in a tent full of ceremonial animal horns. The air smelled sweet from wild sage. This was a tent of honor, he realized. He rose and strode from the tent into the Thunderbeast encampment tucked among the rugged Crags. The sun blazed brightly. Vell's muscles felt tight, and a new energy swelled in his limbs. All around him, Uthgardt he had known all his life looked at him in a new way. They greeted him with eagerness, even with reverence, but with fear as well.

Vell had dreamed not of being somewhere else, but of being something else. That image stayed with him even after the dream itself was gone. Now in his waking, he felt as if something of himself was lost; yet he did not feel empty, but overstuffed. His psyche felt as if some new identity had been crammed into him and was preparing to burst out from his muscles. But what was it?

Keirkrad rushed up to him. Despite his astonishing age, the shaman could move with catlike speed.

"Vell!" he said. His old frame could not keep still, he was so excited. "What do you remember?"

"The eyes of the beast staring at me from above," he said. "And then ... nothing."

"You have been touched by the Thunderbeast," Keirkrad told him, resting a gnarled hand on Vell's shoulder. "Our totem chose you as his vessel. This is the greatest honor an Uthgardt could receive! How do you feel?"

"Different," said Vell. He ran a hand over a tense muscle. "Like I could fell a giant single-handed."

"You have seen the Battlefather's favor as few ever do. Your destiny is assured," Keirkrad said. Through all his kind words, he was peering deeply at Vell with his watery blue eyes, trying to gauge him and figure him out. Vell had experienced this often in his childhood; his brown eyes were so rare among his people. He sometimes found that Uthgardt who seemed to be looking at him were merely looking at his eyes.

At that moment, Thluna arrived. The young warrior commanded enormous respect within the Thunderbeasts, even among those much older and more experienced—perhaps even more respect than Sungar.

"Vell, you have risen!" he said. "Have you further messages for us?"

"Messages?" Vell asked, puzzled.

"The beast spoke through you," Keirkrad said. "It said 'find the living.'"

"'Find the living'?" repeated Vell. "What does it mean?"

Thluna sighed. "If you do not know, we surely do not."

"It means the Thunderbeast wants us to find the living behemoths that still dwell in the High Forest," Keirkrad supplied, chin held high. "Surely that should be clear."

"It is a matter of some discussion," said Thluna. "We had hoped you might clarify."

"No," said Vell, shaking his head. "I'm afraid not."

"Vell has been touched by the Thunderbeast," Keirkrad said. "He may know more—or be capable of more—than he realizes right now. Sungar should keep him close at hand."

"Yes, he does," Thluna said. He lowered his voice slightly. "He plans an expedition into the High Forest, for a select group from the tribe—he's still debating who, but it includes both of you. Do not share this for now."

Keirkrad's ancient, lined face broke into a wide grin.

"The chieftain is wise. I only wish we could have done this years ago."

"But why should I be included?" asked Vell. "I am honored, but . . ."

"Surely the Thunderbeast chose you for a reason," Thluna told him. "It may not have been as simple as delivering a message—Uthgar may plan a further role for you. We shall see. But in the meantime, Sungar has planned something else." Thluna turned from the two of them and addressed the tribe at large. "Hear me, Thunderbeasts!" he cried. Soon dozens of warriors were assembled before him. Thluna's voice was not deep, but he spoke clearly and well.

"Spread the word. Our assembly at Morgur's Mound has been successful beyond our dreams—successful thanks to your faith. An additional pilgrimage will be made. We came here to seek our history and our heritage: to learn something about ourselves by knowing where we have been. So we shall take down this camp and make the path to Grunwald."

A deafening roar came up from the tribe. Keirkrad led Vell aside and up a low hill on the edge of the Crags, where they could look down on the camp being disassembled for the journey to their new destination.

"Vell," he said. "You heard Thluna. We shall go into the High Forest seeking to regain the Thunderbeast's favor for our tribe."

"A task for heroes of legend," Vell said. "I can't imagine myself in that company."

"What man can know his own destiny?" asked Keirkrad. "Yesterday you were but a voice in the chorus, and one weaker than most. Now you shall stand close to Sungar, and have his ear. He shall respect your counsel as he respects that of the boy Thluna."

"And as he respects yours," Vell added.

"Less than you may think." Keirkrad shrugged. "I am an old man." A frown crossed his ancient brow. "We are alike, you and I. I felt the calling of the Thunderbeast at a young age. Once, I left my parent's tent at night and went wandering into the Lurkwood in a blood trance. For days I walked in the cold of deepwinter; not for nothing am I called Seventoes. I saw orcs, ettins, and a hunting party of the shapechanging Gray Wolves, but none of them saw me. By Uthgar's grace, I was invisible to them.

"Then, as I lay in an animal's burrow freezing to death,

I saw a vision of Morgur's Mound—when I first saw the mound itself years later, it was exactly as I had seen it in my mind. Then in the bitter cold of the burrow, the strange, radiant force of the Thunderbeast reached out and touched me, and I returned to my parents and our tribe, warm and with a calling. I knew I would be shaman.

"The priests who answer to me are capable, but lack that special relationship with the beast. I fear for what will happen once I die, and for what will happen to our spiritual life. Perhaps we will become like the Black Lions, worshiping our totem in name only while truly revering Silvanus or Tyr. At least that would be a better fate than that of the Blue Bears, lost to Malar's depravity. Already many members of our tribe favor the outside gods over Uthgar. I have prayed for a true successor. Could that be you, Vell?"

Vell stuttered. "I don't know. . . ."

"I may be able to clarify for us both," said Keirkrad. "I would like to use my magic to look inside you."

Vell stood a bit straighter and silenced a little cry inside himself. "This is well."

Keirkrad's watery blue eyes latched onto Vell's brown ones, and he placed his hands on Vell's bulging forearms. He chanted a few mystical syllables, and his glare grew all the more intense, his blue eyes growing wider and clouding over with a whitish film. Vell trembled silently as the shaman's frail hands dug into his muscles with surprising strength. He summoned the will not to pull free from the old man's grasp as his sour breath enveloped Vell's face in slow puffs.

Then Keirkrad released him and took a few steps back. The shaman's gaze fell to the ground and he shuddered with fists clenched, making twisted claws of his hands.

"What's wrong?" asked Vell. But Keirkrad said nothing. "Tell me," he insisted.

"You're afraid," rasped Keirkrad. The old man wore a disgusted frown. He spoke through his gasps for breath. "I have seen your soul. Why do you fear the gift you have been given?"

✦ ✦ ✦ ✦ ✦

Gan took a deep breath when he arrived at the ditch surrounding Llorkh. Wider than a road, and too deep to climb out of easily, it had been magically dug by Geildarr a few years back. It forced visitors and caravans arriving at Llorkh to visit checkpoints manned by Lord's Men.

The hobgoblin followed the ditch until he reached a checkpoint, a considerable distance outside Llorkh's fortified walls. A black-armored soldier approached him while his two fellows kept watch from a safe distance.

Gan still carried the battle-axe that he and Dray had found. He had spent a dozen days marching through the Fallen Lands and the Graypeaks, and in that time it had scarcely left his hands. He found that he needed it in his grip even when he slept.

Even Gan, with the sentiments of a hobgoblin, felt a wave of disgust as he approached Llorkh. The ditch looked like a cruel gash in the earth, and all around, nature itself seemed to have surrendered to civilization's needs. Bare of trees and grass, the rocky plains were dull and dead. The surrounding mountains bore the ugly scars of mining and forestry. The city walls stood tall, plain, and bare.

"What business have you in Llorkh?" the Lord's Man, called Clavel, demanded of Gan. Though Clavel modeled his speech and manner on the Zhentilar, a certain authority was lacking in his voice as he faced down the huge hobgoblin.

"I wish an audience with Lord Geildarr," Gan said.

"An audience with the mayor?" Clavel said. "For what reason?"

"I fought in his army against the shades."

Clavel placed his hand on the hilt of his sword.

"Geildarr doesn't want you here, hobgoblin. Go back to your tribe. Whatever's left of it."

Before the Lord's Man could react, Gan swung the huge axe. The brunt of it struck Clavel head on, and though he was not badly wounded, the blow was enough to send him flying backward and rolling down to the bottom of the ditch. Two other Lord's Men jumped forward with their weapons at the ready, but Gan lowered his axe.

"I am not here to fight," he said. "I wish to offer this artifact to Geildarr in atonement for my failure, and that of my tribe." He laid it on the ground before the guards.

Nervous glances passed between the Lord's Men. Then, from the shadows behind the checkpoint, an unlikely figure emerged. Small and trim, she moved with the lithe authority of someone thoroughly in control. Her age was difficult to guess, but she appeared to be recently entered into womanhood. Her honey-brown hair hung in a short crop around her smooth oval face. She was dressed in tight black clothing with a sword at her side. The guards' eyes followed her closely. She strode between the Lord's Men and stood in front of the hobgoblin without fear, leaning over to inspect the fallen axe. Her fingers traced its lines.

"Geildarr accepts," she said, and strolled back to the checkpoint with girlish grace. She cast a look over her shoulder at the hobgoblin. "Bring it," she commanded. Gan leaned over and picked up the axe. The woman took a moment to glance down into the ditch as she passed, where Clavel, his robes smudged with dirt, was struggling to claw his way out, bringing more dirt down onto his face with each desperate grasp. She told the other guards, "Leave him down there till tomorrow morning, then demote him two points of rank."

As Gan walked past the guards, he asked, "Who is she?"

One guard wore a lecher's smile as he watched her walk away, admiring the grace and poise in her every step. The other shrank away from the slight woman in nervousness. But they answered together, "Ardeth."

Gan followed Ardeth past the checkpoint and into Llorkh. He had never been in a city before. Most of his life had been spent in the Graypeaks with his tribe: hunting, making war on rival humanoids, and occasionally performing services for the Zhentarim, including this last assault that crushed his tribe's warriors. He didn't doubt that what was left of his people would shortly be destroyed or subsumed by one of their rivals, but he felt only the slightest tinge of remorse. Hobgoblins respected strength, and if strength resided in this Geildarr, it was in Geildarr's service that he belonged.

Llorkh seemed largely unburdened of the decadence his people associated with city living. Whether made of wood or stone, the buildings were spartan and simple, and even the tall one in the center, which he rightly figured was their destination, had little grace in its design. The streets were uncrowded, many of the houses showing decay as if they had been long unoccupied. The people who were visible were largely soldiers—humans or orcs—and downtrodden human workers, their clothes dirty and ragged. This was not a city, he decided, so much as a stronghold, geared for war and defense above anything else.

He respected that.

Bound for the Lord's Keep, they skirted a large square where homes and shops were better maintained. A variety of stock animals brayed in pens here, and many of the caravans that he had sometimes witnessed crossing the Dawn Gap sat under guard.

Soon they came to the Lord's Keep, its guards casting puzzled looks but nevertheless letting Ardeth and Gan through without question. Just before the door, Ardeth pivoted back on the hobgoblin.

"You mean this weapon as a gift for Lord Geildarr?" asked Ardeth.

"This is so," Gan replied.

"And what do you ask in return?"

"Only a place in his army," Gan said, and he looked over the axe he bore. "This is a mighty weapon and it deserves a leader worthy of it. May I not speak to him?" asked Gan.

"He is not here right now," said Ardeth. "But he accepts your gift with great thanks. It is a worthy blade."

"Worthy of a great leader," said Gan, and with great humility, he lay the axe in the dust before the Lord's Keep.

The Dark Sun, together with the Lord's Keep and the barracks, was one of the largest buildings in all of Llorkh: an absurdly oversized cathedral to the Prince of Lies. Its great wooden doors stood several stories high; its nave supported by many thick black pillars of ebon. Geildarr had never seen it more than two-thirds full, not with all the faithful of Llorkh, Loudwater, and Orlbar attendant on important holy days.

When Geildarr strode inside, he felt dwarfed by the immensity of the purple walls, from which the jawless skull—Cyric's symbol—stared at him on every side. A much smaller temple to Bane once stood on this spot, presided over by Mythkar Leng back before the Time of Troubles. But when Cyric took Bane's place after Bane died spectacularly in the city of Tantras, Leng displayed his newfound fealty by ripping down the old temple and building one twice as large on the same spot, mere months afterward.

It amazed Geildarr that Leng could switch allegiances so easily. The transition was easy for Geildarr, of course, for it meant little more than changing the name in his prayers and quaking in fear of a different power. But priests were supposed to have such an intensely personal relationship with their deities. Geildarr had heard about some Banites and Bhaalites who purposely injured themselves after their gods died.

And now Bane was back, bursting from the shell of his son, the puppet, and with Bane's resurgence spreading throughout the Black Network, Cyricist Zhentarim were becoming a rare breed. The Zhentarim, once a secular organization that comprised followers of many deities, seemed increasingly like an arm of the Church of Bane, and the worship of Cyric seemed to be more popular in places like Amn and Thay, where Zhentarim influence was minimal.

Geildarr decided that Leng swapped deities so easily because the god he worshiped was nothing more than a name for the darkness in his soul. What Moritz said made sense: Leng could easily switch to Bane and take the temple with him. He had transitioned so easily to Cyric, and just as easily he could go back. Lord Fzoul did the same, changing his allegiance from Bane to Cyric to Xvim, and he was a favorite servant to each god, blessed with much power.

Geildarr knew what all Zhentarim knew, but none dared say: the bulk of them were interested in power above all else, and worshiped whichever god could best provide it. After Cyric went mad and unleashed a monster army on Zhentil Keep, Xvim the Baneson seemed like a welcome alternative. But Darkhold always remained loyal to Cyric; therefore, Llorkh had too.

Eyeing one of the etched skulls staring down at him from a pillar, Geildarr reflected on his own relationship with Cyric. Certainly he acknowledged that Cyric had touched him in a rare and special way for a wizard, granting him powers to craft and explore magic that few could manage. He owed that much to the Lord of Murder. But did he have such loyalty that he would never contemplate worshiping Bane, or any other god, if circumstances demanded it?

A young acolyte came out to greet Geildarr. "I need to see Leng," Geildarr said. "Fetch him."

"The Master is attending to his studies," the dark disciple told him. Geildarr knew just what that meant. Another dwarf who was part of a conspiracy against Llorkh had been turned over to the temple, and Leng was experimenting with better ways of creating groundlings—the disgusting dwarf-badger hybrids that the Zhentarim used as elite assassins. They were both tinkerers, Geildarr and Leng, though Geildarr liked to experiment with new and better spells and magical items, and Leng devoted his time to finding ways to corrupt good into a dark and degenerate mirror of itself.

Geildarr recalled that the Dark Sun once contained a secret known to few in Llorkh. Rakaxalorth, one of the Zhentarim's loyal beholders, lived in a chamber beneath the temple, covertly operating the Dark Sun alongside Leng. The two functioned together as the Zhentarim's foremost representatives in Llorkh. When a bugbear army—under phaerimm mind control and led by a beholder—assaulted Llorkh, Rakaxalorth came out of his hideaway, flew over the city walls, and joined the fray. Rakaxalorth annihilated the phaerimm's beholder mind slave, and gave his life to do it.

Somehow, Geildarr doubted that Leng would ever do anything remotely comparable in defense of Llorkh.

"He will set his research aside for a moment," Geildarr said to the acolyte. "The mayor of Llorkh wills it." But he was left waiting a long time before Leng arrived.

Leng wore the traditional purple and silver robes of his god, with ornamental handcuffs on the sleeves to signify Cyric's one-time imprisonment in Shadowdale. With jet black hair, pale flesh, and piercing gray eyes, he looked intimidating—enough to inspire the fear and devotion of those weaker than him.

"Mayor," Leng said. "To what do we owe this honor?" His tone was the same as all Zhentarim priests—coldly cordial with a hint of menace.

"I recently received a message from Fzoul," Geildarr said, his voice echoing from the highest rafters of the cavernous church. "He sends his regrets after the failure of our troops in the Fallen Lands."

"Good of him," Leng said. "Has he further instructions for us?"

Geildarr shook his head. "He says that he and Manshoon will review the Shade question before further actions are taken. But I'm concerned."

"Why?" asked Leng.

"You know the workings of the Zhentarim better than I. Fzoul gave us an impossible task—the kind the Zhentarim give to cold initiates. One along the lines of 'assassinate Lady Alustriel' or 'steal Elminster's second-favorite pipe.' Now he wants to punish us for not fulfilling it."

Leng smirked. "Did you give Ardeth Chale such a task? Is that how she earned your devotion to her?"

"Better still, she accomplished a very difficult task of her own volition. Just the kind of initiative I admire." A touch of defensiveness rang in his voice. He went on. "I doubt if all the Lord's Men *and* the muster of our humanoid allies could have shaken the Shadovar from the Fallen Lands.

Even if they had, it would have left us undermanned and vulnerable, even more so than now. This "failure" could be the excuse Fzoul's been looking for to tighten his grip on Llorkh, and that could mean your head and mine." He looked hard into Leng's steel gray eyes as he said this, searching for any reaction that might give him away.

Leng spoke coldly. "If that were Fzoul's plan, he wouldn't need to go to such lengths as the conspiracy you envision. And if he wanted us dead, we wouldn't be here talking about it."

"Perhaps you're right," said Geildarr. "But in any event, I feel the order of the day is appeasement. Start thinking—anything short of bringing the City of Shade crashing to Anauroch."

"As you command, Lord Geildarr," said Leng. But Geildarr knew he would do nothing. Geildarr noted a twitch of Leng's pale lips as he bowed in farewell.

As Geildarr walked back to his keep, he analyzed his information. He didn't trust Moritz, and he knew it was possible the gnome was mixing truths and lies as part of Sememmon's game, or some unknown agenda. For that matter, he had no way of being sure that Moritz was still on Sememmon's side. If Leng were disloyal, Geildarr would need to find out for himself. And if Leng needed to die, the act would need to take place without casting suspicion on Geildarr.

When Geildarr reached the Lord's Keep, he found his promising protégée Ardeth Chale waiting for him in his study, a mysterious smile on her face. She had taken some apprenticeship from him as a wizard, and though her power was progressing steadily, she seemed far more interested in honing her skills of cloak and dagger. So far, she had proved extremely valuable in helping protect Geildarr's rule.

"Something has just arrived," she said, endearing mischief dancing in her eyes, "that should be of great interest to you."

"What is it?" asked Geildarr.

"A hobgoblin arrived in town today. One of the Skalganar tribe and a survivor from the Fallen Lands."

"I wasn't aware there were any survivors."

"He thinks he might be the only one," said Ardeth. "But Gan—that's his name—wants to work for you. On his way back, he found something he decided to bring to you. An axe."

Geildarr sniffed. "Nobody accuses hobgoblins of being much for brains, but an axe? Didn't anyone tell him I'm a wizard?"

"Somebody must have." Ardeth stepped aside, revealing the axe lying on the zalantarwood table behind her. Geildarr walked up to it and leaned over to inspect the axe's design.

"No noticeable markings," he said. "But it looks dwarven to me. And nothing modern."

"I'd wager on Delzounian," said Ardeth. Geildarr perked up at this. Delzoun was once the mightiest dwarf kingdom of the North, on par with the modern Great Rift. A neighbor of Netheril, it fell almost fifteen hundred years earlier.

"How did this hobgoblin get such a thing?" asked Geildarr.

"He said he found it in the Fallen Lands, lying in a field of dirt. An unlikely story, but the weapon is definitely magical. It had some hold over him, that was plain to see, but at the same time he seemed eager to give it to you—to a great leader, he said. I got the sense he felt he was unworthy of it."

Geildarr stroked his chin. "A great leader, eh? A fine judge of character, this hobgoblin."

Ardeth smiled. "I subjected the axe to magical examination—as well as I could manage. I don't sense that it is intelligent in the conventional sense. But I think it might have shaped Gan's attitude, nevertheless."

"What else did you learn?"

"Only a name—Berun's Axe. It would clearly benefit from further examination."

"Both magical and scholarly, yes," said Geildarr, running a finger over the weapon's blade. "And what of our hobgoblin friend?"

"You could still hang him for failure."

"No," said Geildarr. "I don't think I will. If he wants a place in my army, he has it. Find him a spot in the barracks, far enough away that nobody important has to smell him." Picking up the axe, he said, "I'll need some time alone to cast a few spells. Divining the history of an object can be demanding and time consuming. I trust you can handle any important town business in my absence."

Ardeth's face lit up like the sun. "Yes, indeed," she declared, and vacated the study.

Geildarr laid the axe on the desk and retrieved some components for a spell that would reveal its legend. Whether chance or fate had brought the axe to him, he was very pleased. It would give him an enjoyable mystery to mull over while waiting to find out if Fzoul wanted his head.

CHAPTER 3

Four generations before Vell's birth, a Thunderbeast hunting party had discovered one of the secrets of the North—a crumbling dwarven hold in a clearing in the Lurkwood's south. According to the songs faithfully repeated by the tribe's skald, Hazred the Voice, it was named Grunwald after a warrior who single-handedly slew a frost giant in this place, echoing Uthgar's final defeat of King Gurt. The Thunderbeasts saw this as an omen.

The tribe spent many happy and productive years in those stone ruins, though some said that they gave away their souls. They cultivated a strong business in lumber, established relationships with cities such as Mirabar and Nesme, and even began worshiping gods other than Uthgar.

On this day, fog covered Grunwald like a white shroud. Silently, Thunderbeast warriors walked among oval stone buildings that had been their homes, their turf roofs now overgrown with grass and moss. The warriors were alert and on guard. This place, once home, might conceal unknown dangers.

The rest of the tribe waited in relative safety not far away, under the watchful eye of some of the tribe's warriors. Vell reflected that scant days ago, that group would have included him, but now he was at the chieftain's left hand, and the most revered shaman of the tribe seemed to dog his every step. Vell wondered what kept Keirkrad so close to him. Was it respect, or fear?

Vell knew Grunwald as well as any of them, though he had not seen it in four years. Over there was the place where he played as a child. In that direction lay a shaft to the mysterious tunnels beneath Grunwald, where strange monsters were said to lurk, though nobody ever really saw one. That structure was the Stone Bow, where outsiders could find lodgings for themselves and their horses—often in the same stall. The Hand of the Justice lay near, and more.

Vell felt a twinge of melancholy. He felt as if he were seeing a reflection of the Grunwald he knew. It had always been a ruin, but it had never felt dead before. Once it bustled and sang with the lives of the Thunderbeasts, but now Grunwald was bare: a discarded rock pile, a sickening parody of civilization, counting house and all. And when Vell looked at the pallid faces of his fellow Thunderbeasts, he knew they felt the same way.

They envied those who had stayed behind for safety. This place would never elicit the same sentiment again.

Sungar pointed upward at the most prominent building in Grunwald, the stone keep called the King's Lodge. It had probably been several stories higher at one time, but three serviceable levels were still intact. The structure served as feast hall and dungeon for the tribe, and throne room for its chief. Its main entrance lay at the top of a stone stair, over which steel hooks still hung with the skulls of their enemies: orcs, goblins, and some dishonest merchants who had come to Grunwald.

"Come," said Sungar. "Let us pay our respects to the chiefs of times past."

But as he took a step toward the King's Lodge, Sungar's eyes caught sight of something falling from high above the lodge. It was a coal-black feather, fluttering in the light breeze, but it was no normal feather. It was much larger—nearly as long as a short sword. Sungar let out a hoarse war cry, and the tribe jumped to alertness, readying their weapons and fanning out to face potential foes from all sides. The war cry was echoed by the sharp shriek of a great bird, and answered by other cries from the surrounding Lurkwood.

From the top of the King's Lodge, a giant raven took wing. Astride its back was a lean barbarian woman, ritual war paint streaked across her cheeks and arms. She directed her mount to fly a graceful circle around the assembled Thunderbeasts below, as if daring them to let fly their arrows and spears. As the sky filled with more giant ravens and their riders, cries of "For Ostagar!" and "Death to weaklings!" filled the air. Arrows burst from the narrow windows of the King's Lodge.

The Black Ravens despised outsiders more than any Uthgardt tribe. They had special hatred for any tribe that bore the taint of civilization, and that meant the Thunderbeasts. This was the Ravens' Runehunt—they had challenged themselves to achieve the utter ruin of another tribe. They never could have laid siege to Grunwald when the tribe was strong, no matter how many times the Thunderbeasts besieged their strongholds and destroyed their aeries. But times had changed, and the Ravens now believed that the Thunderbeasts were weak and ripe for destruction. Such was the natural order. Just as the weaker members of a wolf pack were removed by violence or winter, so too were tribes eliminated. The Black Ravens considered it a sacred duty to cull the weak.

In a flash Grunwald became a battlefield. The huge ravens dodged the arrows and hammers of the Thunderbeasts while swooping in to snap and slash at their faces. Massive beaks claimed a number of eyes as the beating of great wings disturbed the fog that hung over the dead settlement. War cries blended with the birds' incessant squawking and mixed with screams of pain as arrows arced down from the King's Lodge, embedding in warrior flesh.

Brandishing a mighty warhammer, Sungar charged forward up the stone stairs to the entrance of the King's Lodge, its thick stone door firmly shut. Other warriors surged forward to join him in banging and slashing at the door.

Keirkrad chanted a few syllables and raised his hands. A wind boiled up that tore through the fog and disturbed the air above. Though not strong enough to blow the ravens from their places, it was enough to surprise and slow them so that a well-placed spear and a hail of arrows brought two ravens plummeting from the sky. When they hit the ground, Thunderbeast warriors were ready to finish off bird and rider.

The raven riders were not so many that the Thunderbeasts could not defeat them, but the arrows raining from the King's Lodge were a serious threat. What had been the Thunderbeast's strongest defense was now potentially their destruction.

"Train your weapons to the Lodge!" Thluna shouted, hurling one of his hammers at the upper window. It sailed neatly through, though whether or not it met its mark on the other side, he could not tell.

Vell focused on one detail amid the confusion—a single blue eye staring out from an arrow slit in the fortress. He concentrated and threw his spear at it, but it missed, striking just to the left of its mark and bouncing off the wall. Below the eye, he saw thin lips twist into a smile, and an arrow flew from the window directly at Vell. He didn't have time to blink before it struck him between the eyes.

But Vell barely felt it. The arrow bounced off his skin as if it had struck iron. Vell gulped in confusion and whirled to face Keirkrad. The shaman's skin was covered with brownish, gnarly scales, for he had invoked a power the Thunderbeast bestowed on its priests. Keirkrad gasped and mouthed Vell's name through the noise. When Vell looked down at his hands, he realized that they too were covered with brown scales. His heart jumped at the shock, but he felt something else flowing from his core, overwhelming his fear. His senses began to cloud, and the confusion of war faded, replaced by the perfect clarity of rage.

Keirkrad made slow steps toward Vell, and with each step, the ground around him shook—an effect of his shamanic power. The walls of the King's Lodge vibrated and trembled, dust rising from the ancient dwarven blocks.

A giant raven swooped down and snapped the neck of a Thunderbeast warrior in its thick beak. Sungar's hammer blows began to crack the stone door of the Lodge. Another Thunderbeast cried out as an arrow sank into his skin. The Black Ravens above cursed the name of Gundar and called for the tribe's destruction.

Vell stared intently at his hand and the inhuman skin that coated him like a suit of armor. But he was not wearing it—it *was* him. Vell turned his back on Keirkrad and faced the King's Lodge. He knew what he had to do.

Vell marched up the stone stairs. One of the orc skulls above him slipped from its hook and shattered on the ground.

"Get clear of the Lodge," Vell said, pushing men aside. He locked eyes with Sungar and said, "Trust me." Vell walked up to the stone door. Unflinching, he walked through the damaged portal, which crumbled and fell all around him.

Inside, four Black Raven warriors gasped at the approaching figure covered with dust and scales. Before they could react, Vell grasped two of them by the necks and slammed their heads against the wall with a hard crack. The other two drew their swords, but Vell fended them off barehanded, grasping a sword arm in each hand and squeezing with inhuman strength. The Black Ravens fell to the floor squealing in pain.

Vell ignored them and walked through the vacant stone hall that was once the tribal feast hall. The structure now trembled and crumbled with each of Vell's thunderous steps. As he passed huge depictions of the Thunderbeast adorning the walls, the totem seemed to look on as Vell moved. A few Black Ravens slipped into his wake, but he paid no attention to them or their arrows, which simply zipped past him. Vell made his way into the next room, which he remembered as Gundar's throne room. A simple stone seat, long unoccupied, was the only furniture in the chamber.

Vell picked up the throne, held it high over his head, and threw it at the wall. It broke through, dislodging stone blocks and sending streams of dust from the floor above. Vell didn't even blink as the ceiling caved in on him.

The assembled Thunderbeast warriors watched in awe as the whole face of the King's Lodge crumbled and collapsed in a deafening waterfall of stone. A few screams from the Black Ravens punctuated the noise, but were silenced quickly. Stray pieces of debris bounced toward the Thunderbeasts, but the bulk of the building fell inward and away from the onlookers. A huge cloud of dust billowed up and coated all of Grunwald in a white cloud, thick and oppressive.

The shock felt by the Thunderbeasts was nothing compared to that of the raven riders above them, who watched so many of their tribesmen disappear in the rain of debris. Their birds spooked as the terrain beneath them vanished. The creatures circled uneasily, leaving them unprepared for the hail of arrows that emerged from the dust, and letting missiles plunge into their wings and underbellies. Some threw their riders and flew off into the Lurkwood. Finally, the rest of the Black Ravens retreated, demoralized.

One of the raven riders fell through the dust and landed hard on the ground. A Thunderbeast readied an axe, but Sungar cried, "Halt!" The chieftain ran to study the enemy, whose blood gurgled at his lips. Sungar held a warhammer at the ready.

"You are impure," the Black Raven rasped through his failing breath. "You are weak."

"Not so weak as you think, it seems," said Sungar. He sank his hammer into the Black Raven's brain.

As the dust settled in Grunwald, and the skies cleared

of Black Ravens, a mighty cheer rose up from the tribe. Soon after, all eyes turned toward the rubble of the King's Lodge.

"Is this why the Thunderbeast gave Vell its power?" asked Thluna. "So that he might save us on this occasion?"

"Truly, songs will be sung of his sacrifice," Sungar said.

"He might still live," said Keirkrad. He rubbed his skin, now restored and supple.

The tribe set upon the rubble, digging through it for any trace of Vell. They detected a quiet weeping, like the mewing of a kitten. The strongest of the tribe's warriors were needed to lift the rocks that pinned the youth. Although Vell showed no visible injuries, tears stained his cheeks. The tribe stood staring at him, not knowing what to say.

Sungar and Keirkrad stepped in. "Arise, my son," the chieftain said. "You are our salvation this day, and there shall be mead and flesh to celebrate." But Vell lay still and silent, his brown eyes darting. Not a scratch marked his body, but he was wounded, as if he had witnessed all the pain in the world.

❧ ❧ ❧ ❧ ❧

"A thousand lines of doggerel and I'm no closer to understanding this axe," Geildarr complained. His study was littered with handwritten notes scattered on tables and pinned to the walls, and the subject of it all—the battle-axe—still lay across his desk. Ardeth lingered on a few notees.

"Black feathers fall at the open blade," Ardeth read. "With the name of Uthgar on the lips of both friend and foe, eggshells shatter under the kingly might. A revenge is repaid near the sacred site." Then another: "Tharkane's hands on the shaft as the nations clash under tree the eldest. Blue Haloan's blood spoils the foliage. The people of the forest look on but do not present themselves."

"Interesting spell, this one," Ardeth said. "I thought you'd simply cast it and it would tell you what you need to know about the item. Naïve of me."

"Divinations, my dear," said Geildarr, "are like Alaundo's Prophecies. They always make perfect sense in the clear light of hindsight. Understanding them beforehand is more difficult. The problem here is that this axe obviously has a very long history. I think it goes back as far as Delzoun, and it hasn't been lying in the dust for all those years, by any means. It's had a very active life. Many stories." He rested his hand on the axe head, curling his fingers over the blade enough to feel its sharpness.

"Learning the stories is just the beginning," he went on. "The legending spell doesn't always tell the truth—just the legends people tell, or used to tell."

"And those can be untrue," said Ardeth.

"Right. And sometimes the legends leave out the most important parts of a story. Each new casting gives me a fuller understanding and allows me to ask more probing questions, but the problem in this case is that there's so much story to cover."

"You do have quite a library on the next floor," said Ardeth. "Is more research necessary?"

"I've called you here for research," said Geildarr, "but not the kind that uses books. Let me show you what I know. I've sorted the notes into several categories." He indicated a pile of scribblings on the desk before him. "First, my discoveries about the axe's creation. It was forged in Delzoun and given as a gift to somebody who helped rid the dwarves of an enemy. But the rescuer had powerful enemies of his own." Geildarr rubbed his chin. "I'm going to try some other divinations about this figure, but I suspect that he's the one called 'Berun.' There's a Berun's Hill south of Longsaddle, related or otherwise.

"But here's what interests me the most. There are various hints that Berun is some sort of leader of men, guiding his people west from 'fallen skies, dead gods, and rising sands.' Sounds like Netheril to me—some mass migration after Karsus's Folly. This one—" Geildarr scanned his desk and snatched up the appropriate note "—may describe new dweomers being woven into the axe that ties it to something else, some kind of object or artifact that alters the axe's power." Geildarr read his scribbling aloud. "Joined as one the axe and heart by the stout folks' spells, a link forged cannot be undone. Swells the power of both, and both in Berun's hands now leave the underland." Geildarr smirked. "Bad poetry, but intriguing divination."

Ardeth giggled. "A Netherese artifact?" she asked. "Do you know anything more?"

"I'm still attempting some divinations. But beyond the important bits about the axe's creation, most of the legends describe typical adventuring stories—beheading dragons, slaughtering giants, that kind of thing. The clear majority of what I've uncovered is of this sort. Who knows if they're true?"

Geildarr drummed his fingers on the table. "But it scarcely matters. The sheer volume of the tales means the axe has had a very active history. I've even gleaned that it's been in the hands of one of the barbarian tribes from up north," Geildarr said with a smile, and he produced an old book called *Tulrun's Totem Tales of the Beast Shamans* from amid the piles of notes. "I think I've identified it as the Thunderbeast tribe."

"An Uthgardt tribe," Ardeth said. "But don't they shun magic? Isn't it unlikely that they're hoarding Netherese magic after fourteen hundred years?"

"They had this axe until fairly recently," said Geildarr. "How they lost it and how it ended up in the Fallen Lands is still a mystery to me, but my spells have given me a few references to fairly recent events. And while axes are a fairly standard barbarian weapon, Tulrun's book talks about the chief of the Thunderbeasts—who called himself King Gundar—owning an impressive axe, the symbol of his leadership." Geildarr closed his hand around the axe's shaft. "Perhaps this is the very same."

"So the other artifact that's linked to this axe," Ardeth mused. "What do you know about it?"

"I'll keep trying," said Geildarr. "I don't know much about it yet. Perhaps I'll have more answers once you get back."

"Get back? From where?"

Geildarr smiled. "There's an old friend of mine I haven't thought about in some time. Arthus Tyrrell. He knows plenty about the Uthgardt. That's if you don't mind a trip outside of Llorkh."

"Not at all," said Ardeth.

"You'll need to move quickly." Geildarr stood and walked across the room, snatching from the wall a primitive bone dagger, carved with a sharp point. He tossed it to Ardeth and she caught it by the hilt. "Be sure to give him my best. The skymage Valkin Balducius just came in with a caravan from the Keep—I'll have him escort you." Geildarr hesitated a moment, then said, "There's something else I want to talk to you about, something you can't mention to anyone. It could mean my neck if you do."

"What's that?" asked Ardeth.

"You know who Sememmon is?"

"Of course," said Ardeth.

"A . . . person loyal to him paid me a visit recently, and not for the first time."

"Gods," said Ardeth. "Did you alert Zhentil Keep?"

"No," said Geildarr. "What good would it do? If they haven't been able to catch him with all their resources, a tip from me isn't going to help."

"Who visited you?" asked Ardeth. "What did he want?"

"His name is Moritz. He's a gnome, and an illusionist."

"Truly?" Ardeth giggled.

"No comic trifle, this gnome," said Geildarr. "He's a slippery creature. He's probably as versatile an illusionist as you'll find. No one has ever known him to engage in violence personally, but there are many deaths on his head nonetheless. He's served Sememmon for years, but I wouldn't be surprised if Fzoul still has no knowledge of his existence.

"Let me tell you a story. Moritz—I like to call him Moritz the Mole, burrowling that he is—comes from the village of Hardbuckler." Ardeth knew of this gnome settlement—somewhat south of Llorkh, it served as a stopover along the caravan route between Llorkh and Darkhold. "Or so I believe . . . it's possible that it's all just an elaborate deception Moritz has woven. I suspect he does such things for his own amusement. He was trained in the smoke arts of illusion—but he found the way of Baravar, the gnome god of illusion, too modest; not a path to the power he wanted. He learned about Leira, the Lady of the Mists, and pledged himself to her worship.

"So he left his people and met some human illusionists, who ultimately directed him to a place called the Mistkeep—I don't know where it is. He studied with the Leiran mistcallers there, learning spells, improving his power. Of course, by this point, there was no Leira. Cyric had killed her, and since then, he grants spells to her worshipers in her place. Most Leirans don't care, may not even believe it, or they think the entire world is just one big illusion. But Moritz was a gnome, and he thought differently. He stopped praying to Leira and prayed instead to Cyric. And Cyric gave him a vision."

Geildarr settled into a comfortable chair. "The vision bade him home, so Moritz went back to Hardbuckler in disguise. He found that he felt no sympathy for his people, not even his own family, and when he discovered Zhentarim agents working in secret to take over the town, he helped them—essentially handing over his own folk to Darkhold. His actions brought him the notice of Sememmon, who stripped away the illusion he wore and insisted that Moritz tell him the whole story. Pleased, Sememmon decided to make Moritz into the most secret of his agents, using him as an infiltrator, yes, and as a mole."

"Nice story, Geildarr," said Ardeth. She smiled slightly. "Kinda reminds me of something."

"I thought it might," said Geildarr. "Not many people know it, believe me. I repeat that the story may not be true—but I heard it from Sememmon himself one night over too many ales. Anyway, not long after Sememmon fled Darkhold, Moritz popped up here—Sememmon must have given him some sort of teleportation device, or perhaps he's exploiting illusion cleverly. He came to talk me into joining Sememmon's side. To do what, I'm not entirely sure—cower under a table somewhere with his master and Ashemmi, maybe."

"But you wouldn't do it. Would you?"

"I haven't yet, have I?" Geildarr asked. "But I mention it because . . . the last time he visited, he mentioned you."

"For true?" asked Ardeth. "What about me?"

"Nothing memorable—just a mention. That's what puzzles me. He must have had a reason. Maybe he'll try to get at me through you." Geildarr looked down at his desk a moment. "He probably sees you as a weakness of mine."

"But we're not lovers," said Ardeth.

"You and I know that," Geildarr said with a lukewarm smile, "but not everyone does."

An uncomfortable silence hung over Geildarr's study. Then Ardeth turned to him, gripping the dagger by its carved bone hilt.

"About Arthus Tyrrell, then," she said.

A lone creature, a tangle of roots, vines, and leaves, wandered through the high valley by moonlight. Spawned in the bubbling bogs of the Evermoors, it plodded east through the Silverwood and spread its taint and rot through the valleys at the feet of the Nether Mountains. The grass withered and died where it stepped. Natural creatures—the bears, elk, and red tigers that inhabited these heights—fled at its presence.

But then something arrived to challenge it. A man with thick, hard muscles, armed with nothing but his own strength, stared at the creature, waiting. He stood still and silent in the moonlight, facing down the shambler. A creature of pure instinct, it stepped forward and opened its rotting arms to welcome the barbarian.

The barbarian stood still and accepted the embrace of those putrescent limbs. He let the shambler seize hold of him, feeling its acid sting his flesh. The barbarian gritted his teeth and tried to hold back, but the change came over him nonetheless; his skin changed to scales within the shambler's grasp. The great rotten plant tightened all the more, but strong arms dug into it from within. The barbarian locked his eyes on the twin pools of green that served the shambling mound for vision. He clenched his muscles, and—with a mighty scream—flung his arms apart. The shambler's body was torn asunder.

Vell sat alone in that meadow till the sun rose, the rotting remains of his enemy lying all around him. The scales had left him, but the feeling did not. Eventually, Keirkrad arrived.

"It was not difficult to find you," Keirkrad said. "I needed only to follow the trail of dead ogres and trolls. Sungar may have let you take your leave of the tribe after Grunwald," Keirkrad went on, "but I'm telling you now, your tribe has even greater need of you than before."

"I do not feel like a member of the tribe now," Vell told him.

"You mean you feel better than the rest of us?"

"No!" Vell thundered, rising to his feet. "How could you ask such a thing?"

"You dare raise your voice to a shaman?" Keirkrad snarled. Vell shrank away like a chastised child. "Have you found enlightenment out here, away from your people? Has the beast given you guidance?"

"No," Vell confessed.

"That's because you're not following its instructions. It did not tell you to set yourself apart from our tribe. The beast despises such arrogance, and the more you resist the call, the worse your anguish will become. Uthgar is an accepting deity. Why else would he allow himself to be worshiped through so many different forms—the Thunder-beast, the Sky Pony, the Black Raven, and all the others. Perhaps in Uthgar's halls at Warrior's Rest we shall all be united as brothers, friend and foe alike. But the beast does not accept defiance of its instructions."

"You said the beast had a greater purpose for me. A destiny. That I was set apart."

"That may be so," Keirkrad admitted. "But you seem to believe that the gift of Uthgar was meant for you. This is not so—the gift is for our tribe. You are merely the vessel. I know the burden you bear. Perhaps I alone can help you through it. I have spent my life serving the beast and

Uthgar, and I know full well what you're feeling."

Vell shook his head. "You say you know, but how can you?"

"I should have left the world decades ago," Keirkrad admitted. "I feel unnatural, an aberration. Some call me 'Uthgar's freak.' My skin crawls with age. Sometimes," he smiled grimly, "I wish I could just die, but if I live still, I must have some further function. I have not yet fulfilled my role for our tribe, for Uthgar. I must keep living until I do."

Vell looked Keirkrad square in the eye. "It's not the same thing. I don't know who I am any more. I feel the most precious part of myself slipping away."

"You have power, Vell!" Keirkrad shouted. "You've saved our tribe already, and you can save it again. Our tribe faces a crisis that goes far beyond a few Black Ravens with too much ambition. It's what brought us to Morgur's Mound. You carried the message—'find the living.' "

"I don't remember saying that," said Vell. "But I do remember what happened at Grunwald. I remember exactly how it felt as my mind lost control of my body. The scales took my will with them. I don't know who or what brought down the King's Lodge, but it was not Vell the Brown."

"It's a rare gift to have the Thunderbeast act through you. Such an honor to be our totem's vessel!"

Vell turned away. "Then the beast made a mistake. It chose too weak a vessel."

Keirkrad placed his ancient hand on Vell's shoulder. "The beast makes no mistakes. Do not doubt yourself—place your faith in the divine. If it chose you, that *must* mean you're strong enough to accept the burden. Pray to the beast for strength."

"I pray that it takes this power from me."

Keirkrad snarled. "It is not for you to question this! Sungar makes plans for our expedition into the High Forest. You cannot refuse your destiny any longer."

"Do you hate Sungar?" asked Vell.

The question took Keirkrad aback. "What do you mean?"

"Gundar made him chief instead of you," Vell said, overcome with an inner strength that made him speak words he would never dare to say otherwise. "You scheme to take his place. This is known to all. But you're too old. So you need a champion to become chief and act on your behalf . . ."

"Insolent child!" Keirkrad shouted so sharply that it echoed off the valley walls. "Your gift is being corrupted by the wickedness in your mind. That is why you cannot bear it; you refuse to turn your will over to your totem. Let the Thunderbeast into your heart and you shall know peace again."

Each word cut Vell like a dagger and sucked away the strength he felt. He fell on his knees before the shaman, supplicant and weeping for forgiveness.

❖ ❖ ❖ ❖ ❖

In a way no one had expected, the trip to Grunwald proved worthwhile for the Thunderbeasts. Not only did it provide a taste of the warfare and the prideful thrill of victory that some of them craved—it also helped erase Grunwald from their collective memory. Everyone realized that it was not the place they once knew, and it would never be home again. They made the path back, some to whatever corner of the North they claimed as their hunting ground, most following their chieftain to a pleasant bend of the River Rauvin, east of Everlund. They were free once again to roam and move with the ebb of the seasons and the herds of deer and rothé, but mostly they stayed at the river, in what was inevitably known as Sungar's Camp.

Life slowly returned to normal. Tents were pitched again, children played among the meadows, and the hunting teams brought home elk, deer, and even a ghost rothé—considered a good omen for the upcoming expedition.

Sungar met with Thluna in his tent. "I have chosen the men I need with me in the High Forest. I want you to inform them of the honor. We will need the druid Thanar as a guide in the forest, as well as Hazred the Voice, and the warriors Grallah, Torgrall, Hengin, Ilskar, Stenla, Flagdar, Delark, and Draf the Swift. Tell them to make themselves ready. Once Keirkrad returns with Vell, we shall not delay."

"Very well," Thluna said. "But I ask that you reconsider. I think my place is with you. There are others that might act as chief."

Sungar shook his head. "I cannot deprive my daughter of her husband for such a long time. And I trust no one more than you to lead the Thunderbeasts."

"How long do you think the quest shall last?" asked Thluna.

Sungar shrugged. "Days, months, years. The Thunderbeast has sent us on an epic task, and such glory comes at a cost. This task could claim all our lives."

A Thunderbeast arrived at the tent flap. "Forgive me, chieftain," he said, "but a civilized outlander has arrived at our camp seeking to speak with you. She claims to have an offering for your audience."

"She?" asked Sungar. "A visitor from Everlund?"

"I think not," came the answer. Sungar bade him to bring her, and he and Thluna heard whispers outside. When she stepped forward, they realized why.

Dressed in comfortable traveler's leathers with a slender sword dangling from her waist, the woman was tall and almost as solidly built as Uthgardt women. Long-limbed and agile, there was something pleasantly deerlike about her. Black hair flowed down her shoulders in curls, but the hue of her skin transfixed them most. It was considerably darker than most folk in the North, certainly among the insular Uthgardt. Only a few southern merchants who visited Grunwald over the years had displayed such a dusky skin tone.

"Sungar, son of Moghain, I greet you," she said. Astonishingly, she spoke in the tongue of the Uthgardt! Though her accent slightly favored the Common tongue, her diction was flawless.

"What magic is this?" asked Thluna, having seen translation magic at work before.

"You may wonder that I speak the language of your people. I am not skilled at it, but I hope I have learned enough not to insult. I am Kellin Lyme, daughter of Zale Lyme." Her words and her posture were appropriately respectful for someone seeking an audience with a chief of the Thunderbeasts—even those born to the tribe could have done no better. In her hands she carried a parcel wrapped in wolf skin. She laid it at Sungar's feet and unwrapped it, revealing a large piece of old bone.

"What is this?" asked Sungar, this time in Common. He leaned over to pick it up.

Kellin joined him in Common. "A piece of bone from the Thunderbeast itself, stolen more than a century ago by unknown raiders. It has been away from your tribe too long, and now I return it to you."

Sungar inspected it closely. "This was stolen from Morgur's Mound? How did you come to own it?"

Kellin swallowed. "My father purchased it from an antiquarian in Baldur's Gate. It has spent several decades in the archives of Candlekeep, Faerûn's greatest library."

"Library?" asked Thluna. "Those are for books—why should it hold a bone?"

"Candlekeep collects many things. My father spent his life learning about tribes like yours. It was his specialty. He visited your tribe at Grunwald once, met with King Gundar, and even drank in the King's Lodge with victorious warriors who had broken an orc horde near Shining White."

"Yes," said Sungar. "Yes, I remember. I was young then, and I could not understand why one of the civilized folk would want to learn our customs. But I remember him as a good man, nevertheless."

"You honor his memory," said Kellin graciously. "I follow in his footsteps. I am a sage like him, and I, too, study your people. You interest me very much and I've made it my life's work to learn more about you." With some hesitation, she added, "And yet, I have not met an Uthgardt until today."

"This is difficult to believe," said Thluna, looking at the newcomer warily.

"You may fetch your shaman or a priest of your tribe and let him test my intentions," she replied, "but let me explain them first. On the night of Highharvestide—your Runemeet—my sleep was disturbed by a rattling sound in the archives. It was this bone, dancing in the box that held it, and when I touched it, I felt a flash in my mind, bidding me to come to your aid. It told me that you were in great danger. I wanted to help."

"Help?" asked Sungar. "Why should you want to help us?"

"Many asked me the same when I left Candlekeep," said Kellin. "But I felt that I had no choice. So vivid was my summons that I felt my mind would never feel right again if I ignored it."

"So you think that the Thunderbeast called you—an outsider—to our aid?" asked Sungar, looking her hard in the eye.

"I don't know if the Thunderbeast did," she admitted. "But someone did."

Sungar probed her eyes for a long while. "She speaks the truth," he finally told Thluna. "I need no priest to tell me that. But you, woman, are still a mystery. Where you're from, these studies of which you speak—I know nothing of these things."

"I can explain it all," said Kellin, "if you will listen."

"Perhaps I do not care to hear your explanations. We do not tolerate the presence of your kind more than necessary. That you know our customs does not change this. I cannot allow you to taint my people and introduce your ways."

"I am not here to proselytize!" Kellin insisted. "I do not want to change your way of life. Far from it. To tell the truth . . ." Uncertainty spread through her limbs and her posture fell, her shoulders slumping, and she dropped the formal manner of her speech. "I don't entirely know why I'm here. I had hoped you might give me some idea." Her dark eyes shone with warmth.

Glances passed between Sungar and Thluna. Sungar spoke in Common again, speaking her language almost as well as she spoke his.

"You are a new piece in a mystery which vexes our tribe at present. If the Thunderbeast sent you, if you're here to help, there must be a reason. There are many things we'd like to know right now."

"Then let us find them together," Kellin suggested. "I know much of your tribe's history—more than is recorded in your songs. I've come hundreds of miles to see you. I'd hate to think it was a waste."

Sungar leaned closer to her. "Perhaps you're a test of our strength. A temptation sent by the Thunderbeast to see if we would accept your kind of aid. We've accepted outsiders into our company before, and it has ended badly. Maybe the beast wants us to sacrifice you, the way we sacrificed outsiders in centuries past. If you know our history so well, you should know that I'm telling the truth."

Kellin trembled slightly but stood her ground and held her head high. "It's always difficult to know a god's will," she said. "Perhaps as an outsider, it's my role to make up for the failings of the past. Or perhaps it's just to teach the Thunderbeasts a lesson in humility."

"I suppose you've read that our tribe responds to strength, both of arm and of character," said Sungar. "Well, daughter of Zale, you've proven your mettle. Thluna, arrange a tent for her on the edge of camp, away from the others." Sungar looked at the sword at her belt. "I trust your weapon is not for decoration."

She grinned confidently. "I know which end is which."

Sungar had to smile at that. "Good. You may have some use for it soon."

CHAPTER 4

In the shadow of the twin stockades that dominated Newfort, Arthus Tyrrell arrived at his modest home after a hard day of work. His features were weathered and his hands were calloused, but he never wondered for a moment if he had made a mistake in coming to this inhospitable frontier town. Dwarfed by the mountains that surrounded it, Newfort was founded and largely occupied by settlers from Zhentil Keep. Now, they worked hard to carve out a life for themselves in the North.

Tyrrell closed his door behind him. He was alone; his wife and two children were not yet back from their work at Stauvin's Mill. A few steps from the door, he noticed something lying on his table—something resembling a large, white knife. He walked to it, grabbed the dagger, and held it up to the light. He gasped. He had seen it before.

"Is it true," came a voice, "that you dealt the

death blow to the Great Wyrm?" Tyrrell spun around to see a pretty face smiling at him from a shadowed corner.

"Who are you?" he asked, taking a step forward. But he was silenced as she raised a crossbow from the darkness and sent a bolt zipping past his head to embed in the wall beyond. He stood very still as he looked at her—a petite woman, dressed all in black.

"My name is Ardeth. No one saw me enter your home," she said with a coy smile, "and no one will see me leave."

"Where did you get this?" he said, holding up the dagger.

"Geildarr Ithym sends his regards," the girl said.

Tyrrell sighed. This was his worst fear realized. His past with the Zhentarim had caught up with him. He had never been a member of the Black Network, but he worked *for* them on occasion. Years before, at the behest of Llorkh, he and his fellow adventurers had sought the Great Wyrm Cavern high in the Spine of the World. It was the most sacred site of the Great Wyrm tribe of Uthgardt, and they had to slaughter and torture a great many of the barbarians before they learned its location.

When they finally reached the cavern, they slaughtered the benign dragonlike creature Elrem—the Great Wyrm tribe's totem, shaman, and chief in one. They claimed Elrem's considerable hoard for their Zhentarim masters. The bone dagger was a mundane item of considerable antiquity, presented to Geildarr much later. Geildarr believed that it dated back to the earliest human habitation in the North, many thousands of years before even Netheril.

"I have a family," said Tyrrell. "A wife and children. Kill me and you're taking a father and a husband away. Surely even you Zhentarim have some feelings about that."

"The only thing I care about right now is the Uthgardt," Ardeth said. "Geildarr tells me you're something of an authority on the subject. If you want to live, I recommend you answer my questions."

"The Uthgardt," said Tyrrell. "You're threatening me for information on the barbarians?"

"As implausible as it may sound, yes. And unless you're

willing to die to protect that information, I'd recommend telling me all you know. For instance, the significance of the name 'Berun.'"

"He's a figure in the mythology of some tribes," Tyrrell stammered, drumming his fingers on the table in his nervousness. "Sometimes he's conflated with Uthgar. There's a Berun's Hill near Neverwinter Wood, and Beorunna's Well was probably named for the same person."

"Is this just mythology?" asked Ardeth. "Is it possible he actually existed?"

"Possible. I don't know much about it, but some sages think he might have been a Netherese warrior who led an exodus to the North after the fall."

"Netherese," Ardeth repeated, savoring the word. "Geildarr will like that. Is there anything special about an axe in these legends?"

Tyrrell shrugged. "They're barbarians. There's always an axe. That or an especially large club. For the cracking of skulls."

"Such a wit you are," Ardeth said through pursed lips. "Now, what can you tell me about the Thunderbeasts?"

"Thunderbeasts?" Tyrrell thought a moment. "Thought to be the most civilized of all the tribes, though I don't recommend saying that to their faces. They hate wolves for some obscure reason—they regard them as a ritual enemy. Orcs, too. Something to do with the Gray Wolf tribe, probably. Their totem animal is something called a behemoth, or 'thunderer'—a big lizard of some sort, possibly one of those dinosaurs that live down in Chult. There may even be one of those creatures still alive closer to home—they say that the lizardmen in the Lizard Marsh . . ."

"Where can I find them now?" asked Ardeth. Even though his life was under threat, she sensed a general willingness to cooperate. Perhaps the threat was unnecessary—once a Zhentarim supporter, always a Zhentarim supporter. Or perhaps this erstwhile scholar was so in love with the sound of his own voice that he welcomed any opportunity to hear it. She added, "And by 'them' I mean the Thunderbeasts, not the lizards."

"Well, for about a century they lived in a place called Grunwald, up in the Lurkwood, making a living at some sort of trade. No other tribe has ever dealt with the cities of the North so directly, except possibly the Black Lions, who've recently cast their lot with the Silver Marches wholeheartedly. Some of the other tribes hated the Thunderbeasts for settling down and wanted to destroy them, but others respected them for the power they commanded."

"You say they lived in Grunwald," said Ardeth. "You mean they don't now?"

"No. Their chief for many years was named Gundar. He outlived all his sons, and the story goes that as he was dying, he had a choice between two successors—the old priest Keirkrad, who wanted to stay in Grunwald, and a warrior called Sungar, who represented a faction of the tribe who wanted to abandon Grunwald and go back to their nomadic roots. The dying chief chose Sungar, though some thought that he was too senile to make the decision properly. But Sungar is now chief. Because his succession came under odd circumstances, some in the tribe question the validity of his rule.

"If you're trying to find them, don't try Grunwald. I heard recently that they cut a deal with the folk of Everlund. The Thunderbeasts are living somewhat east of there, along the Rauvin, and they've agreed not to raid the town or harm trading interests as long as Everlund does not extend too far in their direction. Basically, they've both agreed to leave each other alone, except in the face of common enemies. That essentially means orcs—barbarians need little justification to fight orcs."

"This . . . Sungar . . . how would one recognize him?" asked Ardeth.

"Well, like I said, the tribe hates wolves. Sungar's nickname is 'Wolfkiller.' Many of them wear wolf skins, but when dressed for ceremony, the chief probably gets the fanciest—they favor black. Or alternatively," Tyrrell said through a grimace, "you could just ask every barbarian you see. That way, you're bound to find him sooner or later."

Ardeth smiled coldly. "Is there anything else you'd care to tell me about them?"

"Well," said Tyrrell, "there's one thing. I hesitate to mention this—I don't know if it's anything more than silly rumor."

"I'll be the judge of that," said Ardeth. "Talk."

"Apparently, about two and a half years ago, around the same time the Phaerimm War was happening, some members of the Thunderbeast tribe—Sungar included, and maybe Keirkrad, too—were on an orc hunt down in the Fallen Lands." Tyrrell watched Ardeth's eyes narrow at the mention. "I see you've heard of it. Well, when they came back, most of the tribesmen were dead and those still living were missing a great number of weapons, including a very special axe."

"How did you hear this story?" demanded Ardeth.

"From a logger here in Newfort, but he claimed he heard it from a barbarian named Garstak, a former Thunderbeast who left the tribe not long after this. Sungar and the others refused to discuss what had happened, but word got out anyway, and it led to some internal strife. This Garstak—according to the logger, anyway—refused to say much more, but said that he thought his tribe was too debased and was doomed to weakness and ruin. He said he was going to go up north to try to join the Black Lion tribe, for he thought they had the nobility he founded lacking in his own people. And that's all I know."

"Do you know where I might get more information?" asked Ardeth.

"Oh, I don't know . . . you might ask the Thunderbeasts themselves."

"I just might," said Ardeth, letting out an odd giggle. "I thank you for your help, and Geildarr thanks you."

"I hope he does. Here's his dagger back." He tossed it, and the weapon landed on the floor at Ardeth's feet with an unceremonious clunk.

"No," she said. "It belongs to you." She picked it up and hurled it at his face. Tyrrell dodged too slowly and it struck him in the neck. He instinctively grasped at his throat as blood flowed down his chest. Ardeth stood watching as he attempted a few steps toward her, but he collapsed from the pain and blood loss before he could reach her. She smiled like a naughty child as his bloodstained hand reached in her direction and grasped only air.

"Thanks for the help," she said as she leaped over Tyrrell. Within heartbeats, she was through his door and gone.

Through the haze of death, and the blood dripping in his eyes, Tyrrell saw a new face. Was it real, or was he dreaming it? he wondered. The image spun—a huge red nose on a shrunken face.

The face spoke. "She's very good, isn't she?"

Without moving to help him, the gnome waited until Tyrrell rattled with death. Then he reached over to extract the bone dagger from Tyrrell's neck, freeing a tide of blood that swelled the puddle on the floor.

What am I doing here? thought Kellin. Children lurked outside her tent to try to get a glimpse of her, so exotic a creature was she in these northern lands. They regarded her little differently than they might a dark-skinned visitor from Zakhara—any place outside the North was the same to them, and any visitor who looked different was an object of curiosity and fear.

Kellin liked and respected Sungar, and Thluna seemed like a man far beyond his years, yet with boyish wonder and enthusiasm. But they were the only Thunderbeasts she'd spoken to in the days since she'd arrived. She'd taken her meals with the tribe, but they seemed scared of her, especially when she spoke to them in their own language. The women particularly looked at her with disdain, as if she were there to steal their men—as laughable a notion as that was.

Kellin could hear the voices of those who had tried to dissuade her from coming here.

"I can understand it perfectly," one of the Candlekeep lorekeepers told her. "Your whole childhood was spent safely locked away here, while your father wandered the world in search of adventures. But such a venture is foolhardy and dangerous." Kellin's denials hardly even convinced herself.

She heard footsteps approaching outside her tent and instinctively reached for the hilt of her father's sword.

"May I speak with you?" came a deep voice, speaking uncertain Common.

Kellin stood and opened the tent flap. She instantly knew who the man was by his brown eyes, but from the stories she'd heard, she hadn't expected him to look quite so gentle and innocent.

"Vell the Blessed," she said, using the Uthgardt tongue. "I've heard a lot about you. I am honored that you've come to see me."

"The honor is mine," Vell said, staring deeply at her face. He stared so long, in fact, that he pulled away in embarrassment. "I'm sorry."

"No," she laughed. "It's fine. I've gotten the same reaction from most of your people."

"Your parents . . . where did they come from?" asked Vell.

She admired his directness. "My mother was of Tethyrian blood. I've inherited something of her skin tone, and hopefully some of her good sense as well." She smiled. "My father was born in the Moonsea region, in a place called Melvaunt."

"I see," said Vell, though Kellin suspected she'd named a few places he'd never heard of. "Our chieftain tells me the Thunderbeast sent you here."

"All I know is that when I touched that piece of bone, I heard a message of some kind, and it led me here."

"Will you be coming into the forest with us?" asked Vell.

"I don't know," Kellin confessed. "Sungar says he hasn't decided, and I haven't decided if I should."

"I hope you do. We can protect you."

"I can fight," said Kellin, half-smiling. "So can the women of your tribe—they've proven it many times in your history. But I'm not sure if my place is on this expedition. I don't really belong."

Vell reached over with a clumsy hand to comfort her in her uncertainty.

"Do I belong?" Vell asked. "I'd never have dreamed to be invited on such an expedition as this. Sometimes I wonder why the spirit chose me. The entire tribe was assembled at Morgur's Mound. Why didn't the beast choose Sungar as its vessel, or Keirkrad the Shaman? Did it pick me at random out of all the Uthgardt there? Even an outsider responds to the beast's summons better than I."

"Gods, don't think that," said Kellin. "It hasn't been easy for me. That moment on Highharvestide, I felt a nagging dread wash over my body and settle in my stomach. I haven't been able to get rid of it. That's just a taste of what you must have experienced." Vell nodded. She was the first person to try to excuse his weakness. It felt good, but he instinctively mistrusted it for coming from an outsider. "But what's interesting is, it's starting to fade now that I'm here. It's crazy that I'm here, but somehow it feels right, too. Am I making sense?"

"Yes," Vell said. "And I'm glad you're here." Then Keirkrad appeared behind him, seemingly popping out of nowhere.

"I, too, would like to greet our new arrival," the shaman said.

"Oh," said Vell. To Kellin, he whispered, "We shall talk again," before walking out of the tent.

Keirkrad stared at Kellin. She found his eyes unnerving— they were blue as the sky, and so piercing and unwavering. His body appeared frail and crumpled, and he was hunched over like some gargoyle. A brisk wind disturbed the flaps of the tent, and Keirkrad looked almost as if he'd blow away with it.

"I trust you are shaman Seventoes," Kellin said. "Sungar has told me of you."

"He has told me about you," Keirkrad said. He stood very close to her, and she could see a brown film coating his yellowed teeth. "No matter how much you've heard about our tribe's penchant for hospitality at Grunwald, you should know that those times are passed. We no longer consort with outsiders. You are not welcome here."

"I'm here because your totem spirit guided me here," Kellin retorted. "I should think that I would be treated with the greatest courtesy."

Keirkrad sniffed. "Southern humor translates poorly to our tongue. You may think the Thunderbeast sent you here, but I shall be the judge of that. I remember your father well. For a month he lived as we lived in Grunwald. We tolerated him because we thought him an amusing diversion—an outsider who wanted to know our ways. We did not realize he had made himself our chronicler as well, that he put us in books. What death befell Zale Lyme?"

"He died in his sickbed," said Kellin.

"A suitable death," Keirkrad said. "Unheroic."

"Your King Gundar died the same way, as I understand."

Keirkrad ignored her comment. "I just got back from retrieving Vell, who thought to abandon his people in their time of need. I hope his moment of weakness is over. Sungar says you will come with us into the wood. He is my chief and I will not question his wisdom. But I will not let you taint the mind of Vell or any other Thunderbeast with your ways."

"I've spent my life studying the Uthgardt, as my father did," Kellin told him. "The last thing I'd want to do is to change you."

"Have you brought books with you?" asked Keirkrad.

"Yes," she said. "Various reference works that might help me understand what's happening to your tribe."

"Let me see one of these books," said Keirkrad.

Warily, Kellin went to the corner of her tent and picked up a thick volume from her collection. Keirkrad snatched it and flipped through it, idly running his fingers over the lines of dense text. There were occasional illustrations—line drawings of costumes and tribal emblems. He found one sketch of King Gundar himself. At that he snapped the book shut.

Keirkrad looked at the leather-bound cover.

"What does this say?" asked Keirkrad, tracing the embossed title.

"It says, *Customs of the Northern Barbarians*." She hesitated before adding, "By Zale Lyme."

"Oh." Keirkrad looked up at her. "Your father wrote this?"

"Yes," she said.

Keirkrad tore the book to shreds. The binding snapped under his bony hands, and he ripped the pages free, tossing them to be caught by the breeze and scattered all over the camp.

"You may come with us if you want," Keirkrad concluded with a bitter sneer. "But leave your so-called civilization behind. The Thunderbeast doesn't want it."

❖ ❖ ❖ ❖ ❖

That evening, before a roaring fire at the clan hearth, the skald Hazred sang a song of Uthgar. It went on for a long time, like most longer epics, but Hazred's voice never faltered and his memory never failed. When he concluded, Kellin stepped forward to take the skald's place before the assembled warriors, their grim faces lit by the orange flicker of the fire.

"I, too, have a story to tell," she said. "I know it is a tradition of your people for newcomers to tell a story. It does not have a song, but I would never try to usurp the place of your magnificent skald. I'm not practiced in your language, but I shall do my best.

"I'm rarely called upon as a storyteller," she said, smiling. She scanned the crowd and her eyes connected with Sungar, Thluna, Vell, and finally Keirkrad, who stared at her impassively from across the fire. Kellin had first wondered if she might tell them a story from their own history, about the figure known variously as Berun, Beorunna, and the Bey of Runlatha. But Kellin had thought of something that she hoped would work better.

"Let me tell you a story from my own life," she began. "Many of you met my father, Zale Lyme, when he visited

Grunwald many years ago. He studied all the Uthgardt tribes, largely from afar, but yours was the only one that welcomed him.

"I didn't realize until after his death how little I truly knew my father. The bulk of his life was spent away on one expedition or another, and when he came back to me and my mother, he spent most of his time preparing for his next journey. But he enthralled me with stories of faraway places and all the things he learned, all the people he met. And before he died, I told him all this. With his blood and his stories inside me, what choice did I have but to follow in his footsteps?" Kellin paused a few heartbeats, gauging the interest of her listeners. Around the campfire, all was still.

"A few years ago, I went on my first expedition, to the island of Ruathym far away in the Trackless Sea. My father was there many years before, and I went to verify his findings. I was looking for information on Uther Gardolfsson, as Uthgar was called before he came to these lands. He was Thane of that distant isle before he came to the North all those centuries ago. And as I walked the place where Uthgar was born, where he was educated, I realized something. I was not only walking in Uthgar's steps, I was walking in my father's as well. And that helped me understand why he admired your people so much.

"I was born and raised amid stone walls, a world of books and learning. I'm anathema to your way of life, but I realize that makes me respect it all the more. Many civilizations rose in the North and later fell, till only scholars like myself remember their names. But through all that there were the Uthgardt, living more or less as you do today. You are the finest of survivors. Even when the Silver Marches are dead and gone, just another name on a roll of dead kingdoms, the Uthgardt will live on, living the same as you do today."

A roar of applause came up from the tribe. Sungar walked forward and stood with Kellin—a silent gesture of her acceptance by the tribe at large. She caught Keirkrad still wearing the same blank expression as before, but she discovered Vell smiling widely.

❧ ❧ ❧ ❧ ❧

Wings beat in the night, so softly that no one below heard them. The riders on the hippogriff's back heard a dull roar of excitement rise as they made quiet circles above the barbarian encampment, lit by the flickering red and orange of its bonfire.

"I wonder what's going on down there," said the skymage Valkin Balducius, his forehead furrowing beneath his jet black bangs. He was smiling wickedly at having spent so much time with Ardeth over the last few days, even if most of it was just ferrying her around. Now to engage in this strange endeavor alongside her . . . it would make for a good story, if nothing else.

"They're barbarians," said Ardeth. "They're probably celebrating a new record for most spines snapped or something."

"Which one do you suppose is chief?" Valkin asked her.

"There by the fire," said Ardeth, pointing to a dimly lit figure beneath them. "With the beard. Only chiefs are allowed to wear black wolf pelts like that."

Valkin looked back at her. "Just how do you know that?"

She smiled coyly. "I know a lot of things," she said. "Now speaking of wolves, are your pets in position?"

"Ready on your word," Valkin said. "May I say, Ardeth, this mission has proved a lot more interesting than guarding caravans across Anauroch has ever been. Maybe afterward, you'll tell me the real reason we're doing this. Abducting barbarian chiefs . . . not standard Zhentarim activity."

"Geildarr wants him," Ardeth replied. "That's all you need to know for now."

"Hmm," Valkin said. "I spent all morning flying over the Nether Mountains finding dire wolves for this little project, and you still haven't thanked me."

She turned back to him and smiled a transfixing smile.

"Perhaps I'll thank you later," she said.

He cursed himself for being so damned malleable, all the while admitting that he couldn't do a thing about it.

Wolf howls suddenly filled the night, ringing like a knell through Sungar's Camp. The festivities ceased instantly. Mugs filled with mead spilled on the ground as warriors hurried to draw weapons. No war cry and no chief's orders could call the Thunderbeasts to arms faster. These were not the cries of normal wolves, but of the great dire wolves that wandered the wilderness.

"She has brought wolves upon us!" cried Keirkrad, pointing a finger in Kellin's direction, but he was scarcely heard among the uproar. Families were roused from their tents and ushered to the camp's center, and horses were pulled from their corral to the center of camp as well. Mothers armed themselves with bows and formed a tight circle around the children. More howls came from the west, the north, then all sides. Torches were lit, armor donned, and weapons readied.

Kellin searched for Vell, dodging huge barbarians as they rushed back and forth, trying desperately to form a perimeter around the camp before the onslaught began. But as she navigated the confusion, she felt a strong hand on her shoulder and was spun backward, directly into Vell's face.

"This is no random attack," he demanded. "Some mind guides it. If you have anything to do with this . . ."

She shouted at him in fury. "You and Keirkrad both?" Vell shrank back at the force of her reaction. "Why would I have wolves attack your camp while I'm in it? I can help you fight," she said, reaching for the blade she wore at her side. The howls grew closer.

"Save your mettle for another time," Vell said. "Stay with the children." And he turned toward the edge of camp.

At that moment a dire wolf bounded into the lines, very close to Kellin and Vell. Kellin was startled by the suddenness of the attack, but Vell dashed between her and the wolf. Thunderbeast axes and swords quickly brought the creature down, but not before it had bitten a warrior in two with a single snap of its huge jaws. Another wolf came, then another, all charging into camp with suicidal fervor, their huge eyes glowing and drool glistening on their white teeth. The weapons of the Uthgardt dug into fur and flesh, stopping the wolves only at the cost of brave lives. The howling in the distance did not cease.

"Some wizardry is at work on their minds," said Kellin. But when she looked at Vell, she gasped at the transformation that was overtaking him. Scales sprouted from his skin as he vanished into a rage, and Kellin watched reptilian slits grow in the place of his soft, brown eyes. She extended a hand to feel his scaled skin, but he pulled away.

"No," she heard Vell croak. He fell to his knees, gripping at his face with both scaly hands. "Not this time."

"What if the chieftain should die in the attack?" asked Valkin, projecting his voice over the noise of the battle below.

"I suppose I'd leap down there and save him," said Ardeth. Valkin didn't doubt that she would.

It was quite a spectacle. Wolf after wolf tried to ram its way through the barbarian line and was slaughtered in the process. Valkin's magic willed the creatures toward the center of the camp—the beasts had nothing in their heads except a desire to get there and to kill anything in their way. Ardeth kept her eyes locked on the bearded chief who seemed well prepared to stay alive himself, hacking away at fur and claws.

The dire wolves were not so powerful that the tribe was in danger of destruction, but they served their true purpose well. They had been summoned only as a distraction.

"So when do we do it?" asked Valkin, tugging impatiently on the hippogriff's reins.

"Patience, skymage," said Ardeth, a cool night breeze tousling her hair. "When you have the luxury of choosing when to strike, always strike when the opponent is weakest."

"Did Geildarr teach you that?" asked Valkin.

Ardeth ignored him. "Barbarians are strongest when they rage. We wait till that subsides—after all their foes are killed."

"You mean," said Valkin, "we wait until they think they're triumphant, then hand them an awful defeat? A delicious idea."

"Why, Valkin," Ardeth replied. "Where did you acquire so cruel a mind as that?"

"Spending some time with you, my dear," Valkin said. "It rubs off."

He felt the squeeze of Ardeth's arms around his waist as she giggled away, so adorably, so madly.

Like waves against rocks, wolf after wolf charged the Thunderbeast lines. Some were skewered by archers, but many broke through. Barbarians were torn apart by vicious claws or snapped in two by massive jaws, and blood, of both wolves and men, ran in streams across the camp. A few torches had been knocked from their staves and several tents had caught fire. Some of the braver children ventured forward to try to extinguish them.

Vell choked back his anger and summoned every fragment of his will to contain the beast inside him. He knew some would call him a coward—Keirkrad would certainly scold him for abandoning his tribe in its time of need—but he did not trust his other self. Vell still feared that if the beast within him were released again, he would not be able to tell friend from foe.

In the chaos and cacophony that consumed Sungar's Camp, and despite his distorted senses, he could hear Kellin's voice pleading with him.

"Trust yourself," she begged. But how could he?

"There's a power in you," she said quickly. "I don't

understand it. Not even Keirkrad understands it. But I know what it's like to have something within you that seems on the verge of controlling you. You have to learn to control it instead."

Vell looked at Kellin through his lizardlike eyes, wondering what she was talking about, and he saw that the concern on her face was genuine. He looked back at his hands and realized that they were his again. The scales had receded. He stood uncomfortably and looked her in the eye. He wondered how to thank her, but when he opened his mouth his words were not his own.

"What are you?" he asked.

A strange silence settled over the camp all at once. The clinking of armor and weapons ceased, and the howls ended. The enemy was defeated, and the camp was safe again.

"Victory!" Sungar shouted, thrusting a fist high into the air. All eyes turned to him.

In that moment, something appeared in the darkness above. A tiny point of light fell from the sky over the camp, looking no more dangerous than a shooting star in the distant heavens. But Kellin knew better.

"Turn away!" she shouted as loudly as she could, spinning away from it and slapping her hands over her eyes. But Vell's instincts misled him and he turned to look instead, just in time to stare into the heart of the burst.

The speck exploded into a brilliant wave of light that washed over the camp, a thousand times brighter than the midday sun, before it dissolved back into the dark of night. In that horrid instant Vell saw the night vanish, and watched as many of the Uthgardt closest to the impact collapsed unconscious. Most of the barbarians were too late to protect their eyes and now screamed, unable to see. Behind him, Vell could hear the cries of children. Torches fell to the ground and burned the grass, leaping and raging toward some of the tents.

But Vell's eyes had looked into the flash and withstood it.

Kellin uncovered her eyes and turned to join him, just in time to see a winged beast swoop down from above. The warriors stumbled and groped, blind or dazed, and did not notice as the creature closed its talons around the unconscious form of Sungar and lifted him into the air. The hippogriff bore two riders—a honey-haired young woman and an older man. It lifted off with Sungar firmly in its grip.

Kellin extended one hand. A bolt of silver-blue energy burst forth, rocketing across the camp and striking the woman just as the hippogriff rose. It blew her from her place and she fell to the ground, landing amid a group of semi-conscious barbarians. The woman dazedly propped herself up and shot Kellin a dirty look. Then she drew her sword and sank it into a defenseless Uthgardt's heart, twisting his body to place it between herself and Kellin.

The revelation that Kellin was a spellcaster was lost on Vell as he watched the hippogriff rise into the night, Sungar in its talons. In perfect fury, Vell called upon all that he had previously held back and fought against. He bid the scales to come, and with them, whatever powers that so terrified him. Like a dammed river bursting free, they came in a torrent.

❀ ❀ ❀ ❀ ❀

This was supposed to be easy, thought Valkin as he tugged on the reins. He turned his mount to circle back to the camp that he would be so happy to leave behind.

It hadn't taken much for Geildarr to talk Valkin into this scheme. Everybody who'd visited Llorkh in the past two years had heard about Ardeth. She was Geildarr's protégée and some said something more—an uncomfortable thought. At the very least, Valkin thought that a few days alone with her would be good for much discussion over ales at the Wet Wizard.

He could hardly leave her to be murdered by barbarians.

But when the hippogriff came about, Valkin found himself staring into the black, slitted eyes of a great lizard. Indistinct in the dim light, it seemed to him that a new hill had grown up beneath him, its serpentine neck reaching up so high it was almost at his level.

"What in all the Hells!" shouted Valkin. His hippogriff shrieked and stared, closing its claws more tightly around Sungar. Valkin did nothing to discourage the hippogriff as it wheeled about and flew. He looked back, and the behemoth was running after him, the sound of each step rolling off the Crags and crashing like a waterfall. It was gaining on him.

Valkin yanked the reins, taking his mount higher and higher to escape the colossal beast's reach. When he looked back, the barbarian camp was visible only from the fires burning in the distance. He led the hippogriff into a dive to the left, and as he passed alongside the rampaging behemoth, he lit up the night with a lightning bolt that danced between his fingers before streaking to the behemoth's bulky middle.

Letting out a dull but deafening moan of pain, the lizard's legs collapsed beneath it. It fell to the ground with force that rumbled the entire vale. But it was not dead—far from it—and Valkin could already see the creature straining to rise again. He had, however, slowed the monster, and that gave him his chance.

"I must be mad," he muttered as he tugged the reins, directing his hippogriff back to the camp.

Distant rumbles roiled in the distance. Like a thunderstorm crashing all around them, the ground rolled and shook in the Thunderbeast camp. A great mountain of scales rose among the barbarians and was gone and away in a flash, some of the dazed and fallen crushed under its huge feet. Kellin and Ardeth ignored the distraction as they illuminated the night with colorful spells—red and gold shimmers and bursts of magic flying from their fingertips and coursing through the chaotic camp. Kellin did not know what was happening out in the darkness, but she feared for Vell as a lightning blast crackled through the sky in the periphery of her vision.

The dazed barbarians were beginning to recover around Ardeth, and she tried to finish them with a quick flash of her sword or by sinking her foot into their exposed necks, crushing windpipes. But there were too many, and as her human shield rocked under each new magical assault, the corpse weakened and collapsed into pulp. Cursing, Ardeth pushed free of the barbarian hands that grasped at her slender legs and arms. She made quick leaps in Kellin's direction, her sword at her side. Through the darkness she bounded and wove past the barbarians with strange grace, reaching Kellin too quickly for her opponent to react. Kellin tried to dodge her, but cried out as Ardeth's sword caught her shoulder.

Kellin stumbled backward, blood spilling down her sword arm. She drew her father's blade from its sheath but could not hold onto it, and it fell to the ground. In the flickering light of the fire, she could see her opponent's pale oval face twisting into a wicked smile, her sword held at the ready, but before Ardeth could finish off her opponent, a strong hand gripped Ardeth's forearm and twisted her around.

The distant rumbles became closer again, somewhere off in the night.

Keirkrad's blue eyes bore through Ardeth, staring at her from beneath a layer of scales, the sour stink of his breath washing over her. Silently, he released her forearm and instead clamped onto her shoulders with both hands, squeezing with all the magical strength of his altered shape. But Ardeth twisted and slithered within his embrace, freeing her hands just enough to drive her sword into the shaman's magical hide. It sliced deep and embedded. Keirkrad gulped back the pain, but he did not release her. His fingers dug down to her bones, and she let out a high-pitched yelp.

So intense was Keirkrad's blood fury that he did not feel the breeze of wings beating just above him. He was unprepared for the bolt of magic that struck him from above, battering him into unconsciousness in an instant. Keirkrad's form remained stiff as he collapsed, Ardeth still locked within his embrace.

As Kellin prepared a spell, Valkin shot a purplish bolt in her direction that exploded as she dived frantically. The blast hurled her backward by more than half a dozen sword lengths. As a number of Uthgardt warriors charged, Ardeth wriggled free of Keirkrad's unconscious grip and grasped Valkin's outstretched hand above her.

In a single motion he pulled the woman up. She settled behind him on the hippogriff, and it lifted into the night sky just as Uthgardt arrows and hammers sailed in their direction. But with Sungar still in the creature's talons, the warriors dared not strike the hippogriff. The battered tribe could do nothing to stop the beast from flying away, their chief caught in its grip.

"Do you know anything about this?" Valkin demanded of Ardeth. The ground rumbled again, but he couldn't see the creature that had attacked him as he peered through the darkness. "There's something out there. It's huge, and it almost knocked me out of the sky. What is it?"

"I think it's what some call a dinosaur," said Ardeth. "Or what that tribe calls a thunderbeast."

"What's it doing here?" Valkin asked. "We're a long way from Chult."

"I don't know," said Ardeth, peering over the side of the hippogriff into the darkness beneath them. "Perhaps our captive knows. The whip will tell."

As the thunder of heavy steps approached behind them, Valkin tugged on the reins. The hippogriff, tired and overburdened, angled upward but gained elevation only gradually.

"We need to get back to Llorkh alive first," the skymage said.

"Perhaps we need a distraction," Ardeth suggested. She reached out and stroked his ear gently, a lover's gesture.

"What kind of distraction?" asked Valkin, curious.

As an answer, Ardeth delivered a blow to the side of his head with a clenched fist, precisely where she had stroked. It took Valkin's breath, and as he tried to turn, she pummeled him again, knocking him from his place on the hippogriff. The last thing he saw of her was her smiling face as he tumbled down into the darkness.

Cursing, Valkin mouthed a single command that slowed his fall to a safe speed. But the thunderous steps were getting closer, and just as he landed on the grass, something fast-moving and massive emerged from the darkness. Valkin died wondering which spell could save him from being trampled under a behemoth's massive foot.

CHAPTER 5

Geildarr strolled through the halls of his private floor of the Lord's Keep with a stack of books in his arms, headed for his study. As always, he surveyed the artifacts displayed on the walls and his table. He stopped short as he realized that one was missing. A chuckle came from behind him, and he was not surprised to turn around and see red-clad Moritz standing in the hallway. In his hand he clutched a small stone cougar that he was inspecting with little interest.

"I'll never understand your interest in these things, Geildarr," Moritz said. "I can understand the magical artifacts. They have real power. But cutlery from Athalantar? Coins from Ostoria? Dwarven house decorations from Ammarindar? Mundane, useless relics of failed civilizations—what is the point of those?"

Geildarr reached out his free hand and snatched

the statue away, placing it back on the pedestal.

"I thought you were in hiding," he said. "Not deeply enough for my taste."

"You have no idea," said Moritz. "But honestly. Wherein lies the appeal?"

"I don't have to explain my interests to you."

"I suppose not," Moritz said, cocking his head, "but you just might need to explain yourself to the inaptly-named Manshoon Prime. You sent one of his precious skymages on a mission that he won't be returning from. That may delay the new caravans across Anauroch considerably."

"You mean Valkin Balducius is dead?" asked Geildarr. "How?"

"A lizard stepped on him." Moritz smiled widely at Geildarr's reaction. "Ardeth will explain when she returns. Let me say this—I wouldn't turn my back on that minx for anything. She'll kill someone just to show herself she can."

"So you were spying on her," Geildarr said. "Why?"

"You might say I'm acting as an interested spectator in this whole new endeavor of yours. My attention is being rewarded. It's just taken an interesting turn. There's some real power at work here. Magical power. The kind the Zhentarim would like to have their hands on."

"And the kind Sememmon would like to have too," said Geildarr. "Or at least to keep such a thing away from Zhentil Keep. So why not go find it yourself?"

"It's not really what I do," said Moritz. "It's more what you do. Why should I do it when I can get you to do it instead?"

Geildarr slammed down the stack of books on the nearest table with as much force as he could muster and turned on the illusionist, waving an accusatory finger.

"I don't work for Sememmon! He's nothing now—a pathetic rat hiding in a dark hole somewhere with his elf whore. If you were smart, you'd give him up and look for a different master."

Moritz's face flushed with rage. "Do you think you can afford to be so arrogant?" The gnome's nose turned as red as his clothes. "You think yourself secure as mayor of Llorkh—so did Phintarn Redblade before you slit his throat. Traitors surround you. The Dulgenhar Conspiracy could have taken this city from you. It took a little girl to save your rulership. You've managed to offend the Zhent leadership at exactly the wrong time. You worship the wrong god. And I haven't mentioned the Shadovar, who probably aren't too fond of Llorkh either. I trust you've heard what happened to Tilverton. When the axe—the proverbial axe, not the one sitting in your study—comes down, just who do you expect to save your skin if not Sememmon?"

Geildarr broke himself away and paced the hallway, cursing loudly as he wondered if there was anything Moritz said that he could refute. "What if..." he muttered. "What if..."

"You won't be able to sit on the fence much longer, Geildarr," Moritz said. "It's your choice, of course."

"What if that hobgoblin had never brought that axe to Llorkh?" asked Geildarr, mostly to himself. "What if I hid those clues, forgot all about everything?"

"Then how will you explain getting a skymage killed while abducting a barbarian chief?" asked Moritz. "You're past burying it now."

"True, but what if..."

Moritz tapped his cane twice against the floor. "It says something about you that when faced with a difficult choice, you start thinking of ways to avoid making it. Let me say this—you may be on the verge of finding an artifact that makes all of the items your Antiquarians have pulled from old ruins look like the toys they are. I'll be watching closely to see just what you do with it."

"And let me guess," said Geildarr. "If I give it to you, you'll reward me richly. Or some other equally vague offer."

"I couldn't have termed it better myself," Moritz answered. "And while you're speculating, what do you think will happen to you if you should give it to my enemies instead of me?"

Geildarr stared at him wordlessly. A bead of sweat trickled down his temple.

"A silent threat is always the most potent. If I learned anything hanging around with Zhentarim all these years, that would have to be it!" Moritz vanished, but his laughter still echoed off the stone walls.

When the sun rose over Sungar's Camp, it shone down on a shattered people. A quiet haze of disbelief had settled over the camp, now littered with bodies of Uthgardt and wolves, damaged by fire and force, and leaderless. Its bravest blood had been taken away, but why, by whom, and to what place they did not know. The healers attended the many wounded, but much more would be needed to heal the Thunderbeast soul.

Battle was a way of life for the Uthgardt. It was their primary drive and purpose for being. But usually the enemy was known—an orc horde, a rival tribe—something they could understand. They had no way of knowing who their new enemy was. A bead of light had dropped from the sky and blinded most of them, knocking some into unconsciousness. They couldn't fight such dishonorable tactics.

Their chief was gone—not dead, but taken. Leadership of the tribe fell to his son-in-law, but Thluna was so inexperienced and so young—perhaps even subject to the temptations of the outside world. Already there were whispers that an older Thunderbeast—possibly even Keirkrad, still unconscious from the magical attack—would be a more appropriate choice.

Kellin awoke with rain drizzling onto her face. Barbarian women tended to the wounded all around her. No one would speak to her or accept her offers of help. She walked the camp as an observer, searching for a friendly face but finding none. She bound her own shoulder wound where that foul girl had slashed her, hoping that one of the healers might tend to it properly later on. She asked nearly everyone about Vell, but eventually put pieces together from overheard conversations. No one had seen him, and the thunderous steps had not been heard in the valley since dawn.

She found Thluna in the center of the camp, clutching his young wife Alaa, her eyes flowing with tears. Thluna stroked her glossy black hair. Kellin placed a hand on Thluna's shoulder and to her surprise, he did not cast her off. Thluna spoke to her in Common, which Kellin guessed Alaa did not know.

"Her father has been taken," he said. "And I cannot do anything about it. I cannot live up to my responsibilities as a husband, or as a chief's heir." Kellin now saw him not as a strong barbarian warrior and chief to his tribe, but as a scared, confused boy, grappling with things far beyond him. "Who would do this to us?" he asked.

"Do you know of the Zhentarim?" asked Kellin.

Thluna raised his head and nodded. "Was this their work?"

"Perhaps. They're known for their wizards on winged mounts," Kellin said. "And for stirring up local monsters to dislodge or weaken their enemies. They're not often active in the Silver Marches, but they have a stronghold south of the High Forest, in the town of Llorkh."

"Why are we their enemy," asked Thluna, "when we have scarcely heard of them? What could they want with Sungar?"

Thluna summoned his strength. "We must do what Sungar was preparing to do," he told Kellin, stroking Alaa's hair. "She won't like it, but I must. Very soon. The Thunderbeast gave us our mission, and we must achieve it."

"Will you take my aid?" asked Kellin.

Thluna looked away.

"Shaman Seventoes lies unconscious across the camp," Kellin said. "And even if he were whole, you are chief and not he."

"You do not understand," Thluna said softly. "We do not tolerate civilized people. And we do not cooperate with those who shape magic. We know where that path leads."

Kellin's brow furrowed. She was missing something—

something they weren't telling her, something not founded in ancient doctrine but in recent experience.

"I assure you, there is nothing corrupt about my magic. It does not come from a book—my magic is as innate to me as my ability to breathe."

Thluna looked at her.

"You will have my answer soon," he said at length. "We will not be leaving for several days. Our warriors must heal, and we await Vell's return. He is our hope and our prayer. I believe our tribe's survival rests on his shoulders now."

"That's an awful lot to place on him," said Kellin.

Thluna closed his arms tighter around his weeping wife. "If he will not save us," he said, "then I cannot imagine who will."

No place on Faerûn was more mysterious than the High Forest—or at least it seemed that way to the inhabitants of the North. It was a holdover from ages past when such great woods dominated the face of the world. It held elves, treants, dragons, drow, and only the gods knew what else. Why did it still stand after millennia, with encroaching civilizations all around it, all craving lumber? The High Forest had a way of conquering those who sought to do it harm.

In the minds of many, the High Forest threatened to swell in the imagination and become the very embodiment of the unknown. But there it stood, all too real, and churning out mysteries beyond invention. Though most gave it a wide berth—only a few roads skirted close enough even to see the edge of the trees—anyone living in or traveling through the southern end of the forest knew of the Star Mounts. They could be seen from many places in the North, and it was reckoned that they were almost as tall as the highest peaks of the Spine of the World. Shrouded in cloud and lore, they were perhaps the most tempting secret of the infinite mysteries that the High Forest kept so well.

These peaks occupied the thoughts of Llorkh's mayor.

From the westward balcony attached to his study in the Lord's Keep, he stared in their direction even though they were out of view. Perhaps, he mused, his destiny would be decided there.

"The Sanctuary," he muttered to himself.

"What?" asked Ardeth, stepping next to him. "What sanctuary is this?" She was still battered and bruised from her fight in the barbarian camp, but now, with a long rest and some time in Geildarr's private baths, she was recovering.

"Sanctuary," he repeated with a smile. "All of our hard work may be realized in that little word. Come." He led her down the hallway to his study, where the axe still rested on his desk amid stacks of books and papers. He snatched up a note containing the details from one of his divination spells.

"I had almost given up when this came to me in a spell. It'll be interesting to see what Klev can extract from the chieftain, but perhaps capturing him was unnecessary." He held the parchment out to her and she read:

> *Blood flows from the heart of secrets, where shepherds tend to scales. The axe is the key that pulls back the false and reveals the old Sanctuary in Vision's long shadow. The brave shall find the forgotten source.*

Geildarr couldn't stop beaming.

"What does it mean?" asked Ardeth.

"It's simple," he said, grasping a book and flipping to a faded sketch of the Star Mounts. Each peak was marked with human and elf names. On the far right was a mountain labeled Mount Vision.

"Here," Geildarr said, pointing his finger. "This Sanctuary lies somewhere in the vicinity of Mount Vision. More importantly, the Star Mounts are the source of the Heartblood River." He quoted, " 'Blood flows from the heart of secrets.' Whatever it is we're looking for, it should be near here." He poked the diagram with his finger.

"But shepherds tending to scales," asked Ardeth. "What riddle is this?"

"Perhaps it's more literal than that," Geildarr said. "Tyrrell said that the Thunderbeasts worship a behemoth, a great lizard of legend. And what attacked you may be the same, or some godly incarnation of the same."

"I'm lucky to have escaped it," said Ardeth.

"Truly," Geildarr said. "It's a shame Valkin couldn't have as well."

"He came back to save me. I owe him my life."

"You've done me no favors by returning without him," Geildarr said. He kept his tone steady, making no obvious judgments, but Ardeth sensed the anger underneath.

"Would you be happier if I had died instead?" she asked, her voice rising in pitch only slightly, but enough to make Geildarr feel the intensity of her words. "I'm not Zhentarim, after all. Manshoon wouldn't need to know, or care, if I had died."

Who is master here, and who is the apprentice? Geildarr thought. But he kept his frustration in check.

"That's not what I meant," he said. "But this has made the situation all the more desperate for me." He rested his hand on the battle-axe. "You'll shortly be going on another mission, if you're well enough. And this time, I wouldn't be unhappy if your party returns a member light."

The tribe assembled at nightfall in the camp's center. All expected that Thluna would give them some impassioned speech, saying that challenges let their tribe excel, or bidding them to trust in the Thunderbeast's will. But perhaps Thluna knew that speech-making was for another time, for he spoke simply and honestly. Kellin stood on the edge of the assembly, keeping an eye on Keirkrad, who had recently awakened. But throughout the day there had been no signs of Vell, and those barbarians who went combing the valley for him found nothing but a great many large indentations in the ground.

"Our destiny awaits us inside the High Forest," Thluna said. "Our future will be decided there. Our trail is set by the Thunderbeast itself. But our enemies are many, some of our strongest warriors are lost, and this camp must stay strong. When he designed this quest, Sungar did not foresee this calamity, and I can't follow the plan he had set. My place had been to remain in camp, but the chief of the Thunderbeasts must lead this journey. In my stead, Hauk Graymane, bane of orcs and Blue Bears, hero of the Red Ridge, shall lead with all his wisdom." A cheer went up on behalf of Hauk, one of the tribe's most respected elders.

"Sungar also wanted Hazred along with him on this expedition," Thluna went on, facing the skald. "He is the Voice, the keeper of our stories and our soul. I know Sungar's reasons, but I cannot now deprive this tribe of its skald. Hazred is the history of this tribe, which is now more important than ever for safekeeping.

"Some of you wonder: what of Everlund and our pact with them? It may well be that our unseen foe no longer has any interest in this camp, but it may equally be that the attack of last night is just a taste of what they mean for us. Still, it is important that we stand on our own, now more than ever. Let only the direst circumstances compel you to retreat to Everlund's door."

As shouts of encouragement came out of the assembled tribe, Kellin felt a swell of admiration for Thluna. He was nervous, that was certain, but he faced the tribe with the undeniable authority befitting a chief. Kellin knew Sungar would be proud if he were here. But was Keirkrad? Like some ancient, shriveled turtle he stood, passing silent judgment but never betraying anything on his features.

What followed was a hunting ritual Kellin had read about, and was delighted to witness firsthand. Thluna called the name of each man chosen for the quest. Each was showered with a litany of titles and accomplishments, many of them better suited to gods than men. The stout warrior Hengin was praised as "the vengeful arm of Uthgar," the scout Draf as "faster than the white rabbit and as unseen as a ghost," and Keirkrad was hailed as "the Thunderbeast's greatest blessing upon our tribe." Not even this drew a rise from the shaman.

With the roll completed, Thluna turned his eyes to Kellin. "Lastly, there is the matter of Kellin Lyme." His voice was soft, almost apologetic, and Kellin knew what he was going to say. "We must thank her. She delivered to us a lost piece of our heritage, and she helped us in our battle last night, taking the wounds to prove it. And more, she's done what perhaps no outsider ever has—offered her assistance to us not for any personal gain, nor compelled by pressing circumstance, but only because she thought it the right thing to do." Thluna's voice was almost breaking.

"But in conscience I cannot allow her a place with us. We are Thunderbeasts, and it's all the more important— now that our tribe faces so much crisis—that we strive to keep ourselves free from outside influence. So go with our thanks."

Kellin nodded. She understood, but she flushed with anger when she saw a smile cross Keirkrad's lips. Then the hush over the camp was shattered by a loud "No!"

Everyone turned to find the source, and their eyes fell upon Vell at the camp's edge, striding closer. He appeared just as he had before—a young Uthgardt warrior—but his countenance was different. Passed again from man into beast and back, his presence resonated with a new authority—one that awed and terrified the Thunderbeasts. The assembly of barbarians parted as he strode forward toward Thluna, and fear washed over their faces.

"The Thunderbeast chose us *both*. You need us *both*." The passionate certainty that flowed in his words as he contradicted the chief was palpable. Kellin felt it as a tingle down her spine. Only Keirkrad dared step forward to confront him.

"Vell," he said, "it is your not your place . . ."

"Deny Kellin," Vell said, "and you shall not have me either."

"Do we need you?" asked Keirkrad, limping up to Vell.

"The Thunderbeast never decreed for you to come along into the High Forest."

"Nor did the beast ask for you," Vell shot back. Gasps were heard from the Uthgardt at this verbal attack on the shaman.

"Fellow warriors were crushed under *your* feet last night," said Keirkrad. "Tell me, Vell, are we all to fall victim to the powers you cannot control?"

"I need you all," Thluna spat out quickly. "Vell, Keirkrad, and Kellin. All three and no less. This is my last word, and I will hear nothing more of it." Keirkrad made fists of his trembling hands and frowned at Vell as he walked away.

Soon enough, the center of camp was deserted but for Vell and Kellin. She approached the warrior, fighting to steady her own shaking hands as she did so. Why was she feeling this way? she wondered. She sensed that all of the uncertainty and vulnerability she had seen in Vell before was now gone, and she just didn't know who she was talking to.

"Vell," she said, scanning his brown eyes, which were seemingly harder and deeper than before. "I don't know how I can thank you."

"Why thank me?" he demanded. "Thanks to me, you may die, for a cause you don't believe in and a people who don't want your help. I've helped make that happen." His voice was thick with bitterness.

"I've made my own choices," Kellin said. "Vell, what happened? Do you remember anything . . . anything from your transformation?"

"Not much. Like a dream mostly forgotten, or a night lost to mead." Vell shook his head. "I don't think I'd like to remember more. I wasn't Vell any longer. I was something else, to whom my life as a man was nothing but a shadow of a memory. I don't even know how I found my way back home."

Kellin reached out and clutched at his hand. He instinctively pulled away, but then let her take it.

"You did the right thing. You fought for your tribe," Kellin said.

"And so shall I again," said Vell. "This is the Thunder-beast's price. It is ransoming my own soul. That's how it is assured of my service."

"Is that really how you see it?" asked Kellin. She saw a flicker of uncertainty in Vell, and this pleased her. He did not wear his dark cynicism well.

Vell's muscles tensed. "Keirkrad is right. I killed some of my own people last night—Thunderbeasts are dead by my actions."

"The blame is with the wizard who knocked them uncon-scious. Would not those warriors have laid down their lives to protect Sungar? That's exactly what they did.

"I can't pretend to know what you're feeling," she con-tinued, "but I too have felt things inside me that were beyond my control. When I was a child, I felt magic flowing through me in search of an exit. To stay sane and become who I am, I needed to understand it, tame it, and make it part of myself."

"Then you're what the outside tongue calls a sorcerer?" Vell asked. "Such children have been born into our tribe in times past. They were left to die in the Lurkwood." Kellin twitched. "I don't think that was right," Vell hastily added.

"But that would have happened if I had been born into your tribe," Kellin asserted.

"Yes. You would have been deemed impure and too dangerous to live."

"Is that much different from the way things are now?"

Vell looked around the camp, where suspicious eyes ducked and hid from his accusatory gaze.

"They rejected you," he said. "You came from a world away to help, and they spurned you. Perhaps they don't deserve salvation."

"Vell!" protested Kellin. "These are your people. I wouldn't have come here if I thought that about them."

"Why did you come?" asked Vell. "I still cannot fathom it."

"What reason would suffice?" Kellin said, asking her-self as much as Vell.

"Might it have to do with your father?" Vell asked.

"Most assuredly," Kellin replied. "But not in a way you might think. I never knew him as well as I wanted to, and now I've followed his ways and gone several steps beyond the path he trod. He revered your tribe above all the others. I remember so vividly the stories he told me of his time in Grunwald."

"And you won't have any such stories to tell," Vell said sadly.

"Maybe not." Her smile awakened all the dark beauty of her face. "But somehow I'm not upset to be here. In the end, I wonder if I will gain more understanding than he ever dreamed of."

Vell stood silently, then he finally allowed himself a smile. "I look forward to counting you as my companion, Kellin Lyme."

His formality brought a broad, open laugh from Kellin, and she repeated it.

"And I, you, Vell the Brown." As they parted in the fading light, each of them felt a bit stronger and a bit more certain about the task to follow.

CHAPTER 6

Sungar awoke in the dark, with the stench of human waste assaulting his nostrils. He hurt worse than from any beating he had ever taken. His flesh was ripped and torn, his ribs ached, and his mouth was dry and filled with the acrid taste of blood. The only light he could see was the flicker of a torch somewhere down the hall, its light dancing on the thick steel bars of his cage. His cell looked out on the featureless walls of a passageway.

Yet somehow, he found the strength to rage. He rose to his feet, let out a hoarse war cry, and assailed the walls and bars with his fists and feet. If anything had been near enough to smash, he would have demolished it as he vented his rage, but there was nothing, and so he slammed his weight against the bars again and again, challenging his unseen captors to come and confront him.

As his energy left him, and he collapsed into a defeated heap in his cell, it occurred to him that the bars survive the prisoner much more readily than the prisoner survives the bars.

Only a small shower of pebbles broke free from the walls where he had battered them. Sungar reached out to gather them up in his weak hands.

"If yer finished," came a whispered voice, "I'd like to welcome you. If you can call it a welcome." The voice was low and gruff and came from the cell next to Sungar's.

Sungar could barely speak—his throat was parched, his energy sapped. He leaned against the stone wall.

"Where is this?" Sungar asked.

"We're residents of the Lord's Keep. Dignitaries and other important folks guesting in Llorkh get to stay in the Lord's Keep, and so do we. I'm guessin' their rooms are nicer."

"Llorkh," repeated Sungar. "Where is Llorkh?"

"You don't know it?" said the voice. "Then I really can't imagine what yer in here for. Just who are you?"

"Who are you?" demanded Sungar.

"I'm Hurd Hardhalberd. Who are you?"

"You're a dwarf," Sungar said.

"Excellent guess," said Hurd. "And now it'd be polite to give me yer name in return."

"Sungar. Of the Thunderbeast tribe."

"Thunderbeast?" the dwarf said in surprise. "Uthgardt?" He took Sungar's silence as confirmation. "I used to meet with your people when I worked up in Mirabar. Bought yer timber now and again."

"Are we near Mirabar now?"

"No," Hurd told him. "I guess you don't get to look at maps very often. Llorkh's well on the other side of the North, nestled pleasantly among the Graypeaks like an open wound oozing Zhentarim corruption throughout Delimbiyr Vale. We're south and east of the High Forest, if that means more to you."

"Is that anywhere near the Fallen Lands?" asked Sungar.

"Aye, rather near," Hurd said. "Why do you ask?"

There had to be some connection, Sungar knew. The

decisions he made in the Fallen Lands had set the stage for all of this—the Thunderbeasts' disfavor had drawn them to Morgur's Mound where powers were bestowed on Vell, and the attack on his camp couldn't have been coincidence. And now he was here in this dirty hole, with no company but a nattering dwarf.

If it had been King Gundar in the Fallen Lands, Sungar wondered, would Gundar have done any differently?

"Fine conversationalist you'll be, I'm sure," Hurd said. "But you really have no idea why they've brought you here?"

"I don't even know who 'they' are."

"I can help with that part," said Hurd. "They're the Zhentarim. Or some arm of it, led by the fop wizard Geildarr, who murdered the rightful ruler of this town long ago, chased out most of the dwarves, closed down the mines, and handed Llorkh over to the Black Network."

Few in the North had not heard of the Zhentarim, even among the insular barbarians. Sungar knew that warriors loyal to the Zhentarim had slain the Great Wyrm—one of the most respected of the Uthgardt beast totems—just to scavenge its treasure hoard.

"One thing's fer sure," said Hurd. "If they brought you here, they have a reason. You should be able to figure it out soon enough, once Klev's assistant asks you his questions. He's the chief torturer down here. You'll know him when you see him. One of them half-breeds of men and orcs, made of the vilest parts of each."

"He'll get nothing out of me," Sungar said.

"That's what I thought," Hurd told him. "But I spilled my guts, puking it out till there was nothing left. That was in the first months of my stay here. But listen to this: afterward, Klev's assistant told me that they already knew everything I'd said. Klev took it from me while I was unconscious, using magic. He just did it again for the pleasure of seeing me break. I don't know if he told me the truth, but it could be that every secret you have, you've already given up. It's been a year since then, and they still torture me again every now and then. They know I have nothing else to say, but they do it anyway."

"Have you ever thought about killing yourself?" asked Sungar.

"I plan to," said Hurd. "Every morning I wake up thinking that this'll be the day. But it never is."

"Cowardly dwarf," Sungar shot at him, though he instantly wished he hadn't.

"Maybe I am a coward," Hurd replied. "But I don't see what my death will accomplish. Llorkh's on the verge of big changes, one way or the other, and I want to stay alive long enough to see what happens. So kill yourself if you want," Hurd went on. "But don't do it just to prove you're braver than a dwarf."

Sungar welcomed the thought of the lash; it would be punishment either for the past betrayal of his tribe or his future betrayal of its secrets. He knew that either way, he would earn the ire of the Thunderbeast and the shame of dead King Gundar.

❧ ❧ ❧ ❧ ❧

Five men marched silently to the main door of the Lord's Keep and were shown through immediately. The strangers were a common enough sight in Llorkh, but even if they hadn't been, few guards would have dared question them. Their features were worn and battered, and though they were fairly young, they looked as if they had lived many lifetimes of danger and strain in their years. The Lord's Men opened the great iron doors and nodded to them as they passed. They climbed several flights of stairs, finding their way to Geildarr's purple-curtained audience chamber, where they were greeted by a person they'd come to appreciate much in the last year.

"Welcome back," said Ardeth, embracing each of the Antiquarians in turn—Bessick, Vonelh, Gunton, Nithinial, and Royce Hundar.

"I can't tell you how glad we are to see you again, Ardeth," said Royce, their de facto leader, and the most handsome and dynamic of the bunch. His ready smile was disarming but weary. "We're puzzled about the reason Geildarr pulled us back. We think we were close to something big in Highstar Lake."

"Have no fear," said Ardeth. "Highstar Lake is child's play compared to where you men are going. You're all about to be sent on the mission of missions."

"Well, what are you waiting for?" asked Vonelh, the company's wizard. "Tell us about it."

"And spoil the suspense?" Ardeth grinned. "Don't worry. Geildarr will explain everything soon. We first need a few more people to arrive for this briefing. You'll have companions on this mission."

"Gods, no!" protested the heavyset warrior Bessick. He wore his usual maniacal grin and toyed with his favorite weapon—a heavy spiked chain. "Not more of those damned Lord's Men! Doesn't Geildarr remember what happened last time?"

"I promise," said Ardeth. "No Lord's Men. You'll have more interesting companions." On that note, she vanished through a door and left the Antiquarians wondering just who would be joining them. A short time later, the answer arrived. Their eyes grew wide with disbelief and they dropped their heads.

Mythkar Leng nodded in vague satisfaction at their display of supplication.

"I trust you can explain what I'm doing here," Leng said.

"Forgive us, Strifeleader Leng," said Royce, "but we are wondering the same. We would be honored if you were to accompany us on this mission."

"What?" demanded Leng. "What mission?"

"We don't know," Royce told him. "Geildarr has just recalled us for some important new mission."

"Ardeth said that we're waiting for somebody who'll come with us on this mission," said Nithinial. "We're honored if that's you." He was a half-elf, lean and small-boned, though most folk he met learned quickly never to bring up his elf heritage. His companions still told the story of a man who hurled an ethnic slur at Nithinial from across the Ten Bells tavern and found his hand nailed to the wall by Nithinial's expertly-thrown dagger.

"What?" Leng hissed. "Geildarr summoned me to a meeting. He said it was a matter of critical importance to the Zhentarim. He wouldn't dare send me on one of his fool's errands!"

"Indeed I wouldn't," said Geildarr, walking through the door with Ardeth beside him. Behind them came an armor-clad hobgoblin, so tall he had to duck to pass through the doorway. In his hands he held a massive axe and he walked deliberately, as if he invested each step with momentous reverence. The effect was hilarious, and the Antiquarians had to hold back laughter.

"You'd better have a good explanation, Geildarr," said Leng.

"Trust me, I do," the mayor answered. "Gan, if you'd like to put that down." The hobgoblin laid the axe on a table in the audience chamber's center and backed off to a corner where he stood as still as a statue. "Welcome back, men. Gunton, perhaps you'd like to look at this."

Heavily-bearded Gunton walked forward to look over the axe. "Dwarven," he said, and looked up at Geildarr. "That much is obvious. Could it be Delzounian?"

Geildarr patted his shoulder. "Your instincts do not disappoint, my friend." Geildarr was clearly excited about the news he had to share, but wanted to delay the pleasure of revealing it. "Here's a brief history lesson." At the priest's sneer, he said, "You'll have to bear with me, Mythkar. You'll understand why in a moment.

"We all know about Netheril, the Empire of Magic from so long ago. Anyone who hadn't heard of it before should be acquainted with it now, ever since the Plane of Shadows spat up its last survivors. Netherese magic was so great that it could make cities fly, transform lands, and accomplish other feats that the Weave simply doesn't support any longer. When magic failed during Karsus's Folly, most of the artifacts made by the Netherese mages were lost. As you can imagine, any exception to this catastrophe is of great interest to me, and to the Zhentarim. This axe, with a tangled history behind it, is as old as Netheril, and I believe—" he slowed for dramatic effect "—it will point the way to the lost magic of the greatest archwizards Faerûn has ever known."

Geildarr ignored the derisive laughter coming from Leng's direction and continued. "One of the cities of fallen Netheril was called Runlatha. A man whom history recalls only as 'the Bey of Runlatha' led an exodus to the west, taking the wealth of their fallen home with them. Along the way, they were hounded by a tanar'ri named Zukothoth . . . a nalfeshnee, I believe. For a time they took refuge in the dwarven realm of Delzoun, where the Bey acquired an axe—this axe, so graciously brought to our door by our hobgoblin friend Gan, who sensed the power in it and brought it to the right place."

Geildarr swelled with self-importance. "The Bey and his group wove dweomers into the axe that linked it to a powerful artifact from Runlatha. The axe is a key that will reveal the artifact's hiding place when brought into its proximity—a place simply called 'the Sanctuary,' which I have divined as lying just outside of the Star Mounts."

The Antiquarians exchanged glances in their excitement. They'd never set foot in the High Forest and knew the legends about it—the Star Mounts, especially—better than anyone.

"I see that catches your attention," said Geildarr with a smile. "But this power has been lost to the people who possessed it in the centuries since. The Bey used this axe to defeat Zukothoth and died in the process. In time, his followers became the Uthgardt, and this axe became a ceremonial weapon of the Thunderbeast tribe. Even the god Uthgar is said to have wielded it at one time, perhaps when he was a mortal Northlander. But two years ago, the tribe's chief, Sungar, decided to leave this ancient object of power, this priceless piece of their heritage, in the Fallen Lands. Barbarians have never been the best reasoners."

"What kind of artifact is it?" asked Royce. "The one that is linked to the axe?"

"I don't know exactly," Geildarr admitted. "But because the Runlathans to go to such lengths to hide it, it must be important. Its own innate magic capably kept it hidden all these centuries, after all. It's something the Zhentarim will be pleased to possess, I'm quite sure."

"How do you know all this?" Leng asked.

"Divination magic has uncovered much, along with research in my library. The rest we owe to Ardeth." He placed a hand on her shoulder. "She consulted one of the few experts on the Uthgardt living in the North, and she kidnapped the chieftain Sungar, who's currently a resident of the lower floors of the Lord's Keep."

"So that was the mysterious mission on which the sky-mage died?" asked Leng. "By Cyric, Geildarr, you can't imagine that they will ..."

"Skymages are plentiful, at least compared to powerful Netherese artifacts," Geildarr shot back. "I don't doubt that Fzoul will forgive all, if you succeed."

"You honestly mean to order me along with these mercenaries?" Leng demanded.

"No. I wouldn't presume to order about a high priest of Cyric. But I hope you might choose to go, once you hear this." At that, Ardeth stood and told the story of the attack on Sungar's Camp, or at least her version of it. When she finished, expressions of new interest were on the faces of all assembled, except for Gan, who looked puzzled.

"From what we've learned from Sungar," said Geildarr, "the creature that attacked Ardeth and Valkin was probably a member of their tribe who was recently given extraordinary powers by their giant lizard totem animal."

"You mean from Uthgar," said Leng. "These totems they worship are just different faces of Uthgar."

"Was I right?" Geildarr asked him. "Does the knowledge that another god was taking notice draw your interest?"

Leng shrugged. "Uthgar is a minor power. Cyric pays little attention to his activities. But if Uthgar has truly invested enough power to turn a man into a behemoth." He trailed off, leaving his awed expression to convey the rest.

"What's more, the Thunderbeast gave his tribe a message to find the living behemoths," said Geildarr. "It could be that this Sanctuary of which I spoke was designed to hide the last dinosaurs of the North, and that the magic of Runlatha is sustaining it. Unfortunately, Klev tells me that Sungar knows absolutely nothing about the Sanctuary."

"Living dinosaurs," said Royce, looking to his fellow Antiquarians and gauging their reactions. "It takes a lot to find something we haven't seen."

"I'm amused by the prospect of dinosaurs in the High Forest," said Geildarr, "but I suspect Leng could find a more interesting use for them than I." He could already see dark thoughts breeding in the priest's eyes. "I'm already working on a way to contain them in the Central Square."

"You don't expect us to herd them back here, do you?" asked Bessick.

"No," said Geildarr. "I'll leave that to Ardeth."

All eyes turned to Ardeth, who smiled. "I told you you'd have more interesting companions." The Antiquarians nodded their surprised approval.

"I've almost completed crafting some crossbow bolts that will tag the beasts and teleport them back here to Llorkh, where they'll be magically contained," Geildarr explained. "As the unfortunate skymage Valkin found out, the behemoths are very dangerous, and I don't recommend engaging them directly once you reach the Sanctuary."

"But how do we get there?" asked Gunton. "I don't want to seem the naysayer, but the dangers of the High Forest are legendary. We definitely couldn't approach the Star Mounts by air, even if mounts were offered. Only the aarakocra who live there are said to know how to navigate the winds properly. Dragons lair in the Star Mounts and with the way the dragons have been behaving lately, we daren't take that approach. We'll want to avoid the Dire Wood too, and I'm guessing we wouldn't be very welcome along the Unicorn Run."

At Gunton's mention of the Unicorn Run, Geildarr studied Leng intently. The priest started at the mention of this famous stronghold of the fey world, said to be jointly blessed by the Seelie Court and all the nature deities of Faerûn. The Run, some said, was the wellspring of all life on Faerûn. A twitch ran through Leng's upper lip and it curled into a snarl. Leng's eyes glossed in thought. Though Geildarr was himself touched by Cyric in a special way, it disturbed him to wonder what Leng had in mind for that most beautiful of places.

"I think the safest route is parallel to the Run, starting somewhat north of Zelbross," Geildarr said. He reached into his robes and produced a silver coin that he tossed directly to Vonelh, his fellow wizard. "This detects powerful ... well, powerful good magic. It should help you stay an appropriate distance from the Run. Keep a careful eye on it."

"That I will," said Vonelh with a smile, as he pocketed the coin.

"This could be the most epic quest we've been on," said Royce. "It won't be easy." But he was beaming, and the rest of the Antiquarians were as well. This was the sort of thing they lived for.

"I'm working to find you more allies," said Geildarr. "The Zhentarim have some contacts with groups inside the forest, and I may be able to recall an old favor from Heskret, Bloodmaster of a werebat tribe."

Ardeth walked over to the big hobgoblin and tugged on his arm. "How about it, Gan?" she asked. "How'd you like to go to the Star Mounts?"

"Does it mean I get to keep the axe?" he asked.

"Well, it means you get it for a while, anyway," said Geildarr. To the Antiquarians, he added, "Someone has to carry it, after all."

Gan stepped forward to the table where the axe rested, gripped it, and lifted it so quickly that it hit the ceiling, leaving a notch where it struck. Ignoring that, Gan asked, "When do we leave?"

CHAPTER 7

The northern edge of the High Forest was just south of the place where the Thunderbeasts made their camp, but the tribe rarely came within sight of it. Even in the short time they had inhabited Rauvin Vale, they had noticed the curious phenomenon of the woods creeping forward, gaining steadily each moon, in their direction and that of Everlund. Now the party under Thluna's command stood at the edge of the wood, but barring their access to the majestic trees stood a wall of brambles and brush. The growth was nothing that could not be overcome with sword and axe, but served as a clear signal that they were not wanted in this place.

"The treants are not our enemies," said Thluna. It was the first word any of them had spoken in the time since they had left the camp.

"But they may not prove our friends, either,"

Keirkrad retorted. "They guard their forest zealously."

"Turlang's generosity is legendary," said Thanar, the green-robed Uthgardt druid. "He is called Turlang the Thoughtful more frequently than Turlang the Terrible. We are no enemy to his wood. His treants will surely allow us passage if we prove the purity of our motives."

Of all her companions, with the exception of Vell, Thanar intrigued Kellin the most. The majority of the Uthgardt were stoic warriors, silently following the orders of their chief without discussion. Perhaps that was easiest for them. She understood that Thanar lived most of his life away from his tribe and had thrust himself into the elements of the North in an attempt to cleanse the civilizing influence of Grunwald. At the same time, as a druid and a member of one of Silvanus's druid circles, he had doubtlessly dealt with more nonhumans and had a broader understanding of the world. What must it be like for him to have returned to his tribe after such an absence? If only she could speak to these people—such research she could accomplish, and such personal curiosity she could satisfy. Her father had so many advantages over her.

Only Vell seemed comfortable around Kellin, and she was glad for that. He often walked next to her, perhaps symbolically to the others—or perhaps for other reasons. Certainly, Vell knew he was needed by the party, and he knew that perhaps this meant more leeway for him. Kellin was afraid for him, though. The estrangement he felt from his tribe—and from himself—was clearly wearing at him.

Keirkrad had not spoken to Kellin in several days. Certain warriors—Grallah, Hengin, Ilskar, and Draf— were clearly more loyal to Keirkrad than to Thluna and had followed suit. Dressed in brown rothéhide robes, the old buzzard occasionally cast Kellin sidelong glances of disapproval, especially as she walked with Vell. She couldn't forget what Vell had pointed out—those born into the tribe with magical ability were put to death, and such rules were enforced by shamans like Keirkrad. She'd learned as a scholar not to judge other cultures by the standards of her own, yet now she found that next to impossible.

Under Thanar's direction, the barbarians drew their weapons and cut away the brambles, slashing through vines and thorns until they had cleared a path to the forest. As if by instinct, each of them paused to gaze at the legendary woodland. The High Forest was dominated by leafy trees, here favoring birches, silverbarks, and the eerie dusk-woods whose slate gray trunks pointed straight to the sky without many branches. Most of the Thunderbeasts had been raised among trees in the Lurkwood, but that forest was composed of pines and spruces. Even the smells were different—where the Lurkwood was permeated with the heavy piquant fragrance of pine, what lay ahead smelled of something sweeter and more heady, an aroma teasing to their senses.

The year was well into Marpenoth, the month of leaf fall, and even this magically-charged wood showed the impact of the season. The ground was covered with coppery fallen leaves and many of the limbs above were bare. The autumn would give way to another bitter northern winter, like so many the Thunderbeasts had endured. This time, though, the tribe feared the winter might be different, that the tribe might not last till spring. Winter never failed to cull the weak.

They walked with caution across the forest floor, which lay covered in moss and fallen leaves, scarcely daring to disturb a tree branch lest the wood's masters be offended. Ahead, the solid ground became moist and marshy, and revealed a row of small pools, covered in lily pads and alive with jumping frogs.

"These were put here deliberately," Thanar said.

"Have you been here before?" asked Kellin.

"No. But how could they be otherwise? Look how even they are. The treants have placed them here so they can use the water against fires."

"The treants," repeated Keirkrad. "We're truly to put our faith in such creatures as trees that walk?"

"Perhaps they're listening to you even now," Thanar said. "There's no telling which of these trees might be a silent treant. This is their wood, shaman Seventoes, and they are aware of everything that happens herein." Thanar was not a worshiper of Uthgar and was less intimidated by Keirkrad than his companions.

"Let them watch," said Keirkrad, casting wary glances at the oaks around them. "All we need from them is our passage."

"No," said Thluna quietly. Contradicting his elder and shaman was not in his nature, and it showed in his voice. "We need more than passage. We need the treants' help."

They pressed on, and in time the woods grew darker, damper, and cooler. The only light was that which flickered down from the treetops, now looming so high above. They heard occasional rustlings from the underbrush and saw flashes of movement in the periphery of their vision, and wondered whether they detected animals or some intelligent inhabitant of the woods. The remaining light faded as the foliage grew thicker, and the forest around them gradually turned from green to blue. The color was not that of the trees, but of the light reflecting off strange bloblike forms on the ground and on the bark of trees, so many that they carpeted the forest as far as the eye could see. Thanar kneeled to inspect one of the blobs and marveled that it was slowly moving across the forest's mossy floor.

"What is it?" asked Thluna.

"Some type of fungus," said Thanar. "I've never seen anything like it. It is told that the treant Turlang has made a home in his wood for many animals and plants at risk in other parts of the High Forest—these creatures may be among them."

"In that case," said Vell, "I recommend we avoid stepping on them."

This was the first he had spoken all day, and all eyes turned to him. A few breaths later, everyone broke out laughing. Uthgardt belly laughs shook leaves from the trees. It was a relief to all to hear Vell make a joke.

They walked on through the strange blue-tinted wood, following hills and ravines until they came to a strange clearing where daylight once again greeted them. They found themselves at the foot of a massive oak that dwarfed all the other trees they had seen. Its great gnarly roots twisted high above the ground as if they were ready to rise up and walk. Although they had prepared themselves for the unexpected, the Uthgardt still jumped in shock as they spotted a craggy face staring at them from high up on the tree trunk.

"Who dares test the patience of my kind?" the treant asked. Its voice was deep, low, and rich with age. "Who intrudes on our domain?"

Thluna stepped forward. "We beg your forgiveness, noble Turlang ..."

"I am not Turlang!" the treant rumbled, thrashing thick branches, gnarled and ancient, that suggested arms. Roots rose from the ground as if preparing to stride forward. "I am Duthroan, not the Deeproot. I cannot pretend to his age and wisdom. A strange party I see before me. What manner of beings are you?" A great hand swung down and pointed a wooden finger at Vell. "I have seen many things. Many ages have passed since my seed set root. But I have not seen the like of you. What are you?"

"Perhaps you could tell me," said Vell.

"You are a man," the treant said with great deliberation, "yet not a man. There is a sense to you, like something I knew in ages past. Great power is sleeping in you." The bark across its brow furrowed in its contemplation.

"Some of you are channels for energies. Power comes to *you* from the Weave," Duthroan indicated Kellin with the point of a root, "and to you from the divine." The root swung toward Keirkrad. "And to you from nature itself," Duthroan rumbled, pointing at Thanar. It paused. "But you are not a channel for power, but a repository."

"A repository," repeated Vell.

"There is danger where you walk. Danger even to this forest while you are here, if your power should wake and grow beyond your control. Why have you come?"

Thluna spoke. "I am Thluna, chieftain of the Thunderbeast tribe. We are here ..." But before he could finish, Duthroan raised up his roots and slapped them against the ground.

"Thunderbeast!" Leaves showered from Duthroan's branches as he shook them in anger. "The scourge of the Lurkwood? We treants know that name! The only Uthgardt ever known to fell living trees, even to sell them for profit? Not even the demon-tainted Blue Bears dared such a thing." In that heartbeat, all feared that their quest was over, that Duthroan would expel them from the forest—if not kill them outright.

"That is the past!" Thanar shouted. "I am a tender of nature as well, and I was appalled at my tribe's actions. I left them to wander the wilds of the North. I bathed in freezing rivers to purify my soul, to burn off what I considered a decadent, destructive way of life. Now the tribe has gone back to the true path, and I have rejoined them. Grunwald is rubble, life in the Lurkwood is far behind, and no more trees shall be cut down by the Thunderbeasts."

"Scant seasons have passed since this withdrawal," said Duthroan. "We who have lived ages recognize that such changes are not always permanent."

"Then the few generations they spent logging the Grunwald must seem like an eyeblink to you," said Kellin. "And is it not true that the Thunderbeasts once lived in the High Forest?"

"That is so," said Duthroan. This was a surprise to most of the Uthgardt present, though they had heard tales of life in the High Forest in their legends. "Before yellow-bearded Uther came to the North and tempted you out."

"You knew our ancestors as they lived and breathed?" asked Thluna, awestruck at the thought.

"They seldom dared enter our part of the wood," the treant said, "for they feared us. They made their home in the south."

"What of the behemoths?" asked Keirkrad. "The great lizards. Our totem has sent us in search of them."

A new expression crossed the treant's craggy features and he roared in excitement.

"You are one of them!" he shouted at Vell.

"One of whom?" demanded Vell.

"The behemoths! They roamed our woods once, great

gentle beasts with necks that reached the highest tree-tops. But I have not known their like in a millennium, until today."

"I don't understand," Vell said. "How am I like them? I am a man, not a lizard."

"Some things cannot be explained easily," Duthroan said. "You cannot tell me you have no sense of what I mean."

Grim-faced, Vell nodded.

"Perhaps your kinsmen of the forest know of this," Duthroan said. "Perhaps I should take you to them, and let them decide what to do with you."

"The Tree Ghosts," said Keirkrad. They were the youngest of the Uthgardt tribes, an offshoot of the hated Blue Bear tribe. When the Blue Bears fell into savagery, evil, and the worship of Malar, the Tree Ghosts took their own strange path, devoting their lives to searching for a tree. They believed that the original ancestor mound of the Blue Bears, called Grandfather Tree, was lost somewhere in the High Forest. Most Thunderbeasts believed that Grandfather Tree was nothing more than a myth, and that the Tree Ghosts chased a shadow. But in their rare encounters with the Tree Ghosts, the Thunderbeasts found them to be friendly, if strange. They admired the Tree Ghosts' singular purpose and drive, something the Thunderbeast tribe often seemed to lack.

"They've spent many decades collecting the lost lore of the High Forest," said Kellin. "They may have the information we seek."

"Where can we find them?" asked Thluna.

"The way cannot be shown," said Duthroan. "The way is secret. But there is another possibility." His great wooden hands reached for a knot on his side and drew forth a number of small leather flasks. "Quaff the dew these contain. It will take your senses and your wits for a time, so we trees can deliver you to their company. Then the choice will be theirs to decide your fate."

"And if we refuse?" asked Thluna.

"Then I will ask you to leave Turlang's Wood and never return." Duthroan's tone carried the unspoken threat of what might happen if they defied his instructions.

Thluna stood silently, weighing his options.

"The Tree Ghosts are noble," said Thanar. "We would not be wise to offend our only likely allies in the whole of the forest."

"And our time may be short," Vell said. "If we must leave Turlang's Wood and seek another route into the deep forest, we could lose months."

"I agree," said Thluna with some reluctance. He turned to Duthroan. "We accept your offer."

Keirkrad moved close to Thluna and spoke directly into his ear. "You cannot listen to this. This creature cannot be trusted—this is a tree that walks. The Tree Ghosts associate with elves and—gods know what else. Dealing with such beings will be at the cost of our souls."

Something cracked in Thluna. Although young and accustomed to deferring to his elders, he turned on Keirkrad.

"Who is chief here?" he demanded. Keirkrad sniffed and shrank away, making claws of his ancient hands.

The treant passed the flasks to the Uthgardt. "One gulp," he said. "No more." One by one, they lapsed into a trance and stood like brainless undead, eyes wide open, until only Vell and Kellin waited to drink. She could scarcely imagine what he was feeling at that moment. Perhaps he felt that his will had been wrested from him already, and he saw this as another incident of the same. Or perhaps he welcomed this oblivion as a rest.

They took their swigs in unison and lapsed away together.

The true chief of the Thunderbeast tribe lay on the floor of his cell, barely conscious from torture. His own rage had been used against him. His torturers had known of the barbarians' anger, capable of making them powerful, reckless, and all but unstoppable. That state stripped emotion and doubt, and replaced it with the purity of thoughtless rage. Clearly, his torturers knew of this and used it to their advantage. Bound to a cold metal table in their dimly lit chamber, Sungar had been allowed to rage and was left untouched. Only when it was over, when the purity of the fight was gone, when Sungar was susceptible to all the doubts and insecurities of his world, would they go to work. No resistance was possible. Unbidden, his mouth would open, and all the secrets of his tribe would flow forth.

Only the occasional comforting words of the dwarf in the next cell kept Sungar tied to reality as his mind threatened to float away on a sea of wrath and shame. Hurd would laugh even though he had been imprisoned for so long, subject to tortures equal to Sungar's. At times Sungar wondered if Hurd was real, for he never saw his face. Was he just another trick of his torturers to keep him from suicide, or—worse yet—a trick of his own mind?

Two guards, swords at their belts, entered Sungar's cell and propped him up. Weak as a kitten, Sungar could do nothing to resist. He expected they were taking him for another session under the cruel glass-studded whip of tusk-faced Klev, but instead they washed him and put him in clean clothes. Sungar was far too weak to complain, but he croaked, "Why are you doing this?"

"We can't have you smelling like a dumb animal, even if that is what you are," one of them explained through a grin. "You're meeting the mayor."

Now, dressed in silk breeches and a starched white shirt, the finest fashions of Waterdeep, he was marched up a flight of stairs that wound back on itself at each landing. He was delivered into a narrow dining hall. Great decadent paintings decorated the walls, a white cloth covered the table, and cold iron chains bound him to his chair. A strap around his forehead held his head in place against the chains. He felt his feet on a plush carpet. Above his head, a magical light cast unflickering shadows over the walls.

He was left there a long time—he heard a bell sound outside, and later, another. Finally a man entered and took a place opposite him at the table. Somewhat rotund and red-faced, middle-aged with a receding hairline, he was dressed in sleek purple robes. Even if Hurd hadn't mentioned it, Sungar would have known this man was a wizard. Something about him was sluglike; his features were so soft, as if weather had never touched him. This was a man who never used his body for anything. He would be ill-equipped for physical combat, Sungar knew; he could snap the man's neck in an instant, were it not for his deceitful magic.

"Chieftain Sungar," he said with an over-wide smile. "I am pleased to meet you at last. I'm Geildarr Ithym. I'm the mayor here in Llorkh, and you are my guest.

"I regret the necessity of your restraints. I hope that in time I will be able to host you unencumbered. Perhaps you'd like to sample our civilized cuisine—it goes far beyond the berries and roasted joints you're probably accustomed to."

Sungar said nothing.

"You might come to enjoy the pleasures of civilization in time," said Geildarr. "You scowl at the word." Geildarr repeated it, savoring every syllable. "Civilization. The name for everything your people despise. But do you even know what it means?"

Sungar spat onto the table before him. He heard rustling behind him and knew that guards were ready to abuse him if he misbehaved. But Geildarr silenced them with a casual wave of his hand.

"Klev told me you've been very cooperative in his interrogations," Geildarr went on. "But there's one thing I still don't understand. It concerns the axe you left in the Fallen Lands. The exact reason you thought to get rid of it is of great interest to me." Geildarr's gaze became intense. "The wizard named, according to you, Arklow of Ashabenford, demonstrated the axe was magical, so you threw it away. This seems to me—but admittedly, I'm no expert on Uthgardt honor—like an act so petulant as to befit a three-year-old child, not a mighty barbarian warrior.

"I realize you shun magic in all of its forms. I respect that—even a seasoned wizard like myself starts to hate the stuff every now and again. It grows boring when I use it too much. It loses its wonder. However, using a weapon infused with magic isn't quite the same as commanding magic.

"It was your choice to toss it away, to leave it there in the dust. It might have gone for the rest of eternity without anybody finding it. But through a happy accident, or perhaps divine will, somebody did. Sungar, do you know the name Berun?"

Sungar said nothing, but he knew his reaction gave him away.

"Of course you do. He's an important figure in your legends. Well, one of the tales of him was more than legend. That axe you wielded belonged to him."

Sungar scanned the mayor's face. Clearly he was enjoying himself; he was a torturer of another kind. Was that the whole reason for this show? If so, it told much about Geildarr. A true leader, one secure in his power, would not feel the need to taunt the helpless.

But, Sungar wondered, could Geildarr's words possibly be true? Could the weapon of the chiefs have come from the most ancient figure of their history?

Geildarr smiled. "Better still, it's possible—I can't be entirely sure about this, admittedly—that it was also once wielded by Uthgar himself. If this magical axe was an unholy, corruptive influence, as you seem to think, it certainly must have drawn some of the great ones into its web.

"Perhaps you should re-evaluate your relationship with magic. It seems to have been with your tribe from the very beginning. What do you say to that?"

Sungar kept his lips tight. In different words, this was the same argument put to him by the mage Arklow. Worse, Geildarr had a rather dramatic way of showing him up. Limp from weakness and chained to a chair, the only defiance he could manage was silence. Geildarr didn't seem disappointed.

"Mull it over some," he said. "We will speak again. There's no reason we can't be friends. We have much in common, as we are both leaders of men. Your stay in Llorkh needn't be unpleasant. You could have women, food, wine, and all the comforts available even to me. You could be a resident on this keep's highest floors instead of its lowest."

"You will die," said Sungar, though he simultaneously berated himself for playing Geildarr's game.

"Oh?" said Geildarr. "Who will kill me? You? Your people? You should stop thinking that way now—no good holding on to false hope. But you should know this: that axe of yours now resides in the hands of a hobgoblin—a dirty, smelly hobgoblin whose dim mind somehow recognized it as a weapon of legend better than you ever did. But it's far more than a weapon. If only you had realized, you could have kept it safe. Now my people carry it to the depths of the High Forest, where they will use it to rape the history of your tribe."

Geildarr leaned a trifle closer across the table. "And when they do," he said, "it will all be your fault."

In the dark woods of the High Forest's southern reaches, a series of low-slung tents stood pitched in a small clearing. The remnants of a small campfire smoldered in the dark, lighting the twisted trees that surrounded the camp. The Antiquarians felt uncomfortably close to the stands of white-barked trees that marked the edge of the Dire Wood like albino sentinels. That day they had seen an example of the "wizard weather" that sometimes roared out of Karse Butte—a fireball arching over the treetops before exploding into a rain of bloody snow. This part of the forest had obviously been scarred by such phenomena. The trees were tortured, screaming shapes, warped and ugly, and the fact that some of these trees might be sentient and keeping a close eye on them did nothing to help the group sleep better.

Late in the night, Gan stood watch at the camp's edge, clutching the greataxe tightly. He was so happy when Geildarr told him he could wield it again that he almost wept. "But I'm not worthy of it," said Gan. Geildarr told him that he was to wield it as an agent of Llorkh's mayor, and so when Gan held it, it was as if Geildarr carried it.

"Do you know what the axe is?" asked Ardeth. Gan was surprised; he hadn't known she was awake and now she was standing next to him.

"What do you mean?" asked the hobgoblin.

"Did no one tell you?" she asked. "It was once the weapon of a great leader and warrior who lived thousands of years ago. He died in a battle against a demon, giving his own life to save his people."

"Was he a human?" asked Gan.

Ardeth nodded.

"My kind have no such great leaders," Gan lamented. "Word came to us that a hobgoblin named Glargulnir wants to make himself a king of all our people, as Obould united the orcs of the Wall. But humans make the best rulers."

"Why do you have so little faith in your own people?" asked Ardeth. "This Glargulnir could prove a great ruler."

"As great as Geildarr?" asked Gan.

"Let me tell you about Geildarr," said Ardeth. "He may be a great man, but he is mayor of Llorkh only because more powerful men across the desert allow him to be. If they changed their minds, he would be gone in an instant."

Gan frowned. He had allowed himself to build Geildarr up into an authority beyond question. This he could not believe.

Ardeth pointed at the largest tent, from which they could hear Mythkar Leng's snores. "In a way, Geildarr even answers to him."

"The priest?" asked the hobgoblin.

"As you saw for yourself, Geildarr couldn't order him on this mission. It's not always so clear as that. In some ways, Leng is Geildarr's superior, but in other ways, Leng answers to Geildarr."

"But what if the priest were gone?" asked Gan.

Ardeth looked over the camp to make sure all was silent.

"Let me tell you something," she whispered to Gan. "But you can't let anyone else know."

The hobgoblin nodded.

"We know that Leng has been scheming to overthrow

Geildarr," said Ardeth. "He wants to become mayor of Llorkh, and he's willing to kill Geildarr to achieve this."

Gan's face showed almost no reaction. With as much calm as he could muster, Gan said, "We must kill him."

"It's not as easy as that," said Ardeth. "This isn't a hobgoblin tribe—we can't openly murder our enemies. But if we give our enemies enough time and a little help, they may just take care of the job on their own. I have a plan, and I could use your help."

Before she could say more, a loud crashing came from the woods. The trees parted like waves, drawing away as a great treant stepped into the clearing. Propelled by its long roots, it reached the tents with frightening speed. Its heavy, gnarled arm reached out and released water that drizzled onto the campfire embers, eliminating all its heat and light with a hiss.

The Antiquarians crawled free of their tents, and Mythkar Leng, dressed in simple brown robes that concealed his identity and power, did the same.

"You dare make fire in our wood!" the walking tree declared.

Royce took the lead. "Grant us your pardon, woodlord," he said. "The night was chill and we burned only dead wood we collected as we passed through your forest."

Huge green eyes studied him intensely. "Fire cannot be permitted," the treant said. "What business do you have among these trees?"

"We seek the Star Mounts," said Royce. "We want nothing but safe passage to them."

"A dangerous destination. I've seen many outsiders pass this way bound for those peaks, but they seldom return." He stared down each member of the group. "I've never seen a party as this. A hobgoblin in your midst, and clutching such an axe—what am I to think?"

"You can think whatever you will, treant," Leng hissed. "So long as you let us pass."

A wave of dismay passed through the Antiquarians. They had hoped to talk their way past the forest giant without incident. Leng spoke without fear or respect to a creature so much larger than they, and so imposing. He destroyed the image that he was an ordinary traveler.

The treant thought for a long time. An eternity seemed to pass as its oaken features remained still. Any onlooker would have mistaken it for an ordinary tree. Then it said, "You may pass, so long as you give that axe over to me."

Gan clutched the battle-axe tightly and brandished it over his head in challenge. But a clever root crept around and yanked it from his hands. The Antiquarians drew their weapons, and Ardeth pulled her slender sword from her belt.

The axe swiftly vanished among the treant's higher branches.

"That was not an axe for cutting wood," Royce protested. "We need it returned."

"Leave my forest and it shall be yours again," the treant threatened.

"Do you believe you can make threats?" asked Leng. "We could make kindling of you. I understand that in Thay, the Red Wizards have devised a way to corrupt your kind into twisted trees in their service. If only I knew how to do that."

The treant let out a low, reverberating war cry. Its roots snaked out toward its foes, who slashed at them with their weapons. Leng surreptitiously slipped backward. Vonelh unleashed a spinning, whirring collection of magical blades that cut into the treant's trunk. Bessick held a root in place with his raw strength, while Ardeth sliced at it with her sword. Nithinial and Royce readied their crossbows and launched their steel quarrels at the treant's face, but then they heard Leng behind them mutter, "If we are not permitted fire..."

Royce spun backward, leaping toward the priest, but he could not stop Leng from what he was doing. A fiery column burst from the air above and rained down onto the treant as if from heaven itself. It enveloped the treant so that every limb was awash with fire that leaped and coursed along its body, incinerating leaves and burning away bark. The roar of the blaze overwhelmed its screams as its body crumbled away.

Ardeth and the Antiquarians could do nothing but try to jump free of the wave of fire that coursed down the treant's trunk and over its writhing roots. The axe fell from its grasp, crashing atop one of the tents and flattening it.

The treant's instinct to protect nature—especially its woods—was overwhelmed by its agony, and it clambered into the open wood, flames leaping from its branches and igniting neighboring trees on the clearing's edge. Before it could escape the clearing, Bessick swung his heavy spiked chain and snagged the treant along its trunk. A swift yank pulled it backward, tumbling to the ground and sending Gan and Ardeth scrambling as it landed in a crackling inferno of leaping flames and blazing heat. The group darted back to the edge of the clearing, though the quick-spreading flames would soon threaten them again.

"Take cover," called Vonelh, before spreading his arms and muttering a few arcane syllables. The sky exploded in huge hailstones that pelted the clearing and the trees surrounding it. They hissed and sizzled as they struck the roaring flames and melted, and soon the clearing was a mess of soggy ash and wet, burnt debris. The remains of the treant were lost among the charred fragments of inanimate trees. Several of the tents and much of the group's equipment was irretrievably lost.

Royce, leader of the Antiquarians, spun to confront Mythkar Leng. His natural deference to the high priest was forgotten on this occasion, and his face was red from the heat and his anger. "We were close to talking our way out of this. That's what we do—that's how we survive. If you hadn't confronted it ..."

Leng smiled smugly, unapologetic. "Would you care to finish that sentence, Hundar?" he asked.

Royce checked himself, but his tone was completely insincere. His shoulders hung, and he let his sword fall to the ground at his side.

"You could have killed us all," Royce said. "You may yet."

Leng could have slain Royce where he stood. He needed no weapon. Leng could merely lay a hand on Royce, and take his life. Royce was practically inviting him to do it. Ardeth prayed that he would, and give her an excuse to sink her sword into the priest's back. Likewise, Nithinial, Gunton, and Bessick all had weapons ready. But Leng's smile vanished.

"We still have a mission, do we not?" he said. "A few crushed and waterlogged rations don't change that. I can create food and drink, with my god's grace. We have our weapons and our wits. The Star Mounts await, and soon we'll find out if Geildarr's Sanctuary is a myth or not." With that, as if nothing had happened, he led the way into the forest.

Behind his back, looks passed between the Antiquarians and Ardeth, while Gan stepped through the muck to reclaim the fallen axe. Inside, Ardeth was beaming. What luck! she thought. With all of them on one side, it would be no trick to finish the priest. The only question was, which form of death would be most appropriate?

CHAPTER 8

Such beautiful music, thought Vell as he woke, but it was only the wind whistling through the trees.

No, he thought. One tree—*the* tree. He could see it, almost feel it growing.

Half awake, he lay on his back on a carpet of leaves and could not bring himself to look any direction but up. A panoply of shades and tones filled his eyes from the light filtering through the great branches, whose smallest offshoots were themselves the size of trees. Oranges, reds, and golds fluttered and shimmered in those oaken boughs, an ocean of leaves growing crisp and golden—for even this bastion of permanence was subject to nature's cycles.

What beauty! Tears trickled down Vell's cheeks. He felt so humbled under the immensity of it. All of his fears and anger vanished as if they had never mattered and were only faint memories, like the shadow of something that happened long ago. The nagging voice in his breast, the beast inside, fell silent, and for the first time in what felt like so long—perhaps the first time in his life, he mused—he knew complete peace. He would never know if what he was feeling was brought on by the treant's drink, the tree's natural magic, or something within his own mind, but it didn't matter.

No wonder men had spent their lives seeking this place. He knew this to be Grandfather Tree, but he did not dwell on that or any name, including his own. He almost forgot himself, lost himself in heady contemplation. If he had been allowed to lie there, he knew, he might have starved and turned to dust, still looking up at the gnarled trunk that had borne silent witness to the whole of history and more.

Yet he felt no anger when he was roused from his reverie. Thanar came to him and crouched at his side. "They say a great tree structures a goodly part of the cosmos," he said, "and Grandfather Tree is its reflection on Faerûn. I don't know if that's true, but I can think of no better symbol for the nobility of all living things."

As he stood and regained something of his wits, Vell's wonder didn't lessen; it only amplified. He surveyed his surroundings. The tree's size was no illusion. Other oaks, themselves mighty and huge, grew underneath its lowest branches, circling it the way the stone menhirs ringed the altar at Morgur's Mound.

"They spent a lifetime seeking it," the druid went on. "They say they would spend a thousand lifetimes now, keeping it safe and secret."

"The Tree Ghosts," Vell said. "Will they help us?"

Thanar smiled. The simplest gesture was so amplified here that the warmth in his smile struck Vell and lit up his spirit. "They have made no promises as yet. But they trust us."

Vell became aware that other people were beneath Grandfather Tree, some so far away that Vell could tell nothing about them. Others were closer and looking on. He recognized some by their dress as the Tree Ghost barbarians, perhaps some of the same he had met on the outside. Many stood guard as well around the tree. There were others: lithe, brown-clad figures whose skins were coppery tones. By Uthgar, Vell realized. These were elves! For all the exotic folk that had come through Grunwald in the old days, he had never laid his eyes on an elf till today.

Finally, he looked toward the others, still asleep, or perhaps unaware, open-eyed and gawking at the majesty of the canopy above. Only Thluna was not among them.

"They roused me first," said Thanar. "Thluna is meeting with the tribal elders in the settlement nearby. I thought it wise to take you there next."

"Why?" asked Vell. He realized that this was the first time he had ever spoken to the druid alone.

"You transformed into a behemoth, did you not?" Thanar said. "I have transformation powers of my own. I surveyed the Wall wearing a mountain goat's form, but what happened to you goes far beyond. There are rare individuals with abilities that surpass those of any common druid. Apparently one is living in the Tree Ghosts' settlement. Perhaps she can help you understand your condition. She is a flighty creature who comes and goes with her whims, but this young elf promises she will help you how ever she can."

"The Tree Ghosts live among the elves?" Vell asked. The notion amazed him.

"Normally the tree plays host to much stranger forest folk," Thanar told him, "satyrs, korreds, centaurs, and the like. They have taken their leave since we outsiders arrived." This talk of such woodland beings, so remote from his experience, was amazing to Vell.

"We will rouse the others soon," said Thanar. "Let them know this miracle. The Tree Ghosts do not keep it jealously—indeed, they wish all light souls could experience this place—but they are very protective. I only hope Keirkrad will think wisely and keep his dogma in check."

But Keirkrad's face was crossed with a look of naked awe, just like the rest of the group. Vell's eyes settled on Kellin and he was astonished at what he saw. In a state of glorious languor, her bright eyes open and staring at the world, he beheld her clearly as a creature of wonder. She controlled magic; it flowed into her and out, and now he saw her as magic itself, shimmering and glowing with all of its forbidden wonder and power.

What an effect this place had, Vell thought. It banished all that was inconsequential and brought into sharp focus what mattered most. The fog on his brain had floated away; he desperately wished it would never return.

"Vell," said Thanar. "Meet Rask Urgek, of the Tree Ghosts." Vell almost gasped to see the massive barbarian approaching him, wearing a glistening chain shirt. With large ears, orange-tinged skin, traces of fangs, and wiry hair pulled up into a topknot, Rask Urgek was clearly a half-orc. The North crawled with such hybrids, most of who served as mercenaries. They were regarded as the scum of the civilized world and as pariahs within orc tribes; few were allowed to join Uthgardt tribes. No trace of orcish anger appeared on Rask's features. Instead, he showed the warmth and peace of years spent in the company of this extraordinary tree.

"Vell the Brown," Rask said. "Walk with me. Your friends will be safe with Thanar watching over them."

Rask and Vell walked together, leaves crunching beneath their feet.

"Thank you for allowing us to come here," said Vell. He looked up and raised his palms, offering a simple gesture against the immensity of their setting. "I don't know what words could describe my feelings about this place."

"We Tree Ghosts spent many decades searching for this tree," said Rask. "It was the tribe's solitary purpose and drive. When I joined the search, I had a nagging fear that we would find it and it would be a disappointment. How happy I was that it was not so. Our village lies some distance from the tree now. We would not tolerate habitation under the tree's branches, as you would not on Morgur's Mound. Now that we found what was missing, it has not removed our drive but only sharpened it: Grandfather Tree must be kept safe."

"Perhaps that was missing from our tribe," said Vell. "Drive, purpose."

"You have it now, do you not?" asked Rask. "Thanar told me of your mission. We shall help however we can, for your quest mirrors our own. Like you, a hated enemy dogged our steps and meant to reach the tree before us. Look here . . ." He brushed some leaves off a rotten log and uncovered an ancient carving, to Vell a familiar and ominous one—the hulking, destructive Blue Bear.

"Sometime soon, this last trace of human habitation will finally rot away," said Rask. "It is the same with the rest of the world. Stone may outlast wood, but none of our stone menhirs or any of civilization's works will outlive Grandfather Tree."

"We don't know where we're bound," said Vell, impatient with this philosophizing. "Nor do we know why the beast sent us, or for what purpose it's empowered me. And our enemy . . ."

"Your enemy is the Zhentarim," said Rask. "I know them better than I'd care to. My parents were caravan guards on their Black Road, and I made that trip a few times myself. I would wager anything that Mayor Geildarr of Llorkh is part of this. The past is a fascination for him, and robbing it is his favorite hobby. Perhaps he has your chief as well."

"I am not the leader of this expedition," said Vell. "You should tell Thluna."

"We have," Rask told him. "But you are of special interest, Vell." Vell reflected that before Morgur's Mound, no one would have regarded him that way. "Your situation is most peculiar. The nature of your destiny is in question. It requires clarification."

"I agree," said Vell.

"There is magic in this forest that may help you. Nearby, atop one of the mountains that outsiders call the Lost Peaks, lie the Fountains of Memory. It may hold answers. With the Dancing Folks' permission, I think you should visit it and see."

"And Kellin as well," Vell added. "She and I were both chosen by the Thunderbeast. We should go together."

"Kellin, yes." Rask paused a moment. "You've put your-self between her and your chief in the past. It's created tension among your group. Was that what you wanted?"

"No." Vell lowered his head. "Some fear our tribe is being ripped asunder. I want it to stay unified as much as the rest. But Kellin . . ."

"What is she to you?" Rask's tone was vaguely confron-tational. "A potential lover? Your lost twin? Like her father, she has made a study of our tribes and wants us to feel flattered to be the subject of civilized sagecraft. Tell me, Vell. What if we were to keep her unconscious? She would not be harmed and would be returned to your party once you left the tree."

"No," Vell said without hesitation. "You can trust her."

"Can we?" asked Rask, grim-faced. "She will write of our people if she lives to do so. Will she perhaps threaten our greatest secret: our location?"

"She will not," said Vell. Rask inspected him, then an improbable smile broke out on his tusked features. Vell instantly knew this had nothing to do with Kellin, but was a test for him.

"Come my friend," the half-orc said. "Let us rouse the others."

❧ ❧ ❧ ❧ ❧

Something was different in the shade of Grandfather Tree. For the first time, the iciness that the party had carried since leaving Sungar's Camp seemed to fall away. The petty squabbles ceased. They felt not like a group thrust together by the whims of circumstance, but a true band of fellows, united by destiny and a common goal. Even Keirkrad was changed after he broke down and wept at the sight of the boughs spreading above, painting the sky with brilliant hues of autumn.

Kellin was especially awestruck. She held great reverence for the Tree Ghosts' unique ancestor mound, something her father once tried to locate by following the clues of the famed Harper bard Mintiper Moonsilver, who even claimed to have explored forbidden dungeons beneath the tree.

Would that her father could see her now.

Rask Urgek led them to the village of Ghostand just north of the tree, constructed on shadowed platforms above the forest floor in a stand of oak trees. The Tree Ghost chieftain, the grizzled Gunther Longtooth, met them at the camp's edge with Thluna at his side.

"Your cause is just," said Gunther. "We shall help you how ever we can." The roar that went up from the Thunder-beasts scattered the birds from the trees above.

The mood was light that evening as the travelers put aside the heaviness of their task for the morrow. Mead and elven wine flowed freely, and soon the Tree Ghosts, who had faintly distrusted the outsiders, were as brothers with the Thunderbeasts, and even the elves seemed like long-lost friends. Copper-tressed Faeniele Eshele, the de facto leader of the elves here, was as close an advisor to Gunther Longtooth as the Tree Ghost elders. She was all but an honorary member of the tribe herself. The camp, well hidden and safe in the deep woods, was transformed into an impromptu feast, one that brought great bliss to the weary visitors. No fire lit this place, but strings of luminous lichens and magical lamps bathed the festivities in a warm glow. Wood elf minstrels blended their flutes and strings with the Tree Ghosts' Uthgardt sagas, a warm meld representing the friendship and accord their two races had found in this strange place.

Keirkrad chatted with Gunther, a fellow of his genera-tion, and with whom he was faintly acquainted from some dealings in the past. Thanar spent his time with lithesome Hala Spiritwalk—the Tree Ghost shaman—as well as some other druids visiting Grandfather Tree, some elves, and even one of the great red-furred creatures known as an alaghi. Ilskar, Hengin, and the rest found company among Tree Ghosts warriors of various ilk, and Kellin found a surprisingly appreciative audience in the Tree Ghosts' skalds and loremasters.

There was much laughter and happiness among the trees

that night, together with dance and music, good food and mellowness. Perhaps it was a god-sent calm before great struggles to come, but it was precious peace nonetheless.

Vell was sampling some elven brandy when Rask Urgek approached him. By then, Vell was almost used to seeing orc features on a fellow Uthgardt.

"Vell," he said. "There's someone I'd like you to meet. This is Lanaal Featherbreeze."

Before him stood a lovely elf maiden, seemingly young in appearance, though Vell was well aware of elf longevity. Her skin was not the coppery tone of most of the elves in the village, but was tinged a rich bronze, and her hair was a cascade of golden curls. She wore a simple green dress and blue feathers in her hair. Something was very different about her—more than just her clothing and skin tone. Vell could sense it. The other elves were naturally slight, but Lanaal seemed light and fresh as a spring breeze.

"I'm very pleased to meet you, Vell," she said, clasping his hand. "We have much to discuss."

"Then you're the one Thanar told me about," he said.

She nodded. "Let us find a quieter spot to talk." She took Vell by the hand and—moving with graceful ease—led him up a ladder to a higher platform. He scanned the gathering one last time and saw Kellin watching him as he vanished into the trees.

Soon they reached Ghostand's highest platform—a terrace among the treetops, where the clear night sky curled above them, and a thousand bright stars shone down on them. Lanaal stood and looked up at it.

"I like to see the sky," she said. "Sometimes I lose track of it, living under the treetops."

"Pardon me for asking," said Vell, "but you're not like the other elves here, are you?"

"No," Lanaal said. "Most of them are wood elves, and I am one of the sun elves. And you, Vell. You're not like the others."

Suddenly self-conscious, Vell turned away. "Not all Uthgardt have blue eyes, though most do."

"I was not speaking of your eyes." Lanaal reached out

and touched his face, turning it back toward her. "But tell me about them."

"My mother had brown eyes, and so do I. My tribe has called me Vell the Brown for as long as I can remember. They were rarely cruel, but they never let me forget it either."

Lanaal nodded in understanding. "As a child I climbed to the highest window of my parents' mansion and jumped out, without fear, to the shock of all watching from the street below," said Lanaal with a mysterious smile. "Imagine how shocked they were when an eagle swooped down to stop my fall!

"For me, the body of an elf is an accident of birth. I belong up there, in the open sky. So many decades I spent struggling to cope with this encumbering form. No amount of education could purge the avian spirit inside me. I hated my body, and for many years shunned the company of elves and humans. Only among birds did I feel real peace. I can tell when they're present, and talk with them. Sometimes I think I can even sense their thoughts and feelings. I came here hoping I might find something that would help me keep my sanity. And I did."

"The tree," said Vell.

"A beacon of peace for all who see it." Lanaal smiled. "In its shadow, I have learned that I can take the form of a bird—any bird I know of—from a titmouse to a giant falcon. And when I wear this, my elf form, I feel better about it, for it's my choice. The freedom of transformation saved me. My mind stays the same, regardless of the body it's in, and bird or elf, that body *is* Lanaal. It took me a long time to realize that."

Vell stayed silent for a time, choosing his words with care. "You say you felt this way from childhood. Do you know why you are this way? Why you?"

Lanaal shrugged. "Perhaps a gift from Aerdrie Faenya, goddess of air. Some have speculated so. Others suspect a kind of throwback to an ancestral elf, something like the avariel, our winged brethren. For me, it matters not."

Vell frowned. "You do not care why you are this way?"

"I don't think a search for meaning would be fruitful," said Lanaal. "I live my life as it is. You will be happier if you do the same."

"But you have always been this way," said Vell. "For me, a change came when the Thunderbeast entered me at Morgur's Mound. It was thrust upon me."

"I did not choose this either," said Lanaal, "but I've learned to live with it, to embrace it. I suspect you're similar to me. I know there are others—rare individuals born with the souls of horses, snakes, or even fish."

"So is that it?" asked Vell, a touch of bitterness entering his voice. "I have the soul of a lizard? A lizard none of my people have ever seen—is that not strange to you?"

"Let me ask this," said Lanaal. "Do you feel lonely, even among your companions? A dull ache, an emptiness in your soul that you don't know how to fill?" Vell didn't have to nod. "Perhaps that's because you are not with your true kind—the behemoths."

"Behemoths are not my kind!" Vell shouted.

"But you can transform into one."

"Only once," Vell said. "I don't know if I could do it again."

"How did it happen?" asked Lanaal. "Tell me about it."

"Our village was under siege," he said. "Our chief was captured by the enemy. He is still missing. I knew of the power in me and I thought there was something deeper, and this time I reached in and drew upon it. Then, I lost all control of myself. Forgot myself."

"That can happen," said Lanaal. "I remember one time early on, when I became a lark and spent days as one before I even remembered that I was an elf. For you, I would guess it is tied to your nature as an Uthgardt. Your famous rages involve a clouding of the senses, correct? Perhaps you should attempt a transformation at a moment that's less critical."

"I'd be happy never to have that happen again," said Vell. "When you turn into a bird, I'm certain that you do not kill your companions."

"Is that what happened?"

Vell nodded sadly. "Several of them, crushed under my feet."

"The only way you can prevent that is to learn control." Lanaal frowned. "For all I know, it will leave you soon. But if it doesn't, you'll have to accept it as your own. You'll be better for it. I used to feel like there were two souls in my breast, an elf and a bird. But then I realized there was just one—mine, which is *both* elf and bird."

"No, Lanaal." Vell's eyes were dampening. "It's different for me. I'm cursed. It tears me apart from inside. I could lose myself for good. When I changed back, I spent the night wandering the dark fields alone, trying to pull together every scrap of my identity. You don't understand."

"Yes," she said, her eyes warm with compassion. "I do."

The night wore on and the merriment with it, fading to the mild but persistent happiness of inebriation. Thluna spent much of the evening speaking with elves, drawing out any rumors or legends they knew about behemoths, or about the Thunderbeasts' tribal history. From Faeniele Eshele, a wood elf in the camp, he heard a strange story alleging that a behemoth had been spotted many centuries before, grazing in a swamp alongside the Heartblood River. But when an elf party arrived to investigate, it was gone—not only the behemoth, but the swamp as well.

Those elves were uncomfortably close to the Dire Wood and were not inclined to probe deeply, but one elf wizard grew intrigued and cast a spell to search for magical illusion. He found skillfully hidden magical emanations that implied a large concealed space, but was unable to reveal it. They suspected that it may have been some relic of a lost civilization, one of a great many strewn about the High Forest—possibly the elves' own Eaerlann.

"This is only a rumor, you understand," said Faeniele. "But I will contact Reitheillaethor and ask if anyone knows more. It may be within the memory of some of our elders." Thluna thanked her profusely.

Later, as Thluna relaxed beneath a great oak, having consumed some of the Tree Ghosts' hearty ale, Kellin came and slumped down next to him.

"Have you learned anything interesting?" he asked.

"Yes," she said, her speech slightly slurred. "Very interesting indeed. How about you?"

"I think I might have learned where we're going."

"Wonderful," said Kellin. "And Thluna?"

"Yes?"

"Isn't it time somebody told me what happened in the Fallen Lands?"

The question hung in the air, unaddressed. Thluna felt a kind of shame as he thought about it. But it was only right that she should know. "Yes," he said, and told the story as honestly as he knew how.

CHAPTER 9

It was midnight at the Wet Wizard tavern. Fueled by a new shipment of Tanagyr's Stout from Zhentil Keep, discussion turned, as it so often did in Llorkh, to Ardeth Chale. Lord's Men, locals, and visiting merchants and their caravan guards all had their say.

"My younger brother played with her as a child. She's a local girl. Taken an odd turn, that's for sure . . ."

"She does everything Geildarr says, but really she has more power over him than the other way around."

"Word is that she and Royce's band have taken off on one of Geildarr's crazy missions. What's weirdest of all is that Mythkar Leng's gone along with 'em . . ."

"Word about her has even reached Zhentil Keep. Geildarr thinks of her as his Ashemmi."

"Ardeth is the loveliest thing I've ever seen. What I wouldn't do for a chance to . . ."

"What annoys me most is the way she exerts her authority over the Lord's Men, without rank or position to justify it."

"Geildarr thinks he owes her everything. Some renegade dwarves would have taken over Llorkh if it weren't for her . . ."

"A Zhent skymage went off on a mission with her. She came back alone, riding his mount. What does that tell you?"

But all turned to hushed silence when Clavel Foxgray came into the tavern, his cheeks already rosy with drink. The Lord's Men shut up immediately, and the rest followed suit, wondering why.

"Let me guess," said Clavel, sneering. "You were talking about Ardeth."

A half-orc caravan guard snickered and asked, "What's yer beef with her?" Clavel provided the answer.

"A hobgoblin knocked me into the ditch with an axe," Clavel said, leaning against the doorframe to keep his balance. "I can live with that. Somebody would have gotten a rope and let me climb out. Oh, I'd have been laughed at a bit, but I would have laughed, too. Except Ardeth came along and told them to leave me there all night, then demote me. She's no place in the chain of command, but her word is law. So I'm back on the night watch, two years of seniority stripped away by Ardeth's whim. So—" he smirked at the half-orc "—so that's the reason conversations about Ardeth tend to go sour when I walk in."

The assembly in the Wet Wizard was silent as Clavel strode over to the half-orc's table. "That's too bad," Clavel continued. "I have quite a lot to say about her. The big question is this—does anybody know exactly what goes on between her and Geildarr? She lives in the Lord's Keep, does she not? On his floor or somewhere else? Because the image of that fat old slug of a mayor and that lithe demoness turns my stomach like nothing else. Or maybe they deserve each other."

"Clavel," said one of the other Lord's Men. "Perhaps

you've had a bit much to drink . . ."

"Not nearly enough," Clavel slurred. "Like the rest of you—well, any of you who've seen her—I'd very much like to spend a little time in the dark with her. But the difference is, at the end of it, I'd want to sink a dagger into that sweet breast of hers!"

"That's quite enough, Clavel," shouted a Lord's Man, jumping to his feet. He and a companion grasped Clavel by the neck and hauled him out into the street. Sounds of struggling and fighting drifted into the tavern.

Nobody wanted to talk about Ardeth any longer.

Sungar reached around, his hands weak, and rubbed the lash marks along his back. "Klev never speaks, does he?" he asked, on the off-chance that his neighbor was awake and listening. "He laughs sometimes. Snarls. But I don't think I've ever heard him say a word."

"Maybe he's embarrassed by his voice," said Hurd. "Could be it's high-pitched and squeaky or somethin'."

Sungar laughed. His lungs hurt as he did so, but he was happy; it may have been the first time he laughed since he found himself in this cesspit.

"Or maybe, more likely, he lets his whip speak for him," the dwarf added grimly.

"Are there other inmates of this dungeon?" asked Sungar. "Or is it just the two of us?"

"Probably some in the other wings. Petty criminals, cutpurses, dishonest merchants—people who commit crimes in Llorkh. But they don't last long. They're all executed pretty quickly, or maybe even released if they kiss Geildarr's hindquarters enough. Not so with us—Geildarr likes to keep his important prisoners alive forever. Makes him feel more powerful, I reckon."

"Why you?" asked Sungar. "If all the rest of your people are gone, why are you still here?"

"Don't really know," said Hurd. "I'm guessin' the answer is in Geildarr's mind. As I said, he likes to feel powerful—

there's no power in presiding over an empty dungeon. I was one of Trice Dulgenhar's top men. I'm a plum prize, but not one that's dangerous to keep alive. Simple as that.

"Not long ago, the dungeon was full to the gills with dwarves. One by one they just seemed to disappear. Could be Geildarr released them, but not likely. There were rumors that they were given over to a priest of Cyric, who was trying to corrupt them into groundlings."

Sungar could hear the disgust in his voice. "What are groundlings?"

"Something like a dwarf, but mixed with a giant badger. The Zhentarim breeds them as assassins. It took a nefarious mind to conceive of such a thing. A Zhentarim mind."

"How did you end up in here, then?" asked Sungar.

"You've been waiting for me to ask, haven't you?"

Hurd snorted. "At one time, a lot of dwarves lived in Llorkh, and humans alongside. I lived here in those days. We mined the nearby mountains, but after they started to run dry, a lot of us left. Those who stayed behind were eventually captured by the Zhentarim.

"Those black-hearted Zhentarim murdered the old mayor, Phintarn, and put in Geildarr instead. Truth is, they weren't interested in mining but wanted this town as a caravan stop on the Black Road 'cross the Anauroch Desert. What dwarf miners were still here mostly left, especially since Mithral Hall was open for business again.

"But some of us clung to the dream of liberating Llorkh from its captors—the damned Zhentarim. We formed a circle dedicated to it, set up spies in Llorkh, and made allies among the humans living here. Our leader was Trice Dulgenhar, as great a dwarf as I've ever known.

"Then we thought we saw our chance. When the phaerimm burst out of Evereska, Llorkh was under siege from a whole army of bugbears. Even the beholder they kept in the Dark Sun died in the fighting. And better yet, since the Zhentarim was still reeling from Shade's return, they weren't rebuilding Llorkh as fast as they could. We thought that if we moved quickly we could seize Llorkh, and with help from Secomber—and maybe even the Harpers or the

Lord's Alliance—we could keep it out of Zhentarim hands for good. Make it a beacon of light and good in Delimbiyr Vale, rather than the dung heap it is now."

"So you invaded the city?" asked Sungar.

"No," said Hurd, his voice trembling. "One of our human allies sold us out. A mere slip of a girl called Ardeth, the dark-hearted bitch. She brought Trice's head to Geildarr and revealed our entire plan, on the eve of us carrying it out. The Lord's Men stormed our hideaways and rooted out our allies. It was a massacre. Those of us who survived found ourselves down here, subject to Geildarr's whims."

"Why did she do it?" asked Sungar.

"Who knows?" Hurd said. "For power, coin, or Geildarr's confidence, maybe. What's for certain is that she fooled us all. We knew she was no real help to our movement, but we tolerated her for her enthusiasm. She was very pretty, very young . . ." He trailed off, leaving no doubt that he considered himself personally responsible for letting all this happen.

There was no anger in his voice, which puzzled Sungar. Perhaps it had all been shorn from him by Klev's torments. Perhaps this was why he stayed alive—not out of cowardice, but as a penance.

"You are not to blame," Sungar said. "She is."

Hurd snorted. "But what revenge is possible now? Oh, I thirst for it, perhaps with all the rage your heart could muster. But who can I blame but myself?"

Sungar made a fist and banged it weakly against the stone wall. Fragments of the wall dislodged. Who else can any of us blame? he thought.

The Star Mounts were dimly visible, hints of their fog-shrouded majesty hiding in the distance. Gan could tell that even the Antiquarians, for all they had experienced and all the places they had visited, held them in particular regard.

"Perhaps the mystery of all mysteries in the North,"

Royce called them, adding, "and we're in the business of seeking out mysteries." But Gan also noticed the fear they showed as they pressed ever closer to the legendary peaks.

A mystery unto herself was Ardeth, who showed no fear, little wonder, and none of the relish for cruelty that Leng displayed. Gan, unfamiliar with the conventions of human beauty, thought her ugly with her pale flesh, slight form, and her narrow hips that were grossly unsuitable for childbearing. Still, he recognized the effect she had on the human men.

Gan had some sense of the politics in the group, even without being told. He knew that they wanted Leng dead—Ardeth primarily, and now the Antiquarians seemed to be wordlessly supporting her. He could see it in their eyes and detect it in their manner. But they couldn't kill him openly. Leng and Geildarr had masters, and they would be displeased. The particulars of their plan were lost on Gan's brain, but he resolved to play his part nevertheless, and he took pride in what he was about to do on Ardeth's behalf—a most delicate task.

Mythkar Leng had disappeared into the woods quite some time earlier to attend to nature's call, and eventually the group dispatched Gan to check on him. He did so, axe in hand. When Gan found him, the priest's back was to Gan and he was bathed in a sepulchral green light.

"What are you doing?" the hobgoblin asked.

Leng spun about, only mildly perturbed by the interruption. Dangling from his finger was a skeletal green cage. Within, a small creature with blue flesh and cricket wings silently screamed as it cowered in the center. Leng smiled a sadist's smile as he brought it closer to the hobgoblin.

"What is this?" asked Gan.

"A grig," Leng explained. "One of the many varieties of fey that clog this part of the forest. Or rather, it was a grig not long ago."

Within the cage, a change overtook the fairy. Its wings turned to those of a bat and its flesh churned and boiled, sprouting coarse fur. Leng lifted his finger and the magical cage vanished. The creature sprinted off into the woods, a foul parody of what it once was. Moss withered and died where it passed.

"Your power must be very great," said Gan.

"I serve a most powerful god," Leng told him. "Far beyond whatever monsterous deity you venerate."

"Maglubiyet," Gan said quickly. "Maybe a human god would be more powerful."

Leng chuckled. "It's odd that your kind are so inherently servile. You need to be led, and you look for the most powerful leader available. This is commendable, but shortsighted. Tell me, Gan, does it bother you that your function on this mission is simply to carry something?" He poked a finger against the axe head. "You're the most hideous butler I've ever laid eyes on."

Not understanding the insult, Gan said, "I offered my service to Geildarr, and this is the task he assigned me. He is a great leader, and I shall not question."

This provoked a roar of laughter from Leng. "Such loyalty! My advice to you, hobgoblin, is to forget about Geildarr. He is a mediocre man of earthbound ambitions. Many years ago he confessed to me a desire to become part of the Zhentarim's Inner Circle. And he never did anything to make that happen. He is more an administrator than a true leader."

"What do you mean?" asked Gan.

"He is weak. This very expedition is a sign of his weakness. The magic we're looking for—he doesn't want to keep it for himself, but wants to give it away to his superiors. A great man would not perform such errands at the behest of those he hates. A greater leader would remake the world in his image, not hold onto the inglorious scrap of ground he calls his own."

"Are you such a man?" asked Gan.

Leng said nothing.

"Your magic remade that grig," asked Gan. "Why did you do it?"

Leng frowned in puzzlement. A high priest of Cyric did not expect to be questioned for the reasoning behind his actions, so Leng did not have an answer.

"Such creatures disgust me," Leng finally said. "They lock themselves away from the world to flit about in their pools and glades—what purpose do they serve?"

"Why not simply kill it?" asked Gan.

Shrugging his shoulders, Leng answered, "I wanted to see what would happen. What Cyric's power could do to a creature of such purity. What such corruption would yield."

"Were you satisfied?"

Leng almost beamed. "I was."

"I've heard tell of a place not far from here where the fey rule," Gan said, trying hard to sound guileless.

"The Unicorn Run," Leng spat out, as if he were speaking a vile oath. "All know that name. It's the place we're avoiding."

"What would your powers do there?" asked Gan.

Leng shook his head slightly. "I don't know," Leng said.

There was a quality to Leng's voice that Gan couldn't put a name to, but it terrified him more than all of the battlefield atrocities he had witnessed in the Fallen Lands and throughout his life. It was something that went far beyond simple malice to a deep-set desire to corrupt and to destroy.

In that moment, Gan wanted to bring the axe down on Leng, to slice him apart just as he had that Zhentilar fool in the Fallen Lands. Could he act in time? What foul magic warded this priest? To think he could accomplish all that Ardeth wanted, all that Geildarr wanted, with a single swing.

But no—it would not be right. It would upset their plans. It would be beyond his place.

Leng looked down at the hobgoblin's fingers clutching the axe's shaft. A dark chuckle rolled out of his throat as he walked past Gan and back to where the others were making camp.

Kellin strolled under the autumn haven of the great tree and the peacefulness put her in a reflective mood. But then, she thought, when was she not in a reflective mood? Members of the Tree Ghost honor guard were stationed at intervals beneath the tree, but she felt alone nevertheless— an island in the deep shade. She thought about everything Thluna had told her—how Sungar had acted to preserve his tribe's beliefs at such a terrible cost. Now, Thluna feared he was doing the same thing: compromising, cooperating with an outsider—even a spellcaster—and selling off what it meant to be a Thunderbeast.

Here she was, leading them down that path. Threatening to destroy everything that her father was determined to document and help preserve.

She almost jumped when Thanar approached her.

"I didn't mean to disturb you," he said.

"It's all right," she answered. "I was just doing some deep thinking."

Thanar cast a glance up at the leafy expanse above them. "This place can have that effect."

"It must be hard to know you have to leave it so soon."

Thanar ran a hand over his bearded face. "It's better we leave soon. The tree has its own magic. There is a danger that we all might wish to linger in its shade and never accomplish our mission."

"I feel its pull," admitted Kellin. "It's not evil, nor good. It just is. That's its appeal—it doesn't need to be understood. It exists so far from civilization's works, apart from even the Tree Ghosts. No matter how much they revere it, it would exist without them. There's a seductiveness in its simplicity. I could get lost in it if I let myself. Such a pleasant fate, to remain here forever, thinking . . ."

"Contemplation may turn to sloth," Thanar said. "And we cannot allow ourselves to lose time."

"Where is Vell?" asked Kellin, changing the subject.

"I believe the elf maid has taken him into the forest to explore his shapeshifting powers. Does that make you jealous?" She was taken aback at the bluntness of his question. "It is best you acknowledge such feelings . . ."

Kellin cut him off. "Another matter best explored at a later time. Tell me, Thanar. I sense you don't despise me the way the others do." She found it perplexing that he had left Grunwald because he thought his people had become too decadent, yet he was the most tolerant of her—the city-dwelling member of their group.

"Why should I despise my sister?" asked Thanar. He turned to the tree's great trunk. "We may be from different branches, but we are linked nevertheless. All living things are. From the deepest root to the highest bough, we are all one tree."

"I like that," Kellin answered, lowering her head. "I wish everyone thought that way. Some sages follow your line of wisdom. They think all life originated in one place and continues in what some call the Endless March—changing, adapting, and improving—in much the same way that farmers improve their livestock through breeding."

"I've heard of such thinking," Thanar said. "Do you believe it?"

Kellin shrugged. "It's not my area. It makes sense to me, though. And it cuts to the heart of what you said: that all of life may have a common origin and therefore be linked."

"I need no sage to tell me that. I feel it." He asked, "What god do you revere?"

"Principally," she said, "I worship Oghma. Why?"

"The Binder of What Is Known," he said, repeating one of the titles of the Lord of Knowledge. Kellin was faintly surprised Thanar knew of it, that he even knew of Oghma. She supposed it made sense for him to know of a god so opposite to his world view. "Tell me, why should the world be bound? Is not everything dead once it's bound? Once it is written in books or scrolls, it no longer lives in nature."

"I'd rather think that it will live forever if it's written," Kellin answered.

"And our tribe?" Thanar probed. "If we are destroyed, will we live forever in your father's books, or those you will write in the future?"

"You will be remembered," said Kellin, "by anyone who cares to remember you."

Thanar caught a fallen leaf. It was dry and withered, and he crushed it in his fingers.

"Perhaps that's better than nothing," he said.

"You're not like the others," Kellin pressed. "I understand you lived apart from the Thunderbeasts for many years. Do you consider yourself a member of the tribe?"

"Still the sage." Thanar smiled mysteriously. "Do you mean to put my answer in a book?"

"I can't promise I won't," said Kellin, smiling back. She felt much more comfortable with him.

"I spent many years away from it, truly," said Thanar. "But I was born a Thunderbeast and a Thunderbeast I remain. Even if the rest of the tribe withered and died, and I spent a lifetime in the Spine of the World, never seeing another human or speaking another word aloud, a Thunderbeast I would stay."

"Yet in the past you sought to distance yourself from your tribe."

"Others have done worse. Thluna's closest friend left the tribe to join the Black Lions, a matter which weighs heavily on him. The Black Lions' way holds much appeal for the young Uthgardt, it seems. I wonder, in Garstak's soul, does he still think of himself as a Thunderbeast? As for myself, after all this is over—and assuming I still live—I may choose to leave them behind for good. I hold that my tribe is something I carry around inside my heart."

"I'm worried about Vell," Kellin admitted. "He doesn't feel much connection to his tribe. Not now."

"Not ever," corrected Thanar. "He was one of the silent. You have seen them—Hengin, Grallah, Ilskar, and Draf—our warrior companions who follow their chief's orders absolutely and who seldom speak. I would wager that in their depths, they do not identify with their tribe as they feel they should, and that this is a matter of private shame. Many generations have pressed on in such anguish."

"What worries me," said Kellin," is that Vell doesn't have anything else solid to hold on to."

"He'll have his own choices to make," said Thanar. "We must have faith that he'll make them properly."

Kellin looked up at the vast canvas of Grandfather Tree's leaves and was lost again in its beauty and majesty. "Do you think it would be all right to stay here a bit longer?" she asked.

Thanar smiled. "I don't think it will do any harm," he said, and together they lingered and marveled at the tree's everlasting dignity, undiminished by the nagging hollowness they felt in their hearts.

❀ ❀ ❀ ❀ ❀

Vell flinched as the scales took him. Like an arrow to his brain, the change came, and he could feel all of his flesh awaken with thick natural armor, making his limbs heavy.

What scared him most was how natural it felt.

Two trolls were bearing down on him, their green flesh stretched taut over jagged bones. The woods were bright here, the trees spaced far apart and the sun shining brightly above. This was the reason Lanaal had lured the trolls here, where the space was open enough to accommodate even a behemoth.

Lanaal was here, Vell knew, perched somewhere in the trees above, watching and waiting. Within his blood frenzy, his eyes were clouded over with the insensibility of rage, but he could still hear a sharp, shrill bird call—Lanaal goading him forward, daring him to call on his full transformation. But he held back, even as one of the trolls wrapped its huge hands around his neck and twisted.

Vell clapped his hands on the troll's forearm and squeezed tight, ripping the arm free of his scaled neck. He kicked the troll's left knee then the other, sending it tumbling backward onto the leaf-covered forest floor. Before it could recover, he jumped onto it with all of his weight, landing with both feet on the troll's chest. Troll bones snapped under his impact, and he watched its hideous face as the shock hit home, it eyes bugging out and its mouth spewing forth a plume of thick green liquid that splashed over its face.

Vell knew he shouldn't finish the fight too swiftly. Though his sense of reasoning was weakened in his state, he had no intention of drawing the death blow yet. He was enjoying himself. When Vell shifted his attention to the other troll, staring up into the green-gray face topped with a wiry shock of black hair, he saw something he never would have suspected: fear.

The ground trembled around Vell as he walked. So it was with the beast shamans of his tribe when they called on the powers of the Thunderbeast and grew armor of scales.

Vell commanded the tremors to cease, to see if they would. And they did.

Hopping off his downed victim, Vell strode toward the troll slowly and it stepped backward, watching him intently and bracing for the attack. Armed with nothing but his own scaly strength, Vell plunged forward toward the troll's middle, delivering a forceful punch. The troll withstood the blow and struggled with Vell, raking its claws through his tribal robes, ripping them to find any skin beneath not protected by those thick scales. Finding none, the troll brought its fist to the side of Vell's head. The blow echoed like thunder through his skull and sent him flying against a fragile tree nearby. The trunk cracked behind him as the full brunt of his weight struck. The tree toppled into the clearing with a mighty noise.

The first troll's regenerative powers worked to knit its shattered bones together, and the monster rose to confront Vell again. With his feet against the stump of the broken tree, Vell wrapped his arms around the fallen trunk and spun it in a circle, its branches breaking off as it struck other trees. This brought complaint from the treetops above, and even in his rage, he thought of Lanaal in bird form, likely dislodged from her perch.

Facing the two trolls, his arms still around the trunk, Vell used it as a caber, hurling it full on against the trolls. It struck them both in the midsection, knocking them both backward. Like a great pin it rolled, over their chests and faces, stripping its bark on their rough skin. And like an engine of destruction, Vell was on them, tearing into their bodies with foot and fist.

A high-pitched trill sounded above him, and Vell was partly drawn out of his blood fury to remember what he was here to do. Standing tall and straight, he summoned the heart of his courage, not the courage that compelled him to fight monsters, but that which let him look into the most frightening things lurking inside him. He clapped his eyes shut and searched his depths for the will to leave his body behind and fully accept the scales' embrace.

Vell's throat went dry and his mouth filled with the acrid taste of growing fear. Troll breath washed upon him, but he paid it no mind; the danger would make it easier, he decided. The beast within must emerge—this was life or death, just as it was when Sungar's Camp was under siege. His blood coursed faster and thicker through his veins, his pulse throbbed in his neck like a drum beat, but the beast stayed sleeping. Vell's mood disintegrated and his energy with it, and when he looked down at his hands they were pink flesh, the scales retreating as suddenly as they had come.

And two enraged trolls were bearing down on him.

A sword fell from above, landing with a thud at his feet. Vell reached down and grasped its hilt. It was an elegantly curved elven blade, thinner and lighter than he had ever used, but it cut deep as he sliced a neat slash through a troll's neck—blood poured down its bare green chest. With a cry and a rush of air, a gigantic falcon swooped down next to him, tearing at the other troll's face, claiming both of its eyes with its sharp talons. Blind and howling, the troll batted at the bird and stumbled through the wood, bashing into trees as Lanaal circled and occasionally dived to strike again.

How long has it been since I fought as myself? Vell wondered. He felt good as he tore into the troll again and again, moving quickly to avoid its blows. A glorious swell filled his senses, and his heart awakened to barbarian joy. The troll clawed at his arm and wounded him, and he welcomed this too, the human pain and the feel of blood trickling down his body. To defeat the troll without his powers? A greater achievement by any account, he decided, slicing through his foe's leg and sending it toppling to the ground.

At last, he drew a small vial from a pocket inside his deerskin robes, also a gift from Lanaal. He uncorked it and emptied the contents onto the troll's ugly features.

The liquid hissed and bubbled down the troll's face, trickling off its chin onto its chest. It instinctively tried to soothe its wounds by wiping at them, but this only burned its hands as well. Its skin melted on its face, leaving gruesome black-green flesh showing underneath. Its features damaged by the acid and far beyond regeneration, the troll stopped struggling and collapsed on the forest floor.

Spinning around to find the other troll, Vell discovered that Lanaal had transformed back into an elf to finish off the lumbering monster. From her robes she drew a few darts and—with strength surprising for her thin form—drove them into vital places on the troll's body. Each of them leaked acid that seeped into its body. Its agonized cries were deafening as it melted from within.

Lanaal walked over to Vell. "Vell," she said. "By the Winged Mother, what went wrong?"

But Vell couldn't stop smiling. "I haven't felt this good in a long time. That was invigorating, fighting with my own body, my own skills. With the Thunderbeasts I rarely face foes except as part of a horde. I had forgotten the joy of it." He looked down at the demolished troll. "My kill, not the Thunderbeast's."

Lanaal frowned. "You tried to turn into the behemoth," she said, "but you lost the partial transformation that you had already achieved. How did this happen?"

"I think it rejected me," said Vell. "Whatever's inside me did not care to rear its head. Perhaps it did not deem the situation serious enough."

"Or perhaps you did not call it properly," Lanaal said. "Not seriously enough. You talk as if it's something else. You need to think differently. Acknowledge that it is another side of Vell."

"Are you in my head, elf?" asked Vell. "Do you know

what I feel? Keirkrad, Kellin, Sungar, you, and everyone else think they know better than me. But who among you looks through my eyes?" He clenched his fist in anger—not the barbarian rage that he could sate with violence, but something much more complex and difficult to drive off.

"So you consider this experience a failure," said Lanaal.

"No." Vell smiled. "My eyes are clearer now. I tasted battle and felt alive again. No thanks to the enemy inside."

"It's not an enemy, Vell!" Lanaal protested. "Just a resource. A powerful one for good or ill—it will destroy you if you don't make it obey you."

"It's a demon," Vell proclaimed. "One I must strive to cast out."

Lanaal breathed heavily, her bronze-tinged face streaked with redness. "It may not be possible to remove it, Vell," she warned.

"I will strive nevertheless," Vell promised. "Thank you for helping me, Lanaal. I hope I can still call you my friend."

"Have no fear," she whispered. Her smile was filled with concern. "I will help how ever I can. But if you are seeking answers to your puzzle, I don't know if I can help you any further."

"There may be other possibilities," said Vell. "Rask mentioned something about the Fountains of Memory."

CHAPTER 10

Sprites fell like hostile rain. The Antiquarians, Leng, Ardeth, and Gan held their ground against waves and waves of them. The sprites were joined by grigs playing their dreadful fiddles, gossamer-winged pixies, and even some of the seldom-seen nixies. The fey climbed the trees, dived down on the party below, and launched their arrows. The battlefield rang with the grigs' discordant music.

"If we were to surrender," Ardeth shouted through the cacophony, "do you suppose they'd stop playing?"

Amid a duskwood grove carpeted in damp moss, the fey ambushed them and pressed the attack, seemingly unconcerned about their massive casualties. Each swing of Gan's greataxe killed five of them at a time, and the blades of Nithinial and Royce swung unceasingly, slicing the small, fragile creatures with ease. Ardeth crouched with her crossbow and targeted the pixies with her deadly bolts, while Gunton used a net to trap them, then finish them with the point of a short spear. Fey blood pooled on the forest floor. Bessick swung his chains, snagging wings and ripping sprites apart with their cruel spikes. Vonelh blasted the creatures with huge gusts of wind that blew their arrows astray and toppled the smaller sprites, their wings beating hopelessly as the air funneled them hard against the trees.

"If only I could drop a fireball and let them all burn away," Vonelh said, but he knew the danger to the trees was far too great.

Leng was responsible for the most damage. Laughing and cackling with the dark energy of an asylum inmate, he took perverse glee in killing his attackers slowly and painfully. Deep blue bolts of cold erupted from his hands that withered the sprites at a touch, their wings shriveling until their desiccated flesh seemed to slide off their bodies. Leng released dark waves of despair and grief that set some of them weeping. Walls of thorns erupted to rip them apart, and he conjured disembodied black claws that tore into the tiny grigs and pixies as a cruel child might torture a butterfly, plucking off wings and ripping bodies apart.

A flail hung at Leng's waist, and many magical items were concealed in his clothing. But he had no interest in fighting with anything but his spells.

The Antiquarians watched Leng's depredations in awe. He wore an expression of joy as he went about his vile work; his face showed no concern that they were fighting for their lives. This was sport for him; his companions even suspected that Leng could readily kill all the fey with much greater speed, but instead he was drawing out the pleasure, challenging himself to find new and crueler ways of slaughtering them. He almost seemed disappointed as the number of fey around them declined. Whether the large folk were really killing the small ones or if some had decided to flee—fey being notoriously fickle—they could not tell.

"The pixies may be waiting for us to let our guard down," warned Gunton, skewering one on the end of his short spear.

Although equally as small as the grigs, the pixies were far more dangerous foes. Leng and Vonelh tried to wipe out the creatures' invisibility with spells, but the small folk easily crouched unseen in the distance and fired their arrows.

No fewer than ten grigs sprang cricketlike from various places at Vonelh. They all struck his upper body, prodding him with their tiny dagger-points. The surprise was enough to knock the wizard off his feet and disrupt the spell he was casting. Nithinial rushed over to help him, but not before five pixies took wing and buzzed over Vonelh's prone body.

A well-placed sweep from Bessick's chains tore most of them out of the air with cruel accuracy, but as Nithinial rushed to help Vonelh to his feet, he noticed the mage was in a strange state. His eyes darted wildly, and he looked at his companions as if he'd never seen them before. At the same time, all of the pixies, grigs, and nixies hovering on the battle's edge seemed to turn tail and vanish into the forest.

Vonelh opened his mouth and began to chant some arcane syllables.

"Their magic has scuttled his mind!" shouted Leng. "Stand clear." He spun to face Vonelh, took a few steps, and laid his hand on the wizard's exposed forearm. As soon as he made contact, all life left Vonelh. His face and body went slack and he fell to the ground without ceremony or grace, his lifeless eyes staring up at his companions.

"What have you done?" howled Nithinial, standing only inches from Leng.

"He was going to drop a fireball on us all," Leng said calmly.

Nithinial swung at Leng's throat with his dagger, but he never made it. A few words from Leng, and the half-elf was paralyzed, a mask of anger frozen on his face. The dagger was nearly at Leng's neck, but the priest did not flinch.

For a few moments, silence fell over the group as everyone tried to come to grips with the scene. Leng took a few steps back from the others.

"You didn't have to kill Vonelh," said Royce, stepping

around his corpse and the living statue that Nithinial had become. The leader of the Antiquarians stepped forward, his sword lowered in a subtly threatening posture. "You could have dissolved the magic on him."

"Or perhaps I would have failed, and we would all be dead," said Leng.

"You have ruined this mission," Bessick shouted, stepping next to Royce with his chains ready. "If you hadn't killed that treant, we wouldn't have every damned fey in the woods on our trail."

"Oh," Leng replied. "No, there's a different reason for that. Is there not, Ardeth?" He bent over to pick up the blue-tinged corpse of a nixie, took a few steps, and tossed it down at the young woman's feet. "Let's ask Geildarr's official representative among us. Why are we really on this mission? Nixies don't stray far from their waters. So tell us all," he spat as he looked into her dark eyes, "just how close are we to the Unicorn Run?"

Ardeth showed no reaction, only matched Leng's steely gaze. But Gunton, Bessick, and Royce all let out gasps of surprise.

"Your hobgoblin's dedication is admirable," Leng went on, sending Gan a glare that made the hobgoblin grip the axe more tightly. "But his thespian skills leave something to be desired."

Gunton rooted through Vonelh's robes and found the silver coin Geildarr had provided. It was glowing slightly. "Are you saying that this is a lie?"

"Deliberately designed to mislead us, to send us off track, yes," said Leng. "You may as well acknowledge your deception, Ardeth. Geildarr isn't here to protect you now." On cue, Gan stepped between her and Leng.

Leng only laughed. "Do you require further demonstrations of my power?" he asked, turning to face Royce. "Perhaps this one should fall next. Maybe that would be the best way to show for certain who leads this expedition now."

"Are you saying that we were never meant to go to the Star Mounts?" asked Royce.

"Perhaps you, but not I. As it happens, I don't care what's at the Star Mounts," Leng hissed. "This Sanctuary, Netherese magic, big lizards—there's a much more tempting prize on the way. Geildarr counted on me thinking this way. He expected me to go to the Unicorn Run and die." He craned his neck and peeked at Ardeth behind Gan, smiling. "Isn't that the case?"

Leng rambled on in an arrogant tone. "Perhaps all of you together could defeat me. Perhaps not. Myself, I'd prefer that you live. You're useful to me, every one of you. There's no reason we should be enemies now. Why do you perform Geildarr's tasks for him? For gold or power? Why not choose a greater glory? You can carve yourself a place in legend if you fight by my side."

"That's not what we do," said Royce, knowing his words would have no effect. "We're mercenaries and treasure-seekers. We're not crusaders."

"You're nothing but Geildarr's errand boys. This is a chance to become something else. Warriors of myth, maybe. Every child knows of the Unicorn Run. Perhaps soon they will know of the brave men who invaded the loathsome bastion, crippled it, and polluted it beyond repair."

"It won't work," said Ardeth.

"The sweet maid speaks!" Leng shouted. "What has Geildarr's pet to say?"

"You will die," she said. "You overestimate your powers, Leng."

"Don't you mean 'our powers'?" Leng asked. "But fear not. I feel quite certain that when I challenge the forces of the Run, my god will stand behind me and make me a vessel of his full power."

"What god is that?" asked Ardeth. "Bane or Cyric? You are a traitor to every god you've served."

Leng scowled. Apparently, he had no idea that anyone knew of his conflicted loyalties.

"I think," he spat, "if it means the end of the Unicorn Run, the two will find a common ground, and all the other gods of darkness besides. I will enjoy all their favor, and I shall have my victory."

Leng spoke with mad credibility, and the Antiquarians did not know what to make of his claims. Could this be possible? What was certain was that Leng was a terrifying enemy. In some ways, Vonelh was the strongest of their group, and Leng had killed him with a simple touch. Already lacking one member, they could not afford to lose any more, or it might prove impossible to escape the High Forest alive. Perhaps it was best to do as Leng ordered.

Royce locked eyes with Ardeth, trying to communicate his confusion.

Nithinial's paralysis ended abruptly. Still trembling with rage and clutching his dagger, he prepared to lunge at Leng again. Wildly, the half-elf squeezed his dagger's hilt until his hand bled, waiting for the word.

It came from Ardeth. "We should move on before the surviving pixies return."

"Where are we heading?" asked Leng, folding his arms across his chest.

Ardeth lowered her head in a false gesture of deference. "The Unicorn Run, of course."

Leng ripped off his brown robes and let them fall among the dead fey. Beneath were the purple and silver robes of a high priest of Cyric. He wore them proudly as he led his reluctant troops toward death or glory.

A great white goose ascended out of the High Forest, the trees swaying beneath her. Lanaal, transformed, carried Vell and Kellin on her back, each of them gripping feathers to stay in place. Above the tree canopy, the immensity of the High Forest sprawled below them. Their destination, the squat green mounts called the Lost Peaks, was a familiar visage from some vantages north of the forest's edge. Vell found his attention turning south to another group of mountains, a range he'd never laid eyes on before. Immense and towering, they were an arresting sight even to one raised in the shadows of mountains.

"What are those?" Vell asked Kellin. He could not take his eyes off them.

"The Star Mounts," Kellin told him. They looked out of place somehow—mountains in the most unexpected of places—as if some god had dropped them there on an odd whim.

"That's where it is," Vell said.

"Where what is?" asked Kellin.

"The place we're bound for." He didn't understand the words even as they came out of his mouth.

"How do you know?"

Vell looked deeper, harder at the mountains, staring into them. "I just know," he said.

Soon they alighted on a grassy plateau in the Lost Peaks, at the foot of a rocky peak that revealed a series of caves. The plateau was high and the air crisp. A fresh breeze was blowing. Dozens of pools with pristinely clear water dotted the plateau, undisturbed by any breeze. Lanaal flapped her great wings, and as she folded them, she transformed into the familiar shape of an elf. The trio could see more pools just inside the caves, illuminated from within by some sourceless light. These were the Fountains of Memory.

"So?" asked Vell, walking over to one of the pools. "What do we do?"

"Hala Spiritwalk said not to do anything until a korred guide arrives," Lanaal explained. "Most especially . . ." she reached over and grabbed Vell around the middle, dragging him away from the pool, "she said not to look into the pools till he gets here."

"Aye, good advice that is," came a voice. Vell, Kellin, and Lanaal all turned to find a little man standing directly in their midst, the top of his head barely reaching their chests. How he had arrived, none of them could say, though as soon as he appeared, a strong animal stench filled the air. His chest was covered with brown curly hair, and he walked on goat's legs with cloven hooves in place of feet. A small bag dangled at his waist, and a brown loincloth scarcely concealed his crotch.

"Welcome, friends," he said. He danced a circle around

them, kicking and twisting those ungainly legs with strange grace. His dancing seemed as natural as walking. "My name is Tylvis, First Terpsichorean of the Clovenclan." He gave a little bow and stopped before Vell.

Looking to the others for confirmation, Vell bent his knees slightly and extended a hand, which the korred grasped in his hairy palm.

"Thank you for letting us come. I am Vell of the Thunderbeasts. This is Kellin Lyme of Candlekeep, and Lanaal Featherbreeze, late of Evereska."

"Lovely ladies both. Human and elf, one of yellow hair and one of dark." He winked at Vell. "The best of all worlds.

Welcome to the Fountains of Memory!" Tylvis declared with a robust smile. "Many come seeking this sacred spot, and we don't usually mind. They come seeking knowledge, for this place remembers everything that happens in this world of ours. Mostly we let them slip by and stay unseen. No idea whether they find what they're after."

"What are they?" said Kellin, looking into one of the pools. It did not reflect the blue sky above, and when she craned her head out over it she could not see herself. The pool showed only an impassive, shimmering blueness. "How did they come to be?"

"Nobody knows for sure," Tylvis said. "We think our god Tapann made them, but he's not telling. They show images of other times and places. There's no predicting what they'll reveal. Sometimes the past, sometimes the present. But be wary—we've seen weak-minded humans, and even one or two elves, decide to jump into the pools. They never come out. Maybe they're swept away to the place they see, but we sure never see them again."

"Maybe they die," said Vell. "Drown."

"Could well be," said Tylvis. "I'll feel bad if you decide to take an unplanned swim. Otherwise, look! See what they have to say. Maybe nothing, maybe something. But look. Look and see."

"Those pools in the caves?" asked Vell. "Are they different from the ones on the plateau?"

"Hmm." Tylvis stroked his bearded chin and made an odd little hop on his goat legs. "Don't know, 'cept that of all those who vanished into the waters never to be seen again, the bulk vanished in there."

"That's where the most intense visions occur?" asked Lanaal.

"You could say that," said Tylvis. "Myself, I don't know."

"What do you see when you look in the pools?" asked Kellin.

"Oh, I never look in them," said Tylvis. "Nothing in there I need to know. The past, the present . . . what do such things matter to the Dancing Folk?" His smile was mysterious, unreadable—did Tylvis speak the truth, or some merry joke only he understood? "But you three go ahead. Make sure you stay on this side of the pool."

"That's all you have to say?" asked Lanaal.

Tylvis smiled a trickster's smile. "What more would you have me say, elf? So many have come here seeking wisdom—I don't know if they get it or not. So good luck. Hope you don't see anything you'd rather not have known." With that, the korred turned and hopped away down the plateau.

"Do we trust the goat man?" asked Vell. "If this place is sacred to his god, then why leave it so accessible—and why doesn't he treat it with more reverence?"

"Korreds are an irreverent kind," said Kellin. "Not all religions regard their sacred places in the way the Uthgardt do."

"Better yet," Lanaal added, "it may be that this place isn't sacred to Tapann at all. Rumor has it that his followers keep their own sacred fountains secret, and encourage all others, even their allies, to believe that these are the sacred ones."

"I wonder what they are then." Kellin found a pebble at her feet and cast it into the nearest pool. The stone sank, but not a ripple disturbed the pristine surface. "More clear than any mirror."

"I've never looked into a mirror," Vell said. He remembered a time that a foreign merchant in Grunwald presented a mirror to Gundar as a token of his generosity. Gundar accepted it in gratitude but refused to look into it, and later turned it over to Keirkrad to be destroyed as an affront to Uthgar.

"Vanity is one of civilization's primary flaws," Kellin admitted.

"Mirrors don't always reflect the whole truth," Lanaal cautioned Vell. "They can mislead. I spent my early life looking into mirrors and seeing an elf staring back."

"I will look into the pool alone," said Vell. Acknowledging each of the ladies with a nod, he walked into the cave, to the pools within.

When he was out of earshot, the two women stood alone together for the first time, silently assessing each other.

"In some ways, you are more a mystery than Vell," Lanaal said. "I can't understand what compels you to keep the company of barbarians who disdain your very existence."

"The Thunderbeast chose me," Kellin answered.

"It called you, perhaps, but you chose to answer. Uthgar is not your god—what is his summons to you? When you set out from the halls of learning, did you truly feel a personal interest in this particular barbarian tribe?"

"Yes ... no ..." Kellin rubbed her eyes. "My father ..."

"Memory," Lanaal said, as if the word contained all the answers, and she spread her arms wide to indicate their setting. "It can be clear or faulty. It can tell the truth or deceive."

Taking a deep breath, Kellin walked to the nearest pool and gazed down into the water. And what she saw made her flush with embarrassment, and feel rage in her bones.

The caves had a light of their own, shimmering out from those strange pools. It cast eerie rippling shadows over the low cave ceiling, though Vell could not see any movement in the water itself. This was the kind of mystical place that alternately repelled and attracted the average Uthgardt—

repelled him because of unknown magic, yet attracted him for the warm intimacy of the mystery, and the feeling of being wrapped in history. Vell bent over the nearest pool and found himself staring into his reflection.

So that's what I look like, he thought. He was not so different from any other Thunderbeast, and even his brown eyes did not distinguish him. All faded, and only his eyes remained as the water shimmered and he was looking into another time. It was another face, but somehow he knew it was his, or rather, that of an ancestor who remained tied to him from the spirit world. The sun was shining brightly behind him onto a spectacular white city, and he was garbed in robes of gold marked with ornate symbols.

A wizard. He was descended from a wizard.

The vision told him something else. This scene was surely not one of Ruathym, the rocky isle that was the home of Uthgar's mortal line. More likely, it was an image of his ancestry from his other line, stretching back to the Empire of Magic. Often he wondered if his brown eyes marked a stronger concentration of that blood. Most Uthgardt tribes denied that history, the Thunderbeasts included; it was a matter of shame to believe that they were spawned by those decadent magicians.

Vell leaned closer. The wizard melted away, and his eyes were set instead into the sunken sockets of a great lizard, one of the Thunderbeasts or behemoths that the tribe used in their art, or occasionally to tattoo upon themselves. It was the creature Vell had become. There was no human intelligence in those eyes—this was an animal, nothing more. It looked closely at him, as if staring through time back at Vell.

It turned and lumbered through a thick forest. The great beast planted a foot next to an oak sapling, struggling to grow within the dense underbrush. Vell realized with a shock that this must be Grandfather Tree. He knew it. While all of the other trees that stood around it, much greater trees, had died and gone, it remained. What force blessed it with such permanence? Before his eyes, it sprouted higher and higher, spreading its limbs wider and wider until they blocked the sky.

Now ripples disturbed the pool, each beginning at the center and bringing with it a new image. The scenes passed with such speed that Vell could not inspect each one closely. He saw images of heated battles, of a wide-shouldered man with coal-black hair. The dark-haired warrior wielded a greataxe and hacked at a shaggy demon on a mountainside. Then came a scene of that same axe cutting the neck of a behemoth on a vast green hill, but in the hands of a warrior with yellow hair and a bright yellow beard.

The axe! Vell recognized it immediately. It had been the weapon of the chiefs of the Thunderbeasts, both Gundar and Sungar. Sungar had disposed of it some years ago after he learned it contained arcane magic. Vell did not know what to make of this—he was not in the Fallen Lands when it happened—though many took this as a signal that Sungar was an unfit leader.

"Tell me more," Vell said to no one. As if on cue, a new image unfolded—one he knew well. It was Morgur's Mound on Runemeet. Vell saw himself, the bones of the beast hovering above him. He saw his lips move, and though he had no memory of the event, he knew the words: "Find the living."

Another ripple, and the axe appeared again. It was in a different hand, an inhuman hand—the hand of one of the huge goblinoid beasts, a hobgoblin, decked out in armor. The pool revealed a purple-robed man and four other men, humans all, together with a small human woman dressed in tight black leather. He knew her. The man and the beast in him both knew her.

Vell clenched his fists in anger. He wanted to jump into the pool. Perhaps it would transport him there and let him crush the woman who had kidnapped Sungar, and who had eluded him on a hippogriff's wings. But he remembered Tylvis's words of caution and held his ground.

The party of seven was walking along the banks of a river with forest all around. More water, he thought, as he saw the pristine flow rippling in the sunlight. He recognized the high mountains towering over them as the ones Kellin had named the Star Mounts.

For a long time he stood there, staring at the water which now showed nothing, not even his own reflection. He wondered if he would ever see himself again.

When he stepped outside the cave, Kellin started like a child caught in a forbidden act. She was in conversation with Lanaal, but they both silenced at the sight of him.

"Vell," Kellin said, trying to appear calm, though her eyes were red and her cheeks stained. "Did you see anything?"

"Yes," he said, walking over to her. "So did you."

"No, I . . ."

He stopped near her. "Tell me," he said.

"It helped explain why I'm here," she said, casting her eyes to the ground. "My compulsion to help your tribe."

"What do you mean?"

"She's atoning," Lanaal supplied. Her hand stroked Kellin's shoulder. "Atoning for a wrong she didn't know of until now."

Vell shook his head, not understanding.

"I saw Morgur's Mound in my vision," Kellin said, her throat becoming dry. "And my father. He read a counter-spell that cut through the magic protecting the place, and he took a piece of the dinosaur bone." She looked up into Vell's eyes. "He lied when he said he bought it in Baldur's Gate. He stole it. He was a—" she choked, "—a vandal and a desecrator."

"But you're not," Vell said.

"But my father . . ."

"Apparently the blood of mages flows in my veins, but I am no mage," Vell said.

Kellin looked into his brown eyes.

"Sometimes ancestry is something to be overcome, not embraced," Vell continued. "All the same, I don't recommend you tell Keirkrad about this."

"I should say not!" cried Kellin. She wrapped her long arms around him, something he didn't expect. He could feel the warm trickle of tears onto his shoulder. "Tylvis was right," she said. "The Fountains of Memory can show you things you don't want to know." Forcing a smile, she asked, "But what did you find?"

"I was fascinated by what I saw," Vell said. "Few answers and many more questions, but at least now I have seen the faces of our enemies."

"Truly?" Lanaal asked.

Vell broke his embrace with Kellin and nodded to the elf. "One of them is the woman who abducted Sungar. She travels with a group of companions, and from what I saw, they're much closer to our destination than we are." He pointed south to the horizon, to those incongruous mountains.

CHAPTER 11

They say the gods walk here," Nithinial said. With each foot planted in the muddy earth edging the Unicorn Run, they might have trod in the steps of the immortals. The thought was not comforting to any of the Antiquarians. This was a place where they did not belong.

They had spent quite some time marching along the banks of the famed Unicorn Run. They made no attempt to conceal their presence, but they saw no signs of life here, godly or otherwise, beyond the occasional shalass fish jumping in the waters. Certainly there was no sign of the unicorns, nor of the numerous fey believed to make this area their home.

Leng walked like he belonged there, or at least as if he thought he did. It was odd that such a dark priest could walk through such a famously hallowed place with no ill effects—the

Antiquarians wondered if he were trying not to show any harm to himself, or if he were truly powerful enough to resist the effects. He haughtily sniffed the air as if all of the crystalline beauty of nature had no effect on him, indeed, as if it were disgusting to him. The blue purity of the cool, slow waters might have been like a slap to the face to the rest of them, but not for Leng. He would pollute it, destroy it.

Leng was disappointed that they had not yet seen any unicorns. "I had hoped this place which bears their name would be thick with them," he said, not so much to his companions as to the Run itself, and whatever ears might be listening. "I sacrificed one in the temple once. My acolytes captured it in the Southwood. Cyric was especially pleased with that offering. I sliced its horn off, ground it to powder, and used it to devise something special. You will see soon enough."

The fog-shrouded Star Mounts were stretched out before them now, but they still seemed an eternity away—a place they would likely never reach. The Antiquarians had been together for many years and knew each other's moods well. With Vonelh left to rot in a duskwood grove among a pile of dead fey, killed by a supposed ally, they were certainly at their lowest moment. Royce and Bessick walked slumped, defeated; Gunton could not stop himself from talking; and crazy anger blazed in Nithinial's almond-shaped eyes. His elf nature, rising to the surface in the presence of the beauty of the Unicorn Run, was the only thing stopping him from a violent act against Leng.

This was supposed to be an epic quest, but this type of epic did not fit their own modest definition. They did not revere Cyric, spending most of their prayers on Shandakul—a fellow wanderer and explorer of ancient dungeons. They recognized in Leng a truly epic evil. If he had epic heroism to match, this could be a terrible time for the North, for all Faerûn even. They certainly did not want to die fighting on behalf of the Mad God's priest, but neither did they want to lose more members to his whims.

What did Ardeth think? A cool mystery, she was

obviously not a willing party to this detour, but there was no obvious fear in her face. Unfortunately, they could not draw strength from her composure the way the simple-minded hobgoblin could.

"The fashion in Secomber is to say that at the head-waters of the Run lies the Glade of Life, where the gods live and dance as mortals do," said Gunton. "Others claim that it's the birthplace of all the races of Faerûn, and that no further race could ever come to exist if the Glade were destroyed."

A faint roar drew them upstream, the sound growing louder and louder until they rounded a rocky bend to find a true place of legend before them. The roar of the falling water was deafening, yet it appeared as gentle as the mist that softly drifted down from the rocks high above, and the high grassy plateau surrounding it. They all stopped, stunned at the sight of this waterfall. Even Leng stood agape. He merely stared into the rushing waters, the gentle spray misting his strangely calm features.

"The first of the Sisters," said Royce. The Sisters, a set of waterfalls along the Unicorn Run's upper reaches, were famed for their beauty and natural majesty. For once, the legends did not lie.

"I thought no sight could displace Highstar Lake as the most beautiful my eyes have seen," Gunton said, gripping his bearded chin. "The alchemist Amanitus wrote . . ."

"Quiet, fool," shouted Leng. The calm on his face vanished as he spun to face the trees that lined the banks. With a quick incantation, a pair of black, disfigured hands appeared in the air before him, disembodied and sharp-clawed, and in a flash they flew out into the green wilds. When they returned, they were clamped around the slender arms of a naked woman with greenish hair. She resisted wildly with flailing limbs, her eyes wide in terror. The claws released the dryad at Leng's feet, dropping her flat on her face. Leng drew the flail from his waist and brought it down with all his force onto the dryad's head with a stomach-turning *crack*.

The Antiquarians winced. The wreck of the dryad's

body shriveled before their eyes and lay motionless.

"Was that necessary?" demanded Royce. "Obviously, they know we're here."

"I prefer my women without skin the texture of bark," Leng hissed, his eyes alighting on Ardeth.

"What threat is this place to you?" Royce pressed, determined to speak, though it might mean his death. "Is it a threat to Llorkh, or the Zhentarim, or to the church of Cyric? You want to destroy this because it is beautiful, or simply because it offends you?"

The twin claws flew over to hover at Royce's neck.

"Isn't it reason enough," began the priest. "To accomplish what even Fzoul would never dare?" He turned to face the waterfall again, and dipped into a pocket deep in his robes. He produced a small crystal vial filled with viscous liquid. He tossed it in the direction of the waterfall and with its own speed it flew, vanishing into the waters.

"It is said no force can pollute the Unicorn Run," said Gunton.

The claws vanished as Leng folded his arms over his chest. "We shall see. Now you shall see what I made of that unicorn's horn."

Before their eyes, the crystalline purity of the waters became specked with spots of brown that coursed around the bend like a patch of filth, spreading its disease downstream. A fetid cesspool stink filled the air. Nithinial bent over and retched on the rocky shore.

Leng chuckled at this. "Your elf blood is showing, cur," he said.

A churning brown-green sludge manifested at the foot of the waterfall, its oily menace spreading across the river. What this substance was, none of them knew, but it bubbled and crawled on the surface of the Unicorn Run like a sheet of pain. Dead fish floated to the surface, their flesh rotting away on their bones.

"I hope this pleases you, Leng," Ardeth said. "You've taken a place famous for its beauty and serenity, and you've remade it in your own image."

Leng spun back to cast her an acid glare, but as he did

so, the slime parted on the river like a curtain. Fresh water bubbled up, neutralizing the black putrescence. The thick bog of sludge weakened, and soon patches of blue broke through the inky ooze, then whole streams of clear water.

The Antiquarians breathed sighs of relief.

"Are you satisfied now?" Ardeth asked. "It seems, sometimes, the legends speak true."

Leng snorted, his pale skin flushed red, and his muscles tensed. He swung his flail down on the dead dryad at his feet, again and again. Brittle bones were smashed and rivulets of amber blood flowed down the Run.

At last, Leng swung the flail, dripping with fey blood, high into the air.

"Does this place hold nothing but disappointment?" he shouted, his voice hoarsening as he projected it over the waterfall. "Show yourselves! Where is the godly might? They say the nature gods walk here, but where are they now? Mielikki, Eldath, Shiallia, Lurue, and all the fey gods whose names I never bothered to learn—will you let me march into your domain unopposed? And where are the Unicorn Queen's children? Do you fear me so much that you must hide away? If you want to fight me, fight me now!"

A whinny was heard from the forest. As the group looked around at both banks, they could see hints of movement within the woods and patches of white—were they the unicorns, or was it just a trick of the light? Then the sound of trotting hooves came from both sides of the river, quickly growing louder.

The Antiquarians drew their weapons and tried to follow the sounds and movements in the forest. As soon as they caught a flash of white horn, they were distracted by a neigh or a clomp from elsewhere.

"There must be dozens of them," said Gan.

"Do not attack," Ardeth said tersely, her eyes darting to each Antiquarian and to Gan. "Do not help him." Leng ignored her. Perhaps he could not even hear her. His eyes and face were red with anger and hate, and he stared into the wall of water before them.

The low roar of the water increased to a scream like a

hurricane. The spray from the waterfall intensified, hitting them like hailstones. Storm clouds gathered overhead where the sky had been blue moments before, electricity dancing from cloud to cloud. The Run flowed higher, faster. A wind began to howl, a mix of anguish and a war cry. They felt something whirl around them, some presence, some intelligence.

"Nature is in revolt," Nithinial whimpered to himself. The half-elf drew his dagger from its sheath and ran it along his palm, drawing blood. The pain helped him focus.

With a mighty clap, a lightning bolt coursed down from the clouds above, aimed at the spot where they all stood. But the energy could not penetrate Leng's layers of defenses, and danced like a wreath of fire above their heads before dissipating harmlessly.

Inside the waterfall, something large began to move. The surface of the falling water rippled and changed, slowly taking shape.

"At last!" Leng cried through gritted teeth. "It has come to face me!"

A creature stepped out of the moving curtain, as tall as the waterfall itself and composed entirely of the rushing water, bound in place by some great force of magic. With slow, stately steps it walked out of the waterfall, inexorably moving toward them. It rippled and changed, taking shape.

A gigantic unicorn.

"Obvious choice," Leng said through gritted teeth.

"What is it?" asked Gunton. It splashed forward, its aqueous horn nodding up and down with each step.

"It *is* the Unicorn Run," Leng said. "The fey spirit of this place—all of its power embodied in a single form."

"How do you fight such a thing?" asked Royce.

"You don't," Ardeth supplied, watching as it came closer.

Leng pulled down a column of flame from the sky, just as he had done to the treant. The fire met the water and coursed along the liquid surface of the unicorn, drawing sharp hisses and releasing a vast plume of steam that rose into the air. The great unicorn shrank back under the attack, clearly harmed in some way, but still came closer.

"What do we do?" shouted Royce to Ardeth. His eyes darted to the banks—everywhere he looked, a unicorn seemed to emerge, showing that the way was barred. "I doubt that this matter is open to discussion, and the unicorns will kill us easily!"

"Don't fight," Ardeth repeated, never taking her eyes off their vast foe.

Their enemy transformed. Its flesh morphed from water to stone, becoming a huge living cliff of brown and red rock, casting a long dark shadow. Its four feet seemed to be planted directly into the ground beneath it. The ground did not shake as it walked; rather, the earth seemed to swell up to embrace it when it stepped on the shore, as the water had when it stepped in the river. All the elements of nature were the same to this creature—its mastery over them was equal.

Leng drew out hidden wands from inside his robes and blasted the rocky beast with bolts of magic. It withstood each strike. The rocks beneath the Antiquarians' feet changed to soft clay, swelling up around their boots. At once, the waters of the river rose until the group was standing ankle deep in the cold water, sending shocks to their brains.

Bessick cursed, turning to Ardeth. "Just what should we do?" he thundered. "If you have all the answers, tell us!"

Ardeth answered with a single word. "Wait."

An unholy purple radiance surrounded Leng's hands, and he cast the energy forward against the stone unicorn. It struck its horn, which trembled under the impact, the tip cracking through and hitting the ground hard. It melted away, sucked back into the earth.

But the creature was undeterred and still walked forward, its shadow creeping ever closer. Ardeth stepped back, water swirling about her ankles, and stood close to Gan, who hadn't even raised the axe that now seemed like a part of him.

"I will protect you, mistress," the hobgoblin said.

"I'm afraid the opposite is true," Ardeth replied.

Leng did not notice—or did not care—that no one aided him in his battle as he spent his magical might on this monumental foe. He was someplace else, feeling his god's full power coursing through him as never before. A lightning bolt crackled out, this time originating from one of the stone eyes of the unicorn, bound directly for Leng's face. It never reached him, however, instead bouncing off an unseen barrier and into the sky. Whatever resistance Leng used against the creature's magic, though, would no longer be effective once the unicorn reached him, and its magical attacks would no longer be needed.

Nithinial sprang into action. Something inside his tortured mind snapped, and he leaped into the air, his dagger clutched in his hand. He sank it into Leng's left shoulder, driving it through bone and flesh.

The priest let out a wail of agony louder than the roaring waterfall. The spell he had been preparing was demolished and his concentration was ruined. Instinctively Leng plucked the dagger out of his shoulder, causing a plume of blood to squirt into the air, flow down his purple robes and spray onto his face.

Racked with pain, Leng spun to face his attacker. "You, elfspawn," he cursed Nithinial, bloody spittle flying from his mouth, "have just killed us all." With one hand he grabbed Nithinial's arm and pulled him forward, and with the other he drove the dagger, slick with his own blood, into the half-elf's neck. The blade slid into place, hilt deep. Nithinial gurgled blood and collapsed.

A fist struck Leng on the side of his head. The priest lost his balance. He kept his footing for a moment, but stumbled backward into the rushing river. The fist was Bessick's, and the blow was meant to push him to a proper distance for the move that would finish him. But when Bessick's chain lashed out, Leng, standing waist-deep in the fast running water, reached out and gripped the chain, its spikes driving through his hands. He pulled with all of his magically-enhanced strength, ripping Bessick from his place to join Leng in the Run.

The great stone unicorn kept coming toward them, undeterred.

Bessick took a lungful of cold water and scrambled to regain his footing, but he could not get back on his feet. Leng stepped forward, plucking his hands from the spikes on Bessick's chain, the blood tingeing the water crimson. He pushed Bessick's head down to the river's muddy bottom with his foot, then let the heavy chain go, pinning him in place. Bessick's struggling soon ceased.

Two bolts hit Leng, one bouncing off the bracer on his left arm, the other burying itself in his chest. He looked up at the remaining four—Gan, Gunton with his spear, and Ardeth and Royce with their crossbows held ready. And Mythkar Leng, High Priest of the Dark Sun, standing waist-deep in cold water, blood coursing out of his body, found himself without any further tricks.

"You would kill me to protect that thing?" he growled, waving a weak hand in the stone unicorn's direction.

"No," Royce said. "Because we want you dead."

"We're only here because of Geildarr!" he protested. "He wanted me dead, and . . ."

"Please," Royce protested. "You've given us plenty of reasons to hate you."

"You would murder a priest of Cyric?" he asked, blood dribbling from his mouth down his chin. He raised his shoulders in a pathetic gesture of contrition.

"Somehow," Ardeth said, "I doubt the Lord of Murder will mind."

Royce released another crossbow bolt, this one hitting Leng through his cheek and driving into his brain. Whether it killed him on impact or not they did not know, but he fell back into the fast-flowing water and was swept away by the current, carried off by its fury. The last they saw of Leng was a flash of his purple robes as the Unicorn Run dragged him around a bend.

The four survivors spun to face the stone unicorn, the spirit of the Run, which seemed unaffected by Leng's destruction. It was almost upon them.

"Shall we run?" asked Gunton. "Downstream, perhaps?"

"What good would it do?" asked Royce. All around them, unicorn heads now poked out of the forest—they were utterly surrounded, as well as outnumbered.

"We must stand our ground," Ardeth said.

"What?" asked Royce.

"We must link hands," she said, reaching out to Gan. The hobgoblin took her small hand in his massive one.

"This is how we face death?" asked Royce, his brow furrowed.

"It's how we survive," said Ardeth, hanging her crossbow at her belt and grabbing Royce's hand. Shrugging, his head shaking, he took Gunton's hand as well. The four of them anxiously watched each step of the creature until it was almost upon them. "Patience," said Ardeth, and its shadow fell on them, blacking out the sun like an eclipse. "And don't let go."

There, in that deep black shadow, they vanished, borne away as if on a swift breeze.

The spirit dissipated, shedding its material form. It rejoined the rocks, waters, trees, and air. The woods grew silent as the unicorns slipped away, the threat gone.

And the river kept on flowing, clean and pure.

CHAPTER 12

We can relax now," Ardeth said. All the beautiful colors around them bleached away from the land, replaced with pallid blacks, grays, and whites. The Unicorn Run was transformed to a literal shadow of itself—ripples of dark mingling with flashes of white. The forest around them trembled with gray leaves.

"What happened to the world?" asked Gan.

"It's still there, but we're not," Gunton supplied. "This is the Plane of Shadow." He turned to Ardeth. "You're more of a wizard than you let on."

"I am just an initiate," Ardeth said. "But I have a trick or two. This place isn't safe either. We should get moving. Do not lose hold of me, or you could all be stranded in this place, or lost in one of a thousand worlds." She led the others north, in the direction of the Star Mounts, or rather the massive white peaks that stood in their place, wavering and trembling against a starless black sky.

The experience was unnerving for Gan, as a trembling world shorn of color zipped by them. They moved faster than they possibly could on Faerûn, traveling up the rising hills. Soon the smoky spires towered around them on all sides. Ardeth told the others to be still, and soon the darkness melted away as light and color broke through.

They found themselves standing in a high alpine valley, disturbing a family of curly-horned sheep that dashed away over jagged rocks. The sudden blast of sunlight was an assault on their senses. The ground was rocky with generous vegetation—mosses, lichens, and fragile cedars sprouting from every free spot—and great mountains soared all around. These weren't just any mountains, but the fabled Star Mounts. High on the cliffs they could glimpse blue-purple shapes, like vast crystals.

It took the group several long breaths to admire the place and to let their eyes adjust to the bright light. Winds whistled high above them, but they could feel barely a breeze. The tallest mountains, those that could be viewed even from vantages outside the High Forest, were stern giants reaching up for the gray sky, their snow-capped heights vanishing into the haze. Less apparent from a distance were the smaller mountains that filled the spaces between them, each on par with the Graypeaks around Llorkh. The lower slopes were alive with streams and waterfalls that flowed down into the valleys and eventually became the Unicorn Run.

Ardeth said, "Thank Geildarr for our escape." She reached into her robes and produced a small black gem. She dropped it on the ground and it shattered as if it were glass. "Alas, we'll be forced to use our feet from here on."

"Thank Geildarr indeed!" Royce thundered at Ardeth. "If not for his petty rivalries, there'd be five Antiquarians alive now instead of two!"

Gan stepped forward, lifting the axe just slightly. Ardeth placed a hand on his arm to stop him.

"Spare me, hobgoblin!" Royce shouted. "I'm not going to kill your mistress today. Your glowering and brandishing of that battle-axe didn't intimidate Leng. Why didn't you just bury it in his brain and be done with it?"

Gan snorted and stood up straighter.

"Gan was only doing what I asked," Ardeth said. "Don't blame him."

"Oh, I don't," Royce said. "I blame you and Geildarr. If you wanted Leng dead, we could have devised a plan to slaughter him and hide every trace, if you had only told us."

"Why did it have to be the Unicorn Run?" asked Gunton. "Why did he have to die there?" A quieter soul than his leader, his anger manifested in red streaks spreading across his cheeks and a slight tremor in his voice.

Ardeth said, "We wanted him to choose his own death. It would look better to Fzoul that way. Also, Geildarr wanted Leng to have a death of . . . sufficient grandeur."

Royce laughed madly, the sound echoing off the high mountains surrounding them. "It had grandeur, that's for sure!" He made a fist and banged it against his leg. "And we were just expendable pieces in his scheme?"

"You're mercenaries," said Ardeth. "You are, by your nature, expendable."

"They were all fond of you," Royce said. His eyes were moistening and his voice broke. "Your pretty face, your graceful walk . . . these things put us off guard. But my vision is clear now. Asmodeus's soul is no darker than yours." Unable to stop the tears for his dead companions, he fell to his knees and buried his face in his hands.

"I had hoped we might avoid the heights of the Star Mounts," said Gunton, staring accusingly at Ardeth. "Our mountaineering equipment was mostly destroyed when Leng set our camp ablaze. What remained was in Bessick's pack. It now lies at the bottom of the Run."

"I lived all my life in the Graypeaks," Gan proclaimed. "I know my way through mountains. I will lead the way."

Ardeth looked around. "Which of these is Mount Vision?" she asked. "The Sanctuary should lie to the east of it."

"Well, I'm guessing that we're somewhere deep inside the Mounts . . ." Gunton surveyed the terrain and finally pointed out a distant peak rising over a group of smaller mountains, its tip vanishing into cloud and haze.

"Somewhere beyond that one, I should think."

"Probably ten days' travel at best," the hobgoblin estimated. "Assuming that passes exist."

"We'll need to keep a low profile," said Gunton.

Royce bolted to his feet. "We're still speaking about doing Geildarr's bidding? What makes you think Gunton and I will go along to find this Sanctuary now?"

"You'll still be rewarded if we succeed," Ardeth said. "All the more for your fallen comrades. And if you disobey Geildarr, you'll spend the rest of your life dodging Zhentarim assassins. Moreover, we're stranded here. Gan can survive here better than any of us. This is no time to separate."

Royce cursed, but he knew that her logic was undeniable. This time he had no choice but to do what she said.

"It wasn't supposed to happen this way," Ardeth admitted. "I had no desire to see Vonelh, Bessick, or Nithinial dead. I'm sad to see them so. Only Leng was supposed to die."

"So not all your plans come off perfectly," Royce said, still filled with grief. He looked up at the hobgoblin who towered over him. "She put you in danger too, Gan. She risked your life, and for what? Think about that." He could see something flicker over Gan's stern face.

"I saved your lives," Ardeth reminded Royce and Gunton. "I could have left you to be smashed by that fey juggernaut. But I saved you. Does that count for nothing?"

"It's a start," said Royce with a sneer. "But let this be a promise—if you betray us again, nothing will keep me from slitting your throat. Not the hobgoblin, and not all the lord's men."

"I believe you," said Ardeth. Royce wondered if he saw a shadow of a smile on her lips.

When Vell, Kellin, and Lanaal returned to the village of Ghostand, they found the rest of the Thunderbeast party equipped and ready to forge out again. Many of the Tree Ghosts and their elf guests were present to see them off.

"We know the way," said Thluna. "Faeniele has found our path." He nodded graciously toward the copper-haired wood elf.

"Toward the Star Mounts?" asked Vell.

Thluna's brow furrowed. "How did you know that?"

"I saw it in the Fountains of Memory," said Vell. "And I felt it."

"Truly, the Thunderbeast smiles on us," said Keirkrad. He stepped away from the others, directly toward Kellin. He lowered his head before her, a gesture of contrition that shocked all—not only the idea that he would do so, but that he would do so in public.

"I owe you an apology, daughter of Zale," he said. "Your father was a good man. I have not treated you in a manner befitting his memory. We must set aside our differences for the sake of this mission. I promise things will be different now."

Kellin didn't know what to say. Perhaps the tree's influence could soften even the stoniest of hearts. Even her vast knowledge of Uthgardt customs didn't suggest what to do in this situation. Her cheeks flushed, not the least because of what she now knew about her father.

"Thank you, Shaman Seventoes," she said, clutching one of his ancient, lined hands. "I can only hope that our association will be smoother from now on."

"I promise you, it shall." She looked deep into his blue eyes for any hint of deception and found none. She detected real kindness. Fancy that, she thought.

"We must move quickly," said Vell. "Our enemies are on the march. I saw them in the Fountains of Memory." He described some of his vision; the glimpse of the seven walking along a river.

"That river would be either the Unicorn Run or the Heartblood," explained Faeniele. "Either way, they're a good deal closer to your destination, which lies close to the Heartblood's headwaters. You must seek out three great phandar trees growing in a triangle, lying in a shadowed valley at the Star Mounts' eastern reaches. If this story is more than a legend, there you will find the lost swamp and your totem behemoths."

"We will leave soon and move quickly," said Thluna. "And we take with us a new guide."

Rask Urgek stepped up to join them, dressed for travel and clutching a battle-axe of his own. "Your chief has generously consented to walking with a half-orc."

"Walking with a fellow Uthgardt," Thluna corrected him.

Rask smiled, his orc fangs creating an unnerving grin. "I have a history with the Zhentarim," he said. "I was born into their service. This may be a chance to wash them from my spirit at last."

Gunther Longtooth, chief of the Tree Ghosts, spoke. "We will miss Rask's presence here, but we understand his motives. May Uthgar smile on you and speed you to your destination. We have a gift for you, Chief Thluna." He held out a sturdy wooden club with the Tree Ghosts' emblem carved onto it. "This weapon is carved of old oak that grew in Grandfather Tree's shadow. It is enchanted by the Tree Ghosts' grace. Wield it wisely."

"I am humbled by the honor," said Thluna, taking the club and feeling its weight.

Before they were ready to leave, Lanaal spoke to Vell and Kellin alone.

"I mean to help you more," she said. "I'd come with you, but I think I can help more from afar. In this forest, there are others like Vell and myself who might know more. I will seek them out, and I will find you."

"You've helped me enough already," Vell said.

"The more I learn about you, the more I learn about myself," she said, planting a kiss on his cheek. She turned to Kellin and said, "Take care of him for me," smiling wistfully. Then she transformed into a falcon and flew up past the treetops and away.

More good-byes waited to be said.

"If you should ever decide to visit your cousins of the wood again," Gunther told the Thunderbeasts, "know that you will be welcome."

When the Thunderbeast party forged out again, they knew they left behind a small piece of joy in the High

Forest's depths. They never could have imagined keeping company with elves! Now they had accepted a half-orc as one of them. The rules of the outside world didn't apply in the forest depths. Every one of them was changed by Grandfather Tree's grandeur and the Tree Ghosts' hospitality, and it created a most curious effect: they marched into the unknown with a new sense of unity.

"Do you blame your gods, Hurd?" Sungar asked. Five days had passed since his last meeting with Klev, and he felt almost entirely healed. He felt that the time would soon come for Klev to return and strip away all of his strength again.

"Blame them?" the dwarf answered. "For what?"

"For you being here," Sungar answered, lying on his back in the center of his cell, staring at the stones of the ceiling for the thousandth time. "For your rebellion failing. Surely you thought they were on your side."

"The Morndinsamman and I have exchanged some harsh words," Hurd answered. "I don't think they mind."

"Do you hate them?" Sungar asked. "Do you think they let you down—betrayed you?"

"I can't deny having some thoughts like that. But the gods can't do everything for us. See, the god whom I feel closest to now is Gorm Gulthyn. He was Trice Dulgenhar's god—Trice was a *barakor* of the Lord of the Bronze Mask. Not a lot of people know what I'm about to say, and I surely shouldn't be telling you. But who are you going to tell?

"Gorm's fate is tied to the fate of dwarves on Faerûn, and as our strongholds fell, he grew weaker and weaker. The fire in his eyes, it is said, grows dimmer with each fallen nation and city. To fight to reclaim them, like we fought to reclaim Llorkh, is a holy war to help reverse his fate. Or so Trice said.

"Even our gods suffer defeats, Sungar. But they endure them. So must we."

"I suppose," said Sungar, and he asked no more questions. He thought of Uthgar's defeats: losing the Blue Bears to Malar, the Elk tribe to Auril. Each must have been a piece of him cleaved away. And the other dead tribes of old, remembered in the skalds' songs—the Red Pony and Golden Eagle had supposedly vanished into the Underdark forever.

Were the Thunderbeasts bound for a similar fate?

So often Sungar's mind went back to that day in the Fallen Lands. Geildarr's words were insidious. And he wondered whether following Uthgar's law might be leading the tribe down the road to destruction.

And if so, did that mean Uthgar willed it?

CHAPTER 13

Laying her crossbow on a rock, Ardeth kneeled at a fast-moving mountain stream at the foot of a tall peak and filled her waterskin. The inglorious task gave her a welcome moment to herself, away from Royce's cynicism and Gan's toadying. If only she could do without them!

This mission was not going entirely according to plan, she had to admit to herself. But she would not let herself be dismayed. The Sanctuary still awaited.

She heard a strange noise behind her and spun to face it, snatching up her crossbow. It was a sort of flapping sound, but when she turned, she saw nothing. Then she heard it again, behind her still, and swung around to see a red-feathered birdman, just shorter than Ardeth, staring at her from across the stream. Its wings were folded, and it clutched a javelin in one three-fingered hand.

"What are you doing here?" it spoke in a chirping voice, its head darting from side to side.

"We are merely passing through the Star Mounts," Ardeth said.

"My people were slaughtered and dispersed by the green dragon Elaar," the creature said. "Your kind call him Elaacrimalicros. Are you here to slay him, or to aid him?"

Ardeth recognized the birdman as an aarakocra. She had seen drawings of them in Geildarr's study. She shook her head. "We have no interest in your struggle . . ."

"If we are to survive—" the aarakocra lowered its javelin and pointed it in Ardeth's direction "—then we need magic and weapons. We demand . . ."

Ardeth fired her crossbow, launching a bolt directly toward the aarakocra's feathered belly. But the missile never reached its target. It was deflected in midair by magic and bounced into the stream. Suddenly smiling, Ardeth took another shot at the aarakocra's head. It sailed through as if it were fog and struck the rock face behind it.

The aarakocra vanished. In its place stood a creature half the height of the illusionary bird. Ardeth cast a disgusted look at a red-clad gnome. The aarakocra's spear shrank and became the blackwood cane that Moritz carried. Impressive, Ardeth thought.

"Well met, Ardeth Chale," he said. "You've confirmed what I always suspected: it is in your nature to go for the kill."

"Moritz of Hardbuckler." She never changed the aim of her crossbow. "Fancy encountering you here."

"Charmed, sweet lady," he said, tipping his red tricorn. "So good to speak with you at last."

"I take it this isn't the first time we've met."

"Met, maybe," Moritz said with a chuckle.

"Now comes the part where you make a portentous threat before vanishing on the spot?" asked Ardeth. "Geildarr forewarned me. The feathers were a nice touch."

"Rather, I wanted to commend you on securing the death of Mythkar Leng for Sememmon and myself," Moritz told her, taking a step closer to the quick-running stream.

"He was a most inconvenient enemy."

"I wasn't aware he was your enemy," Ardeth answered. "And I'm quite sure I didn't do it for Sememmon's sake."

"All Zhentarim are Sememmon's enemy," said Moritz. "At least all those faithful to the Keepers."

"Does that include Geildarr?" Ardeth asked. "Why doesn't Sememmon kill him?"

"Is that your answer to everything? Why shouldn't I kill you, then?" Moritz shrugged. "You find it easier to kill a man than to let him live. Isn't that so?" He reached into his robes and produced a bone dagger, the same one she had used to kill Arthus Tyrrell. He tossed it into the stream and it gave a small splash. "He wasn't lying about his wife and children—but I don't expect that moves you any. Did you kill him to silence him? Surely not. Who would have known about your visit? The Thunderbeasts? Or was it only because you knew you could? I bet you'd slaughter the surviving Antiquarians and that great beast who carries the axe, if only you didn't need them."

Ardeth glowered at the gnome. "Where does a weakling get the nerve to lecture me on the evils of violence?"

"You intrigue me. You intrigue Geildarr, too. But unlike him, I'm not blind to what you truly are." Moritz stood straighter. "Perhaps I should bring him up to date."

Ardeth's eyes darted about uncertainly.

"What do you want from me?" she asked, staring down at the primitive bone dagger lying in the stream.

"If you find what you're looking for at this Sanctuary," he said, "whatever powerful remnant of fallen Netheril it may be, it cannot be allowed to enter the desert." He spoke blandly, for he did not need to put his threat into words. When she looked up, he was gone.

Ardeth thought about the ancient dagger. Made of bone, it probably had a long history, but what did that mean? From Elrem's cave, to Llorkh, to Newfort, this insignificant token of the past had been on quite a journey. Perhaps it deserved to lie here, undiscovered, for the rest of time.

She reached down into the cold water to claim it, but when she touched it, it vanished.

❧ ❧ ❧ ❧ ❧

"Under other circumstances, this would be a fascinating place to explore," said Gunton. The group sat around a campfire, devouring a meal of roasted mountain sheep.

"The heart of mystery," agreed Royce, admiring the vista of the mountains in the failing light. He added, "The others would have loved to see this," not bothering to hide his sadness.

In the few days that they had traversed the Star Mounts, the surviving Antiquarians felt both at their best and worst. While they could not forget their dead companions, they were also doing something they had always wanted: exploring the hidden places of Faerûn and plundering their secrets. They could think of no more enigmatic place than these peaks. They had already seen the legendary crystals, large as houses, growing from the upper slopes and catching the light to cast blue and green patterns all through the valleys. There were towers, too—strange, needle-thin white ziggurats rising from high mountain spurs, far too high to be accessible.

Were the towers long abandoned or inhabited still? What treasures might they contain? Perhaps they were as old as Netheril, or contained artifacts more mighty than those they sought at the Sanctuary. But for Royce and Gunton, the mysteries of the Star Mounts would remain mysteries.

Two long days of walking had placed them just beyond one of the smaller mountains that stood in their way. To their great unease, they found themselves relying on Gan, who indeed had an excellent sense of navigable passes and could forage for food. The three of them sat around the fire, carving up their latest meal.

"My mistress is overdue," said Gan, scanning the valley for any sign of Ardeth.

"Ardeth can protect herself," said Royce. "Probably better than any of us. Honestly, Gan, I don't understand you at all. Geildarr's responsible for sending your whole tribe to die needlessly in the Fallen Lands. But you serve him nevertheless."

"I sought out strength," Gan replied.

"I wouldn't have guessed that servility was a hobgoblin trait," said Royce, safe in his assumption that Gan wouldn't understand the word.

"This was after you found Berun's axe?" asked Gunton.

"Yes." The hobgoblin's hand involuntarily reached out to touch the axe's shaft as it rested in front of him.

"I wonder if it's an effect of the axe's magic," said Gunton. "It's a weapon of great leaders—the Bey of Runlatha, and from what Geildarr said, even Uthgar."

"I wield it on Geildarr's behalf," Gan explained. "He is a great ruler."

"Yes," said Royce, "so you keep saying. That must make it so. But what are you getting at, Gunton?"

"This is speculation, but . . ." Gunton stroked his beard. "Perhaps the axe responds to its wielder. When wielded by a leader of men, it might confer great power. But in the hands of a born follower . . ."

Gan looked puzzled.

"An interesting speculation," said Royce. "But would that mean . . ."

Suddenly, Gan pointed into the sky. Gunton and Royce looked up to discover the largest dragon they'd ever seen, a vast mass of green scales silhouetted against the evening light. The carcass in its claws was enormous. Huge hairy legs dangled limply, but the dragon's meal was beyond recognition. As large as a cottage, it dripped blood into the valleys below.

Without flapping its wings, the dragon soared through the Star Mounts, higher than even the mysterious towers. The size of it left Gan, Gunton, and Royce staring agape; the dragon's apple-green form was as large as a galleon on the Trackless Sea. There was no question that they were looking upon a dragon of legend—an ancient wyrm that made all of the North its hunting fields. Royce muttered its name: "Elaacrimalicros."

The sighting of the dragon did not set their minds at ease. They knew of the ongoing Dragon Rage burning throughout Faerûn.

Gan jumped to his feet, snatching up the axe and scanning the valley for his mistress.

"Ardeth!" he shouted.

"Quiet!" Royce whispered. "She's probably taken cover, just like we should."

But it was too late. Though the dragon was several mountains away, its face turned in their direction, locking its gaze on them across all that distance. For an awful second Elaacrimalicros flapped its wings, breaking its glide, then changed its mind and rose on the drafts out of view, behind one of the great mountains.

"Thanks be to the Helping Hand," said Gunton, putting his hand over his heart.

"His hunger outweighed our intrusion," said Royce. "But now Elaacrimalicros knows we're here."

"How long till he comes out again?" asked Gan.

"Did you see the size of him?" said Gunton. "Do you think even a feast that size will keep him satisfied for long? And if he's afflicted by the Rage . . . this is not good news."

Gan lifted Berun's axe into the air.

"Let him come," Gan said. "The axe craves dragon blood! For Geildarr's glory, I will slay Elaacrimalicros myself, then haul his head back to Llorkh as a trophy!"

Gunton and Royce looked at Gan with a mix of concern and amusement. Was it the axe's influence that gave him this wild confidence?

"If it's all the same," Royce said, "I think we should get out of these mountains as swiftly as possible."

Under the guidance of Rask Urgek, the Thunderbeast party traveled through the deep woods of the High Forest. The leaves on the trees rippled like fire. Only occasionally did a glimpse of the fog-shrouded Star Mounts, their destination, appear through the dense canopy. They made good time, and the ground became more level as they traveled farther south, as if it had been smoothed by some ancient woodworker's plane.

Three days of travel had passed without incident, but late on the fourth night, their rest was disturbed by a cacophony of high-pitched squeals in the woods.

"Bats," said Rask. Only traces of Selûne's light filtered down through the leaves, illuminating the thick trunks of the overgrown trees. Flashes of movement teased their eyes, and soon the whole forest seemed alive with them.

"Are they dangerous?" asked Thluna.

"The High Forest is home to some carnivorous bats," Rask said. "But they live far to the northeast, in the area of Hellgate Dell and Stone Stand."

"The most dangerous part of the High Forest," Thanar elaborated. "Only marginally more dangerous than the rest."

"There must be thousands of them," said Kellin, watching the trees. The swarm came closer and closer, and they could see an occasional bat darting overhead.

"They find their way by sound, do they not?" Keirkrad asked Thanar. The druid nodded. "Then I know a simple way to keep them away." The shaman motioned with his ancient hands and suddenly, the chiropteran squeals seemed to cease, and with them, all sounds of the night.

"What did you do?" asked Vell, but his question was answered when he opened his mouth and no sound came out.

Kellin smiled. "Clever," she mouthed, and even dared to pat Keirkrad on the back.

Their camp was unearthly, deathly quiet. The bats, perceiving the silence as something solid, avoided the protective shell around the Thunderbeasts. Though the area above was thick with bats, Keirkrad's spell had created an island of calm.

Then the silence turned deadly. Without warning, a jagged spear hurtled down from the trees above. Crudely aimed in the darkness, it nevertheless found an unsuspecting Thunderbeast, striking his chest and driving deep. Grallah collapsed backward, blood trickling from his mouth. Thluna and Hengin reached him to deliver aid, but they could only lower him to the leaf-strewn ground. Grallah's lips moved, but no one could hear his dying words—perhaps a final prayer to Uthgar. The others scanned their dim surroundings, especially the branches of the trees. Amidst the shards of moonlight, they saw flashes of movement, larger than the bats—man-sized forms swooping between the trees.

"Werebats," mouthed Rask.

The group knew that if they huddled closely, they would be easy targets. Worse the lycanthropes didn't seem to be inhibited by the magical silence. A few Thunderbeasts broke away to put their backs to the tree trunks, forming a perimeter.

Vell looked at his hands, seeing flesh and not scales. He summoned the scales and he felt the restless behemoth spirit within him eagerly rising to the surface. He grimaced at first as the lizard scales sprouted and crawled across his flesh, but it was not painful. Lanaal's teachings have had an effect, he thought. He understood the advantage of calling on these powers, but worried about feeling so natural while wearing a behemoth's skin.

Every inch of his human form was quickly covered with a layer of brownish scales. Vell walked away from his group until he was beyond the protection of Keirkrad's spell, finding tumult outside. The air was warm and humid from the swarm of bodies. Dozens of bats immediately set upon him, landing so tightly that his whole body seemed to writhe with their presence, but their teeth could not penetrate his natural armor. He reached out and grabbed handfuls of them, crushing them in his grip.

A figure swept down on him from the trees—a slender, human shape with thick bat wings and sharp white teeth on a hideous rodent face. Kellin jumped beyond the silence and, inspired by Keirkrad's manipulation of sound, howled in the werebat's direction. A tremendous shriek tore from her throat: a low-pitched boom of fantastic intensity that echoed off the trees. The blast struck the creature in midair and sent it careening against a tree, its thick claws grasping at its enormous bat ears. Vell ran over to it and delivered a bare-fisted blow to its head that crushed its skull. Its crumpled, leather-winged form collapsed in a twisted heap. All around, stunned bats plummeted from the sky like fat raindrops.

Unnoticed, a strange pellet fell from the trees. It landed next to Keirkrad and erupted into a mesh of thick, gooey strands like spider silk that wrapped around the ancient shaman, binding him in an instant. Within the sticky wrapping, his hands were held in place and his mouth was covered. The more he struggled, the tighter he was bound within the cocoon.

Ilskar and Draf ran over to slice through Keirkrad's bonds, but another flock of bats assailed the party. The new attackers were as large as dogs, with triangular bodies and red fur. Like their smaller brethren, they lost their ability to navigate inside the magical silence. They panicked and lashed out with spiny tails, drawing blood wherever they struck. Thluna bashed one solidly with his Tree Ghost club, damaging its wings then crushing it under foot. Ilskar and Draf tried to cut Keirkrad free, but their blades were useless against the thick webbing. They turned away from Keirkrad to fight the new enemy.

Amid the confusion, two werebats swooped down from the treetops. They gripped the strange webbing that held Keirkrad and tried to pull him aloft. Rask hit one of them solidly with his battle-axe, but it bounced off the lycanthrope without leaving a mark.

Thanar clapped Thluna on the shoulder and turned him toward the werebats assaulting Keirkrad. Thluna swung his club at one of the struggling werebats, catching it just above its knee. The werebat released its grip on Keirkrad and turned to face Thluna, silently hissing and snarling. Thluna struck again with the enchanted club, sending his victim to the ground on one knee. At the same time, a red-tinged globe of magic struck the other werebat on the head, crimson streamers reaching back to Kellin's fingers. The werebat released its grip on the webbing and flew off to the shelter of the trees. Still bound, Keirkrad tumbled unceremoniously to the ground, rolling out of control and landing with his face planted in the dirt.

Outside the silence, Vell found himself assailed by two werebats. Their speed and flight kept Vell off balance. Dozens of bats swarmed around him until he could hardly see. Thanar slaughtered one of the night hunters with his sword before rushing to join Kellin.

"They're not trying to kill us," he called over the clamor of bat shrieks. "They want Keirkrad." He watched Thluna finish off a werebat with a blow from the Tree Ghost club. The other warriors slashed their way through the remaining night hunters.

Kellin nodded in agreement, looking over at Keirkrad's bound form. "Did they bind him because he's the most powerful of us?"

Thanar shook his head. "They probably thought he was the least powerful. We need to free him."

Thanar and Kellin rushed to the shaman, spun him onto his back, and dragged him out of the magical silence so they could try their spells on the magical webbing. He was still conscious, and his ancient blues eyes darted about in fear. Before Kellin and Thanar could even begin to weaken his bonds, more werebats appeared from above. Kellin quickly conjured a bright blue bolt that blasted through a werebat's thin wings. Thanar summoned a powerful blast of wind that tossed the creatures astray, but more came, flying down and striking, then retreating to the trees and sending more of the smaller bats down on them. Knowing they could not endure much of this, Kellin and Thanar gripped the webbing and hauled Keirkrad back into the shell of silence.

"It won't last," Kellin called, just before her words were swallowed up again.

Vell stood alone outside the protective silence. He succeeded in grabbing one of the werebats, and he squeezed its neck until its huge rodent eyes went dim. Ignoring the other werebats, he leaped into the silence. The world within was deceptively calm. Werebats swooped around the edges, testing its limits and baiting those within it, baring their sharp teeth and begging the barbarians to rage and rush out into danger. The night outside writhed with the bat swarm. An occasional night hunter bat darted into the silence but was swiftly dealt with by the weapons inside. The radius of Keirkrad's spell no longer felt like safety or comfort. Their attackers would soon overcome the fragile barrier.

With communication nearly impossible, the group had difficulty forming a strategy. Kellin drew her father's enchanted sword and passed it to Rask, who dropped his battle-axe to the ground. The barbarians fanned out around the incapacitated Keirkrad. Before long, the silence dissolved, and the cacophony of the outside world assailed them.

Immediately, bats and werebats swept in. Kellin unleashed her ear-piercing shriek again, deafening a host of bats and stunning a number of the werebats. Thanar launched a strong wind that filled outstretched wings and sent numerous bats flying backward, crashing against trees. Vell snatched a werebat from midair and drew it into a tight hug, crushing it with the full force of his strength against his scaly body. The warriors swung their weapons, but only Thluna with his club and Rask with Kellin's sword were able to harm their attackers. The bat swarm filled the air, confounding the senses with their loud shrieks. The horrific mass teemed inward so the defenders could hardly move without their limbs brushing against hairy bodies or leathery wings.

It was a doomed effort. More werebats appeared above, then swooped down and wrapped their claws around the webbing that bound Keirkrad. Before anyone could turn to his aid, the shaman was lifted into the trees and away.

The other werebats followed, vanishing swiftly. The defeated Thunderbeasts were left to hack their way through the thick bat swarm, till at last it dissipated with the first light of day.

The stink of bat guano assailed Keirkrad as he was deposited on a rickety wooden platform in some uncharted corner of the High Forest. For a long time he lay on his back, staring up at the tree tops and the impassive sky beyond, silently calling on Uthgar for aid. At last the webbing around him melted away, though his hands remained stuck to his sides and his mouth was still glued shut. Two figures arrived and pulled him to his feet. One was female and one was male, and both were slight, with coppery skin and elf ears.

Elf werebats, Keirkrad thought, but in this form, they did not look like the elves he had met around Grandfather Tree. Something in these faces was twisted and batlike.

The werebats gripped Keirkrad firmly by the arms and led him across a crude wooden walkway built in the heights of the trees, concealed from view below by thick undergrowth. Bats, large and small, flitted through the trees around him. Perhaps some of them were werebats too, Keirkrad thought. This was a disgusting place, caked with guano, peopled by creatures with scant interest in cleanliness: a rank parody of Ghostand, the Tree Ghosts' village among the trees.

The two werebats led Keirkrad to the middle of a larger platform and let him drop to his knees.

"What have my children brought me?" spoke a strange, high-pitched voice.

On the surrounding trees, Keirkrad noticed crude trophies. Among various animal remains, he identified a hybsil's antlers and desiccated elf ears nailed into the bark. At the end of the platform sat a werebat perched on a crude wooden throne amid piles of offal. Its vast wings were folded against its middle. It was naked but covered with matted fur, and its face was a hideous amalgam of bat and man: a snarling mouth with sharp teeth and grossly oversized ears. Two red eyes stared at Keirkrad.

The werebat stepped from its throne and walked over to Keirkrad, its long toenails clicking against the wooden floor.

"Shaman Seventoes," it pronounced. "What a boon they have brought me. And they had no idea who you were! What luck! What luck!"

It leaned in closer to Keirkrad, bathing him in its foul breath. A pink tongue snaked out to lick its long rodent teeth.

"Do you remember me, Thunderbeast? I am now called Heskret, but I had another name. We met in battle. Have you forgotten? Beneath Thranulf's Height. Do you remember?"

The werebat transformed before Keirkrad's eyes. His wings drew into his sides and vanished, his face twisted and contorted, and the fur vanished from his chest and revealed human skin. A white-haired man stood naked before Keirkrad, and on his shriveled upper chest was a huge tattoo, one that Keirkrad recognized all too well. It was the crude form of a hulking bear.

The Blue Bear! Every barbarian believed that the most hated Uthgardt tribe had utterly perished in the fall of Hellgate Keep. Keirkrad remembered the man who stood before him—a war chief whom he and Gundar had battled long ago. The fighting was long, with many casualties on both sides, resulting in a costly victory for the Thunderbeasts. It was whispered that the Blue Bear war leader feared to return to face punishment from his chief and vanished into the forest to seek penance from Malar.

"Do not misunderstand," said Heskret, now speaking with a human voice. His blue eyes locked onto Keirkrad. "I am not Blue Bear, though I was Blue Bear. My former tribe proved weak and perished, but my new tribe lasts still. Now I serve nothing but the Black Blood."

He walked closer and planted a finger on the strands of webbing that held Keirkrad's mouth shut. But instead of removing the obstruction, Heskret made a fist and punched the shaman in the side of the head. Weak and exhausted, especially at his advanced age, Keirkrad tumbled sideways, his head slamming hard into the wooden floor. When Heskret unsealed his mouth, all Keirkrad could do was drool blood onto the floor.

A clawed finger stroked Keirkrad's cheek. He knew without looking that Heskret had taken his werebat form again.

"You have lived how long now?" Heskret snarled, leaning closer till Keirkrad could feel his warm breath on his face. It stank of raw meat and rot. "They say Uthgar prolonged your life so grotesquely because he had some destiny in store for you. I wonder if this is what he had in mind."

Keirkrad cried out as he felt sharp teeth take a chunk out of his cheek.

CHAPTER 14

Tremendous winds pelted Ardeth, Royce, Gunton, and Gan as they slowly navigated a high mountain pass. A vicious thunderstorm had slowed them; the gray mists above had let out their store, dropping a sudden deluge that turned the mountain slopes into slides of pure mud. The foursome lost much time hunkering in sheltered spots, and their object, Mount Vision, had disappeared into the haze. The wind howled so loudly that they could barely hear each other, their clothes were soaked through, and all the while they looked over their shoulders for Elaacrimalicros to drop out of the rain clouds.

While the rain was at its worst, and they took refuge in a hollow at the base of a steep cliff, a black figure stopped at the mouth of their cave, barely visible in the gloom. Everyone grasped weapons, and Ardeth pointed her crossbow at the intruder.

Through the rain, they saw the outline of huge wings. The wings disappeared as the strange creature approached, and a copper-skinned elf stepped out of the murk, dressed in animal leathers. Short and slender even for an elf, his dark hair was matted and unkempt. His red-streaked hazel eyes darted back and forth before settling on Ardeth.

"Ardeth of Llorkh?" he asked, barely audible over the raging winds outside. His voice was high-pitched and raspy, decidedly not like any elf any of them had encountered before.

"Yes," Ardeth answered cautiously.

"I smelled your scent on the wind. I am here on behalf of the Mayor of Llorkh."

"Thank the gods," Royce gasped. "I didn't suspect Geildarr would have contact with the wood elves."

The elf let out a disgusted grunt as his answer.

"You're a werebat," Ardeth said. "From Heskret's tribe. Geildarr told me there was a chance he could recruit aid from your folk." There was no relief in her voice, only suspicion, and she kept her eyes locked on his face, scanning for any insincerity.

"My name is Halzoon," the elf said, looking at the group, his neck twitching. "I am to offer myself as your guide."

"No deva, but a winged savior nonetheless," said Gunton.

"Where are you guiding us?" asked Ardeth.

"Three great phandar trees in a triangle, alongside the Heartblood River. That is what you seek."

"How do you know this?" asked Royce.

"Heskret extracted it—" he drooled and chuckled, "—from an Uthgardt shaman."

"You know the best way to the Sanctuary?" asked Royce. "These passes are difficult to navigate."

"Forget the passes," the werebat hissed. "Forget them! I know a better way."

"We don't have wings," huffed Gan.

"Not above the mountains, goblinoid. Below them."

"There are tunnels?" asked Royce.

"Yes," Halzoon said, rubbing his cheek against his shoulder. "Many tunnels, all through the mountains.

Dwarves built them long ago. Harpies made their nests there. But not any more."

"How do we get in?" asked Gunton. "It'd be a far better option than waiting here for Elaacrimalicros to eat us."

Halzoon pointed upward. "An entrance farther up the mountain. Winds are terrible up there, but with care, you should make it."

"Thanks be to all the gods," Royce said. "I'd hug you if you didn't stink of guano."

The elf werebat chuckled at Royce's joke. "I will lead you," he said. "Heskret commands it."

"What was his name?" Ardeth demanded.

"Whose name?" asked Halzoon.

"The barbarian shaman you captured," she said. "What was his name?"

"His name was Keirkrad." A cruel smile crossed his face and he let out a high-pitched cackle. "We were lucky to get that one. Heskret was pleased. He had some unfinished business with that one."

"Keirkrad," she repeated. The answered satisfied her, and she lowered her crossbow.

The ingress on the mountain that Halzoon described was higher and more remote than anyone expected. Ardeth and her companions summoned every scrap of will and endurance to climb through the driving rain and the roaring wind to reach shelter again. They found a knee-high drop onto an enclosed platform, its base full of water, and a stone passageway leading into the mountain.

"Fascinating," said Gunton when they ducked into the dry passage. "A landing platform. The dwarves who lived here must have used flying mounts, just as they do in the Great Rift."

Ardeth lit a torch, and by its light they could see the fine stonework of the passageway. Dethek letters were inscribed in the wall and from them, Gunton translated the name of the place: Onthrilaenthor.

"Ancient mines," said Royce. "Built by dwarves, but with a clearly elf name. Most curious. How far is our destination?" he asked Halzoon.

"Two, three days," the werebat said. "I don't know why you want to go there. I know the place, and there's nothing to say about it."

"We have a key," said Gan, holding up the axe.

Halzoon scratched his head, uninterested.

"And you know exactly where we're going?" asked Gunton.

Halzoon nodded. "I scouted these tunnels for Bloodmaster Heskret. I know the way."

"I can only hope that a werebat will have good senses underground," said Ardeth.

"We Antiquarians have experience in tunnels as well," boasted Royce, but Halzoon soon humbled Royce and Gunton. He led the foursome through a maze of ancient tunnels, shored by the occasional stone pillar. The werebat frequently stopped to sniff the air or turn an ear to a vacant passageway, apparently navigating on sheer instinct. Some of the tunnels were coursing with wind from the outside, while others were silent as if they'd not been visited in millennia.

Halzoon was a strange creature. He was more bat than elf, clearly. His posture was stooped, and he was a mass of tics—he could not keep still for a second, scratching, twitching, and sniffing.

"You said there are harpies here," said Ardeth as they climbed down a twisting staircase deep into the bowels of the mountains.

"No," Halzoon answered.

"But you said ..."

"Harpies lived here, but no more. Scared off, they left and are all gone."

"What scared them off?" asked Gunton.

"The dragon."

"Dragon?" Royce said. "You mean Elaacrimalicros?"

"No!" Halzoon insisted. "Onskarrarrd."

"Who?"

"Deep dragon. He moved here after the fall of Ched Nasad last year. Onskarrarrd lairs down below."

"Tremendous," said Royce, dropping his voice to a whisper. "We're evading one dragon above, only to intrude on another one below. You might have mentioned that."

"No worry," said Halzoon. "He is sleeping now."

"How do you know that?" asked Ardeth.

Halzoon pressed an ear to the wall. "Can't you hear?" he asked. "He's snoring!"

"You should have mentioned this," Royce said, new anxiety in his voice.

"Why, human?" asked the werebat. "Would you have preferred to stay out there?" He squeaked with laughter.

The Uthgardt pushed their way through the High Forest with new urgency. The Star Mounts drew ever closer, cold and forbidding, and their clouds spread out to douse them all with hard rain.

No one said much since Keirkrad had been taken. They wondered whether the werebats had been hired—most likely by the Zhentarim—to capture one of them for interrogation, perhaps to learn where they were going.

"Malar," spat Thluna. "Blast his hide."

As they pushed through the pouring rain, Thluna vividly remembered a single day on the cracked earth of the Fallen Lands. All their troubles seemed to stem from that day. The wizard Arklow had spoken of creatures called the phaerimm, monsters of magic who could ensnare the mind of any creature. Thluna had feared that would be their fate—the Thunderbeasts would be made vassals to another foul power.

But with Arklow's help and directions, the Thunderbeasts had slaughtered the dark naga who led the phaerimm forces and fled as a massive orc army fell into infighting. Their victory was swiftly tangled with defeat, as Arklow revealed that magic lay in many of the tribe's weapons, including Sungar's ceremonial axe. The Thunderbeasts responded by leaving those weapons in the Fallen Lands.

Thluna looked at the oaken club he now clutched, given to him by Gunther Longtooth. It had hurt the werebats when other weapons had not. Thluna knew that the club must be magical, just like the axe. But he would not dream of disposing of it. It was a gift. Moreover, it was an outstanding weapon.

"When we were seeking out Grandfather Tree," Rask told Thluna as they walked together, "we knew that the Blue Bears were doing the same. We did our best to give them false leads, lure them into traps, counter them wherever we could. And, thanks be to Uthgar, we reached the Tree before they did. But at the same time, our enemy helped legitimize our quest."

"What do you mean?" asked Thluna.

"Think of what we're doing now. You quest for your living behemoths. This might seem foolhardy to outsiders, something important only to your tribe. But clearly, this is not the case. If the Zhentarim want your secrets, your secrets must be very important indeed."

"I had not thought of it that way," said Thluna. "The Zhentarim have taken great interest in us. Why? Aren't we beneath their notice?"

"A mystery indeed," Rask confirmed. "Nothing moves the Zhentarim but power. I knew their workings all too well . . . they are brutal and cruel, and Geildarr is a petty despot. But contrary to what some would say, they do not practice their vile ways for no reason. They want power, and for power they hoard their coin and whatever else magic can find."

"Magic," Thluna repeated fatefully. At the core of all the evil in the world, he decided, there was magic.

"A mystery indeed," the half-orc repeated. "I only hope we live long enough to solve it."

"I never thought I had anything to hide," said Kellin softly.

"What's that?" asked Vell. They walked together through the underbrush, the Thunderbeast party fanning out around them. Rask and Thluna walked in the lead while Thanar held back, scanning the woods for signs of anything lurking among the trees.

Kellin swallowed. "Until recently, I never had secrets— not any that anyone would care to know. I was as open and forthcoming as anyone could be, and that felt like freedom. When I came to your camp, I kept part of myself hidden, but I could justify that to myself. I knew that if I revealed that I was a sorceress you'd reject me, and my journey would end before it began."

"You were right," Vell affirmed.

Kellin forced a smile. Keeping her voice low, she asked, "But am I right this time? What I know about my father ..."

"Has nothing to do with you. You are not your father."

He cast her a sideways glance.

"A curious statement from an Uthgardt," she said. "Tell me about your father, Vell."

Vell stood a little taller. Out of pride? Kellin wondered. "He fought with King Gundar. He died when I was young, fighting perytons in the Lurkwood. He was buried with honor outside Grunwald."

"My father's body was burned, and his ashes spread into the Trackless Sea at Candlekeep. He wanted to unite with the sea, with everything." Kellin frowned. "As I keep my father's shame a secret, it becomes my shame. Maybe I should tell Thluna."

Vell thought about it. "Thluna's younger even than I. He's already proven himself less rigid than Sungar. But all the same, I would not do it. Not now."

A tear rolled down Kellin's cheek. "Why should I bear his shame?" She laid her hand on the hilt of the sword she wore. "I took him as my teacher. How he fooled us all. Even Keirkrad said he was a good man." Vell could see she was holding back her emotions, and he put a hand on her shoulder.

"What will you do when you return home?" asked Vell.

"I'll have to reveal what I've learned to the Candlekeep

monks. It will cast doubt on all of his research. His entire work could be discarded, his books culled from the libraries." She looked up at Vell. "Or perhaps not—I hope not, for most of my work is built on his work. But what I've learned *must* be brought forward, must be revealed."

"You could keep his secret," said Vell. "Only Lanaal and I know, and neither of us will reveal it."

Kellin shook her head. "Oghma is the god of knowledge, and he teaches that knowledge is the most valuable thing. But that doesn't mean it should be hoarded. It should be freely available to all. I'm not able to start keeping the secrets of thieves."

"You're brave," said Vell. "All my life, I was taught that civilized outsiders were dishonorable and full of deceit."

"Not all, but some are," said Kellin. "Your tribe has seen this. Likewise, most of civilization thinks of the Uthgardt as stupid and bloodthirsty. But I always knew better."

"Because of your father, no doubt," said Vell. Tentatively, he added, "I'm intrigued by what you said about Oghma. Does he truly spurn all secrets? Even those we carry in our hearts?"

"Well, mostly it concerns the facts of the world," said Kellin. "Some things are meant just for the individual. The church of Oghma values self-knowledge as well, and sometimes that means privacy. In fact, on my twelfth birthday, the Lorekeepers revealed to me my True Name, a secret name meant to contain the truth of me."

"Does it?" Vell asked.

"I wondered at first how it was meant to," she admitted. "It frustrated me. I thought this was a weakness. I thought I was supposed to understand. I struggled to grasp the meaning, the reason this True Name was for me. I probed deep, contemplated many questions. There are moments when I seemed on the verge of understanding, but it always lay just outside my grasp. Then I had an epiphany. I realized that the struggle for understanding held more meaning than the name ever could." She smiled with a serenity that Vell admired and envied.

"So what name is it?"

"I can't tell!" she laughed. Vell was thoroughly disarmed. "A lady must keep some secrets for herself."

"That's all I wanted to know," said Vell.

"If I had secrets of the heart?" asked Kellin. "Be assured, I do."

"I am glad of that," Vell answered, a smile on his face. It filled him with confidence that perhaps, when all of this was settled, another world might be opened up for him.

But the pressure inside his mind could not be ignored. It was growing stronger with each step closer to the Star Mounts. Gods, he thought. I would not be here if it wasn't for my affliction, the Thunderbeast inside.

He placed his hand on the side of his head, trying to weigh his thoughts.

It's leading me around, he thought.

CHAPTER 15

Sungar's world was a blur as two guards tossed him back into his cell. He'd had another session of Klev's ministrations. They grew more brutal each time, Sungar was convinced, and now his body was raw and torn as never before. Falling limply on the hard cell floor, he heard one of the attendants say, "Sweet dreams, chief." Then Sungar drifted away on the pain.

A hand reached out to grasp his. When he opened his eyes, Sungar found himself staring into the craggy, bearded face of King Gundar.

He was not lying in the prison cell in Llorkh, but on a warm, grassy field, with an open sky sprawling above him. His wounds were gone—not healed, but gone—as if they had never been. Gundar's familiar, smiling face, so strong and so benevolent, beamed down on him. This was not Gundar as he lay dying in Llorkh, but the vibrant man Sungar had fought beside so many times, now decked in mail as if newly returned from their victorious raid on Raven Rock.

"Arise, Chieftain of the Thunderbeasts," Gundar said.

Sungar accepted his hand and pulled himself to his feet. He could see the Spine of the World towering in the distance and knew that he was just south of the Lurkwood. Open spaces, a clear sky—he drank in all of those things he had feared he would never see again. But this place was strangely unreal: the colors more vivid, the rose-colored sky so much closer to the ground. Sungar wondered whether he was receiving a vision, or if he was hallucinating. One would be a true gift from Uthgar, the other the meaningless babble of a crippled mind.

"I fear I am chief no longer," said Sungar. "Perhaps I was never meant to be."

"I chose you," Gundar said. "All of my sons were dead. On my deathbed, I named you my successor—not Keirkrad, nor any other."

"And by doing so, you confirmed my decision to withdraw from Grunwald."

Gundar shrugged. "Our people thrived in Grunwald in some senses, but in others, we festered. Perhaps a return to nomad ways was wise."

"I strive to make all of my decisions wise," said Sungar. "But my decisions have brought us here. Our tribe is in ruins, and I am nothing but a prisoner. They must have been a fool's decisions. I misled our people."

"Do not be so certain," the old chief said. Sungar saw that Gundar held the battle-axe. Better it be in Gundar's grasp than a hobgoblin's. "It is possible to make no mistake, and yet fail."

"What would you have done?" asked Sungar. "I've asked myself that a thousand times. That day, in the Fallen Lands. I can't deny that I felt satisfaction as I threw the axe." He reached toward the phantasmal battle-axe and rested his hand on its blade. "The civilized mage thought himself better than us—he thought he could make us abandon our principles because he said so. I proved him wrong."

"You were interpreting Uthgar's law," said Gundar.

"So did the Black Ravens when they tried to destroy us in Grunwald," Sungar said. "They thought they were doing his work. But that day, I had motivations other than serving Uthgar."

"So you think this is Uthgar's punishment?" asked Gundar. "Do you think Uthgar placed the axe in that hobgoblin's hands and sent him to the door of a great enemy—all to teach you a lesson?"

Sungar flinched. "That shows a lack of humility, I confess. I am curious . . . if you are dead, do you have access to Uthgar's will?"

Gundar smiled mysteriously. "That *is* a question. Are you so certain that you are speaking to someone beyond the grave? Honestly?"

"Who could ever be certain of such a thing?" asked Sungar. "Is it humble to think so miraculous a visitor would come to me?"

Gundar let out a roar of laughter. It felt entirely right—exactly how Gundar would have reacted in life. "M'boy, the Chieftain of Chieftains isn't punishing you. Uthgar is trying to help you, and he is acting to help your tribesmen. Don't be afraid for them. Nor should you be afraid for yourself. If death awaits you, face it proudly in a manner befitting a chief."

"Should I kill myself, then?"

Gundar's blue eyes locked onto Sungar's. He spoke simply, but his words hit Sungar with unexpected weight. "Do not be in such a hurry to die."

The sky began to fade away, the dull gray of the stone ceiling peeking out behind it.

"You haven't answered my question," said Sungar hurriedly.

"About the axe, you mean?" Gundar lifted it into the air. "Uthgar wielded this axe once. Our people gave it to him as an offering in the time when he walked and breathed as a man. Uthgar gave it to Chief Tharkane Scalehide, not as a rejection of our gift, but because he thought it most appropriate that our tribe wield it. The weapon of Berun stayed with the blood of Berun."

"So Geildarr spoke the truth," said Sungar. He desperately tried to keep his eyes shut to the world so that this vision might continue, but it was dissolving despite his efforts.

"Yes," said Gundar, the world trembling around him. "If you had known that this magical axe had been wielded by Berun of old, and even by Uthgar, would you have acted any differently?"

Sungar's eyes flew open. His bloodied lips parted, and his hoarse voice rasped, "Yes, I would have."

When they saw light again, it was through an archway facing north, overlooking the sweep of the High Forest. Royce and Gunton squinted at the welcome light. Their trip through the dark tunnels of Onthrilaenthor had been tedious and exhausting, but thankfully uneventful. Their doorway to the outside lay partway up one of the mountains, cut into the slope of one of the easternmost Star Mounts. Traces of ancient switchbacks cutting down the mountainside and into the forest were evident.

"Mount Vision!" Halzoon pointed up at the peak towering into the clouds. He kept his back to the sun; the bright light was uncomfortable for him. "The place you want is on the other side, down in a valley."

"How far?" asked Ardeth.

"On wings, not far," the werebat mused. "But on legs, another day."

"Very well," said Ardeth. "Take us there now. But I must ask—what is your agreement with Geildarr? Are you to simply lead us there, or are you willing to join us in battle if needed?"

"Hmm," said Halzoon. "Heskret told me to deliver you to the place you seek. He said nothing of fighting."

"I don't understand something," said Royce. "What kind of payment has Geildarr given you? Just what do werebats want?"

"Mmm," Halzoon mused. "Mosquitoes."

Ardeth, Gunton, and Royce stared at him like he'd just dropped down from the Sea of Night. Even Gan seemed puzzled.

"He paid you in mosquitoes?" Royce asked.

"No, silly," said Halzoon, baring his saliva-covered teeth. "He paid us in gold."

Unsure whether to laugh, they just stared at him. At this Gan spoke; none of them could remember him saying anything in several days.

"You will not help us fight, if we must fight?" he asked Halzoon, holding Berun's axe close.

"I am not paid to fight," Halzoon rasped. "And you, goblinoid?"

"There is more to life than wealth," Gan answered.

Halzoon shook his head in confusion. "You, goblinoid, are here for the same reason as I, surely. Zhentarim hired your people . . ."

"I serve Geildarr out of honor, not for profit. Serving for profit ruined my people, and it will ruin yours." Gan angrily slammed the shaft of the axe onto the rock at his feet.

"Then why do you serve him?" Halzoon's hazel eyes looked up at the hobgoblin. "You admit that the destruction of your tribe is on his head. So what has he done to make himself worthy of your loyalty?"

Snorting, Geildarr twisted the axe sideways. The blade caught the light and flashed directly into the werebat's eyes. Halzoon's hands went up instinctively to cover his eyes, and Gan delivered a quick blow to Halzoon's knee. With a yelp of pain, Halzoon fell forward. Gan sank the axe into his back. The werebat twitched a moment then expired, lying face down on the rock.

"Gan?" demanded Royce. "Why did you do that?"

"He was disloyal," the hobgoblin said calmly as he pulled the axe free and began cleaning the blade.

"It's the axe." Royce turned to Ardeth, while casting a nervous glance at Gan. "It has a strange effect on him. Its influence is probably getting stronger as we approach the Sanctuary. Ardeth, did you mean to do this?"

"What do you mean?" Ardeth demanded.

"You deprived us of a fighter. I think you know the effect that axe has on Gan. Even if Halzoon didn't want to fight with us, he certainly did not deserve death," said Royce. "Only the vaguest suggestion of disloyalty, and Gan killed our guide."

"Then we'd best get there quickly, lest Gan hack the two of you into little pieces," said Ardeth with a self-satisfied smile. "Wouldn't you agree?" Hopping over the dead werebat, she led them down the mountain path.

❖ ❖ ❖ ❖ ❖

There was no mistaking the phandar trees that they sought. The group could see their destination long before they reached it. Each tree was taller than a temple spire, far larger than phandars usually grew, with huge masses of tangled branches and green leaves paling to golden. The lonely phandar trees were indeed growing in a triangle straddling the deep blue Heartblood River, two on one side and another opposite. They delineated a large area, perhaps not the size of Llorkh, but certainly equal to a smaller town. No trees or features of any kind lay within their boundary. Between them, the Heartblood flowed down from the mountains and into the forest. Somewhere on its path, it entered the Dire Wood and emerged with a red tint. But here, it was pure, cold, and fresh.

"In Vision's shadow," Ardeth muttered as they looked down on it from their high pass. The sun was setting on the opposite side of the mountain, covering the whole valley in darkness. "Just as Geildarr's divination said. We have found the Sanctuary."

"Something is here," said Gan. "I can feel it. We are very near now."

The light was beginning to fade as they reached the foot of the mountain. Gan's hands clenched the axe so tightly that his knuckles were pale. A steely single-mindedness shone in his eyes. He did not shift his focus off the triangle of land below them.

"What do you feel, Gan?" asked Gunton. "What's it like?"

"Like I'm going home," Gan answered. Without warning he stood up straight and spoke in a voice not his own. Clutching the axe to his breast, he rattled off several sentences.

"What was that?" asked Royce. "Gan, did you understand that?"

The hobgoblin dropped the axe, which clanked to the ground before him. He was white as a ghost, and he could only shake his head in the negative.

"I think I recognize some of the words," said Gunton. "I think it was the Netherese tongue. My spoken Netherese isn't as strong as . . ."

"What did it mean?" demanded Ardeth.

"Like I said, I only know a few words," Gunton answered. "But I'm fairly sure it was some sort of warning. I wonder if it is an automated ward, or if there's someone or something alive in there." He pointed down at the area between the phandars.

Ardeth put her hand on Gan's side. "Gan," she asked. "Can you continue?"

The hobgoblin snorted and bent over to pick up the axe. He raised it high and bolted down the mountainside in the direction of the Sanctuary, so fast that the others could barely keep up.

❂   ❂   ❂   ❂   ❂

Like an arrow from on high, an image struck Vell's brain and split it open. Amid the peacefully swaying trees, the Star Mounts closer than ever, Vell dropped to his knees and let out an agonized scream.

The others rushed to him, but they could do nothing to console him.

"What are you feeling?" asked Kellin, kneeling before him.

"There are so many of us," he said, staring right through her face as if she weren't there. "So many in one place, and so close. We are afraid. They are coming close. We will try to trample them when they arrive. The Shepherds have willed it."

"What do you see, Vell?" asked Thluna.

"A marsh. Trees. And a red light." He spoke quickly, fervently. "So many perspectives at once. Too many!" he cried, clasping his temples. He blinked the vision away, and his eyes locked with Kellin's. "Make it go away," he whispered. "Help me."

"He must be seeing through the eyes of the behemoths," Thanar said. "He said 'we'—he thinks he's one of them."

"We should be moving," said Thluna. "If it's so close he can feel them, it can't be far. We need to get there ahead of this threat."

"Vell," said Kellin. "What else can you tell us? Where is it?"

Vell pointed in the distance, directly at one of the Star Mounts. "There. On the other side of that mountain."

"It will take us days to reach it," said Rask.

"Vell," said Thluna. "Can you go back into the vision? Can you tell us more about it?"

Vell shook his head furiously. "Too many minds," he said. "Lanaal spoke of this—how she can sense the feelings and thoughts of birds."

"Can you focus on one of them?" asked Kellin, placing her hands on his shoulders. "Maybe you're having trouble because you're taking in all of their thoughts at once."

Vell's face was a mask of fear, but Kellin's touch helped steady him.

"Let me try," he said, and he went back inside his mind. He found himself wading through the marsh amid the massive behemoths, perhaps two dozen in all, grazing from the trees—all except three tall phandar trees that they never touched. They knew never to go beyond the phandars. It was not safe there. They had no reason to go there, anyway.

Vell's fear left him, and he pressed on with a sense of wonder and curiosity, pushing more and more of his human mind aside. He bathed in the sensations of the behemoths instead—the taste of the leaves they plucked from the treetops, the warmth of the water around their legs. What trees—like none he had ever seen, thin and tall, swaying in the breeze.

But he also felt a different kind of fear—fear of an approaching enemy.

He loved the behemoths. They were his kind. Part of him was amazed to see these animals that he had never laid eyes on before. But part of him saw them every moment of every day.

In the center of the hidden Sanctuary stood a small menhir marked with ancient runes, rising from the marsh water. Atop it, a bright light gleamed, dabbing the whole Sanctuary in streaks of red. The runes, too, glowed faintly. The behemoths ignored it, but Vell could not.

Magic. The magic that sustained this place.

They mean to steal it.

That's the reason for all of this.

But the Shepherds? Where were they? How would they protect their flock?

Figures were coming down from the mountain. He couldn't see them, but he knew they were there. He'd seen them before, some of them, in the pool.

They carried the axe. The axe would bring it all down. It would expose them and make them vulnerable. It would tear down the magic on the menhir—the magic that concealed them.

He knew it because the Shepherds knew it.

"Who are the Shepherds?" Vell said aloud. His companions in the High Forest heard it and had no answer. He was not asking them, but his true fellows in the hidden marsh of the Sanctuary.

You are, came the answer. He didn't know where the reply came from.

The behemoths arrayed themselves in lines, ready to attack the intruders. He did the same. He wondered if he could control the behemoth whose perspective he shared, but he didn't want to try. The animals grunted and paced.

Why did the Shepherds not protect them?

Vell knew: because they expect me to.

"I've failed them," Vell said. This time, he addressed the humans around him. "They gave me the power so I would protect them."

He heard voices ask many questions, but he pulled away from them, deeper and deeper into his vision. Four outsiders stood at the very rim of the Sanctuary.

"They died to get us here," said Royce as they stood near the northernmost phandar. "Vonelh, Nithinial, Bessick, the werebat ... this expedition even claimed Mythkar Leng." To Ardeth, he added, "This had better be worthwhile."

"I'll try not to disappoint," said Ardeth, her tone somewhere between haughty and flirtatious. She cast a spell to reveal emanations of magic, then narrowed her eyes in concentration. "There," she said, pointing in the direction of the phandar trees. Gan, Royce, and Gunton stared without seeing anything different.

Ardeth drew a number of crossbow bolts from her leathers and slowly loaded one into her crossbow. "Geildarr's gifts," she explained, and held the crossbow at the ready.

"Illusion magic," guessed Royce. "We came all this way to pilfer illusion magic?"

"Don't underestimate the power of illusion, or its value," said Ardeth. "I've recently been reminded of what it's capable of. Anything that can create an illusion this size could conceal a marching army. And that's assuming that it's the only ..."

A voice not his own suddenly rolled out of Gan's throat. "Please reconsider this," it said. This time the language was Illuskan, if an oddly accented and archaic version of it. "Turn away, travelers," it continued. "We warn you again. Our secrets are ours. We keep them with our might."

"And we shall take them with ours," Ardeth promised. "Gan ..."

The hobgoblin needed no instructions. He was seething with anger at the idea of something controlling his body again, and he charged the area sectioned off by the phandar trees, the axe held high over his head. The instant it touched the invisible field, a reddish energy flowed out of the axe; it trembled in his hands, nodding toward the center of the triangle. Shocked, Gan slowed and took a few steps backward just as the axe's energy punched a hole through the illusion. A red pulse burst away and traveled halfway across the field before colliding with another source of magic. The rest of the illusion crumbled around him.

"Vell," said Thluna. "What's happening?"

"They have arrived," Vell answered, though his eyes were still staring into another place. Then he added, "We have failed."

CHAPTER 16

More than a dozen giant lizards ran through the thinly forested marsh of the revealed Sanctuary, toward the four intruders. Their long, snakelike necks leaned forward, and the ground trembled as they charged. Each was larger than several cottages, weighing more than twin dragons. Each step threw up huge sprays of water from the marsh and covered the charging behemoths in a shower of mist. Royce, Gunton, and Gan could only stare, just as they had at Elaacrimalicros. Scaly mountains bore down on them, and they could do nothing but watch.

Ardeth's crossbow sang. Each bolt zipped across the marsh and met its mark. No behemoth would be deterred by so minor a blow, but these bolts were fashioned with powerful magic at no little expense. When they struck behemoth scales, the beast disappeared, as if it had never been.

Ardeth giggled as she watched the magic work. The charging behemoths quickly noticed their disappearing companions and slowed their onrush, turning sideways and exposing more of their flanks to Ardeth's deadly aim.

As the behemoths began to thin out, Ardeth could see a strange standing stone at the Sanctuary's center, the top of which glowed with a beacon of unearthly red.

"Royce," she said. She passed the crossbow to the Antiquarian. "Cover me."

With no further explanation, she sprang forward into the marsh, running like a black streak through the knee-deep water.

Vell's mind cried out as he abandoned perspective after perspective. The behemoths were not dying, he knew, but were being sent somewhere far away where his mind could not follow. He watched the strange girl run through the swamp. He knew her well by now; she had abducted Sungar, astride the hippogriff he had chased through Rauvin Vale. She was also the enemy he had seen in the Fountains of Memory.

He bade one of the behemoths to break away from the others and cut her off before she could reach the menhir. To his surprise, the behemoth willingly, almost deferentially, turned its form over to him. Vell gasped as he found that he directed the creature. His human mind remained in control, yet he felt a strange familiarity with the behemoth's body.

Controlling this animal as if he walked in its skin, Vell rushed to intercept the woman in black, sending great sprays of water up from the marsh. The water slowed her, and Vell had no trouble getting ahead of her. He let out a reptilian cry from his behemoth throat. Her pale oval face wore a determined look.

A crossbow bolt zipped past Vell's head but missed and flew off into the marsh. Fired from a great distance, its aim had gone wildly astray.

Then the woman opened an outstretched hand. A number of black bolts zipped forth and pelted Vell all along his lizard form. He braced himself and let out a tremendous moan. His mind was unaffected, for it was many miles away, but his body succumbed to tremendous inertia. Vell strained to move his torpid legs. He was all but rooted to the spot.

Springing across the water, the woman in black unsheathed her sword and ran close to Vell, using the weapon to rake his behemoth form as she ran, drawing blood from both front legs. Not caring to make a kill, she ran past him, bound for the menhir.

Vell focused harder, pushing away the pain and the paralysis from her magic, and managed to turn and pursue her. He leaped into the air, his forelegs leaving the marsh and sending a cascade of water down on the woman. She lost her footing and tumbled into the swamp face first, losing her sword in the muck, not more than a dozen feet from the menhir with its glowing red light. With a silent scream of success, Vell pushed his massive form onto her, landing a foot on her body, pressing her into the water and pinning her there. She squirmed and struggled against him

Then Vell felt a sharp pain on his backside, and, in an instant, his mind was thrown back to his own body.

Ardeth surfaced in the marsh on all fours and gulped air furiously as the behemoth vanished above her. She was soaked from head to foot. The marsh muck penetrated her leather clothes, and she threw her honey hair back, a slimy weight on her shoulders. The marsh was strangely quiet—perhaps Royce had succeeded in sending away all of the remaining behemoths. She groped for her sword before looking up at the rune-covered menhir towering above her.

Standing at the foot of it was a man. Dressed in pristine white robes, unstained despite the water and muck all around them, he was old—far older than even the ancient Uthgardt shaman she'd battled in the Thunderbeast camp. His face was chalk white, yet his hair was jet black and straight, like that of an Uthgardt. He spoke in the dialect of Illuskan that Gan had used, and had the same voice.

"Why have you come?" he asked. His voice was full of anger and sadness. "Why did you think to test a place that has stayed hidden for so long?"

Ardeth's hand found the pommel of her sword under the water.

"You hide powerful magic," she said. "Magic from Netheril. Did you think you could keep it secret forever?"

"Yes," said the man. "We did."

Ardeth burst from the water, swinging the sword around in a long, graceful slash. The ancient man made no move to resist her as the blade sliced through his middle. She gave him a quick, clean death, and he uttered not a sound until his body fell at the base of the standing stone. He seemed almost glad to die, weary from his centuries as a guardian.

Ardeth sheathed her sword. Planting a foot on the dead man's head, she climbed up the side of the menhir with the grace of a squirrel. Standing at the top, she stared into the source of the red light: a glowing stone object the size of a fist, and vaguely resembling a human heart. It rested in a small indentation at the top of the menhir. Ardeth leaned closer, the light bathing her pale features in crimson. She could feel the energies pouring out of it, washing over her. Ancient magic. Magic from Netheril.

Smiling, she reached down, plucking the stone from its resting place. She heard an audible hiss as she removed it—how many centuries had it laid there, undisturbed? It felt warm in her hand.

The runes on the menhir beneath her ceased glowing.

Ardeth could see Gunton, Gan, and Royce looking toward her from the edge of the Sanctuary, afraid to step deeper into the marsh. The area was missing its behemoths, but Ardeth knew guardians must be near. The man she had slaughtered had said "we."

She would have to finish this quickly.

Ardeth held the stone high in the air within her hand, its light glowing through her pale fingers. She saw Gan raise the greataxe in response. With her other hand, she reached into her soaked leathers and pulled out a crossbow bolt she had held in reserve. Never taking her eyes off her three unfortunate companions, she gripped the bolt and drove it into her palm.

"No!" Royce screamed as he watched Ardeth vanish from atop the menhir, but he was not surprised. He paced for a moment, then took Ardeth's empty crossbow and smashed it against the rocks outside the Sanctuary's edge.

"What happened?" asked Gan.

"You should appreciate this," said Gunton. "She betrayed us."

"No," the hobgoblin said. "No, that can't be."

Human figures appeared all around the Sanctuary. Eight men and women, each of them old and black-haired, made their tentative way through the marsh, bound for the three outsiders. Each was dressed in white robes that became neither stained nor wet as they progressed through the muck.

"We are not without resources, even with the Heart of Runlatha stolen," the nearest of them said in a weak rasp that was somehow projected across the marsh. "You will not be allowed to escape."

Gunton watched them draw closer. "Do we run, or do we try to bargain with them?"

"She would not betray us," Gan said, bewildered.

"Wake up!" Royce shouted. "She has done nothing but betray us! All of our deaths are on her head. That Zhentarim bitch has left us here to die and teleported back to Llorkh with her treasure!"

Gunton raised his short spear, alternating nervous glances between the folk of the swamp and the hobgoblin. "Must we argue, while..."

"Why don't you kill me, Gan?" cried Royce. "Ardeth isn't here to stop you now!"

Gan flashed back to the Fallen Lands, when he had first found the axe. He knew that it was a leader's weapon from the moment he saw it, as surely as he knew that he was no leader. Neither was Dray, that stupid Lord's Man he slaughtered on the plain of dirt. It belonged with Geildarr.

Such a weapon! Though he didn't understand all of what Geildarr had told him about its origins, he understood enough to confirm what he had always felt. This was a hero's weapon. What a privilege to wield it on a hero's behalf!

Doing Geildarr's work, he boldly brought the axe down on Royce. Like Dray, he struck the warrior in the shoulder, and drove the axe downward until the head was embedded deep in his chest. In the last flicker of his companion's eyes, Gan saw not the anger he expected, but sadness.

What have I done? he asked himself.

The hobgoblin's hand went out to stroke Royce's face. Gan felt a pain in his own chest and looked down to see the point of Gunton's spear protruding from it, driven through from behind. He stumbled, turning about. The axe ripped free from Royce's body and fell from Gan's hands, landing with a splash in the marsh.

Gan tumbled backward onto Gunton's spear, which snapped under his weight. The bloody spearhead emerged from his chest. He reached out to grasp it as his body twitched and rattled.

As Gunton looked down on Gan, he saw the hobgoblin's dying face was a mask of confusion and indecision. Some realization must have dawned on Gan in his last moments. Perhaps, Gunton thought, in those last moments the hobgoblin understood the full power the axe had wielded over him.

Gunton choked back tears as he looked at the mangled wreck of Royce's body. He turned to the white-clad men and women still approaching from the Sanctuary. He spread his arms wide to show that he was unarmed.

"He was a brother to me," he explained. "Do you understand what that means?" He repeated himself in Illuskan, more furiously.

"We never should have dealt with a Zhentarim," he continued in Common, not worrying that they might not understand him as they approached with steady steps. "That was our first mistake. It wasn't just Geildarr's coin we craved. He truly seemed to treasure the things we found for him. He seemed as passionate about history as we were. He was hard to resist. We were just as deluded as Gan. May Shaundakul accept our souls despite our weaknesses."

Gunton made no attempt to run as one of the figures stepped out of the Sanctuary before him. It was a woman, her white face as gnarled as a tree branch, jet black hair spilling over her shoulders. She extended a hand, and the axe rose from the water and into her grasp.

Gunton turned his back to her and braced himself. "I am the only member of this expedition not killed by a companion," he whispered to himself, awaiting the axe's impact.

Instead a bony hand clamped onto his shoulder and squeezed. He yelped in pain.

"We have use for you," the old woman said. "You must earn your rest."

Two days passed before the Thunderbeasts arrived, their path clarified by Vell's descriptions. They passed Mount Vision to the east, passing through the forest until they found the remains of the Sanctuary. The strange, thin trees were slowly dying. The cold mountain water from the Heartblood River had penetrated the marsh, and its magical warmth was lost. With the behemoths gone, the region was empty and desolate. Vell's heart cried out when he saw it—it was not the living, vital preserve he knew from his vision, but a drab, ruined, and useless waste.

On the northernmost phandar tree, the crow-pecked

remains of one of the invaders made a gruesome spectacle. He was tied high up on the trunk, his hands severed and lashed alongside him. His head, thickly bearded and with its eyes stolen by birds, rested between his two feet.

"A warning against further intruders," Thluna said, unable to bring himself to look at it for long. "But who left it?"

"The Shepherds," said Vell. "Whoever they are." He looked across the Sanctuary to the menhir and immediately saw the difference. "The red light is gone. The invaders stole it when they stole the behemoths. It must have been the source of the magic that preserved this place."

"It is so," came a voice. A figure appeared from nowhere, white-clad and ancient. He was older even than Keirkrad and looked as if his flesh were ready to slide from his bones. While Keirkrad was unnaturally old, he was preserved by Uthgar's grace, and retained something of his youthful self. This figure made Elaacrimalicros seem young. His skin was mottled, halfway between skin and scales. Yet, despite his vast age, the old Shepherd had jet black hair like an Uthgardt, streaked with only a few strands of white. His eyes were a lifeless brown.

"Your failure is utter," he said. His voice was cold, without compassion. "You of Uther's blood have led us to ruin, once again."

All eyes stared at the strange old man. More of his kind emerged from the swamp, as if they had been hiding beneath the water, or simply melded with the marsh. A dozen appeared in all, men and women both—all of them equally ancient, as if all their life-force had long ago been sucked from their bodies. One of the women held the legendary axe, lifting it with ease despite her slenderness—the axe Sungar had wielded and left in the Fallen Lands two years earlier.

"Who are you?" asked Thluna.

"We are the *Thunderbeasts*," the Shepherd replied, pronouncing the word like a curse. "All others are but pretenders to the noble name." He huffed. "As are you, who dare travel with the blood of an orc—a creature even more debased than yourself." He pointed to Rask.

"This is an Uthgardt of the Tree Ghost tribe you offend," Thanar warned.

"We know of no Tree Ghost tribe, and hold little esteem for any of the Ruathan race that poisoned your spirit twelve hundred years past," the Shepherd said. "Uther Gardolfsson and his island race invaded our lands and polluted our strain."

They all knew that it was Uthgar—called by his mortal name—he defamed, but the warriors did not know how to react. Such a brazen insult to their god provoked wars among tribes, but what war was possible against these creatures?

"What fools we were to place our protection in your hands," cursed the old woman carrying the axe. She stepped from the water and dropped it at Vell's feet, then pointed an angry finger in his face. "You carry the power of us all—we stripped ourselves bare for you! And you failed us."

"Your powers," Vell said, suddenly understanding. "You bestowed them on me at Morgur's Mound on Runemeet." He looked over all the ancient faces. "All of your powers, into me."

"True," the man said. "Many of us have not worn our human forms in many centuries. We had hoped that you, who carry more of the pure bloodline than any other of your tribe, would retain the nobility to handle it properly." He looked at Vell with unalloyed disgust. "A poor choice on our part."

Vell looked him in the eye. "It is only an accident of birth that I have any relationship to you." There was absolute conviction in his voice.

"Let us understand," Kellin said, hoping to diffuse the situation. "Are you descended from the Thunderbeast tribe as it was before the coming of Uthgar?"

"Not descended," the Shepherd answered. "We are they." He looked at Kellin more closely. "And you—you have the blood of dragons. Why do you deign to travel with these mongrels?"

The barbarians looked at her in puzzlement. "Sorcerers

carry the blood of dragons," she said. "Or so some sages say. But how dilute must the blood you speak of be? And does that not make me a mongrel myself? Why praise some and condemn others?"

The Shepherds frowned at her.

"Let me introduce myself," said Thluna. "My name is Thluna, Chief of the Thunderbeast tribe, son of Hagraavan . . ."

"And many dozens of generations past, son of the traitor Tharkane," the Shepherd said, unimpressed. "The same Tharkane who took this axe of legend—" he prodded it with his foot "—and made it an offering to the conqueror Gardolfsson."

"Gardolfsson?" asked Thanar. "Uthgar wielded the axe?"

"Indeed. With it he slaughtered one of our kind, who dared venture forth from the forest to contest him. Several centuries passed before we regained the power lost to us that day. Our fallen fellow's bones surmount Gardolfsson's grave."

"Morgur's Mound," said Vell. So that was it! The bones of the beast were not of any natural behemoth, but of one of the Shepherds transformed into a behemoth. And through those bones, they transferred their powers to him.

All of their powers. No wonder he could not wield them—they were not meant for an individual, but for many persons. Like the treant Duthroan had said, Vell was a receptacle.

"So Uthgar defeated him," Thluna said proudly. "Killed him."

"He did," the Shepherd confirmed. "And so our Thunderbeasts became his Thunderbeasts. But we have kept watch from behind the Sanctuary's walls where we could, through the bones of our fallen fellow, and through this axe. We felt such sadness as our children mated with other tribes and the Ruathans, as our blood weakened into something we no longer recognized. Under Uther's hand, all memories of us were steadily winnowed."

Thluna and his followers stood quietly for a time, letting the words sink in.

Kellin looked down at the axe. "What magic connects you to the axe?"

"Powerful magic and tangled, dragonborn," the Shepherd woman said. "On yonder menhir, until recently, rested the means of our deception—that which kept us and our behemoths secret from prying eyes for many centuries: the Heart of Runlatha, salvaged from that fallen city of magic by the Bey of Runlatha himself."

"Berun," some of the Thunderbeasts whispered among themselves, the name of a great hero in their songs.

"Yes, Berun indeed," hissed the woman. "A name that has floated through the ages misremembered and distorted. The Bey was ancient even for us, his true name lost to history, but it is known that he fled dead Netheril, leading our ancestors west from that fallen land."

"With the Heart of Runlatha," extrapolated Kellin. "And in Delzoun, the dwarves tied its magic to that of the axe you carry. The axe serves as a key," she went on. "It can dissolve the illusions. It can, and it did."

The Shepherdess nodded sadly. "With the axe in his hand, Bey battled the foul three who troubled his people, giving his own life to defeat Zukothoth." Vell realized that he must have caught a glimpse of that ancient battle in the Fountains of Memory, where it rippled like an afterthought. What a wonder! To lay eyes upon the Bey of legend!

"The axe was recovered by his followers and held as sacred, as they tamed the land. The weapon of the truest of heroes, it craves heroism from those who wield it. Its true powers lie dormant in the hands of mediocre men like your chiefs, though it twists the minds of the weak, always seeking a stronger wielder."

"And the Heart of Runlatha?" prompted Thanar.

"It has preserved us."

"And with it gone . . ."

"Yes," the Shepherd said. "We will die."

"A pity," said Thanar. This provoked a dark glare from the Shepherd.

"Magic!" cursed Thluna. "The unreliability of magic!

No wonder Sungar disposed of the axe—would that it had stayed lost."

"Sungar!" the female Shepherd shouted. This was the strongest anger they'd heard from the ancients—she shouted the name like an epithet. "Wolfkiller! The blame is his! Where is he? He left our secrets ripe for the pillage."

"He lies in the hands of our enemies," Rask Urgek said. "We can only guess that, if he lives, he is in the dungeons of Llorkh."

"Llorkh." The name was whispered among the other Shepherds, still standing nearby in the marsh. "This orc-man speaks a name we have heard already," said the male Shepherd, pointing at the soldier displayed on the phandar tree. "That is where our behemoths are, and the Heart with it. The survivor of this invasion, save the dark lady who fled by magic, revealed their plans to us."

"A fine burial you gave him," Rask said, eyeing the disgusting spectacle. "A thousand years of isolation has clearly caused your souls to atrophy." The Shepherds did not blink an eye in response to his insult.

Thluna asked, "Why do you not take your powers back from Vell?"

"They cannot," said Kellin. "Not without the Heart."

The male Shepherd nodded.

"As it always was with magic," Thluna told him. "You relied on it—you based your existence around it. And it has failed you."

"You have failed us," the Shepherd retorted. "You have all failed us."

"I'm curious," said Kellin. "Did you mean to summon me here as well, or was that an accident?"

"It was not our intention," said the Shepherd woman. "Our contact with the world outside this Sanctuary was limited. We could not . . ."

"You could not send clear messages, obviously," said Thanar. "Why say, 'Find the living'? Why not say, 'Come to the shadow of the easternmost Star Mount'? Why not, 'Recover the lost axe'?"

"Our ability to act was limited," came the answer. The

man hesitantly went on. "The shard of your totem that remains in our possession is limited indeed."

"What can this mean?" asked Vell. "What shard of our totem?"

"I can explain," said Kellin. "At least, I'll try. Before the coming of Uthgar, the barbarians of the North—Netherese-blooded survivors from the exodus of Runlatha—worshiped powerful nature spirits rather than gods. This was common in those days. There were fewer gods then, and the conditions of the gods' existence were less stringent, as they were not bound by Ao to their followers. You know the names of these totem spirits— Blue Bear, Black Raven, Elk, Red Tiger, and more, and of course the Thunderbeast. When Uthgar became a god, his tribal followers began to worship him and their totems at once, so they became aspects of Uthgar: fragments of his personality representing different tribes.

"We know that worshipers can be stolen away, as the Blue Bear tribe was by Malar. When none of the Blue Bear tribe worshiped Uthgar any longer, the Blue Bear itself no longer represented him, but became part of the Beastlord instead. So, too, is it possible for new totems to be added, as with the Tree Ghosts," she explained, looking to Rask. "But this place is special. For the most part, worship of the Thunderbeast flowed to Uthgar, but a portion of it trickled here instead. Therefore, the Shepherds have some ability to act through the Thunderbeast outside of Uthgar's authority—perhaps even without his knowledge."

"The Thunderbeast is more legitimately ours than Uthgar's," said the male Shepherd haughtily. "Our claim is prior. We of Netheril's line possess nobility the Ruathan race could never possess."

Thluna paced for a moment, but his youth got the better of him and he delivered a punch to the Shepherd's chin.

The old man crumbled, falling to his knees. "A bold blow," he cursed through clenched teeth, "against a defenseless opponent."

"You deceived our tribe into believing it was given a

summons from the divine!" Thluna shouted. "You have masqueraded as the spirit of our tribe for far too long! We lost warriors fighting your fight for you, and our shaman as well. Our tribe is left weak in a time of danger. Worst of all, you twisted us into believing we were doing Uthgar's work, while instead we were serving ancient rivals of his." He snatched up the greataxe lying at his feet. "You deserve this axe in your skull." He turned and walked away, back toward the pass that had led them there.

Vell caught up to him across the high mountain field. "We must continue with our mission," he said.

"Why should we, Vell?" asked Thluna. "Do they not deserve their fate?"

"They do, but the behemoths do not. They are blameless."

"They are beasts," Thluna replied, but when he saw the anger rise in Vell's eyes, he amended his statement. "Sacred beasts, truly, and in some ways our kindred. But can I justify marching our warriors into a city of darkness? Surely that will bring doom down on our tribe more swiftly."

"And Sungar?" asked Vell. "What of him?"

The question gave Thluna pause. "We do not know if Sungar still lives."

"We do not know that he doesn't. Kellin, Thanar, Rask, and the rest . . . I am certain that all of them will be willing to make the trip to Llorkh. They will not refuse because the journey serves the Shepherds as well."

Thluna closed his eyes and nodded. "In addition to everything else, Vell, the beast inside you . . . they put it there."

"And they can take it away," said Vell. "If we aid them."

"We came into the forest looking for answers. Looking for a destiny." Thluna frowned. "I said that myself, did I not? That our destiny would be found in the High Forest. And so it was. I wonder if we should never have come here."

He cast a glance back at the Sanctuary. The menhir standing at its center looked so much like those at Morgur's Mound and at a dozen other sites sacred to the Uthgardt. The Shepherds seemed to have vanished; how did they live in this marsh? How did they survive? What did they use for food? What would they do now that the marsh was cold and their protection gone?

Next to the great phandar tree stood Thluna's companions, including the three Uthgardt warriors who had come so far without complaint. Ilskar, Hengin, and Draf represented the characteristics of the Thunderbeast tribe: sturdy and solid, largely silent in the face of orders from their chief, and willing to march and die at his whim.

"We have the answers now, wretched though they may be," Thluna told Vell. "How can they be our ancestors? How could we have come from them?" A new thought dawned on him. "What will our tribesmen think if they learn all this? Must we keep the truth from them?"

"A question for a chief," said Vell. "Chieftains face difficult decisions, as Sungar did that day in the Fallen Lands. I was not there, but I heard what happened. Many questioned his decision to throw the axe away, but I did not think it was my place to question that decision."

"He made the wrong choice," Thluna said, looking down at the axe in his hands. "But I understand why he made it."

"This is your decision," said Vell. "We will follow you. Back to our people, to tell them what you will; or onward to Llorkh, a city completely unknown to us, to death or glory, and to that destiny we came seeking."

Thluna forced a smile. "I have little choice," he said, "when you put it that way."

Thluna faced the marsh, and the Shepherds approached him once again. His seven companions clustered about him.

"I have made a decision," he said, holding the ancient axe. "We will go to Llorkh and reclaim that which was taken from you. We will bring it back here."

The Shepherds seemed unimpressed. "Do you believe you can do this?"

"We believe we must try," Thluna answered. "But there is one condition."

"Which is?"

"This Heart of Runlatha obviously holds great power," said Kellin. "Now that the outside world knows of its existence, it will be doubly difficult to keep yourselves secret. All avenues must be closed."

"Therefore," concluded Thluna, "we will leave this axe with you inside the Sanctuary. Forever."

The Shepherds looked at each other then nodded to the Thunderbeasts. "This is well."

"And something further," said Vell. "You must renounce all claims on the Thunderbeast tribe and on our totem. Abandon this 'shard of the spirit' you have used to mislead us. We cannot have you interfering in our affairs any further."

This brought a violent reaction from the Shepherds. "Our claims are older than yours!" one roared. "We cannot forsake them simply because you ask it!"

"It is our price," said Thluna.

The druid Thanar added, "It is not often that fate affords the opportunity to bargain with one's own past."

"You will fail," predicted another of the Shepherds. "You have failed already, and you will fail again. Any bargain is immaterial."

"Then it should not matter if you enter one," said Thluna. "Swear. Who else will help you? Or shall we just leave you here to die?"

They sneered, then with great reluctance they relented with the slightest of nods. "May the gods speed you to Llorkh," one of them said.

"Any god but Uthgar?" asked Thluna. He turned his back to the Shepherds and led his followers away; they did not look back.

CHAPTER 17

The Central Square in Llorkh had been emptied of its usual town market, but now it held more folk than ever. Onlookers swarmed around its edges where the Lord's Men stood guard, all hoping to catch a glimpse of the strange newcomers. The exotic lizards, each taller than the buildings that surrounded them, were tethered by magic. Each behemoth wore an iron ring around a hind ankle, connected by a massive chain to a stone post in the middle of the square. The chains were enchanted to dissolve flesh that touched them, lest any fool try to release the behemoths. The chains were only long enough for the creatures to reach feed bins placed at the square's edges by some brave Lord's Men.

The great beasts occasionally raised their feet, pulling the chains to their tightest and lifting them off the ground, but the chains could not be broken. And as long as the lizards bore the rings around their ankles, they could not lift more than one foot off the ground at any time. The magical formulation had proven to be simple but effective, for which Geildarr was vastly proud.

From the heights of the Lord's Keep, Geildarr enjoyed stepping onto his balcony and watching the behemoths. He never tired of watching them. A honey-colored bird alighted on the balcony's rail and chirped merrily; its cheerful song echoed in Geildarr's heart.

The fate of the behemoths was an open question for Geildarr. He considered dissecting them, harvesting their organs for whatever magical value they might possess, and making armor of their hides. Naturally, the Dark Sun temple wanted the dinosaurs turned over to them, so they could explore corrupting them, perhaps turning them into beasts of Cyric. Geildarr would need time to weigh his options. In the meantime, he just enjoyed their presence. Huge creatures of living, breathing art, they were more of a monument to his success than any statue of Geildarr could ever be.

And yet, these animals were but a side show. The real bounty was the Heart of Runlatha. A piece of Netherese magic from before the fall was worth many more lives than had been spent on the expedition.

"You expect me to discipline you for letting the Antiquarians die," Geildarr told Ardeth as he met with her in his study. "But I will not. I was very fond of them—I know you were, too. I will miss having them crawl through ruins on my behalf. They were useful. But your success—" he gripped the red hunk of magic, its scarlet glow escaping through his fingers, "—does much to counterbalance that loss."

"I'm glad you think so," said Ardeth. "But what is that thing?"

Geildarr smiled and answered, "Nothing less than our redemption."

"You will deliver it to Zhentil Keep, then?" Ardeth asked.

"In time," said Geildarr. "I want more time to study it

first—to see what it truly is. It's clearly capable of weaving powerful illusions, from what you report. Perhaps it even extended the lifespan of the Shepherds you encountered in the Sanctuary." The excitement rose in his voice. "Netherese magic, Ardeth! I've never before had my hands on a piece of magic from before Karsus's folly. I wonder how it survived. This could be magic of the sort Mystra now denies to Faerûn!"

"Fzoul and Manshoon will be very pleased with it, then," said Ardeth. She watched Geildarr's crestfallen reaction to that statement.

"Truly," he said. "It's a shame that the Heart should only be ransom for my preservation as mayor."

"Is not your reign more secure now?" asked Ardeth. "Or did I kill Mythkar Leng for nothing?"

"His death pleases me, for certain." It's a shame the Antiquarians needed to die also, he silently added. He would save that issue for another time, a future blackmail.

"I'm afraid this accomplishment is only delaying the inevitable," Geildarr said. "So long as I answer to Lord Chembryl, my position here in Llorkh is in jeopardy."

"Is there not another option?" asked Ardeth. "What of Sememmon?"

Geildarr sighed heavily. "You give voice to my darkest thoughts. I never liked him, even when he was master of Darkhold, and I answered to him directly."

"Perhaps because of that reason," Ardeth suggested with a coy smile.

Geildarr patted her shoulder. "That could be. But I understood when he fled the Zhentarim, even sympathized. Fzoul has consolidated power to a terrifying degree. The Inner Circle used to battle among itself mercilessly, and that system worked—it kept any one of them from gathering too much power. But the new Manshoon appears to be thoroughly under Fzoul's thumb, and Sememmon is gone. Bane's vision is being stamped on the whole Network. Cyricists like myself will be an increasingly rare breed."

"Sememmon was a coward for fleeing Darkhold," said Ardeth.

"No," said Geildarr. "He was smart." He looked sadly at the Heart of Runlatha, still gleaming in his clenched hand. "This could only buy me a reprieve. I serve as mayor of Llorkh at Fzoul's pleasure."

The golden bird on the balcony chirped, but somehow its song didn't seem as happy as before.

"Do you think Sememmon would be a better option?" asked Ardeth.

"He has kept himself hidden from Fzoul," Geildarr acknowledged. "No minor feat even for a wizard of such resources and power. But I am not interested in living out my days lurking in dark shadows. Moritz would like me to think Sememmon has some plan for overthrowing Fzoul, or destroying the Zhentarim, or carving out some kingdom for himself. Only the gods know if he does, or if he has a prayer of seeing it to reality. He is certainly amassing magic and allies for some purpose."

"He would like the Heart of Runlatha," said Ardeth.

"Certainly." He looked down at the artifact and sighed. "I'm afraid he might try to take it by force, and I mean to be ready for him if he does. But enough of this doom and gloom. A guest of mine must be made acquainted with our new arrivals." He smiled at Ardeth. "He is an old friend of yours. Perhaps you'd like to accompany me?"

❧ ❧ ❧ ❧ ❧

The sunlight seared Sungar's eyes as guards led him through the streets of Llorkh. After so many tendays in a dark hole, the outdoors were no longer his friend. He'd never been in a city before, not Everlund, or Mirabar, or any other. If they all were like this one, he couldn't imagine why anyone would choose to live within city walls. Llorkh stank of desperation and decay. It was drab, and its streets were littered with garbage. From the windows of cottages, common people looked out, their eyes sunken in despair. Armored orcs walked the streets.

Sungar was weak from another beating, his hands bound with iron once again. Two dungeon guards marched him from the Lord's Keep, across Llorkh to the Central Square, but a few blocks away, they put a blindfold on him.

"The mayor's orders," one of them explained. "Geildarr says he wants to be there to see your expression." Sungar did his best not to show any reaction, but when the blindfold came off, he could not help himself.

Geildarr laughed at the chief's surprise and sorrow. "Priceless, priceless, Sungar!" He gestured at the wide square before them. "Thunderbeast, meet the thunderbeasts!"

Sungar wept. These were the living totems that he revered, and like him, they were Geildarr's prisoners. They were myths that were never meant to be real. He would have been overcome with wonder had he seen the beasts in a forest's depths, grazing and roaming, but now, interred like living statues in this square, the sight was a tremendous blow to Sungar. Incomprehensible sadness showed in their massive eyes. Sungar tried to make a fist, but his fingers were too weak.

A young woman stepped up to Sungar. Small and dark-eyed, she wore a smug smile, and she strode up to him flaunting her lack of fear.

"I brought them here," she said. "Just like I brought you here."

Sungar knew her name and spat it. "Ardeth." The traitor to Hurd's conspiracy.

She was surprised. "You know me? Oh yes—you learned it from the dwarf."

"Uthgar will destroy you," Sungar said. An unexpected feeling of peace flooded up inside him.

"Will he?" she asked. "Trice Dulgenhar said that Gorm would do the same, just before I chopped his head off. Why is it that only the most obscure gods have it in for me?" She giggled.

"And you, Geildarr," Sungar said. "You will fall. This precious city of yours will fall." He nodded toward the behemoths. "The buildings will topple under their strength."

He did not feel as if the words were his own any more.

They flowed from his chest unbidden. Across the square, amid the enslaved behemoths, a ghostly figure flickered—King Gundar.

"Vague proclamations of doom from a barbarian chief," Geildarr said. "What a shock."

"You have stolen our birthright," Sungar went on. "This theft will not be tolerated. My tribe will arrive to reclaim them." And he believed it. He knew it.

Geildarr leaned close to him, so Sungar could feel the mayor's breath on his cheeks. "We took more than just these dumb beasts. Ardeth claimed for me an object of power from before the Fall of Netheril."

Geildarr was so close—if Sungar were less weak, and he not been bound, he could have killed him with his bare hands. But he felt no compulsion to do so. His anger left him. The specter of King Gundar in his vision smiled widely.

"I will watch your fate unfold," he told Geildarr. "And it will be soon."

Geildarr took a few steps back. "The dungeon usually drives its residents insane," he said, "but not this swiftly."

Ardeth spoke to the guards who stood around Sungar. "Instruct Klev to step up the torture. This pathetic man must be brought to his lowest point."

But Sungar was smiling as they led him away. Gundar vanished into nothingness but left Uthgar's grace behind, and Sungar awaited his captors' comeuppance with giddy anticipation.

A few days' march south of the Sanctuary, the Thunder-beast party continued to make its way through the High Forest. They kept a discreet distance from the Unicorn Run and slipped through the deep woods without incident. As they walked, golden and red leaves cascaded down on them and formed a carpet stretching forward, guiding them to victory or ruin. But the leaf fall was coming to an end, and all around trees stood leafless, their bare branches reaching out and grasping like the thin arms of desperate men.

They spoke very little. Thanar and Rask at first attempted to keep the mood light, though they swiftly realized that this was futile and joined the silence. The Shepherds' revelations had cast a shadow over the Thunderbeasts' entire history. Now, to be doing the work of these loathsome tokens of the past rankled especially. And whenever Vell and Kellin's dark eyes met, they knew without speaking that her thoughts concerned her father—another idol fallen, and another dark secret of the past unearthed so unwelcomely.

Thluna carried the axe, though it was heavy for his lean stature. It was his tactile reminder of their real purpose. It kept his focus on Sungar. He bade Rask carry the oaken club given as a gift by Chief Gunther.

At a quiet, grassy clearing at the forest's edge, next to the quick-flowing Delimbiyr, they came upon a figure standing in the half-light of evening, staring into the distance, robed in rothéhide. They recognized him instantly, even before they saw his face. Thluna yelped when he saw the man. "Keirkrad!"

He turned to face them. A festering red wound crawled across Keirkrad's cheek. His eyes were frozen oceans of blue streaked with lines of bright crimson.

Keirkrad smiled a warped, feral smile, his teeth glistening with saliva.

"The champions come," he said, his distinctive rasp familiar but somehow infused with malice. "Uthgar's champions come marching from the wood of their ancient home." He extended a finger in Vell's direction. "The blessed one," he hissed, "the brown-eyed one—Uthgar's favorite."

"No," said Vell. "No, Keirkrad. You must understand. Uthgar did not choose me."

"No?" Keirkrad's lined brow furrowed. "No? He did not pluck you for glory on Runemeet, on the site of his own death, the most sacred Morgur's Mound? He did not invest in you all the power he denied me?"

Vell shook his head firmly. "I am not of Uthgar's choosing, and this is not glory. This is a curse."

"Again you spurn the honor!" Keirkrad shouted to the sky. "Again you turn away from your god's calling! Is there no end to your gall? I will do his work in destroying you, though I have found a more potent master than Tempus's son could ever be. As a child, Uthgar granted me a glimpse of Morgur's Mound, but cruel and capricious he was, revealing to me the place where I would be undone and betrayed. Now the Beastlord has granted me what Uthgar would not."

Keirkrad snarled, and the red in his eyes spread till his eyes swam in crimson. Huge leathery wings unfurled from his sides and his face twisted and distorted into a drooling werebat. Heskret had inflicted lycanthropy, the ultimate punishment, on an enemy of old. He had not foreseen how the blessing of Uthgar resident in Keirkrad would manifest in his new form. With Keirkrad's mind wrested from his old form, he served his new master with devotion far exceeding that which he had lavished on Uthgar, and Malar responded to this fervor. Keirkrad was no simple werebat, but a nightmare of strength and power.

He was quickly a mass of fur and vast wings. Sharp claws spouted from his hands and feet, his ears grew huge and cupped like a bat's, and his teeth lengthened into glistening white fangs. Most terrifying of all was that he was still Keirkrad. Something indescribable in his movement—the way he held his shoulders and his head—and those watery blue eyes were the same, but now set in a bat's leering face.

The Thunderbeast party fanned out and drew weapons. I am a werebeast of sorts, too, Vell realized for the first time.

Keirkrad advanced in slow steps, his wings dragging on the ground. His eyes locked on the axe in Thluna's hands.

"How is this?" he asked. "The axe reclaimed? Sungar's folly undone?"

"There is much to be explained, Keirkrad," said Thluna. "We Thunderbeasts have been misled and manipulated. Let us explain."

"There is no reasoning with a werebeast," Kellin warned.

Keirkrad let out a throaty chuckle. "For once, the southland whore and I agree. You are weak creatures, all. I have borne witness to the fickleness of your kind all my long life." He scanned the assembled Uthgardt. "The child chief, the traitor druid of Silvanus, an orc infiltrator, and warriors of no particular distinction. You disappoint even so minor and weak a god as Uthgar. Only one among you is worthy of the transformation, of Malar's blessing, and that is purely for the power that resides in you. A repository, the treant called you. Just what is a reservoir, if not a power waiting to be tapped?"

A new kind of anger awakened in Vell.

"You wanted to groom me as your champion to challenge Sungar's chiefdom!" he shouted. "And when I wouldn't, you slandered me instead, told me that I was not worthy of Uthgar's blessing. You openly schemed against the chief to whom you swore fealty—what behavior is this for a shaman? What actions are these for a favored son of Uthgar? I did not betray Uthgar—you did."

The composure drained from Keirkrad's batface, and Vell counted that as a victory. He went on. "And now you would make me a monster? Perhaps I am a monster already." Lanaal's lessons in transformation, which he had resisted, suddenly struck home. When he shed his human form, he largely kept his own mind and volition.

Vell's transformation into a brown-scaled behemoth was more shocking than the first incident. In Sungar's Camp, it had happened so quickly amid such confusion and in the dark of night—it had seemed like a strange dream. Now, in the daylight amid a tranquil setting, it bore a new reality. Vell was gone, or what the warriors knew as Vell, and in his place stood a creature of legend, a creature the Thunderbeasts had been taught to revere. No glimpse of the bones of the beast hovering above Morgur's Mound could have prepared them for the flesh and blood behemoth before them.

Vell stood as tall as the treetops. He felt a strange rush of embarrassment as he looked down on the disbelieving faces of his friends and allies as they rushed to keep clear.

Hissing, snarling, Keirkrad sprang from the ground into the air. His physical weakness was erased by his bat-form, and he landed on Vell's vast face, clamping on with his claws and wrapping his huge wings over Vell's eyes. Vell charged, partly to keep Keirkrad away from the others, and partly to disturb Keirkrad's grip, the ground trembling as he did so. He blindly strode into the River Delimbiyr. A massive splash drenched the river's banks, and Vell waded into the middle of the river.

Vell felt the shocking coldness of the water rush up his massive limbs, reaching his brain with the intensity of a thunder strike. He dunked his head into the water, dousing Keirkrad. All around them, currents and eddies swirled, formed by the sudden intrusion of Vell's bulk. The werebat clung, squeezing more and more tightly on Vell's face; but he could not maintain his grip, and drifted away in the rapids.

Vell watched Keirkrad's huge wings vainly struggling against the water, their fine bones and leathery covering inadequate against the Delimbiyr's onrush. Then the water swirled around him, forming a whirlpool and a wall that protected him, and Keirkrad magically lifted above the Delimbiyr's surface. Beating his wings steadily to dry himself and stay aloft, he looked toward Vell with a perverse grin as he faced the lizard in the middle of the river.

"I am no longer human, perhaps," Keirkrad taunted. "But a cleric I am still." He spat out a prayer, and when Vell tried to urge his vast body to action, he could not move. A vicious torpidity seized his limbs and held him captive in the middle of the river, where the chill still assaulted his senses. He urged his animal body to action, but it would not answer. He was still as a statue, and the cold numbed his senses. He could barely feel his legs beneath him.

How could I have been so stupid? Vell asked himself. He had no way of knowing how long he could maintain his beast form, especially while paralyzed.

When he lapsed back to his human shape, he would be at Keirkrad's mercy.

A loud roar filled the air. A burst of sound caught Keirkrad and blasted him out of the air with such force that he landed beyond the south bank, clapping his clawed hands to his ears. From the corner of his eye, Vell saw Kellin standing on the river bank, Thanar alongside her. He could only guess that they were trying to dissolve the magic that held him.

Keirkrad unfurled his wings and flew across the river, bound for the druid and the sorceress. Thunderbeast hammers and arrows assailed him, but they bounced off as if he were solid metal. When he swooped down to harry Kellin and Thanar, Rask Urgek planted a blow solidly in his face with the Tree Ghosts' club, sending Keirkrad reeling, but leaving him aloft. His nose was smashed, and blood dripped down his face. He let out a high-pitched chirp of pain.

Thluna ran at Keirkrad with the greataxe, but Keirkrad ably dodged, and it slashed through empty air next to him. Too heavy for Thluna to wield properly, the axe went astray, and its head embedded deep in the ground. Keirkrad let out a twisted laugh as he swooped.

"Leave it to a true man to handle such weapons," the werebat taunted. "It is beyond a mere boy such as you."

Rask swung the club at him again, but missed. Keirkrad beat his wings furiously, lifting himself till he was just above the half-orc's head. He lowered a clawed foot, several of its toes missing, to Rask's face with his sharp nails and raked his throat. Before Rask could react, Keirkrad murmured a dark spell. A ravenous maw sprouted from the underside of his foot, a ring of teeth that snapped and sank hungrily onto Rask's chin.

The half-orc screamed with pain. He dropped the club, and his hands grabbed at the werebat's foot, but the fangs only sank deeper. Snarling in pleasure, Keirkrad beat his wings and began to lift Rask off the ground.

Thluna pulled at the shaft of the battle-axe, freeing it from the earth. He took another swing at Keirkrad, more quickly than the shaman had expected. Keirkrad released Rask, letting the half-orc tumble to the ground. The werebat dodged wildly, but Thluna's swing clipped one of his broad leathery wings, ripping it halfway through. Keirkrad flapped his great wings uncertainly. He hissed as he looked down on his enemies, yet he gained control of his flight. Blood ran from his smashed nose and dribbled onto the grass below.

Kellin and Thanar's magic unbound Vell from his paralysis in the Delimbiyr, and he struggled to move his chilled legs. With slow, steady steps, he lumbered to the shore, his vast brown lizard eyes locked on Keirkrad's hovering form. But he was so weak, his energy drained from him, that he felt his behemoth form shuddering and realized it would soon leave him. Soon, he would be Vell again and subject to Keirkrad's scheme. What would happen if Keirkrad succeeded in infecting them all with lycanthropy? Would all Vell's power vanish, or would it be shaped in some hideous new way? What would remain of himself?

In his moments of contemplation and weakness, Vell felt the transformation stirring. He rallied the last of his energy into a charge at Keirkrad. The others dodged to safety as the drenched behemoth thundered across the field. Keirkrad prepared to fly out of reach, but his damaged wing slowed him, and he could not rise high enough before the juggernaut collided with him at full speed. Vell knocked Keirkrad from the air with a swing of his mighty neck.

The world around Vell faded and shifted as he focused on the object of his rage. Brown eyes locked on the two bloodshot eyes that had such little humanity left in them. Even when Keirkrad was at his very worst, he was at least human. Now the elements of his humanity had been sacrificed for this sick taint.

Is this what I will become? thought Vell as he continued his assault. He was no longer conscious of his own body, human or behemoth; that awareness floated away on a sea of desperate fury. All of the anger he had held in check against the Shepherds, and against those of his own tribe who had shunned him for a lifetime, he unleashed on Keirkrad. He sated his need for vengeance against all those who had made him this amalgam of man and beast. He cried, weeping tears of rage for all the blows he had absorbed in his life. His tears dripped onto Keirkrad's snarling face below him.

They dripped from human eyes.

When his senses cleared, Vell found his bare hands locked around Keirkrad's neck, the werebat underneath him, pinned and struggling on the ground. Pulling back in shock, he released his grip just in time for the axe to swing down and slice through Keirkrad's throat. Thluna's blow separated the werebat's head from its body and sent it rolling away.

Vell weakly pulled himself to his feet, wiping streaks of tears from his cheeks. Beneath him sprawled the open-winged remnants of the man who had been their shaman for longer than any Thunderbeast could remember. Vell stared down on the spectacle of ruin, appalled. The ugly bat face rolled to a stop and lay facedown in the dirt.

Thanar rushed over to heal Rask's wound. Much to the half-orc's relief, the druid discovered that he had not been infected with lycanthropy.

"I loved him," Vell reflected. "Our shaman. All my childhood I was told to love him, and so I did."

"That's true of us all," said Thluna. He propped up the axe and cleaned the blade of Keirkrad's blood. "But it was not our shaman of old we just killed."

"Is that truly so?" Vell asked. "I wonder."

Kellin stood near Vell and placed a sympathetic hand on his arm. She felt a tremble as her flesh touched his.

"It's sad that Keirkrad had to die," she said. "But it's for the best."

"There is no doubt of that," said Thanar. "He is the reason I could not make my home in Grunwald. If our tribe is to survive, his type must be consigned to the past." He turned to face Thluna. "And so, chief of the Thunderbeasts, what honor is appropriate for our fallen shaman?"

Thluna thought for a moment. "Keirkrad was our comrade, and his memory will carry much weight among our brethren. When our fellow, Grallah, fell in the deep wood, we could not pause to honor his body. We have scarcely more time now . . ." He looked at the Delimbiyr River. "Burial or fire would be a greater honor, but . . ."

Thanar smiled. "A decision worthy of a chief. Worthy of my chief."

"This all may have been a test," said Rask. A fresh scar, a circle of teeth marks as if from a lamprey's bite, now adorned his chin. "Even the Tree Ghosts knew of Keirkrad and the destiny Uthgar supposedly planned for him—the reason his life was preserved for so long. As a test for us. And we've won." The notion let a contemplative mood settle over the assembled Thunderbeasts. They felt uplifted by the idea that Uthgar had godly plans of such foresight. It might even have redeemed Keirkrad, by justifying his betrayal.

Vell spoke simply but profoundly. "Perhaps, in a way he never imagined, Keirkrad fulfilled his destiny at last."

CHAPTER 18

Sungar smiled though his flesh was raw and his cheeks were flecked with blood. Another afternoon of torture had ripped away all of his strength, but he smiled and laughed through it nevertheless. A trace of light filtered through the tiny window at the top of his cell, casting patterns across the walls, and somewhere nearby a bird chirped merrily, lightening Sungar's spirits.

"It will not be much longer now," he said.

"Can you be certain?" asked Hurd through the wall.

"You said it yourself," Sungar said. "The first time we spoke. Change is coming to Llorkh. And you wanted to live long enough to see it."

"I hope you're right."

"I am." Sungar said. "The old chief has shown me so."

"This place can have strange effects," Hurd

cautioned. "We cannot always trust our senses."

"Simply believe, Hurd," said Sungar. "Even false belief will give you the strength you need when the time comes."

"I want to kill him," said Hurd. "I mean Klev, though I would surely gut Geildarr if given the chance. But Klev, who's brought such pain down on us. I'd love to see him pay. I wouldn't even care about seeing him suffer. That'd be playing his game. The quick death he denied us . . . that would be fulfillment enough."

"Let your anger brew," Sungar advised. "All the rage you've kept in check for all these years . . . now is the time for it."

❧ ❧ ❧ ❧ ❧

The Thunderbeasts made camp in a field of brown grass, south of Loudwater. On Rask's advice, they chose to avoid the towns and major roads as much as they could, for the area crawled with Zhentarim, and they did not want Llorkh to have any forewarning of their approach. Kellin tossed and turned in her bedroll then rose, the full moon dappling her dark skin in tones of silver. Vell was keeping watch, silently staring into the distance.

"How do you feel, Vell?" she asked softly, so as not to disturb the sleeping warriors around them.

"Fine," he said. He turned to her. "As angry as I am at the Shepherds, there is something reassuring in knowing exactly where I stand. I thought Uthgar cursed me with this—he did not."

"But you transformed again," Kellin said. "How do you feel about that? I realize Uthgardt are unaccustomed to speaking of feelings, but—"

"I kept more of my own mind this time," said Vell. "That is good."

Kellin nodded.

"What troubled me is how comfortable I felt in that form." Vell forced a smile. "In a body so foreign, so unlike my own, so huge and scaly—I felt like myself."

Kellin embraced him. This took him by surprise. The

gesture meant more to him than any words of reassurance. In the moonlight, he closed his arms around her as well, and for a long time they stood in a shared embrace, their heads resting on each other's shoulders. He felt warm and welcome in her arms, and his heart beat fast. For the first time in a long while, he was moved by something other than anger. He was of age to select a wife from among the Thunderbeast women, but the warriors of greater repute and importance took precedence. Before Runemeet, he had always hovered on the margins of his tribe, and not only because of his eye color—though that served as a reminder of his differences.

She whispered into his ear, "I would not wish your predicament on anyone. The Shepherds were wrong to do this to you, and you are brave to have borne it this far. You are the bravest man I've known." He began to speak, but she shushed him. "When this is over, if you do not want to return to your tribe, there will be a place for you with me."

"Will we be lovers?" Vell asked. He surprised himself with the question, and he began to recant. "I mean . . ."

"No," said Kellin. "It's an important question. I don't know yet. We'll see how this turns out. Unless you think Lanaal . . ."

"No," Vell said. "Not Lanaal."

"You and she have so much in common," Kellin said.

"And so little in common." Vell moved a tentative hand to stroke the black curls that hung down over her shoulders.

"You don't have to accept my offer," Kellin said, resting her head on his shoulder. "This is your choice. Maybe you'll decide that your place is with your people."

"Up until now," Vell answered, "I had no way to even contemplate leaving. But you had never met me, Kellin. Before Runemeet, before Morgur's Mound, Vell the Brown was an ordinary man, unremarkable in most ways. Take the behemoth from me, and I fear that's what I'll be again."

"Don't think that way," said Kellin. "Look where it's led you. You've traveled far outside the world you knew, met creatures you never could have expected—elves, korreds, treants, and a half-orc, not to mention a sorceress. You've shared harsh words with your own ancestors. These experiences cannot be erased, nor the experience of carrying all this weight. You will emerge a stronger person, and that's how you will stay."

Vell said, "Another thing I'll have to thank the Shepherds for." He let out a soft chuckle that let Kellin know it was just a bitter joke.

Together in the night, with barbarian warriors sleeping all around them, they clutched each other tightly, nothing more needing to be said.

Rask used the tip of his sword to trace a map of Llorkh in the dust at his feet, digging a furrow around it to represent the ditch. He drove the sword's tip deep into the ground at the city's center, to represent Geildarr's manor and the seat of government for Llorkh: the Lord's Keep. The party hid among the foothills of the Graypeaks, keeping a distant watch on the Dawn Pass Trail to the north, where the occasional caravan crawled to or from Llorkh. They crouched in the tall grass that swayed in the wind as larks chirped their autumn songs.

"Much of Llorkh is unpopulated," Rask explained. "Or so it was. I should remind you that I have not been there in many years. The population dwindled after the mines closed, so the town has many untended, uninhabited buildings. Geildarr fortified the walls and built a great ditch around Llorkh.

"We face one major problem," Rask went on. "Llorkh is a Zhentarim stronghold. It is no place to live, though many do live there, poor souls. In truth, it is a fortress for the protection of caravans, and nothing else. Geildarr's Lord's Men number in the hundreds, and with so many caravans passing through the city, the number of soldiers within the walls is usually high. And there are but eight of us."

"We faced a vastly superior force in the Fallen Lands," Thluna said, "and we were victorious then." He looked at Kellin, then at Vell. "We have a magic user, as we did then, and something else of perhaps even greater power."

"I will do all I can to create havoc. With care, I could collapse buildings, stopping many of our enemies," said Vell. "But it may not be enough. It seems Geildarr is a powerful wizard himself."

"More than that," Rask added, "Llorkh houses a large and powerful church of Cyric. If Mythkar Leng still rules there, he is a mighty spellcaster in his own right, and a cruel-hearted sadist. Once, when I was just a child, my parents and I sat in the Dark Sun temple. As caravan guards, it was required that they occasionally sat in on these ceremonies, though none of us revered Cyric. Leng detected our lack of faith instantly. The service included the ritual sacrifice of an enemy of Cyric, in this case a halfling who Leng said was a Harper agent captured in Loudwater.

"I dared to turn away as they disemboweled him on the altar. Leng took me from the audience and flogged me as Cyricists looked on in amusement, not as punishment for my lack of faith, but for my parents' disinterest." Rask paused a moment at the difficult memory.

"At the center of Llorkh is the Lord's Keep, a well-guarded tower of a building. Surely this is where Geildarr would keep the Heart of Runlatha, if he has not yet shipped it to his Zhentarim masters. So you see what we are up against. A bold assault would be suicide."

"We are prepared for whatever our chief wills," said the warrior Ilskar. "It would be a glorious fate."

Thanar rested a hand on his shoulder. "Glorious perhaps, but not smart. What is our mission here? It is threefold: free the behemoths from their bondage, recover the Heart of Runlatha, and rescue Sungar. For the moment, we do not even know if these things reside in Llorkh."

"I can assure you that they do," said a mellifluous voice. They spun to find Lanaal's delicate elf face staring at them from the long grass. The elf laughed.

"I should have known you would put in an appearance at the right moment," said Rask.

"Lanaal!" Vell said. "How did you find us?"

"It's not hard to find someone when you have so many spies." As if on cue, the larks around her chirped louder. "With my own eyes I have seen your chief Sungar, resident in the dungeons under the Lord's Keep. He has been tortured but has not lost his spirit. He believes he will be liberated, and from what I heard, has seen a portent that told him so."

"Praise be to Uthgar," Thluna said, closing his eyes in his relief.

"And the behemoths?" asked Vell. "What of them?"

"You will likely sense them when you get closer, and you will know their agony as if it were your own. They are tethered by magic in Llorkh's Central Square. I have much more to tell, and doubtless you do as well, but this I must say first. Vell, I kept my promise and sought out an old elf hermit in the Arn Forest whose only name is Lynx-Eyes. He is rumored to have an affinity with cats, akin to mine for birds. Lynx-Eyes was obstinate at first, but I persuaded him to help me. He claimed to have an ability I had never heard of before. He says he can not only transform into a cat, but can allow willing comrades to do the same."

Vell's face went blank. Could this be? The Shepherds would surely have mentioned such a thing, unless they didn't know of it, and why would they? How often, in all of their centuries, would they have tried to bestow their powers upon mere humans?

"If true, this could be our answer," said Thluna.

"I could not ask this of you," said Vell. "Even if it is true, and even if I am capable of it, how can I ask any of you to . . ."

"I will accept it," said Hengin unblinkingly.

"I cannot ask you to share my curse," Vell told the warrior, "and neither can Thluna command it . . ."

"We are able to choose, Vell the Brown," said Draf. "We choose this."

"It shall be only for a short time, Vell," said Thanar. "It is the only way."

Rask Urgek smiled, widely enough to show his orc fangs. "I, for one, look forward to bringing as much of Llorkh crumbling down as I can."

A cold autumn wind passed through the silent streets of Llorkh in the dark of night. It chilled the bones of the city's most unwilling residents, the behemoths, who shuddered in the square where they stood imprisoned. A quiet moan of protest from one grew to a low, mournful symphony, as more and more voices joined in, filling the night with the tones of their sadness.

Throughout Llorkh, the poor townsfolk awoke and lay in their beds, hearing this unearthly choir. They had gawked at the behemoths when they had walked the streets of the town, and were sympathetic, for they knew fellow prisoners when they saw them. Some townspeople were old enough to remember the murdered mayor Phintarn Redblade, and the days before Geildarr and the Zhentarim, when Llorkh was an honest mining town down on its luck—a place where dwarves and humans lived together in peace. Their sobs joined the cries of the behemoths.

That night, no soldier slept soundly in the barracks. Halfhearted rumbles were shared about orders to silence the inconvenient beasts, but none could bring themselves to do it. A profound unease they could not name settled into their spirits. Even Geildarr woke in his bed high up in the Lord's Keep, wandered to his balcony, and stared down on the Central Square and his unfortunate pets. His hands trembled as he gripped the railing, and he soon turned away and shut himself back into his room. He fetched the Heart of Runlatha, felt its warmth, and let its red glow wash over his hands. Clutching it to his breast, he settled back into his bed and tried hard to get back to sleep.

So many floors below, Sungar and Hurd shared no words, for none were required. They were ready. The time was upon them—if they had any doubts, they were settled for good once the cries of the behemoths ceased, and suddenly, a signal if ever there was one: a mind many miles away reached out and touched them, soothed them, making them ready for the battle to come.

The two prisoners in the dungeon imagined the warrior gods of their esteem—Uthgar and Gorm—standing together, armored and prepared for war.

An expectant mood settled over the scarred town of Llorkh. At long last, it was on the brink of something new.

CHAPTER 19

The sun was just rising over the vale as Thluna and his tiny army made their final preparations for the impending siege. The Thunderbeasts knew the effectiveness of an early morning attack. The famous siege Gundar led on Raven Rock was waged at dawn, when the watch guards were most weary, and an attack was unexpected. Still, the potential for surprise in this battle was remote.

The success or failure of this attack depended on whether Vell could impart his powers of transformation on the others.

"I can transform myself, I'm sure. But how do I change the others?" asked Vell.

"You voluntarily changed into a behemoth to fight Keirkrad, did you not?" asked Lanaal.

Vell nodded, and swallowed hard. "I know that this should be no different. But what if I simply don't have the power? Your hermit may have been lying. Even if he is capable of this, that is no guarantee that . . ."

"Then we will try something else, Vell," said Thluna. "We have a dozen potent allies imprisoned in Llorkh. You are in contact with them."

"I am. Contact of sorts, that is." Vell could feel the behemoths' every sensation when he let himself probe their minds. From their eyes, he could survey much of Llorkh. Alongside the misery of their containment, he found in them an animal excitement at the potential of liberation. In his mind, he received images of the place they wanted to be—the peaceful idyll of the Sanctuary where they had spent their entire lives. They had never imagined being anywhere else, had never realized there was anywhere else to be. And the Shepherds. They loved the Shepherds. They loved Vell because they thought he was one of them.

"They are ready to fight?" asked Kellin.

Vell nodded in affirmation. They chafed in their bondage, as any creature would.

"So are we," said Hengin. "In whatever body is necessary." He, Ilskar, Draf, Thanar, and Rask stood waiting for Vell to attempt the impossible and make behemoths of them all.

"If it does work," Vell warned them all, "you will find your senses much changed. It may be difficult to keep the consciousness necessary to do your job." He looked to Thanar. "I cannot know how this compares to a druid's wildforms. It's possible that your skills will not prepare you for this."

"I understand that," said the druid.

"I fear that all of you may become what I was the first time," said Vell. "A mindless, rampaging beast. We all know the blood rage. You know what it is like to lose yourself. The purity of that emotion is enticing. This transformation will be just as much, and a thousand times more." He surprised himself with his own eloquence.

"But we must try to lock up our rage. There are innocents in Llorkh. We must fear for them. Our tribe has killed enemy innocents before, but that is not something we remember as glory. Fear for your own minds too. It may be hard to come back. You might forget you were ever human."

A disquieted hush fell over the five as they absorbed Vell's speech.

"Do you still choose this?" asked Vell. They all nodded, but with less enthusiasm. "Keep whatever part of yourself you hold most dear foremost in your mind. That, I hope, will help you keep a level head."

The sun's early rays crawled across the sky, tracing the edges of the mine-scarred Graypeaks. The world seemed so peaceful, as if all of its troubles were vanishing just as the light dabbed the clouds in tones of gentle pink.

"To Llorkh," Thluna said. "To glory or ruin. We have come so far to do Uthgar's will. I can only hope, if we die, that we will die pleasing him." Rather than trumpeting his cry to battle across the plains, as he might when leading a throng of warriors, he whispered it. The moment was private and intimate. His eyes fell on each of his companions: this strange assembly of a bird-souled elf, a southern sorceress, a half-orc Tree Ghost, a druid exile, stalwart Thunderbeast warriors, and this strangest of creatures, Vell the Brown. His eyes shone with love and respect.

Vell's hands trembled as he extended them, one to Rask, the other to Hengin. With Draf, Thanar, and Ilskar they formed a circle of linked hands and sank into concentration. Something rose into his mind unbidden. He thought of Kellin, of the True Name the priests of Oghma had given her. All of her soul-searching could not tell her its meaning, but she said the search had meaning in itself.

Vell delved deeper into his lizard-tainted soul, and found a place he had never imagined.

Clavel Foxgray stood on the city walls of Llorkh surveying the terrain, holding his hand above his eyes as shelter from the cold wind. His purple robe fluttered in the breeze. Clavel avoided looking down at the ditch, the ugly scar on the earth that encircled the city, all the more terrible for anyone who had spent a night sleeping in it.

Nobody ever jeered him for being knocked into the ditch by that hobgoblin. But on that dreadful drunken night in the Wet Wizard, two of his colleagues taught him something when they had to beat sense into him—sense enough to keep his mouth shut about Ardeth.

The low rising sun was at Clavel's back, and as he stared west, the shadow of the wall crawled across the land. The strange and unsettling night, with those huge lizards wailing their lungs out, had left him shaken, and he was happy that it would soon be over.

Through the whistling wind, he could swear he heard a strange sound in the distance—a repetitive pounding. It triggered a faint recollection from his childhood, when the mines around Llorkh were still active, and their sounds echoed across the land. Now they were closed and gone.

Somehow Clavel was reminded of another night, too, when he had also stood on these walls. It was in the month of Ches in the Year of Wild Magic, when the phaerimm had emerged from their underground prison near Evereska. It seemed all the lands west of Anauroch were suddenly alive with danger, with strange monsters enslaving humanoid tribes to accomplish their foul objectives. An army of bugbears appeared out of the Graypeaks to march against Llorkh, led by a beholder. That day, with his city under siege, the walls on the verge of collapse, and bugbear corpses filling the ditch, he felt something unexpected. For a moment, part of him wanted the city to fall. He wanted the whole sad saga of Llorkh to come to an end. A good end, a bad end, it didn't matter. Just an end.

Only for a moment, Clavel felt that way once again.

As Geildarr slept in his luxurious feather bed within the oak-paneled splendor of his bedroom, the Heart of Runlatha clapped to his breast, the glowing red energies of the artifact crept forth and invaded his dreaming mind.

He dreamed he was in Netheril in its last days, walking the streets of Runlatha by night. He was calm, though the world around him was crumbling. The black waters of the vanished Narrow Sea trembled under a heavy breeze. The city buildings were not only damaged by war, but they seemed somehow colorless and stripped of something vital. Clearly they had once been fantastic feats of architecture, but now they were broken and decayed. Bodies were piled in the street, both human and orc. The place stank of rotting flesh, and cries of anguish filled the air. In the distance, smoke plumes rose to the sky.

The magic is gone, Geildarr knew. This is after Karsus's folly, when the greatest arcanist of Netheril—the most powerful and most foolish wizard Faerûn had ever known—had cast an avatar spell to kill the goddess of magic, hoping to gain her power.

Instead, Geildarr recalled, Karsus destroyed all of the arcane magic in the world, sending all the sky citadels of High Netheril tumbling to the ground. Though Runlatha was part of Low Netheril, it too probably had much magic woven into its very structure—magic that failed the moment Karsus cast his spell. Without the protection of the citadels, Runlatha was vulnerable to the masses of humanoid hordes.

Even without Karsus's folly, the Great Desert was spreading, ruining farmland throughout what was once the heart of Netheril. From his own studies of history, Geildarr had decided that the fall of the Empire of Magic was inevitable, one way or another. Karsus merely hastened it.

"We must abandon this city," a booming voice said. Geildarr spun around to see that the world had shifted around him. He was standing in a vast meeting hall, stars peeking through huge holes in the ceiling. Geildarr stood in the middle of a vast mob of humans, all staring forward at a man with coal-black hair, broad shoulders, and a warrior's physique. Some in the crowd wore the brightly colored robes of Netherese arcanists, the spellcasters of old, but most were plainly dressed. The general populace visibly shunned the arcanists, doubtless blaming their kind for the current lot of the world. No one acknowledged Geildarr, either not seeing him or not regarding him as anything out of the ordinary.

Geildarr was thankful that this vision was not coming to him in the Netherese language.

"Throughout what was once Netheril, crops are failing, and orcs and other beasts are massing to destroy the last shreds of our civilization," said the man. "We repelled this latest attack, but at too high a cost. More attacks will follow.

"And the citadels are falling. We can expect no aid from them. We are alone, and we cannot hold Runlatha for long." With a heavy voice, he said, "Our home is not worth saving any more."

Heads bowed all over the room. Geildarr looked around at the thousands of souls around him—men, women, and children—all desperate, all saddened. All looked to this man—the Bey of Runlatha—for guidance.

To Geildarr, the Bey did not resemble a barbarian chieftain like Sungar, but rather a disciplined military general of old Netheril, a strategist, warrior, and leader of armies.

"Karsus's hubris has freed us from the yoke of our Netherese oppressors," said the Bey. "We are free now, and it is our first duty to find and rally others in nearby lands who have also survived. Through luck and companionship, we shall survive and forge a new life far away from this place. Throughout the empire, groups are banding together and seeking out new lands. Some go east, some south."

"Where will we go?" yelled someone from the audience.

"West," the Bey declared. "We shall try the Lowroad. The underground route will have perils of its own, but the dwarves have always been our friends, and they will shelter and protect us, if we prove ourselves to them. Already they have agreed to give us sanctuary in Ascore, and from there we shall proceed west across the Northkingdom, searching for some unclaimed land to make our own. The road will be hard and treacherous, and our enemies will be many. We face even more than orcs and bandits—our leader Shaquintar kept many creatures magically caged for his experiments, creatures freed by Karsus's spell. The most powerful of them, the demon Zukothoth, desires revenge, and he has rallied some of the others to this goal."

"But the tyrant Shaquintar is dead!" came the protests. "And we did not take part in these experiments!"

"It matters not to Zukothoth. He blames the folk of Runlatha. He is another reason that we must move, and quickly. Perhaps we will be able to slip away under his notice."

Not likely, thought Geildarr. He knew that the Bey would eventually go down fighting Zukothoth on the western border of Delzoun.

"Damn Shaquintar to Moander's stinking pit," someone in the audience yelled. "He is dead and gone, yet he will still bring ruin upon us."

"Perhaps he will save us yet. I scavenged the ruins of his manse, destroyed in the fall, and learned that not all of the magic of old has failed."

The dream spun again, and Geildarr was standing at the front of the room, watching as the Bey picked up a small wooden box and opened it. The Bey's stony face was bathed in red light as he plucked free the glowing artifact and held it high for all to see.

"It has survived!" a nearby arcanist cried. "I didn't believe it possible."

"Yes, believe it," said the Bey. "Those of you outside the Arcanist's Guild may not have been aware of the purposes of Shaquintar's experiments. Cruel-hearted tyrant that he was, in his way he loved Runlatha and all who lived here. He wanted to keep us safe, and sensing all this inevitable turmoil, he looked for ways to hide Runlatha from trouble. Shaquintar was not so different from Lord Shadow, but on a more modest scale, tormenting creatures good and evil to achieve his goals. It is said that the beating heart of an angelic planetar was used to create this artifact."

A collective gasp came from the audience at this revelation.

"Shaquintar called it the Heart of Runlatha. It was to be one of several artifacts. The others were meant to move the city to some far-off place. Either he did not create them or they were lost in the death of magic. I do not know how to use this artifact. Our surviving arcanists must try to unlock its secrets. Perhaps when we find a scrap of ground to call our own, it will help us conceal it from the world."

A cry of joy arose from the crowd. The Bey had given them hope. Geildarr admired the Bey's ambitions, but wondered if he ever really thought that they would find a peaceful home somewhere in the North, hidden by illusion. Little did the Runlathans know that they would be scattered and ruined, falling into barbarity and tribalism. All memories, and very nearly all traces of their civilization, would vanish from them, and they would become the Uthgardt.

Naïve, perhaps. Or maybe not—maybe the Bey knew real success was unlikely, but he kept up this fantasy for the sake of his followers. If nothing else, he would achieve a legacy. Some sixteen hundred years later, his name, or a form of it—whether Berun or Beorunna—would be remembered. He wondered if the name Geildarr, or even Fzoul or Sememmon, would last a fraction of that time.

"Now we must leave Runlatha behind," the Bey told his followers. "We must renounce all claims on it, so that our own hearts do not remain here in the ruins but travel with us on the Lowroad and beyond, to wherever the wind might carry us. Let the orcs pick its bones. Let the desert rise and swallow it up. It means nothing to us any longer. Cities fall, empires perish. It has happened before, and it will surely happen again. But we shall outlast the death of our empire."

An inexplicable anxiety rose up in Geildarr's breast, the way it sometimes did in his dreams. He reached out to grab the Heart of Runlatha away from the Bey of Runlatha, and as his hand made contact with the artifact, he woke.

There, trembling in his own opulent bed, the sheets damp with his sweat, he heard the sound of distant footsteps.

With slow, powerful steps, six behemoths walked toward Llorkh. Long serpentine necks bobbed with each footfall. Their steps were synchronized like those of an army marching in time, so that each heavy step sounded like the beat of a great war drum, sending reverberations across the plains. The walls of Llorkh trembled at their approach.

Clavel and the other watchmen atop the city walls stared in disbelief as the brown-skinned lizards came closer. They seemed larger than those Geildarr kept imprisoned in the Central Square. To shocked onlookers, they appeared like vast hills of scale, juggernauts of destruction.

The behemoths followed the wide road, the Dawn Pass Trail, continuing along the same path many thousands of merchant caravans had followed. They marched directly to the west gate of Llorkh: the largest gap in the walls but also the best-defended section. The Lord's Men manning the checkpoint outside wisely retreated within the city walls.

"Archers," Clavel croaked, trying to overcome his own astonishment. He barked to his fellows, "Archers! Fetch the archers!"

"How many archers?" a Lord's Man asked.

"As many as we have!" Clavel cried. "Quickly—wake the barracks! Wake the city!" In the Year of Wild Magic, Llorkh had withstood an attack from hundreds of foes, but could it survive an assault from only six?

Vell walked ahead of the other five, watching purple-clad soldiers, small as beetles, scramble on the city walls. Before long, several dozen archers amassed around the west gate. In all the chaos and confusion, they failed to notice a giant hawk sailing over the unguarded southern walls.

What was this like for the others? Vell wondered. Did they keep their minds the way he did, or were they now the rampaging beast he had been when he killed that Zhentarim skymage outside the camp? With no way to communicate with them, he could only hope they would follow his lead.

The city gates grew closer, and so did the archers defending them. Some of them lit their arrows ablaze, as if it would make a difference.

I've never been in a city before, Vell thought, though he had always been faintly curious about life inside them. Some of the merchants who had visited Grunwald when he was a child told him stories about these faraway places with mysterious names. As near as Silverymoon, or as far as Calimport, they were all the same to him—so far outside of his experience that Vell knew he would never come near them.

A few arrows flew from the top of the wall. The archers were firing too early and the missiles fell short, striking the road in the behemoths' path.

Vell thought, I never considered entering a city in this way.

❖ ❖ ❖ ❖ ❖

The Mayor of Llorkh paced his residence, the Heart of Runlatha still held in his right hand. All of his ancient treasures, hanging on his walls or placed on pedestals, trembled with the vibrations shaking the city.

Ardeth appeared from her door on cue, as she always did. He did not need to summon her. She always seemed to know when to appear.

"I sense Sememmon behind this, Cyric take him," cursed Geildarr.

"Really?" asked Ardeth. "You think Sememmon sent these behemoths to destroy Llorkh?"

"Perhaps, perhaps," Geildarr thought aloud as he marched out onto his balcony. He could no longer see the behemoths; they were now close enough to the city walls that the angle hid them. In the town below, excitement spread as people dashed about in the early morning streets. "He probably made a deal with those ancients you discovered in the Star Mounts."

"But didn't you say he was determined to preserve Llorkh, so he could take it himself later on?" asked Ardeth.

"Yes! No!" Geildarr slammed his left fist down on his balcony rail. "Those damned Uthgardt are clearly involved somehow. The Thunderbeast tribe. Rouse Klev. He needs to have a little chat with our friend the chieftain."

The rhythmic footfalls still sounded from outside the city walls, now so loud that Geildarr could feel them in his bones.

Ardeth nodded. "The Lord's Men will assail the behemoths with all they have. They'll stop them outside the gates, if they can. Perhaps we should join them ... perhaps with our magic ..."

"Some mages are down in the Merchant District, staying with a caravan from Darkhold. We'll see how they fare. If these behemoths should break through the walls, our magic will be needed to fight them here," said Geildarr. He shook his head in disbelief at the words he was speaking.

Ardeth reached out and clasped her small hand around Geildarr's right wrist. "What of the Heart of Runlatha?"

Geildarr looked down at it, its shimmering red energies radiating forth. "It is safe here. The Lord's Keep is warded and defended."

"This place may not be so safe after all," said Ardeth. "I can take it out of the city, deliver it to Zhentil Keep if you will it."

Geildarr peered into the artifact. He felt a hollowness in his breath, and he asked himself, Will all of Llorkh fall over this?

"Netherese magic," he marveled. "All those cities fell, all that civilization was lost. Yet this remains."

"Geildarr!" Ardeth protested. "Are you all right?"

The mayor looked down on her pale face, and a tear rolled down his cheek.

"What do we do?" Ardeth asked plaintively.

"We wait," answered Geildarr.

CHAPTER 20

The behemoths stepped over the ditch as if it were a scratch in the dirt. Each new thunderous step, with its hellish synchrony, kicked up clouds of soil, which the wind caught and blew into a brown haze. Clavel could feel each footfall, vibrating the stone walls all the way to the top where he stood.

Five or six dozen Lord's Men stood ready above the gate, their bows strung and arrows nocked. Without a bow of his own, Clavel stood behind the line of archers, facing outward, trying to stay out of the way, yet remain close to the action. He looked up and saw a murder of crows circling the wall, wings flapping. The birds settled into glides as they navigated the currents.

"Take aim!" the archers' commander shouted.

The crows were flying low. They were ready to pick the carrion, Clavel reasoned. Clever birds.

The archers took aim all along the line. Some hands trembled. The repetitive pounding of the behemoths' steps echoed up their spines, and they did not know if their arrows would even penetrate the behemoths' scales.

Then Clavel noticed something curious. At least two of the crows were holding objects in their feet. The items flashed as they reflected sunlight—they were made of glass. And they were directly over the archers. Clavel leaned his head back and saw another crow hovering right over him, a small glass flask in its feet.

"Get ready!" shouted the commander. The Lord's Men drew back their bowstrings.

Fear arising in his throat, Clavel tried to dive for cover, but there was none to be had. He fell on his belly and desperately tried to roll under the bowmen. He upset their feet and a few tumbled backward, landing on top of him. Two archers lost their balance entirely and fell off the wall with a scream of death.

All along the line of archers, Lord's Men turned their heads to look at the source of the commotion.

The crows released their flasks in unison.

"Fire!" the commander shouted, but not a single bowstring snapped in response. The flasks, which Clavel too late recognized as alchemist's fire, smashed on the archers and the wall. Leaping, roaring flames burst upward, crawling along the top of the wall and raining fire down each side. The Lord's Men closest to the impact let out cries of agony as their clothes erupted in fire, their bowstrings incinerating in their hands. Those farther from the blasts released their weapons and went running to help their fellows, slapping them in a vain attempt to put out the fires.

Clavel rose, a plume of orange flame leaping from his purple cloak, his screams unheard among the chorus of pain. He plunged off the wall, landing as a flaming wreck directly in the behemoths' unchallenged path.

Vell watched as flames decimated the mass of soldiers assembled on the wall. Blazing men tumbled to the ground like a fiery waterfall. He looked upward and saw the crows scattering away from the fires. He silently thanked Lanaal. Her plan had worked perfectly.

The behemoths behind him moved into a line, single file, as they approached the heavy wood gate into Llorkh. Vell stepped onto the flaming ruins of some fallen archers, barely feeling any pain as the blazes were extinguished under his vast feet.

Arrows flew down at them, but the missiles were few, and they bounced off thick behemoth hides or embedded, troubling the creatures little more than pinpricks.

Vell's mind reached out to his imprisoned fellows. He felt their excitement, felt them straining against their bondage even more strongly now that liberation seemed so close.

Shepherd, they seemed to say, *give us our freedom!*

Vell raised himself partly onto his hind legs and kicked the massive gates to the city, the last barrier between him and the behemoths, and the ancient wood groaned. He kicked again, and the whole gate shuddered. A crack raced to split the wood from the point of impact. With one more kick, the door splintered and fell apart.

Vell lowered his neck to pass through the gateway into Llorkh, where a whole city was ready to fight him.

Sungar lay on the floor of the cramped cell, its walls marking the edges of his world. With his ear to the ground, he could feel the vibrations of the huge thunderbeast steps. He smiled.

His two dungeon guards arrived at the cell door. He lay limp and clenched a fist under his body.

"Wake with the morning, chief," said one of the dungeon guards, unlocking the cell door. "Klev requests another audience." He spoke faster than Sungar had ever heard him, the urgency plain in his voice. Looking up, Sungar could see that both soldiers had swords at their belts, though neither of them had their hands anywhere near the hilts.

The instant the first guard walked into the cell, the keys still in the lock, Sungar burst into action. He unleashed all of the anger he had kept in check till this moment. In his clenched fist, he hid all of the dust and pebbles that had fallen from his cell walls during his imprisonment, and he threw it into the guard's eyes.

As the guard tumbled back, surprised and blinded by Sungar's attack, the second guard stepped backward into the passageway and quickly pushed the cell door shut. Sungar grasped his fellow by the hair and slammed him face-first into the stone wall, then pulled him back and let him fall to the ground. With a swift foot, Sungar stamped on the guard's face, and with the single blow the guard's skull collapsed, his head smashed open on the cold cell floor.

In the corridor, the surviving guard desperately fumbled with the keys, glancing with fear at Sungar's raging eyes, gone wild and red with fury. The chieftain made a run for the cell door. The guard jumped backward just as Sungar rammed his foot into the door and sent it flying open, its thick iron hinges trembling as it smashed into the wall.

The guard reached for his sword, but before his hand reached the hilt, Sungar assailed him with both fists. He pushed the guard backward against the far side of the passageway, pummeling him into the stone wall with fast blows. The guard succeeded in drawing his sword, but as soon as it left his scabbard, Sungar snatched it from him and sank it deep into its owner's chest. The guard spat up blood, and his head lolled in death.

The sound of clapping echoed off the dungeon walls. Sungar turned to see Hurd Hardhalberd at the door of his cell. The prisoners looked upon each other for the first time. The stout dwarf was gray-bearded, with long scars down his cheeks, much as Sungar had imagined.

"Good show, Sungar," said Hurd. "Now if you'll be lettin' me out, we'll be ready to cause some serious damage."

Sungar went to his own damaged cell door, where the keys still dangled from the lock. He pulled them out and dashed to Hurd's cell, trying numerous keys before finding one that would turn.

"Grrruuh . . . ," came an indecipherable grunt from the dark passageway. Standing in the shadows was Klev himself, his half-orc features lit by flickering torchlight. A sickly grin crossed the torturer's hideous face, his sharp tusks glistening with saliva. In his hand he clutched a weapon all too familiar to Sungar—his glass-studded lash.

Sungar turned the key and it clicked in the lock. Klev's long whip uncoiled with a resonant *crack* and it snaked through the air, wrapping around Sungar's legs and pulling tight. The barbarian chief collapsed onto the hard ground, losing his sword as he fell.

Hurd burst free of his cell. "I've been waitin' fer this too long!" he shouted as he dashed down the passageway as fast as his legs could move him. He leaped into midair as he reached Klev, colliding with the half-orc and knocking him backward on the dungeon floor in a vicious, reckless attack. Klev released his whip as the dwarf gripped his throat and squeezed.

Klev shoved Hurd's shoulders with both hands, sending the dwarf tumbling backward. The half-orc regained his footing and pulled out a dagger, holding it out before him, daring Hurd to attack him again. And Hurd, unarmed but undeterred, faced him down.

From down the hallway, the lash cracked again, flying directly over Hurd's head so that the dwarf felt its motion as it passed. The whip found its mark as it coiled around Klev's neck, the cruel glass studs digging into his flesh. Klev's hands went up to his neck, his dagger falling from his grip. Before the weapon could strike the ground, Hurd caught it and sank it solidly into the torturer's heart. Klev fell backward with a force that wrested the whip from Sungar's hands.

Hurd spun to face Sungar. "You some kinda expert with that whip?" he asked.

"Not really," Sungar answered, collecting the swords from the dead guards and tossing one to Hurd. "But if a half-orc can swing it, how hard could it be?"

"Be careful to mind my head next time," said Hurd, rubbing the top of his skull. He looked down at Klev, lying on his back in the middle of the dungeon passage. "That felt *good,*" he said, reaching down to give the dagger a final twist as the last light vanished from the half-orc's eyes. "But it won't be half as pleasurable as chopping Geildarr's head off!" He snapped up the sword and raised it to Sungar. The two warriors clanged their weapons together in a gesture of their camaraderie.

In the bowels of the Dark Sun, where Mythkar Leng conducted his vile experiments, a disciple of Cyric paced through narrow subterranean hallways that reeked of burning fur. An acolyte followed him, a huge ebon key in his hand. They had already freed their captive groundlings, the half-badger assassins which Leng had formed from many of the traitor dwarves. The mutants were commanded to attack all enemies of Llorkh, then were sent racing into the streets. The Cyricists knew they would be little resistance against the behemoths, but this was an excuse to let them go to work.

"Llorkh is under siege," the disciple said in a smooth, emotionless tone. "Our temple may soon be at risk. We must unleash our stock to help defend it." To the trembling initiate he added, "It is what Leng would have done."

"Yes, Dark Master." They reached a metal door, warm to the touch. The acolyte extended the ebon key and slipped it into the lock. As soon as the lock clicked, the hallways echoed with an unearthly barking.

As the last behemoth passed through the gates of Llorkh, he paused and swung his thick neck backward to rub against the wall above it. A few Lord's Men still clung to their places atop the wall, and ran in terror to avoid falling off as so many of their fellow archers had.

The behemoths went separate ways as the streets forked, each taking a different direction and plowing through lines of Lord's Men. Some men were trampled under great feet, but most had the sense to step aside. More arrows and spears pierced Vell's hide, and brave swords slashed at his heels and ankles where he passed, but these were of little consequence to him. What troubled him were the cries of pain he heard from the others. They shared his form, but perhaps not all of his magical armor, so impenetrable when Vell held the form of a man or a thunderbeast.

Vell heard a strange blast of wind, and a moment later one of his fellows let out an agonized moan, which was echoed by sympathetic cries from the tethered behemoths deeper in the city. Vell craned his long neck, looking back just in time to watch Hengin, only his neck and head visible across a block of old buildings, collapse to his knees as he was blasted by a magical blizzard. Even as it abated, frost clung to his scales, chilling his blood. The cold immobilized him and the Lord's Men fell on him. Vell could not see the assault, but he could hear the attacks in Hengin's groans as swords slashed at his exposed underbelly.

There must be a mage in that street, Vell realized. Letting out his own reptilian cry, he spun about, his tail sweeping through the street and smashing through the fragile buildings behind him, bringing walls crashing down. Briefly rising onto his hind legs, he pressed his forelegs into the side of the stone building opposite. It collapsed under his weight, and Vell pressed forward, his legs crushing each floor until his feet were firmly planted amid the rubble. The rest of the building collapsed from the damage, kicking up a terrific storm of dust. Tremors spread throughout the neighboring buildings and they shuddered, some beginning to crack and fall apart.

The opposite street was lost in dust and rubble, the enemy mage surely buried and dead, but it was too late— Hengin's cries had ceased. The vast behemoth, a cloud of grit settling on it, lay in the middle of the street, his skin sliced open by the many weapons of the Lord's Men.

Vell's blood boiled, his gentle behemoth form coming

to life, fueled by his rage. Vell felt the rage rising in him but forced himself to hold it back. He needed to keep his senses, if anyone did. He had a mission to accomplish and could not leave self-control behind to stampede off on a haze of seething anger.

The contingents of Lord's Men guarding the behemoths in the Central Square watched in horror as the new arrivals, larger than the ones already held captive, marched into the heart of Llorkh. They seemed to be unstoppable, ripping the city apart where it stood. But one of the six had fallen. The Lord's Men hoped beyond hope that the animals would be torn down by spells or force before they could reach the square.

Three groups of soldiers guarded the Central Square, one at each of the streets leading into the city. Each had only about a dozen men, all looking in the direction of the west gate. Behind them, the behemoths moaned a dissonant chorus. They sang in high throaty tones, strange vocalizations that conveyed all of their sadness, grief, and despair.

From one of the streets sauntered a strange sight—a leather-clad woman with the dark skin tones of the southern Sword Coast. A sword hung at her belt. Surely, she must have been part of a merchant caravan.

"Milady," said one of the Lord's Men. "We recommend you leave the streets. This place is—" his voice trembled, "—is not safe."

"I should say not," she said, and opened her mouth wide. A sharp scream issued from her throat that rang and resounded in the Lord's Men's ears, shattering their concentration. Some of them fainted from the sonic assault; others were deafened, dropping their weapons to clap their hands over their ears. Immediately, a wiry young barbarian wielding a massive axe raced into view from the street. The woman drew her sword, and they leaped onto the Lord's Men.

Together, Kellin and Thluna made short work of the stunned soldiers, he cleaving them with the axe and she sinking her father's sword wherever she found exposed flesh. From across the Central Square, the other contingents of Lord's Men charged, roused from their positions by the battle. As they dashed across the square, past the magical post that kept the behemoths in bondage, the behemoths all raised their tethered feet at once, pulling the chains tight.

The sudden tension lifted the magical chains off the ground, catching many of the Lord's Men across their middles. They were sliced apart wherever the enchanted chains touched them, their gruesomely bisected bodies littering the Central Square. The few who were not snared went bobbing and weaving to avoid the deadly chains, dashing out of the square back to the streets. Then they fled altogether, into the chaotic alleyways of Llorkh.

"Clever beasts," Kellin said to Thluna. The creatures lowered their feet and the chains once again lay on the ground. "I only hope they know friend from foe."

Thluna clapped her on the shoulder, excited for their success. Looking up, he watched a lone crow fly a strange pattern far above, its beak pointed toward the Lord's Keep. "Good luck," he said to her before dashing into the streets, axe in hand.

Kellin carefully stepped into the square. Gingerly avoiding the chains, she reached the central post. It was a solemn gray marker anchoring a dozen chains which led to the rings on the behemoths' hind feet. Spreading her hands over the top of the post, she tried to dispel the magic that bound the chains. Geildarr's spell was strong and fiendish, and it took all of Kellin's concentration and energy to work at unlocking it. She did not hear the fast-moving feet behind her, or smell the sulfurous stink that filled the air. Not until a fiery blast caught her from behind was her concentration lost and her spell scuttled.

CHAPTER 21

Sungar and Hurd burst out of the dungeons of Llorkh with impassioned fury. The two guards at the entrance were startled to be attacked from behind. Sungar caught one on the shoulder with his sword, and Hurd slashed at the knees of the other, sending him tumbling to the ground. Hurd sank his sword into the guard's heart.

The two warriors dashed through the elegant hallways of the Lord's Keep, looking for a staircase to take them upward. They made no secret of their presence—Sungar freely shouted Uthgardt war cries—but wherever Lord's Men found them, the soldiers were swiftly slaughtered. One of the men, run through by Sungar's sword, lay dying against the wall. Hurd held his blade to his throat.

"What is happening in Llorkh?" Hurd demanded.

"Behemoths," he gasped out. "The great lizards. Some have come to attack the city."

"Friends of yours?" Hurd asked Sungar, sliding the sword home.

"I can only hope so," said Sungar.

They rushed through the ground floor. Sungar's rage was in full fervor. Clutching a weapon again, and feeling enemies fall under his blade, made him feel alive once more, reborn from the prison cell. He had feared that all of his Uthgardt instincts had atrophied and vanished, but was thrilled to find his faculties reignited.

Before the great iron doors that served as the entrance to the tower, they found a contingent of five Lord's Men. A massive, sickly painting of Lord Geildarr, clad in purple and surrounded by the adoring people of Llorkh, hung over their heads. The soldiers faced the entrance to the Lord's Keep, their attention on the large, sealed doors, ready for a threat from that direction. Sungar snatched up a vase that decorated the passage and tossed it across the hall into an opposite room. As it smashed, the guards turned to look.

In that moment, the barbarian and the dwarf assaulted them with full strength. Their swords found critical places, and they made short work of their foes. Puddles of blood collected on the red carpet.

"This is the way out," said Hurd, pointing to the large doors. "If you want to leave . . ."

"Why would I?" asked Sungar. "Most likely Geildarr's up there." He pointed to the wide stairway leading upward. Hurd bent over to pick up the head of a Lord's Man, hacked from his shoulders by Sungar's sword. He tossed it up at the painting and it bounced off, leaving a red smear across Geildarr's smiling face. He and Hurd ran up the stairs, leaving bloody footprints on the carpet.

Soon they found the narrow dining hall where Geildarr had met with Sungar to taunt him. Huge paintings hung on the walls, and white linen covered the long table. The chair at the end of the table had iron restraints built into it. All was lit by a magical white sphere floating in the center of the ceiling.

Standing on top of the table was a figure familiar to them both, lithe and slender, dressed in black and holding a leveled crossbow. Sungar knew her face from the night of the attack on his camp. She was the one who had captured him.

Hurd's lip curled into a smile. "We meet again," he said, brandishing his sword.

Ardeth returned his smile and raised her crossbow. Hurd dodged wildly, and the quarrel zipped past him. Sungar jumped onto the table, his feet skidding on the tablecloth. Almost losing his balance, he swung his sword horizontally at Ardeth. She deftly leaped into the air over the blade, flipping backward to land on the chair Geildarr had sat in when taunting Sungar. She leaped again just as Sungar's sword came down, digging deep into the chair's wooden back.

In midair, with the heavy crossbow still in one hand, Ardeth planted a foot against a wall and pushed off, turning to plant her other foot on Sungar's shoulder. Though she was light, the force sent him tumbling away from the embedded sword, off the table, and into the opposite wall.

Hurd snatched up a chair and threw it, striking Ardeth just as her feet touched down on the table. The chair cracked on impact, sending Ardeth tumbling off the table and into a far corner. Her head slammed hard against the wall with an audible *smack*. She lost her crossbow, which struck the wall and broke apart, landing near her on the floor.

Hurd dashed around to confront Ardeth where she lay near the manacled chair. Seeing her lying limp and dazed in the corner, Hurd raised his sword above his head and ran toward her with surprising speed for his short stature, hoarsely crying, "For Trice Dulgenhar! For Gorm Gulythn!"

But as Hurd came closer, he saw a devious twinkle in Ardeth's eye. She slid her hand into the wreckage of her crossbow and came away with a closed fist. She leaped to her feet and charged in the raging dwarf's direction, using her remarkable speed to duck under his sword as he tried to bring it down upon her. In her fist she grasped a single crossbow bolt, which she drove into one of Hurd's eyes. Having penetrated it, she placed her palm on the bolt and drove it into Hurd's brain.

The dwarf's sword fell to the carpet, and his good eye blinked, then stared dully.

Sungar rose to his feet. Seeing Hurd's lifeless body collapsing to the floor, he gripped the hilt of the sword, still embedded in the chair, and twisted sideways. The wood snapped and cracked, and Sungar pulled the weapon free. Spinning to face Ardeth, his rage redoubled and he saw something new on her face—fear.

Before she could reach Hurd's sword, Sungar jumped up, planting his feet on the table with such impact that the whole room trembled. Ardeth skipped away, just before Sungar swung the sword at her from atop the table, slicing through a painting on the wall. Ardeth stopped just before the open door through which Sungar and Hurd had entered.

Her chest visibly rising and falling, she stood like a frightened animal, unsure of what to do next. Sungar stood atop the table, sword ready, waiting for her next move. She was a dangerous enemy, he knew, and an intelligent one. Hurd died because he attacked her in anger, and Sungar would not make the same mistake.

Ardeth turned her back to Sungar, ready to run out of the open door. Sungar moved to follow her, but at the last moment she turned back, pulled into a somersault, and rolled under the table. Sungar plunged his sword downward with all his strength. It sank through the wood, and Sungar put all his weight behind it until it was buried hilt-deep in the table.

All was silent. The magical light above the table trembled, casting nervous shadows over the room.

Sungar jumped off the table, snapping up the sword that Hurd had wielded. He looked under the table, where the darkness was deep. The sword Sungar had impaled in the table was close to touching the floor, but no one was there.

Ardeth was gone.

Vell urged his behemoth form forward through the streets of Llorkh. To his left, he heard a massive crash and hoped that Thanar and Draf were destroying the barracks and any Lord's Men who were still inside. He hoped the two of them would escape with their lives.

Vell seemed to have left the Lord's Men behind. Rarely, a soldier would dare cross his path, but the streets were mostly empty as he continued his dauntless plunge toward the Lord's Keep. In the buildings around him, he occasionally glimpsed terrified townsfolk peering out at him.

Half a dozen strange dogs appeared in the street before him, unlike any Vell had seen before. These curs were slightly larger than the dogs or wolves he knew, wiry and muscular, with fur the color of rust. But their eyes glowed fire, and their hideous faces had such unearthly looks that Vell knew they could not be of this world. Hell hounds, he realized.

More hounds joined the small pack, and together they ran at Vell, leaping and snarling, plumes of fire emerging from their mouths. Vell stamped his feet, trying to trample them, but the hell hounds nimbly dodged, snapping at his legs and feet where they could. Each time they sank their jaws into his flesh, a jolt of pain shot up his leg.

In the middle of the Central Square, Kellin froze, her head spinning as her spell to erase Geildarr's magic collapsed in her mind. She turned to stare a hell hound directly in its blazing eyes. It leaped on her, its huge forepaws striking her shoulders and smashing her against the stone post. Her arms flew back, nearly striking the deadly chains. She smelled the sulfurous stink of the hell hound's mouth as its huge jaws snapped at her neck.

Desperately, Kellin kneed the beast in its underbelly, and as it yelped from the blow, she grasped it around the middle, her hands clawing into its matted fur. With all her strength she flung the dog sideways, hurling it onto one of the chains tethering the behemoths. The hell hound bayed in agony as the magic of the chain melted its flesh. The air filled with the acrid scent of burning fur. The hell hound bounded upward, almost regaining its footing before Kellin drew her sword and slashed through the air. It caught the hound through its muzzle, cleaving its skull apart.

Brazen barks sounded across the square as three more hell hounds entered, running toward Kellin. She extended a finger and conjured four cold blue pellets of magic. They coursed across the square and struck one of the hell hounds, but it kept running. Kellin looked toward the other streets leading out of the square, but hell hounds burst from them as well. She pressed her back to the post, held her sword ready, and awaited the assault.

Not far from the Lord's Keep, Thluna ducked into an alley as a trio of hell hounds rushed by. He hated hiding from an enemy, but knew it was only prudent. Lanaal was fetching another flask of alchemist's fire that she had stolen from a local shop and hidden on the rooftops of Llorkh. Her destination was the guard contingent in front of the Lord's Keep. The fire, they hoped, would occupy the guards, and allow Thluna entrance.

Hell hounds seemed to have the full run of the city, tearing through anything that stood in their way. Thluna slaughtered two with the axe, but the beasts were ripping away at the behemoths wherever they found them. He feared for Kellin, for he could see that the behemoths in the square were not yet free of their bonds.

Thluna heard a strange sound in the dirt beneath him. He looked down just in time to see a hole open at his feet. Thick-clawed hands reached out and grasped him by his legs. He caught a glimpse of a creature like a giant badger—its black-furred snout covered with dirt—just before it pulled and yanked him off his feet.

Thluna fell, grasping the axe tightly in his hands. He kicked his feet hard but it was no help; he was being dragged down into a burrow. The creature dragged him farther and farther until his head was pulled into the hole, his mouth filling with dirt. Thluna kicked and struggled madly. He punched and scraped at the dirt, widening the burrow's entrance to give himself enough room to swing his weapon.

Choking on dirt, Thluna gripped the axe by the end of its handle, managing an unwieldy swing downward. The axe head sank into the dirt, and as the groundling tried to pull him farther, Thluna swung again and again, with as much strength as he could manage. The groundling gripped his legs tighter, its badger-claws digging into flesh, just as the axe broke through the earth, sinking into the creature's head.

Feeling the claws yield their grip on his legs, Thluna released the axe. His muscles strained as he dragged himself free of the burrow. Gasping heavily, he brushed clumps of dirt from his face. Down the street, he heard a small explosion and the crackle of fire, followed by the screams of men.

Thank you Lanaal, he thought, as he spat dirt from his mouth.

Rask Urgek blinked his huge behemoth eyes, trying desperately to hang on to the threads of his mind. As a rare half-orc born to half-orc parents, he had never felt torn between two worlds. Throughout his tangled history and variety of identities—Zhent caravan guard, thug in the employ of the Xanathar's Thieves Guild, mercenary for hire, Tree Ghost adoptee—he had always had at least some idea of who he was. Now, in this animal body, he felt his identity slipping away like dew in the sunlight. This beast form was seductive in its immensity and power. He felt a strong temptation to cast off the troubles of the civilized world, where Rask had lived on the margins most of his life, and even shrug off his duties and responsibilities with his adopted tribe. O, to be a beast!

As he clung to his consciousness, he wondered whether being in this city again played a part in his mental crisis. Every corner of Llorkh reeked with unpleasant memories for Rask, and walking the streets again brought them all flooding back. They fueled his rage but impaired his reason. The smell of the streets was the same, except now it was tinged with the foul stink of sulfur.

A dozen or more hell hounds pursued him, close enough to snap at his tail. They must have come from the under-levels of the Dark Sun, Rask knew, where Mythkar Leng bred them for dark purposes. Leng still stalked Rask's darkest dreams, his gray eyes peering from the front of the temple, seeing through his feigned faith in Cyric.

The Dark Sun. Did he have the power to destroy it?

Rask could make out its single spire from where he stood, and he turned a corner and galloped toward it, his skin crawling with anger. The street trembled as he ran, stampeding through the Merchant District and crushing caravans as if they were egg shells. As the dark cathedral grew closer, the hell hounds on his trail increased in number.

The Central Square was alive with hell hounds, growling, leaping, and barking. They avoided the deadly chains crisscrossing the square, even when the behemoths lifted their feet and pulled the chains higher. The dogs surrounded Kellin as she fended them off with her father's sword and her spells. The fiery blasts from their mouths were unrelenting, and she was wounded and exhausted. Backed against the post, with hounds snarling at her on all sides and bounding over her head to attack from above, Kellin knew she had little hope of defeating them.

The ground shook as a behemoth stormed into the square. Its vast bulk traveled with remarkable speed and care, and it reared back and slammed its front feet down on the hell hounds that harried Kellin, crushing them beneath its great weight. Those massive feet landed mere inches from Kellin, and the vibrations rattled her brain. The remaining hell hounds jumped at the impact, many onto the deadly chains.

Kellin watched as the behemoth transformed, its vast size melting. Soon, standing before her was the green-robed druid Thanar.

"I've never been more grateful to see you," she said.

"Nor I you," he answered. He smiled in wonder, looking around at the chained behemoths crowding the square.

Kellin asked, "How are the others?"

"Hengin fell, and so did Draf." He lowered his head. "The soldiers tore Draf down as we were toppling the city barracks."

"And Vell? What of Vell?"

"I do not know," said Thanar. "Can we free the captives?" he asked, looking up at the trapped behemoths.

Kellin nodded at the post. "Its enchantment is strong, but perhaps we can overcome it together."

Both of them placed their hands over the stone post and began to concentrate, pouring all their energy into dissolving Geildarr's magic.

❖ ❖ ❖ ❖ ❖

Rask's feet burned as he raced through the streets of Llorkh, the infernal dogs at his heels. With his gargantuan strides, he quickly reached his destination. The Dark Sun stood before him—the huge, purple-walled church raised after the Time of Troubles to the glory of Cyric.

In Rask's mind he was a small child again, flogged by Leng as Cyricists looked on and smiled. He felt each lash again, ripping his flesh.

The huge doors to the Dark Sun were closed. Rask pounded them with his huge forelegs until they flew off their hinges. As a behemoth, he shouldered his way inside, dozens of hell hounds following him.

The church trembled at his entry. Pillars shook, and shocked Cyricists darted and dived for cover as the behemoth rushed in. The temple could barely contain Rask, even with its enormous size. His head bumped the ebon ceiling, and he thrashed his tail at the jawless skulls staring at him from every wall. The hell hounds raced into the temple and dashed around Rask, howling and yipping, breathing flames, snapping at him, ripping away flesh in their fiery jaws. The priests of Cyric unleashed their cruel magic upon him.

Rask looked for Leng among the Cyricists, but was disappointed not to find him. He could think of many reasons for the priest's absence, but somehow Rask suspected he was dead. He sighed, wishing he could crush him under his heel, smash his body, grind him into nothingness.

He would settle for Leng's creation instead—the foul temple to the Prince of Lies.

Some Cyricists ran toward the doors to flee, but Rask shifted the bulk of his weight against the doors to block them. All would die together. Rask's vision blurred, and the walls seemed to close in on him. The skulls leered at him, pressing closer. The Dark Sun had always seemed like a giant tomb to him, but as a child, he never anticipated that it would be *his* tomb.

Magical chains tore at him, huge claws raked him. The hell hounds bit through Rask, exposing white bone. The priests stole his vision and tormented him with diabolical spells. Flames lashed over his body. He was dying. Every part of Rask's vast body rang with pain, but he was happy. He was laughing inside as he swung his great tail and threw his body about, upsetting ebon pillars and smashing through walls. Chunks of the ceiling collapsed. Acolytes ran for the exit but found their way blocked by falling debris. Their wailing prayers were not answered by their cruel god.

As the world fell around him, Rask lost all sense of body and place. Amid this destruction, he was at peace. He had a sudden vision of himself in his own half-orc body, resting for all eternity in the shade of Grandfather Tree. The boughs swayed, and the leaves danced. Eternity waited.

When the roof finally let go, bringing down the Dark

Sun in a final, glorious ruin, Rask Urgek had never felt more satisfied.

Thluna swung the axe, cleaving the skulls of the last survivors among the Lord's Men who guarded Geildarr's Keep. Forcing open the great doors, he was surprised to find bodies lying within, slashed by swords. The dead had been dispatched ferociously but efficiently—a hallmark of a raging barbarian.

"Sungar!" he exclaimed. The chief must have escaped, saving Thluna the need to rescue him. On the wall nearby he noticed a painting of a man who could only be Geildarr, standing before a crowd of adoring citizens. Thluna smiled as he noted the blood smeared across his face.

He saw bloody footprints going up the staircase and followed them.

Netheril falling. This was not the same, but it felt just like it. Geildarr watched from his balcony as the Dark Sun collapsed in on itself, the final reservoir of magical strength in Llorkh destroyed. Buildings were falling all over Llorkh, and whole portions of the city were lost to his eyes in the haze kicked up by the debris. Rampaging behemoths went wherever they cared to, destroying whatever offended them.

A small stone cougar in the hall fell from its pedestal and smashed on the floor. It had come from Ammarindar and was almost a thousand years old. It had survived so much, only to break apart now.

His city. They were destroying *his* city.

The citizens of Llorkh, those who were smart, quit their lodgings and ran for the city gates. Geildarr could see them moving through the streets by the hundreds. He looked toward the Merchant District, where caravans were crushed and devastated by a behemoth's destructive passing. Their goods were surely beyond rescue. Perhaps this assault would finally convince Zhentil Keep that Llorkh required a larger garrison.

In all likelihood, however, it would convince them that it needed a new mayor.

Geildarr looked down at the Heart of Runlatha, still clutched in his right hand, and wondered if it gave him that dream to taunt him.

Ardeth appeared to report bad news. "The barracks are gone. At least fifty of the Lord's Men were killed there alone, and just as many in the disaster at the gate. Battles are going on all over the city. The soldiers and Leng's hell hounds are the only ones fighting against the dinosaurs. This was a well-coordinated, intricately planned assault."

"The Dark Sun has fallen," said Geildarr. "Cyric must be mightily displeased with us for letting his temple be destroyed. No rabble of barbarians could be so calculated in a siege. What force can be behind this?"

"I don't know, but Chief Sungar has escaped from his prison. He is racing through the Lord's Keep, killing anything that moves. I only barely escaped from him with my life. No doubt," Ardeth added, "he's looking for you."

"I can handle one rabid Uthgardt," said Geildarr.

Ardeth frowned. "We have far more to deal with than one Uthgardt! Llorkh is being demolished building by building! Have you considered what will happen when Fzoul hears about this? He'll ask questions. He'll ask 'Who brought this on?' 'Why did this happen?' and 'Who do I blame?' You said he was angry that our incursion into the Fallen Lands failed—how do you suppose he'll feel about all of this?"

Each statement drove a nail into Geildarr's troubled mind. "Do you think you need to tell me this? I know!" he howled, banging his left fist against his thigh. "I know!" he repeated, stamping his feet on his red carpet. He let out a scream of frustration that echoed throughout the Lord's Keep. If Sungar did not know where to find him, he did now.

Geildarr's posture collapsed, and he wandered across his study, placing the Heart of Runlatha on a table—the very same zalantarwood table on which the axe had rested when all of this began.

"If only I had more time," he whispered. "If only I could have learned how to use it. It could have kept us secret, kept us safe from Fzoul, Manshoon, and the world. We could have lived together, you and I, hidden away from the world." He looked up at Ardeth, tears streaming from his eyes. "If Sememmon and Ashemmi can hide from the Zhentarim's eyes, surely we could too?"

"This is not a time for dreams," Ardeth spat. "It is a time for decisions."

"Yes," Geildarr said. "Decisions." He walked over to a case on his wall and pulled out a wand of duskwood. Walking back to his balcony, he looked down at the behemoths bound in the Central Square. "There's a good chance our foes are here for my pets, that they want to liberate them. We may want to relieve them of that task."

"Or you could enrage them further," said Ardeth.

"If we are to fall this day," said Geildarr, "let it be a glorious fall."

He pointed the wand at the behemoths, and the wand's magic crackled forth.

Like a key turning in a lock, Thanar and Kellin's blended spells succeeded in undoing the magic in the post that bound the behemoths in place. The sorceress and druid clapped hands in their victory as they watched the chains vanish. The great lizards were free, the rings on their legs now only mundane anklets.

Across the city, Vell felt their freedom and shared it. *We are free, we are saved!* their minds shouted, and they trumpeted in joy. *You have freed us, Shepherd!* Vell knew their pleasure.

No sooner had they raised their necks to salute their liberation than a lightning bolt flashed down from above.

The thunderous impact sent Kellin and Thanar diving to the ground.

The energy arced down a line of behemoths—the half of the herd that only moments before had strained at the limits of their chains along the west side of the square. Vell felt every stab of their pain as if it were happening to him, doubled and redoubled in his psyche until it became unbearable. The force of it brought him to his knees.

Another lightning blast tore down from the Lord's Keep, striking the same six behemoths. They shuddered and collapsed, their huge bulks sending the city trembling as they fell to the ground.

A blast of agony struck Vell's brain as if it carried the force of thousands of tons. Then he felt nothing. The absence was worse than the pain. Six minds fell silent.

The emptiness was deafening.

All of Lanaal's teachings fell to a forgotten corner of Vell's mind. All of his careful control of his behemoth body vanished in an instant. A rage beyond all rage overtook him and he was no longer Vell, but the mindless, rampaging monster that had killed the Zhentarim skymage in Rauvin Vale. No recollection of human consciousness, no sympathy for the blameless folk of Llorkh remained in him. Vell had no way to focus his anger on a single source. The whole city stood around him for one purpose—to be destroyed, a mere plaything to sate his bottomless fury.

Lying on the ground, Thanar and Kellin rolled to avoid the bodies of the dead behemoths that fell across the square. The living behemoths were no less of a hazard; consumed by the same anger that had seized Vell, they rampaged through the square, smashing walls with their huge forelimbs in search of an exit. Thanar and Kellin lay right in the path of a mad behemoth, its eyes inflamed with fury, and unable to recognize friend from enemy. Numb with fear, they scrambled to their feet and dashed toward the street.

Outside of the Central Square, they discovered Lanaal, again in the form of the huge brown-feathered hawk that had lifted Kellin and Thluna over Llorkh's walls. Thanar and Kellin desperately climbed onto her back and she took wing, just ahead of a rampaging behemoth. Lanaal kept low to avoid Geildarr and his lightning bolts, and circled around to the back side of the Lord's Keep.

From their vantage point, they saw the city being demolished from within. They easily identified Vell, larger than the rest, smashing his way through buildings with an unfettered appetite for destruction. Ilskar, also in his behemoth form—but apparently retaining his wits—patrolled the inner side of the walls, appearing uncertain of what to do. The liberated behemoths joined Vell in his rage, bursting free of the Central Square and damaging anything that stood in their path.

Lone hell hounds still roamed the city, but the bulk of them had been killed in the collapse of the Dark Sun. The behemoths stormed streets and alleys, unchallenged. Many of the Lord's Men withdrew and fled the city alongside terrified townsfolk. Crowds poured out of the gates and into the countryside. But Llorkh was far from deserted, and innocent citizens remained in the path of the behemoths' rampage.

"This is wrong," said Kellin. "We have to stop Vell."

"We have to stop Geildarr," corrected Thanar. "And we have to do it now."

Lanaal veered to one side, toward an aerial landing platform jutting out from an upper level of the Lord's Keep. She settled lightly and turned back to her elf body, a short elven blade hanging from her belt.

"Geildarr's private floor is three stories below," said Lanaal. "He was probably firing lightning bolts at the behemoths from his balcony, so I didn't dare land there."

The wind whistled across the platform, almost loud enough to block out the noise of the destruction below.

"I certainly hope Geildarr didn't expect anyone to intrude from up here," Kellin said, trying the door. It was not locked and swung open.

"I guess he didn't," said Lanaal with a smile. "Not his first mistake of the day, but perhaps his last."

The three ran into the keep.

Sungar ran up a staircase to a landing, then up to a higher floor in the Lord's Keep. No guards waited for him here, and the entire complex was eerily silent. Only the cacophony outside bled through, faint and distant as a dream. A long room unfurled before him, lined by mirrors on each side. A narrow table spanned the length of the room, and the whole place was lit by candles that faintly wobbled as the keep trembled with the vibrations of the city.

The barbarian walked slowly forward. Soon his reflection caught his eye, doubled and redoubled into an infinity of Sungars walking beside him. He startled and turned to stare into the mirror, watching his own blue eyes gaze at himself. He studied his face closely. Sungar's beard and hair were streaked with white, a token of his time in the dungeon. With his fingers, he traced the scars and the wounds, still red and tender, that Klev's cruel lash had inflicted on him.

Sungar's rage left him; his fury-fueled energy dissipated. He felt every ache again, every stinging wound along his back and sides. His shoulders drooped, his sword arm fell to his side, and he felt as weak as he had when he was sprawled on the floor of his cell so far below.

He stared deeper into the mirror. Sungar had heard of such things, but he had never seen one before. Other than his reflection in water, he had never seen himself. There was something beautiful about the mirror, as smooth, cool, and polished as an icy mountain lake. Things seemed more perfect in the mirror, even his own face and form.

Civilized vanity, he thought. The shamans of Uthgar often described mirrors as the symbol of civilization's flaws. They represented the tendency to become distracted with oneself, and to become useless and nonproductive. An

Uthgardt warrior was trained not to be drawn into excessive contemplation, but Sungar knew that was happening to him now.

His sword fell from his hand, landing on the floor with a thud. Those blue eyes in the mirror—his eyes, but somehow not his eyes—drew him in deeper and deeper.

Suddenly, the mirror smashed in front of him, a thousand shards falling to the carpet. It shook Sungar from his reverie, his moment of weakness shattering. A familiar axe head was embedded in the mirror's frame. Sungar turned to face its wielder, and his heart soared with joy.

"Thluna!" His cry echoed off the walls. He embraced the boy, pulling him close. "My son! Can it be you?"

"Sungar," Thluna wept. "Thank Uthgar you're alive. Thank Uthgar."

Breaking their embrace, Sungar's eyes went to the axe. "Is this . . ."

"Yes," said Thluna. "It is what you think."

Sungar gripped the axe handle, the head still stuck in the wall.

"We now know that it was once the weapon of Berun himself, in an age past," said Thluna, "and also that Uthgar himself wielded it."

"I know," said Sungar.

"How?" asked Thluna.

"King Gundar came to me in a vision. He showed me that you'd be coming to rescue me."

"And we feared the Battlefather had abandoned us!" Thluna declared. "He never forsook us. He was on our side all along."

Sungar pulled the axe from the wall. It felt comfortable in his hands—better than any weapon he had ever wielded. He offered it to Thluna. "This is for the chief of the Thunderbeasts," he said.

Thluna shook his head. "I am not the chief of the Thunderbeasts. I played that role in your absence, wielding this axe with pride, but only because I knew it was in your stead. This axe belongs to you. Besides, I have my own weapon now." He reached to his belt and drew up the heavy oaken club. "This was a gift from Chief Gunther Longtooth of the Tree Ghosts." He paused a moment before adding, "It, too, is a magical weapon."

Sungar breathed heavily, looking at the axe in his hands. It seemed so long ago since he threw it away on that desolate plain in the Fallen Lands. It felt so good to have it in his hands again. It felt like a part of himself long missing, now restored.

Sungar's strength rose in him again. "To war!" he cried, and together once again, the two Uthgardt dashed through the halls.

* * *

CHAPTER 22

Sungar and Thluna raced up two flights of stairs to a small anteroom. Another stairway led up to a heavy iron door, guarded by a massive metal statue—the top of its head almost scraped the ceiling. The figure was depicted in a suit of night-black armor, with a skull within a sunburst—the emblem of Cyric—etched into its chest.

"This is where we'll find Geildarr," said Sungar.

"How do you know?" asked Thluna.

Sungar pointed up at the statue's face, chiseled, youthful, and as beautiful as a god, but recognizable as Geildarr all the same.

Thluna allowed himself a slight chuckle. But when he reached for the door, the statue lurched into life. Purple fire lit up within its eyes, and it turned to face Thluna. Thluna ducked fast. The statue's arm swung about and slammed against the door behind him with a loud clang. He rolled backward, barely avoiding the golem as it brought its foot down hard, setting the walls trembling.

Sungar swung the axe, striking its left shoulder with a metallic ring and digging a dent in the iron body. The golem swept out with its iron arms, but Sungar jumped beyond their reach. Thluna struck the automaton with his club, denting the metal, but the golem showed no reaction to the blow.

"Strong and physical," said Sungar, dodging another blow from the golem. "No wonder Geildarr gave it his face. It's everything Geildarr himself is not."

❧ ❧ ❧ ❧ ❧

The sounds of battle rang through Geildarr's private floor, reaching his study. "Fighting on our threshold, Geildarr," said Ardeth. "It's time you made a decision."

"Very well." Geildarr tossed down his wand and turned his back on his balcony. Much of the city was lost in a haze of dust from so many destroyed buildings. "The secret passageway, then," he said, looking toward one of his bookcases. "We can slip out of the keep, then . . ."

"Then what, Geildarr?" Ardeth demanded. Her white face was flushed with anger. "Explain to Fzoul that you were chased from the Lord's Keep by an enraged barbarian?"

"The Heart of Runlatha may hold power worth a dozen Llorkhs. I will not turn it over to Sungar, even to save the city." He looked at the artifact, resting on a table. It glowed so serenely and peacefully, even as the world shattered around it. It had survived the fall of Netheril, and it would survive the fall of Llorkh, too. Geildarr extended his hand.

Ardeth reached out to stop him from touching it. "It's not yours, Geildarr," Ardeth said. "I stole it from the Sanctuary, but that didn't make it mine. It's not yours now—it never was."

Geildarr reached out and placed his hand over the Heart, not to clutch it, but to touch it, one last time.

❖ ❖ ❖ ❖ ❖

The golem wearing Geildarr's face struck Thluna with the back of its hand, sending the young barbarian sailing. Thluna hit the wall hard, and the wind was knocked from him, but he held on to his club.

Sungar drove the axe into the golem's shoulder, widening the crevice he was carving into its neck. Its stony face pivoted on its shoulders toward Sungar, and its mouth opened wide. A thick greenish haze flowed out that quickly settled over the anteroom. Sungar raised the axe, but the gas crept into his nostrils and turned his stomach. His eyes watered, and he felt his throat burn as the acid from his stomach climbed into his mouth. The poisonous green smoke filled Sungar's lungs, and he stumbled backward before collapsing at the foot of the stairs. The axe clattered to the floor. His eyes swam with the poisonous taint.

Thluna choked back vomit as the stinking vapors reached him. He buried his face in his sleeve. This was worse than anything he had ever smelled in the forests—worse than a skunk, and far worse than a decaying carcass. Soon the room was lost in the haze, and Thluna heard only silence, broken by the golem's steps as it marched across the room.

Out of nowhere, a powerful wind erupted near the ceiling, sending wild, green swirls through the fog. The haze began to dissipate under the strong breeze, and Thluna could see his surroundings again, just in time to watch the golem step forward, its thick arms ready to pummel the incapacitated Sungar. As he spat the sick taste from his mouth, Thluna saw Kellin pounce down the stairway, her sword catching the golem against its neck.

"Good to see you, Thluna," said Kellin as she slashed at the golem. Her sword ripped slashes in its armor, but the golem was unfazed. Wisps of gas still hung in the air but soon dissolved.

"Likewise, daughter of Zale," said Thluna, smashing his club against the golem's iron with a noise like the ringing of a gong.

Thanar and Lanaal ran down the stairs, grasping

Sungar's helpless form to drag him to safety. The golem reached out a thick iron arm and caught the druid around his middle. It pulled him against itself, crushing Thanar between its arm and its body. Lanaal let out a cry as she heard bones snapping. To her surprise, the automaton focused its purple eyes on her and Sungar, then turned away. Ignoring the intruders outside its room, it confronted Kellin and Thluna, releasing Thanar's shattered form. The druid crumpled to the foot of the stairs next to Sungar.

Thanar's head struck a stair as he landed. "By the Winged Mother, Thanar," said Lanaal, her tears flowing. His entire middle section was collapsed and twisted sideways. Broken ribs pierced his lungs, and a pool of blood spread beneath him. Lanaal reached out a hand to grasp his, but he pulled away.

"Oakfather," he said through gasps, "one last request." He placed his hands on Sungar's unconscious form. "Restore my chief to health and strength. Take his poison and give him vigor. Grant me this, then I'll be no more trouble to you."

His god heard his prayer. White radiance flowed from Thanar's hands and coursed through Sungar's body. Contentment and satisfaction spread across the druid's face as he expired. He died a Thunderbeast.

The deathly pallor slipped away from Sungar's face, and he sat up. He shrugged in puzzlement at the elf maiden standing next to him, but she was scarcely the strangest thing he had witnessed that day.

Sungar looked to Thanar's mangled corpse. Whispering a few words to his fallen brother, Sungar stood and snatched up the axe, dashing toward their metal enemy with restored vigor. Even the wounds of his imprisonment had faded to smooth scars. He buried the axe head into the golem's features and twisted the weapon, ripping apart the ridiculous parody of Geildarr's face.

"Take it," said Geildarr, looking at the Heart of Runlatha. His voice was full of regret. "Get it out of here."

"Where shall I take it?" asked Ardeth.

"Take it to Zhentil Keep. Don't rest until it's in Fzoul's hands, and tell him what brought all of this about."

Geildarr detected a faint trace of glee in Ardeth's voice as she said, "As you command." Ardeth picked up the Heart of Runlatha in both hands. She took a step toward the bookcase that concealed a secret passage out of the keep, but found a red-clad gnome standing in her path, the tricorn atop his head slightly askew.

For a moment all were still, nobody knowing what to say. Moritz smiled at Geildarr.

"So, my friend," Moritz said. "You reveal your true colors at last."

With a burst of speed, Ardeth spun backward and dived, the Heart of Runlatha still within her grasp. She tried to pull herself into the shadow under the zalantarwood table, but Moritz gestured and the table vanished, its shadow disappearing with it.

Catlike, she fell into a crouch and stared at Moritz—or more precisely, at the small shadow he cast. A determined look from the gnome told her not to bother. Ardeth backed away from him, easing up against a bookcase along the far wall, breathing heavily. Her eyes darted to the corners of the room and to Geildarr—not to him, but to his shadow, barely visible in the filtered light of the keep. Then her eyes darted to the hallway beyond the door, from which sounds of battle still rang.

"Moritz!" shouted Geildarr. "What is the meaning of this?"

"I wondered if you might be disloyal," said Moritz to Geildarr, taking a few steps toward Ardeth and twirling his wooden cane. "But no—you have kept the faith. To Fzoul. Whereas Ardeth . . . she knows to whom Netherese artifacts truly belong. Isn't that so?" He flashed her a venomous smile. "Uncloud your eyes, Geildarr. See the truth."

Moritz cast another spell. Before Geildarr's unbelieving eyes, Ardeth's pretty face turned from white to a dusky tone, like that of a Calishite. Her honey-colored hair darkened to a coal black shade. Then even this illusion was stripped away, and Ardeth was laid bare as a pillar of shadow in the shape of a girl. Darkness wafted from her, smoky tendrils snaking from her into the air. The Heart of Runlatha glowed even brighter in her hands—its light against her veil of shadows shining like a red star over her chest.

The shadows reached out to stroke the artifact, enveloping it in a cold caress. It sank inside Ardeth's body, coming to rest where her heart should be. The strength of its glow diminished only slightly. The Heart's red light shone from within its cage of shadows.

"I would've preferred to act earlier," Moritz told Geildarr. "But Sememmon wanted me to confirm your loyalties."

Geildarr's doughy face turned red as anger mixed with embarrassment. She had manipulated him so completely, deceived him so utterly. Geildarr wanted to look away from her but he could not. How did she keep this hidden for so long? She was a shade. A shade! A spy in his midst all this time, a spy from the Empire of Shadows.

No wonder his troops had been unable to surprise the Shadovar in the Fallen Lands.

He had thought she was his new Ashemmi, the creature he could trust in everything. She bought his confidence with the head of a dwarf, and kept it by skillfully accomplishing every task Geildarr assigned to her.

What a fool she had made of him. No, he corrected himself, what a fool she had revealed him to be.

Geildarr raised a hand and an arrow burst forth, sailing through the air at Ardeth. She leaped toward the hallway, the arrow splintering the bookcase behind her, acid spraying from it and singeing tomes and floor. Geildarr bellowed a magical word that locked all the doors on his private floor.

As Geildarr ran after her, Moritz called him back.

"Here. Sememmon's regards." He tossed Geildarr a dagger. Geildarr caught it in midair and realized it was the ancient bone dagger from the Great Wyrm's hoard, the very same dagger he had given Ardeth before sending her after Arthus Tyrrell.

She'd be seeking out deep shadows, Geildarr knew, that would allow her to step into the Plane of Shadow and walk away with the Heart, probably back to Anauroch and the City of Shade. Then the Heart would be lost forever.

Ardeth ran through the hallway, little more than a black streak trailing tendrils of smoke. Pedestals toppled as she passed, Geildarr's precious relics smashing on the floor. Geildarr bounded after her, hopping over each fallen treasure, naked anger compelling his sluggish form to faster and faster speeds. The light of the Heart shone faintly from inside Ardeth—a beacon for his fury. Ardeth didn't bother to exit through any of the doors along the hallway, but kept up her sprint all the way to the hall's end.

Ardeth reached the iron door, her shadowy fingers playing on the lock as Geildarr bore down on her, dagger in hand.

Who am I?
What am I?

Rage was such an utterly pure state. Vell understood everything—the limits of the world were no further than his own perceptions. There was nothing in the universe but what he saw and what he felt. When his human mind floated to the surface for a moment, a wave of confusion overtook Vell that was quickly silenced by the simplicity of rage. The behemoth anger swelled and grew till it encompassed all things, and Vell was pushed down beneath.

A chorus sang inside Vell. Every behemoth was there in his mind along with him, fighting in the streets of Llorkh and leaving a trail of destruction. When another of them fell, he felt the death as if it were his own.

Who am I?
Did I ever really know?

Thluna, Kellin, and Sungar battered the iron golem with club, sword, and axe, chipping away at the powerful construct. Lanaal, helpless against its power, kept out of the way on the stairs.

Kellin chopped at the crevice that Sungar had cloven into the golem's shoulder, and the statue's left arm fell off, landing on the floor at the top of the staircase. Sungar could see the golem's purple lights flickering and fading inside its eye sockets, and he let it follow him to the downward stairs.

"Now!" he shouted. He dived out of the way just as Thluna slammed his club against the golem's back. Unable to balance properly without its arm, and with its magical animation failing, the golem tumbled forward down the stairs with a metallic racket. Sungar leaped over it and came to rest on the landing below. Kellin patted Thluna's back as Sungar and Lanaal approached the heavy iron door leading to Geildarr's private chambers.

Before they could examine the door, it swung open with great force. A rotund, purple-robed mage tumbled out, locked in combat with something dark and vaporous. The wizard struggled with a creature that seemed forged out of pure darkness, yet held the shape and solidity of a human woman. As its dark face howled at them, Sungar and Kellin recognized it as Ardeth, shadows writhing across her face.

Geildarr knocked her to the floor and pinned her against the red carpet under his weight. Ardeth writhed and twisted under his full bulk. He lifted the bone dagger and drove it into her shoulder. She let out an unearthly squeal as it easily sliced her shadow-flesh. When Geildarr pulled out the weapon, he saw a flash of yellow ignite inside her.

He glanced at the dagger in puzzlement. Geildarr had examined it himself years before and found it to be completely ordinary. One of his useless relics, Moritz had termed it.

A realization struck Geildarr. Moritz must have asked Sememmon to weave a new enchantment into the dagger.

Moritz had berated Geildarr for collecting worthless relics of the past—this must be his sense of irony at work.

Geildarr guessed that Sememmon had infused it with the stuff of sunshine.

Sungar and the others watched in amazement as Geildarr struck again and again, sinking the dagger into Ardeth's flesh. Each time he withdrew the dagger, her wails grew louder as explosions of light tortured her dark form from the inside. The bursts of sunlight grew brighter, blanketing the room with flashes of white light.

Finally, Geildarr drove the cruel dagger into Ardeth's face. With a single flash brighter than any sun, her black form disintegrated beneath him. He flopped to the floor, falling flat on the carpet, now marked with an inky black stain beneath him.

The Heart of Runlatha rolled out from under him, toward the door from which he and Ardeth had come. But before the Thunderbeasts could move to claim it, another man emerged from the doorway and picked up the Heart in his hand.

He was tall, handsome, and black-haired, and he wore long blue robes that flowed down to the floor. He held a long staff topped with a black bat in his free hand. He was an imperious, impressive figure; his expression was calm and self-satisfied, showing no fear.

Kellin, Sungar, Thluna, and Lanaal held their weapons ready. But they were uncertain who to fight.

"You may kill Geildarr if you like," said the deep voice of the wizard, as he looked directly at Sungar. "You have every right, and I won't stop you. But know this: he rules Llorkh at the Zhentarim's pleasure. When word of today's disaster reaches them, they will be highly displeased. I'll wager that Geildarr doesn't have more than four or five days to live. And if I know Geildarr, I imagine those last days will be spent in fear and dread as he desperately schemes for a way to save his skin. But the Zhentarim do not tolerate failure, and they can neither be reasoned with nor hidden from. At least—" he added with a dark chuckle "—not by Geildarr. Chieftain Sungar, the torments you endured in Geildarr's dungeon are but a shadow of what Fzoul will inflict on the Lord Mayor."

Geildarr pulled himself to his knees and turned to the tall wizard. "Please," he gulped. "Help me, help me now—" he pronounced the name carefully, "—Sememmon." The name sent a shiver of recognition through Kellin, which brought a touch of a smile to the former Master of Darkhold.

"Do you not think you've had enough chances?" the wizard asked, tapping his staff against the floor, catching part of Geildarr's robe.

"Please," Geildarr said, dropping his face to the floor before Sememmon, gripping the bottom of his quarterstaff in a gesture of submission. If the barbarians would only believe that this was a wizard of extreme power before whom he supplicated himself, perhaps they would be humbled into submission, into sparing him. "I'll do anything you say," Geildarr said. "Protect me, save me—"

"Save your groveling for Fzoul," said Sememmon. "But it won't do any more good with him than with me."

"The Heart of Runlatha," said Thluna from across the room.

"What of it?" Sememmon snapped at the young barbarian.

A nervous shiver ran through Thluna's limbs. "We need it."

"No, my Uthgardt friend, I think not." He looked at the glowing artifact. "When I have a Netherese artifact in my hands, I'm not about to let go of it."

Geildarr admired the economy with which Moritz, in the guise of Sememmon, voiced his threat. He clutched the staff more tightly.

"We will not let you leave with it," Sungar threatened.

"You won't be able to stop me, I'm afraid. Consider your lives my gift to you, and only because you've caught me in a generous mood. You've accomplished nearly everything you set out to do. I'm sure your god is adequately pleased."

Geildarr turned to them from his position kneeling in front of Moritz. "Join me and fight him," he said. "He's not a wizard . . . not the wizard he appears to be. He's just a gnome . . . a gnome named Moritz wearing Sememmon's face. He's an illusion—a weakling gnome! We can defeat him! A gnome!"

Sungar, Kellin, Lanaal, and Thluna frowned, exchanging puzzled looks. Was this true?

This brought a chuckle to Moritz, a perfect replication of Sememmon. "You see the desperate scheming I was talking about?" He looked down at the mayor of Llorkh. "Geildarr, did I ever tell you what happened when one of Manshoon's clones attacked me during the Manshoon Wars? I plucked his beating heart from his chest!"

"Sememmon did that, Moritz," said Geildarr. "Not you."

"Good-bye, Geildarr. Give my best to Fzoul. For that matter, give my best to Cyric." He finished with a smug look and a slight wave.

A moment later, confusion crossed his face. Moritz's illusionary brow furrowed as he found himself unable to teleport out of the Lord's Keep.

"Sememmon isn't the only one who can toy with magic," spat Geildarr. He thrust the dagger at the image of Sememmon, driving it into his abdomen. The illusion flickered and fell, and the stately wizard was replaced by a red-garbed gnome, a blackwood cane in one hand and the Heart of Runlatha in the other. He howled at the dagger, embedded in his shoulder and now sending a cascade of blood down his crimson clothing.

"Attack!" shouted Geildarr.

All looked to Sungar. The chief took one step forward and swung his battle-axe down on Moritz. Moritz lifted his cane to deflect the blow. The blackwood repelled the assault, but snapped in two under the impact.

Sungar felt a strange new energy flowing from the axe. The ancient weapon was closer to the Heart of Runlatha than it had been in many centuries.

With Sungar charging at him, Moritz hopped backward through the doorway and ducked. Muttering an arcane syllable, he vanished on the spot, along with the Heart. His red tricorn hat fluttered to the ground. Sungar stopped, puzzled.

"He cannot teleport from inside the Lord's Keep," shouted Geildarr. "He's invisible."

Faint footfalls were audible from down the hallway as small, unseen feet jumped over the fallen pedestals. Thluna and Sungar bolted after their quarry.

"Where will he go?" asked Kellin.

"He'll try to get outside, especially since he's hurt," said Geildarr, pulling himself to his feet. "He'll try for my balcony or a secret door behind the bookcase down the hall."

"Look after him, Lanaal," said Kellin, running down the hallway after them.

Lanaal raised her sword and rested the curve of its blade against Geildarr's neck. "Not a word, not an incantation, or I take your head," Lanaal promised.

"Fair enough," said Geildarr. He asked her, "How did an elf maid like yourself come to be fighting alongside barbarians?"

"Strange times," Lanaal answered.

"You remind me of another elf woman I met once," he said. "Her name was Ashemmi. Have you heard of her?"

Lanaal said nothing, but raked her short sword against Geildarr's throat, drawing a line of blood.

Geildarr's eyes turned down toward the dark spot on the carpet, stained by the disintegrating shadowstuff of Ardeth's body. If he were truly brave, he thought, why shouldn't he let the elf kill him here and now?

Shaquintar, wizard tyrant of Runlatha, died in the fall of Netheril.

Lucky fool.

Something drove Sungar on as he raced down the hallway, hopping over debris. It was the axe, pushing him forward with its will and giving him a wild new strength. Sungar had wielded the axe hundreds of times before and had never known anything like this. It invigorated him, inspired him. His will and that of the axe were merged, fighting as one. He fancied that he could feel Berun, and Uthgar, and the imprints of all who had ever touched the axe, and that they were wielding it alongside him.

As he reached the end of the hallway, he slammed into a table—an invisible table that had been placed in his way. It dug into his belly and stole the wind from his gut. The axe flew from his grip, landing on the floor in the middle of Geildarr's study.

A faint wind blew in this room, from the wide-open doors to the balcony. Bookshelves lined the walls—Sungar had never seen so many books, had scarcely seen them at all. A passageway built into a bookcase hung open.

On the floor, the axe trembled.

Regaining his footing, Sungar hopped over the invisible table and into the study. He snapped up the axe and prepared to dive after the gnome down the hidden staircase. Kellin and Thluna arrived behind him, shoving the table aside.

But as Sungar leaped toward the passageway, he felt the axe tremble in his hands. A strange red glow enveloped its head.

It pulled him the other way.

Sungar didn't resist, but let the axe guide him, turning with its coaxing until it pointed to a corner of the study next to the balcony.

Suddenly, a burst of red radiance pulsed on the head of the axe. The new energy flowed across the room, and the artifact to which the axe was magically tied, the Heart of Runlatha, pulsed in return. As it had done at the Sanctuary, it dissolved all illusions, all invisibility, slicing through anything that kept the Heart hidden. Moritz the Illusionist was revealed before Geildarr's bookshelf. The gnome staggered from his bleeding wound, and he clutched the Heart of Runlatha in one hand.

Moritz frowned at the barbarian chief and slowly shook his head.

"Sememmon's not going to like this," he said. And with the last of his strength, he ran for the balcony.

Sungar bolted after him, axe raised. The gnome reached the balcony's rail and took a flying leap just as Sungar brought the mighty axe down, burying it deep into the floor. Moritz vanished over the side.

Thluna and Kellin rushed to join him. Sungar smiled, holding up the axe. Blood clung to the blade.

At his feet lay the Heart of Runlatha, clutched within a diminutive hand.

Kellin looked over the balcony just in time to see a falling body vanish into the dusty haze that encircled the Lord's Keep. A trickle of falling blood traced its path downward.

Sungar plucked up the gnome's arm and pried the Heart from its grip. He felt its warmth and held it up to his eye to inspect it closely, as one might a jewel. He turned to face Thluna and Kellin.

"Now," he said. "Is someone going to tell me what this damned thing *is?*"

CHAPTER 23

Was Moritz killed?" asked Geildarr when they returned to him in the anteroom. Lanaal lifted the blade from his neck and stepped back to join Sungar, Kellin, and Thluna, who held the Heart of Runlatha.

"Perhaps not killed," said Kellin.

Sungar held up the severed arm and threw it down at Geildarr's feet.

"His own flesh." Geildarr nudged the hand with his boot. "No illusion. So he escaped?"

"He went over your balcony," explained Kellin. "I saw him vanish into the dust, but I couldn't tell if he teleported or not before he hit the ground."

"You had best hope he didn't escape," said Geildarr. "You will find Sememmon to be an unforgiving enemy. My advice to you is to get rid of it fast. Wait—what am I saying?" He chuckled darkly. "Why am I giving you advice? If you keep it, Sememmon will do things to your tribe that'll make you wish you never busted out of my dungeon."

Sungar punched Geildarr in the face. The mayor's head rocked back and struck the wall behind him.

"Was that blow in place of killing me?" said Geildarr, blood dribbling down his chin and onto his robe. "I wish you *would* kill me. Moritz wasn't lying. There is little chance that the Zhentarim will let me live, and if they do, it will be to endure a terrible punishment, far beyond anything your barbarian justice could comprehend." His words carried a perverse pride.

Thluna looked at Thanar's ruined body lying on the stairway. "Many of our men have died, thanks to him," Thluna reminded Sungar.

"And how many of my people did you kill?" asked Geildarr. "How many of my people are still dying out there, while your behemoths continue to wreck my city?"

Sungar brandished his axe before the mayor. "We will let you live," he declared.

"Somehow," Geildarr gulped, "I'm still glad for that."

The chief of the Thunderbeasts tilted the axe sideways and slammed its broad side into Geildarr's head, throwing his world into blackness.

When Geildarr awoke, he wondered if it had all been a bad dream.

His head spun from the blows he had taken, and his vision was clouded with spots of light and dark. A bright light shone in his eyes from above him. He was sitting in a chair. He recognized the second floor dining hall, damaged from fighting. The paintings on the walls hung askew.

A dead dwarf lay on the table in front of him, covered by the white table cloth.

Geildarr screamed. As he did so, he realized that he could not move his arms or legs, and he screamed louder, panicked. He grasped at the shreds of his wits and looked about to discover the reason for his paralysis.

He was bound to the chair, just as he had bound Sungar.

Through the tablecloth, Geildarr could see that the dwarf's head faced him, one lifeless eye open, the other crushed in its socket. The undamaged eye stared at him through the shroud as if mocking him, blaming him.

He screamed again. It echoed off the walls of the room. He yelled for help, but no one was in the Lord's Keep to hear him.

Geildarr screamed some more.

Finally, he laughed.

Vell saw himself staring at the surface of a pool of water, as if he were submerged and looking up. In the stillness he could see his reflection, but when he reached out to touch it, his image was lost in the ripples.

Who am I? A Thunderbeast, but what does that mean? Vell the Brown, but what does that mean?

A mystery. A mystery worth contemplating.

He stayed submerged in this restful state, thinking about it, until a word sounded in his ears that drew him back to himself.

By the time the behemoths were quieted, a full third of the buildings in Llorkh had been destroyed by the rampaging animals. The number of dead was uncountable. With the Heart of Runlatha in hand, Sungar, Thluna, and Kellin easily calmed the massive creatures. Only four of the twelve that had been stolen from the Sanctuary remained, the rest killed by Geildarr's lightning bolts or lost in the confusion and battle afterward. Ilskar survived the calamity and when he laid eyes on Sungar, joyfully shed his animal body and took the shape of a barbarian again.

But Vell was lost in his behemoth shape. There was no flicker of human intelligence in his eyes. He seemed to have entirely forgotten that he was ever human. Lanaal tried to reach him in the depths of his animal mind.

"I have experienced something like this myself," she said. "Especially after emotional strain—as he must have experienced when the behemoths were killed. Being an animal is seductively simple. He'll return in time." She sounded less than certain about her prediction.

Kellin wondered about the Endless March that sages sometimes spoke of, that she had discussed with Thanar under Grandfather Tree. The March was the eternal progress of life, growing and changing in all its myriad forms, all stemming from a central point that connected all life with a common origin, like the leaves and branches of a tree. But it held a darker implication as well. If humans had once been beasts, was there not something of the beasts in them still? She thought of what Lanaal said, of the seductive quality of being an animal. Part of that must be toxic, as well—how else to explain the Shepherds? They had worn scales too long, their humanity atrophying in their breasts. But if all people were born of animals, and had wisps of animal in them as surely as Vell did, who could say when such spirits might climb out?

As the strange procession—behemoths, barbarians, a human woman, and a gigantic white swan—filed toward the west gate of Llorkh, the survivors of the city gave them a wide berth. The Lord's Men stood warily, weapons at their sides but enclosed in scabbards and sheaths. Sungar and his slow group began the long trek west following the Trade Way, letting the behemoths drink from the River Grayflow and graze from the trees that still bore leaves. The season was turning, and the weather would soon carry winter's chill. To everyone's surprise, the behemoths proved to be sturdy at the march. They even permitted riders, to let all move at a steady pace.

Lanaal, Kellin, and the barbarians all took turns talking to Vell, hoping to ignite his human spark, but

Vell remained silent. By the time they reached the High Forest's edge, Kellin decided the time had come for a new tactic. Clinging to Vell's long neck, she spoke to him.

"Vell, remember when I told you about my True Name?" Kellin said. "The name that's supposed to explain everything about me? The priests of Oghma said that I should never tell it to another person—to do so would give that person power over me. I'm going to tell it to you. I'm sure Oghma won't mind."

She spoke it, and clung to Vell's neck, waiting. Vell plodded slowly after his fellows and Kellin began to wonder if he had even heard her. Then he paused in his step and reared on his hind legs, enough to tilt Kellin from her place on his back. As she slid down his great mass, his scales vanished beneath her and she landed in a mound of golden leaves. Something crashed lightly in the leaves beside her, and Kellin turned to look into familiar brown eyes. Everyone rushed over to greet Vell.

"Welcome back, Vell the Brown," said Sungar, clasping Vell's hands. "You saved all of our lives. Your name will be remembered in the skalds' songs for many generations."

Exactly how will they remember me? wondered Vell.

Kellin smiled at Vell and offered her hand to him. Vell took it and they rose to continue their journey. For a long time, they walked together in silence.

Vell said very little the rest of the way to the Sanctuary, but the difference in him was plainly visible. He walked tall, proud, and confident, with a purpose that he had never shown before. Whatever dark issues swam in his mind, they could not outshadow his new courage and strength.

Their travels through the High Forest were blissfully quiet. Nothing in the woods dared to challenge the mighty behemoths. When they reached the foot of the Star Mounts and found the Sanctuary, they discovered that the place had been all but destroyed by the elements. Cold water had rushed into the swamp from the Heartblood River. The behemoths waded in, heedless of the cold, knowing they were home.

Bony frowns were frozen onto the Shepherds' faces.

They showed no sign of welcome or gratitude.

"Shepherds," yelled Sungar as the ancient people appeared to receive him. Thluna held up the Heart of Runlatha. "You have made a pact with my tribe, and I expect you to keep it."

"Sungar Wolfkiller," said one of the Shepherds. "We meet you finally—the man responsible for all of our woes. Why? Why did you throw away the axe on that dismal plain?"

"I do not have to justify myself to you," said Sungar. "Perhaps I must justify myself to my tribe, but not to you. Will you keep your end of the bargain? For a return of your hideaway and your immortality, it seems like a small price."

"Yes," another Shepherd said, full of resentment. "We give up all claims on the totem spirit, the Thunderbeast, and to Uthgar. We shall never again interfere in your affairs."

"Uthgar will hold you to this promise," said Thluna, turning the Heart of Runlatha over to them.

"I'm sure he will," said one of them, before carrying it over to the menhir.

"There is still the question of Vell." One of the Shepherds stepped toward him. "You are one of us. The behemoths have told us of your heroism and your nobility. Even if you are of Uther's mongrel race, we accept you. You may stay with us if you choose."

"No," Vell said. "I will not stay with you or keep any part of what you have given me. Take the powers away from me."

The Shepherds gasped. They had not considered this possibility. "You would renounce your heritage? But surely you love the beasts as we do."

"I do," said Vell. "Maybe more than you can know. But they are safe now. I know they will be left in your care."

"Those few whom you saved," one Shepherd spat.

"And you wonder why he doesn't want to stay with you," said Kellin.

"But the behemoths are part of you, Vell," said a Shepherd. "Will you give away a piece of who you are?"

Sadness weighed in Vell's voice. "It was never mine. I carried it, but it was never me."

The Heart of Runlatha was restored to its place atop the menhir at the center of the Sanctuary. Its glow brightened, and its red light spread across the swamp.

"In time, its magic will restore all of the damage that has been done," one of the Shepherds explained.

"Can you take these powers away from me now?" asked Vell.

"Come with us."

The Shepherds led him to the center of the Sanctuary. The ancient men and women surrounded the menhir, whose runes now glowed faintly. They linked hands and bid Vell to join them. He reached out and clutched two shriveled, bony hands.

They chanted in Netherese, the runes on the menhir pulsed with magic, and the Heart glowed brighter. Vell cried out as he felt part of his soul begin to rip away. His connection to the behemoths in the Sanctuary—something he had experienced for so long that it felt like second nature to him, like one of his five senses—faded and extinguished.

"It is not too late," said one of the Shepherds. "We can give it back to you."

"No," said Vell, though tears filled his eyes. "Finish it."

The unnatural strength Vell had felt in his muscles for so long was ripped away, and he felt weak as a child. All of the skills and senses that had imbued him on Runemeet at Morgur's Mound were gone. He was the plain, ordinary, and unremarkable Uthgardt warrior known as Vell the Brown again.

But he didn't feel that way.

"We are your ancestors," the Shepherds said as they again gathered before Sungar and the others at the Sanctuary's edge. "We are your history."

"Yet no songs are sung of you," said Sungar. "Perhaps some of the songs our skald sings are about events that never happened. They never tell the whole story, but they hold our tribe together. They preserve the stories we tell about ourselves. You are not part of us.

"And now," Sungar said, "I must return something to you."

Sungar raised the axe and held it high over his head, just as he had that day in the Fallen Lands. "With this locked inside your walls of illusion, you can live out the remainder of time safely, and the North will never again suffer your manipulations."

"Wait," said Thluna, reaching out a hand to stop Sungar. He turned to the Shepherds. "As you took the magic from Vell, can you also take it from the axe?"

The Shepherds cast glances among themselves. "Why do you ask?"

"Could you remove the magic so the axe can never access the Sanctuary?" asked Kellin. "In essence, could you sever the magical connection between it and the Heart of Runlatha?"

"Yes," said one of the Shepherds firmly. "We can. Indeed, we would be happy to prevent the Sanctuary from ever being disturbed again."

Kellin turned to Sungar. "It's your decision. And it will still be a magical weapon afterward."

Thluna said, "But it will always be the weapon of Berun, of Chief Tharkane, and of Uthgar."

"Let it be done," decided Sungar.

The Shepherds gathered around the Heart again. A faint red glow within the axe flared then faded out, marking the weapon's separation from the artifact to which it had been tied more than fifteen hundred years earlier.

Before long, the Sanctuary and all within started to flicker and fade as the illusion returned. "You belong to the past," said Vell. "Stay there."

In a blink's time, the entire Sanctuary was gone, replaced by a huge field at the foot of Mount Vision, marked by three massive phandar trees. For quite a while the six comrades stood there, staring at the untouched landscape before them, the high Star Mounts towering into the sky above. They knew what they saw was false, but there was no way for the eye to see it.

"Where do you go from here?" asked Lanaal.

Sungar answered, "North to Grandfather Tree, if you'd care to show us the way. The Tree Ghosts and their elf companions have done the Thunderbeast tribe a great service. I want to thank them personally, and cement the bonds of friendship between our two tribes. They need to know that Rask Urgek died a hero. From there, to Rauvin Vale. Home to our people."

Thluna and Ilskar smiled at the thought, but Vell did not.

"What do we tell our people?" asked Thluna. "About them, I mean?" He waved toward the walls of illusion that concealed the Shepherds. "Do we hide their existence, just as they have done?"

"If my chief commands it, I will keep the secret till my death," said Ilskar.

"I do not doubt it, Ilskar," said Sungar. He looked at the axe in his hand. "How do we explain to the Thunderbeasts that the axe has come back? Do we lie? Make up some story? I confess, I am tired of lies."

"Why not simply tell them the truth?" asked Lanaal.

"But to know the whole truth," said Vell. "That our ancestors are such creatures as the Shepherds? That we are descended from an empire of wizards?"

"Will we have Hazred the Voice compose a ballad about that?" quipped Thluna.

"What do you think we should do, daughter of Zale?" asked Sungar.

Kellin was taken aback at his question. There was no mockery in his voice. The Uthgardt was truly asking the advice of a trusted and battle-proven ally, and Kellin felt honored. But a wave of guilt rolled over her as she answered.

"My inclination is always toward the truth," she said. "But I also recognize that some truths are too hurtful and dangerous to be spread. You are wise, Chieftain Sungar. I'm sure you will make the right decision."

"I'm sure you will as well," said Sungar. "When you deem to put us in your books."

Kellin smiled.

"Don't worry," said Vell. "I will make sure she depicts you all in a favorable light."

Sungar's brow furrowed. "What do you mean, Vell?" asked Thluna.

"I won't be returning to the tribe with you." Vell spoke softly but firmly. "I'm going south with Kellin. To Candle-keep, or whatever other place we might find ourselves." He turned to face Kellin. "That is, if you'll have me."

She reached out to touch his arm. "Only if you're sure, Vell."

"What?" said Sungar. "Why?"

"I don't know if I can explain myself," said Vell. "Please don't misunderstand me. I am not renouncing the tribe. I am a Thunderbeast, and will always be a Thunderbeast. But all of this has changed me too much. I do not think I can return to my life as it was before."

Sungar frowned with disgust. "You would go to her world instead? The world of cities, of books, of magic—of *civilization*?"

"It is the only place I know to go." Vell's brown eyes met Sungar's blue ones. As much as he wanted to avert his gaze in shame, Vell held steady.

"You know how they look at us there: as savages, as comic brutes, nothing more." Vell wondered if Sungar reacted this way because of what he endured in his imprisonment. "They are not all like Kellin."

"But no chief may press his will in this way," said Thluna. "It is your choice, Vell." There was sadness in his voice, but admiration as well.

"I think it's a wonderful decision," said Lanaal. "Go someplace else, experience something new—what else is life about? It takes bravery and it takes vision. This is a great thing you're doing, the two of you."

"Do you ever mean to return, Vell?" asked Thluna. "Thanar left the tribe as well, but he returned and died fighting alongside us."

"In truth," Vell answered, "I do not know."

Sungar trained his eyes on Kellin. "You would deprive our tribe of one of its warriors?"

"One warrior will not make the difference between victory or defeat," Kellin answered.

"Do you truly think this is the best thing for Vell?" Sungar asked.

"Yes," she said. "As a matter of fact, I do."

Sungar's face reddened and his grip on the axe tightened.

"I don't need your approval, my chief," said Vell. "I have earned the right to my own mind. But I would like your blessing."

Silence hung over them for a long time. At last, Sungar spoke, his voice kindly. "If you want my blessing," he said, "you have it. And as my last gift to you for your services to your tribe, Vell the Brown, I promise you this. I will ask Hazred the Voice to write a song about you, of great length and surpassing beauty. It will tell of your bravery, your sacrifice, and of your valiant death."

FORGOTTEN REALMS®

The New York Times **bestselling author
R.A. Salvatore
brings you a new series!**

The Sellswords

SERVANT OF THE SHARD

Book I

Powerful assassin Artemis Entreri tightens his grip on the streets of
Calimport, but his sponsor Jarlaxle grows ever more ambitious. Soon the
power of the malevolent Crystal Shard grows greater than them both,
threatening to draw them into a vast web of treachery from which there
will be no escape.

VOLUME TWO OF THE SELLSWORDS WILL BE AVAILABLE IN 2005!

ALSO BY R.A. SALVATORE

STREAMS OF SILVER

The Legend of Drizzt, Book V

The fifth installment in the deluxe hardcover editions of Salvatore's
classic Dark Elf novels, *Streams of Silver* continues the epic saga of Drizzt
Do'Urden™.

THE HALFLING'S GEM

The Legend of Drizzt, Book VI

The New York Times best-selling classic for the first time in a deluxe
hardcover edition that includes bonus material found nowhere else.

HOMELAND

The Legend of Drizzt, Book I

Now in paperback, the *New York Times* best-selling classic that began the
tale of one of fantasy's most beloved characters. Experience the Legend of
Drizzt from the beginning!

DRAGONS ARE DESCENDING ON THE FORGOTTEN REALMS!

THE RAGE
The Year of Rogue Dragons, Book I

RICHARD LEE BYERS

Renegade dragon hunter Dorn hates dragons with a passion few can believe, let alone match. He has devoted his entire life to killing every dragon he can find, but as a feral madness begins to overtake the dragons of Faerûn, civilization's only hope may lie in the last alliance Dorn would ever accept.

THE RITE
The Year of Rogue Dragons, Book II

RICHARD LEE BYERS

Dragons war with dragons in the cold steppes of the Bloodstone Lands, and the secret of the ancient curse gives a small band of determined heroes hope that the madness might be brought to an end.

REALMS OF THE DRAGONS
Book I

EDITED BY PHILIP ATHANS

This anthology features all-new stories by R.A. Salvatore, Ed Greenwood, Elaine Cunningham, and the authors of the R.A. Salvatore's War of the Spider Queen series. It fleshes out many of the details from the current Year of Rogue Dragons trilogy by Richard Lee Byers and includes a short story by Byers.

REALMS OF THE DRAGONS
Book II

EDITED BY PHILIP ATHANS

A new breed of Forgotten Realms authors bring a fresh approach to new stories of mighty dragons and the unfortunate humans who cross their paths.

NEW TALES FROM FORGOTTEN REALMS CREATOR
ED GREENWOOD

THE BEST OF THE REALMS
Book II

This new anthology of short stories by Ed Greenwood, creator of the
FORGOTTEN REALMS Campaign Setting, features many old and well-loved
classics as well as three brand new stories of high-spirited adventure.

CITY OF SPLENDORS
A Waterdeep Novel

ED GREENWOOD AND ELAINE CUNNINGHAM

In the streets of Waterdeep, conspiracies run like water through the
gutters, bubbling beneath the seeming calm of the city's life. As a band of
young, foppish lords discovers there is a dark side to the city they all love,
a sinister mage and his son seek to create perverted creatures to further
their twisted ends. And across it all sprawls the great city itself: brawling,
drinking, laughing, living life to the fullest. Even in the face of death.

SILVERFALL
Stories of the Seven Sisters

This paperback edition of *Silverfall: Stories of the Seven Sisters*, by the creator
of the FORGOTTEN REALMS Campaign Setting, features seven stories of
seven sisters illustrated by seven beautiful pages of interior art by John Foster.

ELMINSTER'S DAUGHTER
The Elminster Series

All her life, Narnra of Waterdeep has wondered who her father is. Now
she has discovered that it is no less a person than Elminster of Shadowdale,
mightiest mage in all Faerûn. And her anger is as boundless as his power.

www.wizards.com

THE TWILIGHT GIANTS TRILOGY
Written by *New York Times*
bestselling author
TROY DENNING

THE OGRE'S PACT
Book I

This attractive new re-release by multiple *New York Times* best-selling author Troy Denning, features all new cover art that will re-introduce Forgotten Realms fans to this excellent series. A thousand years of peace between giants and men is shattered when a human princess is stolen by ogres, and the only man brave enough to go after her is a firbolg, who must first discover the human king's greatest secret.

THE GIANT AMONG US
Book II

A scout's attempts to unmask a spy in his beloved queen's inner circle is her only hope against the forces of evil that rise against her from without and from within.

THE TITAN OF TWILIGHT
Book III

The queen's consort is torn between love for his son and the dark prophesy that predicts his child will unleash a cataclysmic war. But before he can take action, a dark thief steals both the boy and the choice away from him.